Kaz Jordyn

A Warped Sense of Uma

For everyone who encouraged me in my writing.

This one's for you.

'Members of the jury, have you reached a verdict upon which you are all agreed?'

'Yes, Your Honour.'

'In the case of the Crown versus Jesamine Vickers, do you find the defendant guilty, or not guilty?'

'GUILTY.'

Daily Record

Judge Declares "Evil Eva" NOT A Danger –
Women's Groups Outraged

"Evil Eva" Rowe, jailed for life in 1997 for her part in a nationwide child pornography ring, left prison a free woman last night, after controversial judge, Hedley Calderfield QC, decided she no longer represented a danger to children, following a three-year programme of rehabilitation and education at Whytemoor Hall prison, Leicestershire. Not for the first time, there were calls for Calderfield to step down, claiming he is out of touch with society.

In the 1990's, Rowe, now 43, was known as the "Bling-bling Candywoman," for the methods she used to lure her female victims, some as young as ten, into posing for photographs at her Hoxton studio, promising them lucrative modelling contracts, fine jewellery and chauffeur-driven limousines – lifestyles most girls of that age could only dream of. She seduced them into believing they were special – chosen, before leading them, Pied Piper-style to their deaths in snuff movies.

A former inmate of Rowe's, who asked not to be named said: "Eva had this way about her. Even though you were utterly revolted by the things they said she'd done, you found yourself craving her attention. She could be charming and affectionate. Within the confines of an institution it was easier to have her onside."

Rowe's departure from the jail, which houses 350 of the UK's most violent female offenders, was met by a baying crowd of several hundred protesters, mainly women, who jeered and threw rotten eggs and tomatoes at the private hire car as she was driven away at speed.

Rowe was transferred to a secret location overnight, where it is thought that she will already have taken steps to change elements of her identity and may be intending to flee the country.

Juliet Anderson, a spokesperson for Women Against Pornography & Violence, said: "This woman kills kids for a living. No amount of rehabilitation is going to change what she is inside. Ask the mothers whose children were murdered to satisfy her perverted lust and greed." When asked whether she still considered Rowe to be a danger to young girls, Anderson advised parents to be on their guard. "Lock up your daughters," she said.

1

Eight years is a long time for a twenty-one-year-old to contemplate spending on the Maximum Security wing of the UK's most notorious women's prison. Especially when you're kept on lock-down for eighteen hours a day. Almost fifty-three-thousand hours spent with only the occasional cockroach for company adds up to one hell of a lot of thinking time.

Fifty-three-thousand fucking hours. It's a good job I've never minded my own company. Odd they allow you to breed cockroaches in your cell willy-nilly, when there are plenty of signs up saying, "No Pets Allowed."

Some people cope admirably with the prospect of a lifetime of incarceration. I wasn't one of them. I quickly learned I don't do small spaces. Eight years of being confined to a cell not much bigger than a dog kennel is enough to send the most resolute of stoics off her rocker.

Yesterday I read about an ex-caretaker's cupboard in Cadogan Place that went for one-hundred-and-seventy grand. It's the size of a snooker table apparently. No room to swing a cat. They've tried. Ouch. The world's gone mad. Or maybe it's just the housing market. It's become so saturated that they're selling starter homes in the city not much bigger than a nine-by-six to young professionals. Pods, I think they're called.

Been up before the beak recently, Madam? Did the court recommend residential care in a secure unit? If so, you may qualify for a transfer to this super dinky little "pod," located in a particularly secluded part of leafy Leicestershire. One careful owner for the past four years. All mod cons (that's enough about the inmates;) compact and bijou with it's own washbasin, loo and (somewhat restricted) views over a large courtyard.

On the downside I have to warn you the neighbours can be pretty darned noisy as people can become when they don't get out much. Boisterous is probably more accurate. Feral some might say, but that may be a slight overreaction depending on how liberal your point of view.

On the plus side there's plenty of room for integration with your fellow "podsters," and on-site facilities include an a la carte restaurant serving a variety of oh-so-slimming meals (trust me, if you've got any sense you'll put away as little as possible for as long as possible.)

There's also free gym membership for the duration of your stay with us. I can also vouch for the fact that it's an agoraphobic's paradise in here, so applications from those minus a penchant for the wild outdoors are particularly well received.

And the main selling point: it's burglar-proof! Virtually. Not many housing developments can boast that.

You see those bars at the window? They aren't simply there, as many misguided people think, to keep us lot inside. No, not at all. They are here to keep us proud residents safe from the scum on the outside. Are you thinking I'd make a half-decent estate agent? Me neither.

Funny how your life can change irrevocably in the time it takes to draw a breath in and let it out again. That's what happened with me. The deed was done in an instant. No planning. Just an execution. I'm not like her – Madam – the woman whose glamorous image graces the front covers of the world's press. A woman who blueprinted her sickening crimes down to the last vile detail, as if she was compiling something as mundane as a business plan.

'Jesamine Vickers.'

I saunter over to the desk in my ill-fitting clothes.

'About bloody time. And my name is Vale.'

Officer Kenton sneers at me. 'Since when?'

'Last Friday, when the change was approved. I'm going back to using the family name.'

'Well nobody thought to inform the likes of us. We're always the last to know.'

'My brief sent a copy of the deed to Governor Grainger.'

'Well there you are, you see. Copies of official documents aren't acceptable. Her Majesty requires the original. Your solicitor ought to know that.'

'Well get Her Maj on the blower and I'll sort it. Look just give me my stuff and I'll be out of your life.'

She shakes her pudding bowl mane at me. 'This puts a whole new complexion on things. I'll have to converse with the Governor's office.'

'But I've got people waiting for me.'

5

'Tough. Sit back down again and I'll try not to keep you waiting too long.' She peers over the top of me. 'Heather Spears!'

'You shouldn't call anyone else until you've dealt with me.'

'I *am* dealing with you. I can multi-task, you know. I *am* a woman.'

'You really ought to try getting a second opinion on that, love. You checked the mirror recently?'

She plops my file nonchalantly into the pending tray.

'That attitude might have earned you respect amongst the down and outs in this place, but I guarantee it won't do you any favours in the big wide world. Now either sit quietly while I make this phone call, or I'll put you on report and you can stay with us another fortnight. How does that suit you, Mizz Vale?'

This Kenton woman has the potential to be more of a pain in the arse than ruddy Strychnine and she was your worst nightmare. I squat down on the bench opposite and while she's busy aggravating some other soon-to-be ex-con, I scratch my initials onto the steel surface with a paperclip.

Fifteen minutes later Kenton clicks her stubby fingers at me, like she's some champagne swilling, city-slicker in a lap-dancing club. I amble across, thrusting my boobs out at her and sucking my belly in, if only to remind her what the inside of a gym is for.

Contents of an ancient plastic bag tumble out in front of me. Several coins that for all I know are probably not legal tender any more. A key-ring with I Heart NY we got when my mother was playing Norma Desmond in *Sunset Boulevard* on Broadway. A metal comb that looks capable of inflicting serious bodily injury, I can't ever remember owning.

'Sign here.' Kenton drops the pen on the board, as if accidentally brushing her skin against mine might cause her to contract something contagious. Like Murderitis.

If there's one thing worse than spending fifty-three-thousand hours in your own company, it's the prospect of seeing the rest of your life go the same way. As the gates clang behind me I look round helplessly for Octavia or Dad or Saint Lizzy. Some bloody hope. As the minutes tick by it becomes blindingly obvious that no-one's told them I was being released early. Only three weeks, granted, but still . . .

The guard grins at me from his sentry box. I am half expecting myself to summon him to open the gates and let me back in again. Presumably they'll be fumigating my chalet ready for the next unsuspecting holidaymaker. Hi-di-bloody-hi, campers.

While I'm pacing up and down a sweatbox arrives with the latest intake. Poor wretched cows. I could write a five volume tome about my experiences inside, only nobody would believe me. Whatever occurred outside these godforsaken walls might as well be on another planet. Everything that happens to you in prison is magnified a hundred times. Even the most trivial things, like someone's hair slide going AWOL, could be the catalyst for a major riot. If you were scared of the school playground darlin', you ain't got a prayer in here, so you had better get used to it.

Those nights on remand in Holloway were the worst. The only thing that has ever come close was my first day at boarding school. The one and only time in my life when I'd tried vainly to cling on to Mother's hand. Never did make friends easily. When the lights went out in the dorm I could hear their upper-class voices banging around my head. Fiona Harding and her eleven-year-old cronies, Maureen, Susanna and Andrea, chanting in unison: *"Jesamine Vickers wets her knickers. Jesamine Vickers . . . wets her knickers."* Like a chorus in a cats' choir. I'm afraid it's one of those names that lends itself easily to ridicule. I won't be sorry to be rid of it.

And I did. Piss my knickers. Frequently. Until the wankers in charge got the message and sent me home. No point in doing that in Holloway. I hear they're trying to make the place more user-friendly these days, with first-night "suites." More like a hotel they reckon. Well a Travelodge anyway. That'll give the right-wingers something to scream about. "Them women are there to be punished – the scourge of society. Let them rot in hell!" Damned know-alls. They don't know sod all, the lot of them.

Unlike, Eva Rowe, who allegedly exited jail in an Armani suit (made to measure – I ask you) sent in by admirer, I'm jogging along very nicely, thank you, in a black nylon T-shirt that keeps giving me static shocks, a pair of faded denims I'd need braces to hold up properly and a padded anorak circa nineteen-eighty-nine. I imagine I must look like a failed trainspotter if such a thing exists. They're not coming, are they? Not one miserable bugger to welcome me home. Wherever that is.

I sling my rucksack over my shoulder and make for the station.

2

I'm good at routine. I'm not good at days like this, when I'm left to my own devices – where I have to make my own decisions – establish new patterns. Prison leaves you numb. Unfeeling. The city skyline has changed over the best part of a decade. Glassier, but not classier. It's huge. Frightening. A mass of weird edifices dotted across the horizon. Give me a one way ticket to anywhere. Heaven? Hell? Who gives a sod?

I sit on the station bench nursing a cup of designer coffee off a cart that's set me back just over two quid. At least inside the coffee was free even if it did taste like rabbits' piss. Ten minutes later, my train pulls in. I'm still not sure this is a good idea, but unfortunately I don't have a Plan B. I can't laugh and I can't cry and I can't remember the last time I did either to good effect. On the old trains if you felt the way I do, at least you could pull the window down and stick your head out and there was a good chance there'd be a tunnel along soon to lop it off for you. Now with these new ones you can't even do that.

I scuff my boots against the seat opposite and a woman who looks like she's wearing one of Mother's hairpieces glares at me. I screw up my fists in my pockets. Wanna make something of it, love? Maybe it's the wig that's riled me. I let my eyes fix on something altogether more pleasant. The perky boobs of a young woman in a tight, bucket-necked T-shirt who's come from another carriage to join us. I squeeze up on my seat and hope she'll take the hint. She doesn't. It turns out she prefers to sit next to the scruffy git in the opposite corner, who looks like he hasn't washed his braided hair for a month.

The train pulls into Birmingham and a middle-aged man wearing a shiny charcoal-grey suit and reeking of pungent aftershave squashes in beside me. That's something I haven't had in a long time. Male company. Can't say I've exactly missed it. He glances at me and half-smiles, like I'm dressed in this get-up for a dare. Some kind of music festival dropout.

He opens his legs wide forcing my knees together. Women don't do that, do they? Not that I'd object if the woman was as alluring as Miss Perky Boobs over there. He flips the catch on his briefcase and pulls out some papers. People's CVs I think. I glare at him sideways-on. His leg is wedged firmly against mine now, like we're stitched together. I want to say something, but the carriage is totally silent. The woman in the hairpiece (or maybe it's her own hair) has been joined by a teenage girl who's reading a novel with a bright pink cover and a title I've never heard of. The scruffy oik in the corner has his headphones on, eyes shut, in another world.

I stand up and plant my trainer on Mr Moron's foot. He doesn't respond. He doesn't glare at me, tell me to fuck off. Nothing. Bit different from being inside, kid.

I weave my way through three busy carriages to the sanctum of the toilet, knowing I have no intention of returning to my seat. I just want some time on my own. Solitary confinement by choice, this.

I throw off my padded quilt and squat on the loo, enjoying the rocking motion – the jiggy-jiggy of wheels on tracks. My hand slides between my legs that all too familiar way. In my (considerable) experience there's nothing rocks you as hard as the orgasm you emit when you're aching to pee. Odd how you can employ the same technique a thousand times and every single time the result comes out different. The same, yet different. Amazing.

Now then, is it to be right, or left? It's right-handed for a quickie, left-handed for when I've got the time and inclination to take things leisurely. Panning for gold right-handed plays havoc with my tennis elbow.

While I'm making my mind up, there's a sharp rap on the door. How frustrating is this? Give a girl a chance to get going, why don't you?

The husky voice says: 'Hurry up mate, you're causing a queue out here.'

Hastily I flush the pan, soap my hands and splash my blotchy face with cold water. When I pull the bolt on the door it's him: Mr Moron. Just him. No queue.

I move for the door but he shoves me backwards and I bang my arm on the sink.

'What's your problem?' he says, his massive frame looming over me. He snatches hold of my wrists, capturing them in his sweaty palms.

As calmly as my nerves will allow, I utter, 'You were rude. You invaded my personal space.' That's what they teach you in anger management classes. State your perspective clearly and concisely. Don't lose your rag.

'Personal space? We're on a fucking train, darling, there is no *"personal space."* There's no bloody space at all. You stamped on my foot. D'you know how much these shoes set me back?'

'Haven't a clue, mate, but you were almost certainly robbed. You look like Coco the Clown.'

'Yeah and you look like something off the catwalk. More like something the cat dragged in.'

'And anyway I didn't stamp. I may have accidentally caught your foot.'

'On purpose, more like.'

'You have exactly ten seconds to back off,' I say, keeping perfectly still, allowing him to hold my wrists in front of me and not struggling.'

'Or what? Or you'll scream? I wouldn't waste your breath. No-one's interested, love.'

'Hang around and we'll find out, won't we? Let go of me. Please. There now, I've said it nicely. There's no need for any trouble.'

He pushes me against the side of the cubicle. I can feel his prick gouging at my groin. He drops my wrists and slides one hand up under my T-shirt.

'You really don't want to do that.'

His hand is on my breast. Squeezing it like it's one of those stress-relief toys.

He breathes in my ear, 'C'mon, you know you want it.'

I lean into him like I'm about to snog him, then drive my knee sharply into his bollocks. He doubles up and drops to the floor. While he's writhing around moaning obscenities at me, I drop my pants and let out what I've been holding in.

Jesamine Vickers wets her knickers.

Jesamine *Vale* . . . pisses on bald tossers' heads.

3

There's a four-by-four on the driveway. Black. What they call a Chelsea Tractor in that neck of the woods. It's all shiny like it's just rolled out of the showroom. The cottage looks as if it's walked off the front of a chocolate box and the garden is immaculate, like it's the result of one of those TV makeover programmes. I have this vision of Lizzy crouched over the lawn in her designer knee pads, carefully manicuring each blade of grass with nail scissors until they are all identical.

I sidle up the crazy-paved path and pull on the chimes. Hopefully they're out. What I'll do is count to ten very quickly and then go. I get to three and hear footsteps approaching. My stomach is gurgling away furiously. The door opens. A large-framed, handsome man with designer stubble and brown tousled hair stands grinning at me.

He says in a lazy Glaswegian drawl, 'Well now, what can I do for you, young lady?'

'I'm looking for Lizzy. Lizzy Vickers.'

'She isn't here. She's at the restaurant. She'll be home in an hour. Can I give her a message?'

'Restaurant? Lizzy, a waitress . . .' I stifle a laugh. 'Don't tell me it's a chippie? A fat-drenched perm is so not a cool look.'

'Bistro . . . pan Asian. She co-owns it.'

'Of course. She would. And you are?'

'Very funny. You first.'

'Long lost relative.'

'Does the long lost relative have a name?'

'Jesamine. Jes.'

'Well would Jesamine Jes like to come in and wait?' He moves away from the door. I step over the threshold. The point of no return.

'You still haven't introduced yourself.'

He lets out a throaty laugh that tells me he's a whisky and cigars man. 'I can tell you're not star-struck. Makes a nice change actually.'

'You're somebody famous, right?'

'Not too famous to make you a cup tea.'

'Only if there's nothing stronger. Anything.'

'Wine?'

'Ta.'

The interior is impeccably tidy like I knew it would be. Exposed beams on the ceiling, powder pink paint in the hall. Little mementos dotted around here and there.

I duck my head into the camomile living room. There's a photo of Octavia and Dad on the sideboard and one of Octavia with some bloke I've never seen before. And one of Lizzy and the bloke who answered the door splashing around in a dinghy. She's wearing a wetsuit. My sister in a wetsuit, what's the world coming to?

He goes through to the compact kitchen and I follow. He opens the fridge and takes out a bottle of Chardonnay. 'Make yourself comfortable.

'So, Lizzy's famous friend, would you like to play *Give Us a Clue*, or are you just going to be dead boring and tell me straight out?'

He holds out his hand. 'Cameron McGill.'

'Pleased to meet you.'

'You too. You still haven't twigged, have you? Is it the stubble?'

I shrug. 'Sorry.'

'*Leith's Country* – Fridays at eight, ITV.'

'You might as well be spouting Cantonese, mate.'

'You must have seen the trailers surely? And there's posters up everywhere . . . shopping malls . . . train stations . . . airport lounges . . .'

'I don't get out much.'

'Where on earth have you been? Planet Zog? '

'And I don't watch travel programmes.'

'It's not *Wish You Were Here*, darlin'. I play Jed Leith, a private investigator with a murky past. Not exactly wholesome. It's altogether more fun playing a baddie. I get fan mail. Women send me explicit photos of themselves in provocative poses. And I've got enough crotch-less knickers in my undies drawer to open a sex shop.'

'Sorry, I'm not big on TV.' I take a sip of wine and feel my cheeks flush. 'This is strong. I don't usually drink . . .'

'No alcohol, no TV, no outside world to speak of . . . you'll be telling me next you've taken a sabbatical from the convent.' His fingers inch across the table like he's about to make an assault on my hand. 'Your top.'

'What about it?'

'You've got one of those electronic tags sticking out. Didn't the alarm go off when you left the shop?'

'Not that I noticed.'

'Whip it off and I'll see to it for you. I've got a handy little tool that'll take care of it.'

'I'll bet you have. You don't waste much time. And here's me thinking all Lizzy's actor friends were natives of Sitges.'

'I'm a teeny bit more than her friend, darlin' – I'm her husband. Three glorious years and counting.'

'Lizzy's remarried? No-one's said anything.'

His eyes flicker at me suspiciously.

'How long exactly since you've seen Liz?'

'Eight years. We used to be close. I'd have thought once bitten . . . '

'Losing Ewan so tragically like that. An accident, wasn't it? I assume you knew him.'

'Better than her.'

'You didn't approve?'

'You'd need to talk to Lizzy about that.'

'I'd rather talk to you.'

13

4

'That'll be her,' Cameron says, as a car crunches onto the drive.

'Two Jags, eh? The pair of you must be doing well.' I knock back my wine and help myself to another. My hands have gone icy cold the way they do when I'm petrified. In spite of what some people might choose to believe about me, I've never been one to court conflict.

Through the crack in the door I see Mr Handsome's lips meet her cheek fleetingly.

'We have a surprise guest,' he says, taking her bag off her.

'Well you'll have to do the entertaining, sweetheart,' she coos in her bird-like voice. My body jerks to attention. Seems weird hearing her again. Like a dream. 'Run me a bath, darling,' she says. 'That blasted Sian didn't show up for yet the third time. I don't give a sod about her personal problems, I'm not some bloody social worker. She's getting a final written warning, then she's out on her ear.'

She strides through the hallway and peers in. She looks porkier than I remember her, in her cherry woollen suit and kitten heels. Or maybe it's because I'm half the size I used to be. She glares over the top of my head without attempting to make eye contact.

'You're not supposed to be out for another month,' she says sharply. 'And even then, you're not meant to be *here*.'

'Three weeks. They needed the space.'

She goes across to the decanter and pours herself a brandy. 'Out five minutes and you're already breaking the terms of your early release. You've got some bloody nerve, Jes, but then you always did.'

'Lizzy, sit down. You're making me nervous.'

'And what exactly do you think you're making me?'

'Aren't you going to ask how I am? Say how well I look on bread and water?'

'They'll sling you back inside without a second thought. Your choice entirely. Nothing to do with me.' She spins round at Cameron who looks totally bewildered. 'Who did she tell you she was?'

'She didn't – exactly.'

'And you let her wander into our home just like that. Typical.'

He rolls his eyes. 'Look would someone mind telling me what's going on here?'

I push my chair back. 'I'm her sister. Younger sister, obviously.'

'She's not my sister,' Lizzy snaps. 'She's not anything to me.' She snatches up her car keys. 'I'm popping out for half an hour. You had better not be here when I get back.'

'Have another drink,' Cameron says, as the door thunders shut. 'Take no notice. You know what she can be like.' He fans his face with his hand. 'Hot-headed.'

'Runs in the family, I'm afraid,' I say apologetically. 'Apart from Octavia who is a trifle colder than the North Pole. If her girdle was on fire it's no guarantee it would thaw her out. The only time I've seen her lose her cool was when Judi Dench beat her to the part of 'M' in *GoldenEye*. She blew a gasket. Trashed her dressing room. Rather gratifying to witness actually.'

'Do I detect an air of bitterness?'

'Not me, mate. I'm well used to the fact that Lizzy is the family favourite and I'm the also-ran. Born to play it.'

'I've always championed the underdog, me.' He rubs his chin. 'Would you believe I've known Lizzy for the best part of four years now and I never knew she had a sister. Bizarre.'

'So how did the pair of you get together?'

'At an after-show party. Leeds. I'm afraid I was screwing your mother at the time, but only for professional reasons you understand.'

'Poor you.'

'Funnily enough, I was playing her son-in law. A bloke who seduces his wife's mother with the intention of inheriting the family's vast fortune.'

'Yeah? Well don't you go getting any funny ideas, matey. Not that it matters to me. I've probably been squeezed out of the will already.'

15

He bows his head to one side. 'You're not upset are you?' He looks like he's ready to make the leap over to my side of the table the minute I give him any encouragement whatsoever.

'Over Lizzy? God, no. I never expected her to lay on the red carpet treatment after all these years. We were fairly close as kids, but well . . . you drift . . .'

'Octavia's never once mentioned you. Liz never talks about you. It makes me wonder what you could have done that's so bad.'

'Going into detective mode are we, Mr Leith?'

'I'm intrigued. And more than a little puzzled that my wife has chosen to keep this a secret from me. And that my mother-in-law appears to have colluded with her.'

'That's what they're like, the pair of them. Now you see how it's been for me all these years. You'll get used to it.'

'So do you intend telling me what all this about, or do you want me to feel totally excluded?'

'I killed someone.'

He starts to laugh then stops. 'My God you're serious. Who? How? Why?'

'You sound like my defence lawyer. Probably best if Lizzy fills in the rest.'

He gets up. 'Tell you what then, why don't I give you a guided tour.'

When she comes through the door we're giggling like old drinking buddies. She gives me a piercing look.

'Still here?' She turns to Cameron. 'Whatever she's told you, don't believe her. She's a compulsive liar. I hope you had the good sense to hide the knife block.'

Cameron looks at me. 'So I know the 'how.''

'Lizzy . . .'

'It's Liz,' she says curtly. 'My *Dizzy Lizzy* days are well and truly behind me. No-one's going to make a fool out of me anymore.'

'Dizzy Lizzy,' Cameron says, winking at me. 'It's got quite a ring to it.'

She looks at him with a pinched expression. 'And you can stop flirting with the Devil.'

16

'I sense I'm in the way.' Cameron opens the cellar door. 'I'll fetch another bottle.'

'Well take your time about it,' Lizzy says. 'Ten minutes should do it. Then she'll be on her way.'

I tip the wine down my throat at a frantic rate, more out of necessity than pleasure.

'How's Dad? And Octavia?' That it's as an afterthought I ask about *her* is only too obvious.

'They're not together anymore,' Lizzy says curtly.

'What do you mean, not together?'

'They've separated.'

'When?'

'November.'

'She came to see me just before Christmas. She didn't say anything. What on earth's happened, Lizzy?'

She shakes her head. 'You'll have to ask her.'

'Poor Dad. Is he OK? Did he leave her? I wouldn't blame him. I'd have done it years ago.'

'No, he's at home. She left.'

'But why? Why would she?'

'And I don't intend turning this into a social event. Like I say, speak to Mum. She's flying over for the weekend.'

'Good of her to make the effort. Bravo.' I clap my hands sarcastically.

'Don't think it's for you. Like I said, we didn't know.'

We parade around the living room, sizing one another up like a couple of mating birds.

I say eventually, 'So how have you been?'

'Oh you know. Grief-stricken. Like all the life has been sucked out of me. What's the point in carrying on? You've got all the answers it seems, so bloody answer me this, Jesamine. What's the damn point?'

'You remember my name then? I thought maybe because you haven't used it in a while . . .'

'If you've come here for tea and sympathy you've come to the wrong place.'

'That's the last thing.'

'So why then?'

17

'Because I didn't know what else to do.' I draw in a deep breath. 'About Lola . . .'

'I might have known. You don't really give a damn about anyone else. This is all about you. Some things don't change.'

'Is she OK?'

'She's happy and healthy. With a family that adores her.'

'How often do you see her?'

'Rarely. We thought it best not to intrude. Eight-year-olds ask an awful lot of questions.'

'Is she bright? Bubbly? What does she like to do? What's her favourite colour? Is it pink? All little girls like pink, don't they?'

'You didn't. You loathed it. I'm seem to remember khaki was your favourite. You had a nice line in camouflage clothes.'

'Is she a daredevil like me?'

'She's not like you. Not a bit. She's studious. Sensible. A wise head on young shoulders.'

'But she *is* happy, yeah?'

'I just bloody told you.'

'There's not a single day gone by when I haven't thought about what it would be like . . .'

She wags her finger at me. 'Don't you go getting any stupid ideas.'

'I'm her mother. She needs me, Lizzy.'

'She doesn't need you. You need her, because you don't have anything else in your life. It's not the same. Go away and get some help. Sort your head out.'

'Tell me where she is . . . who she's with . . . and I'll go. I'll leave you alone.'

She goes to the drawer and takes out a paper knife. She walks slowly towards me, her pale skin shining like an apparition. Her eyes are still. Intense. I can see *his* face. *His* head on *her* shoulders. I want to back away but I can't move. She lays the knife in my hand.

'Make me.'

'What's going on?' Cameron says, as I pop the knife back in the drawer.

'Nothing.' I look at Lizzy. Shock registered on her white face. 'Can I stay the night?'

'Best not,' Lizzy says, businesslike, her composure recovered.

18

'One night. One bloody night. It's all I'm asking guys. Tomorrow I'll go. They're supposed to be fixing me up with somewhere to stay.'

'No doubt you'll get one of the new mews houses in the centre of town,' Lizzy says cuttingly. 'The ones the law-abiding locals can't afford.'

I look her straight in the eyes. 'Either way it'll be more space than I'm used to.'

Cameron says, 'Ah come on, Liz, have a heart. We can't see the poor girl on the street. The return of the prodigal sister. Surely that's a cause worth celebrating.'

'One night,' Lizzy says, her eyes narrowing. 'I mean it, Jes. Don't think you're going to get round me.'

'Can I hug you?'

She runs her hand through her impeccably-coiffed hair. 'Don't push it.' She kicks off her slippers and picks up the evening paper.

'Feel free,' Cameron says, opening his arms to me, so I hug him instead and it was probably the wrong thing to do, as usual. I can sense Lizzy giving me daggers.

'Hey girls I've just had the most fantastic idea,' he booms. 'How about a threesome?'

Ah, so this is what bliss feels like. I settle back onto the pristine Egyptian cotton sheets and yielding divan. Makes a bloody change from a mattress that's like an ironing board and a sheet strip that's only good for roping yourself with. That's our Lizzy for you. Doesn't do things by halves. The best of everything. Even as a child her dollies were decked out in outfits from Harrods. Least that's what I told everybody at school and she never once denied it.

There's giggling coming from the next room. Something I rarely heard at my last place. Piercing screams, yes. Paranoiac rants from the substance users who were withdrawing, eventually subdued by hastily induced medication. Much bellowing across the courtyard – undying love pledged between inmates, their physicality separated by mile-upon-mile of iron and mortar.

The giggling has been replaced by something more serious. He's banging her up, if you know what I mean. Sorry about the terminology, but it's down to years of conditioning. Listening to Mr Macho hammering away with all the panache of a lion butchering a gazelle, doesn't do anything to rouse my libido from its hibernation. I'm imagining Lizzy's face – pale and contorted. Her body as limp and lifeless as Ewan Stafford in a body bag.

Then again, perhaps it's altogether different when you're having passionate love made to you by some superstar of Friday night TV. I'll have to ask her sometime, when she's very, very pissed.

Hurry up and finish you selfish bastard. Don't pretend you're one of these rare breeds that can keep going all night. Shoot your spunk, roll over and let us all get some peace. I clutch the sheet in my moist hands and pull it over my head.

5

My intended shopping spree with Lizzy's Visa card comes to an abrupt halt at the first hurdle when the shop assistant thrusts a hand-held computer at me and invites me to 'Punch in my PIN.'

I stare at him blankly for what feels like five minutes, then I enter Lizzy's day and month of birth: two-six-nought-five. She's never been imaginative when it comes to codes. Even as kids when we used to play Mastermind – the one where you hid coloured pegs behind a wooden screen – not the one with the sinister black chair, Lizzy was always more concerned with creating symmetrical patterns than winning. She should have become an interior designer.

'It's a bit slow today,' he says. 'Always is, first of the month.'

I nod. He drums his fingers on the counter. 'I'm afraid it's been rejected.'

'Computer says no,' I offer. He doesn't laugh. Miserable old fart. Young fart.

'Have another go if you want,' he says. 'Or do you perhaps have another card with you?'

'Isn't there some way of by-passing the code? Can't I just sign?' I wiggle my cleavage at him. It might have worked ten years ago. He looks at me pityingly. Not the effect I was after. I feel like a pensioner trying to seduce a choir boy.

'I'm afraid not. Do you want us to reserve the goods, madam? We can keep them until close of business this afternoon, if you'd care to call back.'

No-one ever called me *madam* before I went inside. It was all *sweetheart* and *darling* and *babe*. And I was always getting wolf-whistled in the street. Propositioned in the local hostelry. Have the years away really been that unkind? Deflated, I stuff the wretched card back in my pocket. 'You're all right, love. I wouldn't want to get you in any trouble.'

What use is a flaming credit card that won't give me any credit? I need a job. Something. Anything. On my way to the library, I amble back through the village gazing luminously into every newsagents window at the little postcards mostly aimed at flat hunters.

At the library help desk, I am confronted by a melon-breasted assistant in a slinky, low-cut gypsy top. This woman's an impostor. For a start she's younger than me. The only librarians I remember from my youth were old enough to be your granny's granny, mooching about in their crinoline skirts and tweed cardies and peering at you severely over their horn-rimmed specs.

'Let me show you to the reference section,' she says brightly. 'Was there anything in particular you were after?'

'December 1999. A murder. Local.'

'Doing some research, eh? Are you a journalist?'

'No. Just interested.'

'You can use the Internet for one hour free of charge. It's normally quiet at this time of day. Do you have any ID with you?'

'Do I need it to use the computer? Can't you scan my iris, or something?'

'I'll need to register you. Usually we need two forms of ID, but I'll take one – credit card bill, driving licence – that sort of thing.'

'I've got a driving licence.'

I pull out a dog-eared scrap of paper and hand it to her. She unfolds it gingerly like it might disintegrate in her hand.

'Gosh, where have you been? You don't have one of the new style licences?'

'I've been away. Overseas. Charity stuff. They didn't require me to drive.'

'Well done you,' she says, slapping my back a little too feistily like I've swallowed a gob stopper. 'It's something I've always meant to do. We all talk about it, don't we? It's only people like you that actually get out into the field and make a difference. You put the rest of us to shame.'

'I'm sure you do your bit in other ways,' I mumble, faintly embarrassed.

'Where were you stationed?'

I'm thinking I need the loo. Urgently. I cross my legs and raise my body up and down on the spot. 'Bog-ota.'

'Blimey, you're brave. The bloody coke capital. I'd have been shitting it. By the way, I'm Gina,' she says, holding her hand out. 'Put it there.'

'I know. It says so on your name badge. I'm Jes.' I place my sticky little paw into her cool hand.

She flips the switch on the computer.

'I was just going to ask if you knew how to use it – silly me. I guess the driving licence made me think we were in some time warp. I'll leave you to it. If you want anything don't hesitate to give me a yell. I'll be at the front desk.'

'Are we allowed to yell in libraries now? Whatever next?' I say, on the way to relieving myself.

She grins at me. 'Figure of speech.'

Several minutes later, I slide the mouse across the mat and the blinking cursor shoots off the screen. The teenage boy next to me giggles. I tilt the screen my way so he can't see what I'm up to.

After farting about for what seems like an age, I manage to click on something that works.

Local Woman Arrested In "Slaughter" Murder Mystery

Police are questioning a local woman in connection with the death of former army chef, Ewan Stafford, at his home in Lower Slaughter on December 28th. The woman is thought to be Jesamine Vickers, the dead man's sister-in-law and daughter of the renowned TV and theatre actress, Octavia Vickers. It is understood that the woman has been remanded in custody pending further investigations.

"Slaughter" Woman Convicted

Jesamine Vickers, youngest daughter of the stage and screen star, Octavia Vickers, has been convicted of murdering her sister's husband, Ewan Stafford on December 28th last year. The court heard how Miss Vickers calmly took a knife to the former army chef. She then proceeded to stab him five times in the chest and abdomen. Forensic evidence showed that the wounds were deep and precise – not the result of a frenzied attack, but of a calculated one, the court concluded.

During the trial, Vickers, 21, offered no justification for her actions that afternoon, but claimed that Stafford was a sadistic bully who had turned her sister Lizzy, 23, from a fun-loving jetsetter and regular on the London social scene, into a virtual recluse, despite Elizabeth giving evidence to the contrary. Vickers has been detained at HMP Holloway, pending psychiatric assessment and further reports.

It's that word "Slaughter," isn't it? It lends itself to situations like this. Why couldn't they have lived forty miles up the road in sodding Chipping Sodbury? Or Sodding Chipbury, or whatever it is the locals call it. My eyes stray to one of the nationals. I pick it up and force myself to read, even though I don't want to.

"Sightings of Evil Eva top two hundred mark"

In excess of two hundred members of the public reckon they've had a brush with Evil Eva Rowe, since her release from Whytemoor Hall prison, Leicestershire, last Wednesday. Rowe has been "sighted" in locations as far apart as Aberdeen, Cornwall and Suffolk. The owner of a Padstow sub post office, Gloria Summers, is convinced the woman who asked her for change of a tenner yesterday lunchtime is the UK's most notorious jailbird.

Mrs Summers said: "It was her, I'm absolutely certain. She was wearing a black trilby, like she'd just walked off the cover of some fashion magazine. Her hair was poking out from underneath. It looked as though it had been dyed recently. She spoke with a West Country accent I thought was put on."

Were you the woman Mrs Summers served yesterday? Are you an innocent member of the public? Come forward and clear your name. Get in touch with our news desk and we'll return your call straight away.

When I get back, Cameron is painting the front fence and muttering to himself.
'First sign of madness,' I say and he jumps. Little flecks of paint splash the pavement. 'Very, *Desperate Housewives* – the picket fence.'

'Shit.' Paint drips off the end of his brush onto his jogging bottoms. 'Are you in the habit of creeping up on people?'

'I didn't. You were in your own little world.'

'Rehearsing my lines. We're filming a Christmas special from tomorrow. You should come along. Banff.'

'Canada? Fantastic. I've always fancied myself as a snowboarder. I do that grunge look so well. Mind you, they do say, it's bloody freezing.'

'Scotland.'

'No time, mate. Sorry. I need to find a job. Unless your team needs a runner. I'll do anything.'

He seals the lid on the paint tin and follows me inside. He puts his brush in the kitchen sink and turns on the tap.

'Don't you dare let on to Lizzy about me putting paint down her sink. She'll go ballistic.'

'I won't tell. Never been a grass. *Snitches end up in ditches* – that's what they taught us inside. It's served me well.'

'What you said just now about a job . . . anything . . . did you mean it?'

'I need cash. I can't exist on handouts.'

'And, funnily enough, I need a assistant.'

I pull up a stool. 'Go on then, interview me.'

'So what jobs have you done in the past? Apart from being an assassin.'

'Excuse me if I don't laugh. I can sell. I used to be the top motor spares salesperson for my local garage ten years back. I'm good on the phone. I'm personable.'

'I can vouch for that.'

'So what do you need?'

'For a start you could help me with my lines.' He goes to the dresser and takes out two bundles of papers. 'You can read, I take it?'

'Cheeky bastard.'

He winks at me. 'Read the part of Ellen – the feisty young farmhand.'

I flip through the pages. 'I'm allergic to cows. And goats. Anything furry's a no-no.'

He grins, 'Ellen's the only woman that won't let Jed have his wicked way with her.'

'Good for her. She doesn't give in, does she? Else I'm not doing it.'

'Read on and we'll find out. From the top.'

25

'Hello stranger. *Original.* What brings you up here?'

'Just checking you're OK. What with all the recent goings on.'

'I lived half me life on these here moors.'

'You can drop the Bristol accent – she's meant to be Scottish.'

'Well it doesn't say that, does it? In the bloody notes.'

'If you'd watched the series you'd know.'

'Ooh-er. Sorry I've been incarcerated for half my bloody life.'

'Carry on.'

'I know how to defend my virtue, Mister Leith. Is this crap set in the dark ages, or what?'

'Helston's still on the loose. He's armed with a sawn-off shotgun. You'll need to watch your step. Mind if I take a look in the barn?'

'Help yourself. You won't find anything.'

'Harbouring a fugitive can result in very serious consequences, Miss Winter.'

'Mister Leith, whatever are you suggesting? Note the fluttering eyelashes. I'm a natural at this game.'

'Most impressive. Come with me.'

'Sorry, Jed . . . Cameron . . . or whatever you prefer to be called, but this is the biggest load of shit ever. A five-year-old could write better dialogue than this.'

'It's the action sequences that make it – the boats. . . the helicopters . . . the car chases. Don't be too dismissive. Once we hit the hay things get a whole lot more exciting.'

I throw the dog-eared script on to the table.

'Sorry, mate, you've had your chance. The calling of the Job Centre is too powerful to resist.'

'OK, let's try something else.' He takes my hand and leads me downstairs into the cellar.

'What are you doing?'

'How about a blow job? For starters.'

'Fuck off. You're not serious?'

'Why not? You can pocket a hundred quid just like that. You said you needed cash. You said you'd do anything. Call it one-fifty. Because I like you. And because I think you'll be good at it.'

'Bloody hell, man, you're married to my sister. The one than hates the very bones of me. What are you trying to do?'

'Cameron is married to your sister. Jed is young, free and gloriously single.' He fingers the zip on his trousers. 'Come on, honey, where are you going to earn that kind of money for ten minutes work?'

I feel hot and cold all over. I shove him away.

'Ten minutes, Cameron? Don't flatter yourself. Didn't you get enough last night?' Even though I can feel my knees trembling, I force myself to walk calmly up the ten stone steps to the kitchen. I open the cupboard, take out two expensive-looking tea bags, drop them into bone china mugs and flip the switch on the kettle.

'Ah, so we disturbed you. I said as much to Liz. Sorry about that. The monthly duties.'

'Not Lizzy – just you. She's quiet isn't she? That's if she was there at all.'

'Just now,' he says. 'I got carried away. Thought I was on the set.'

'So that's what you get up to?'

'No. No I don't. That's not what I meant.'

I make certain I don't eyeball him. In Whytemoor, women got hit on all the time. If the attention was unwanted you just played it cool. Stayed out of the way until the other party got the message. When the place is a cauldron of raging hormones and sexual tension, it is considered foolish to aggravate the situation – akin to pouring white spirit onto a barbecue.

I can feel him hovering behind me. His hot breath on the back of my neck. I take a teaspoon from the drawer and squeeze the tea bags against the sides of the mugs.

'Milk?' Stupid thing to say, Jes. He doesn't answer. I open the fridge. He pulls out a chair and straddles it. I can't bring myself to look and see if he's done up his flies.

He clears his throat. 'It was selfish of me to expect you to do something for me without giving anything back. Selfish and egotistical. I'm living up to my reputation.'

'Forget it.'

'I just thought what with you being stuck inside all that time . . . it must have been hell.'

'I'm fine. Don't I look fine?'

'So what did you do for sex? Get a screw to screw you?' He laughs. 'Come off it. Your hole must be tighter than a cork in a bottle of vintage Krug after going without for so long.'

27

'You're so unbelievably fucking rude. And arrogant.'

'So I'm right. Thought so. Sparked a nerve.'

'Who says I went without?'

'I got the impression you spent a lot of time in solitary.'

'So? I took DIY lessons. It was a progressive regime.'

'Not much fun flying solo – not when you can have company.'

'That rather depends on the co-pilot.'

'Oh I know my away around the territory all right. You won't be disappointed.' He smirks. 'DIY, eh? Feel free to show me if you like. Lizzy's got a yoga mat in the bedroom. Not that it's seen much action. Help yourself.'

He's laughing at me now. If there's one thing I can't tolerate, it's being made fun of.

'How do you like your tea? Don't tell me, hot and strong. Tell me something I don't know.'

'I don't actually . . . drink tea. He opens the cupboard and takes out a malt whiskey bottle and two tumblers. 'You will join me.'

'No thanks.'

'Course you will.'

'Are you always this obnoxious?'

'Let's put it this way, gorgeous, when Jed Leith wants something bad, he usually gets it.'

'But you're not Jed. Jed doesn't exist. Only in the mind of some warped scriptwriter.'

'Oh Jed exists all right. We all have a dark side wouldn't you say? I'll bet you've seen more dark sides than most in your time?'

'All in the past.'

I glance up. He is staring at me intensely. I feel my cheeks sting. He grins, like it's registered.

'I don't know about you, babe, but all this talk is making me horny. We should do something about it. Why don't you come over here and get acquainted with my hard side?'

'Oh I don't know, probably one of a million reasons. Because you happen to be married to my sister . . . I told you . . .'

'We have an open marriage. Lizzy is very understanding.'

'The Lizzy I know isn't like that. She's always believed in fidelity . . . that's what our family is like.'

'You wouldn't believe the times I have to prod somebody on the set. It's a perk of the job.

'That's simulated, surely?'

He winks at me. 'Oh come on woman, this isn't a quick fumble behind the bike sheds. We're both over eighteen. What Lizzy doesn't know can't hurt her.'

I chew my lip. 'OK then, how about . . . because I don't fancy you.'

'Bollocks. Of course you fancy me. Why are you blushing? Jed can be very persuasive. Let me persuade you Jesamine Jes.' He looks at me with that boyish smirk that tells me he's going to get his way. 'Leith's got something for you, baby. Come over here and say hello.'

If the guy's not going to back off what other choice do I have? He gets up off the chair. 'Promise I'll be gentle.'

I offer him my most seductive smile. 'Promise I won't.'

6

'Don't think of knocking,' Doctor Khan says, shaking her ebony mane in my direction and trying not to let on she's startled, even though we both know she is. Physically she doesn't look a day older than when we last saw one another, thirty-four months and five days ago. I'm aware I do every time I look in the mirror. Her body is slim, honed like an athlete's. Not an ounce of fat visible. Her face is unlined, minimally made-up.

But then she ought to look bloody good, didn't she? Unlike the gorgeous Doctor Khan, I haven't had the benefits of a dressing table bulging with Clarins products and unlimited trips to the day spa whenever I felt in need of pampering. One glimpse of this beautiful apparition is enough to suggest my heart valves have been hot-wired to a set of jump leads.

I plant my hands on the desk. 'You've got to help me.'

'I'm so sorry, Doctor Khan,' the receptionist says, bustling in and frowning at me like I've just made a total arse of her. 'She just barged straight past me. I tried to tell her you were busy.'

'It's all right, Dora. I can see it's not your fault. Give me ten minutes, then you can show the next appointment in.'

'Certainly Doctor.'

The door snaps shut.

'Is she menopausal?'

'Please don't do that in future,' she says firmly. 'I might have been in the middle of a consultation.'

'While you're still as professional and unruffled as always. So we have a future. Sounds promising. Tell me more.'

'I must say, Jes, you are the last person I expected to see. How did you find me?'

'The Yellow Pages wasn't exactly bulging with Pashindra Khans.'

'Quite.'

I reach across the desk and she withdraws.

'It's not how you think.'

'You don't know how I think. When did you get out?'

'Yesterday.' I pull up a chair.

'Make yourself at home,' she says. 'Shouldn't you be seeing your probation officer or something?'

'Probably. It can wait. This can't. I didn't get you the sack from Whytemoor. Honestly, I've no idea which vindictive cow stuck the knife in, but it wasn't me.'

Her face softens. 'I'm amazed you're still using that phrase,' she says, her lips curling into a faint smile.

'Slip of the tongue. You're smiling. So you're not still mad at me?'

'I've never seen the point of having regrets. I've moved on to bigger and better things. Onwards and upwards. '

'So I see. Cheltenham, eh? Very upmarket.'

'With extortionate rents to match.'

'I'll bet.'

'So you see, maybe somebody did me a favour, unwittingly.'

'In that case, I only wish it had been me. Why didn't you fight your corner?'

'Because I knew my time had come. I was too radical for their anarchic regime. They wanted repression, I wanted expression – and progression. The women's kick-boxing class was a little too progressive . . .'

'You could have got compensation.'

'I did. I got this place. No amount of money would have made any difference. Sometimes you have to accept that you're in a no-win situation. You have to know when to hold and when to fold.'

'Are you a player?'

'In my youth. My wild student days.'

'Pashindra Khan, the gambler . . . who'd have thought it?'

'So if the only reason you're here is to tell me you didn't get me the sack, then I believe you. Happy?'

'Ecstatic. But it's not the only reason I'm here.'

'Oh.'

'I need your help. Professionally I mean.'

'Unfortunately I don't have time for Twenty Questions, so . . .'

'I've done something. Something really naughty, except . . .'

31

Her eyes drift away from mine. She starts tapping away on her computer keyboard.

'OK, you really don't have time for me.' I move to get up.

She closes the lid on the laptop. Leans back in her leather chair. Flexes those slender fingers I've spent many a restless night fantasizing over.

'You've done something naughty, except . . .'

'Instead of feeling guilty about it, it gave me a buzz. A kick. My sister's husband . . . he's cheeky and good-looking . . . and famous as well. He really fancies himself. We got into a bit of a situation.'

'What kind of *situation*?'

'He offered to bung me a hundred and fifty quid in return for a blow job. I acted like I was insulted. I wanted him to beg. Then he came over all apologetic . . . said like we should do something mutually beneficial. He thought I was an easy target because in his arrogant opinion, I was sex-starved. He pressured me . . . tried to brainwash me into thinking it was OK. That Lizzy wouldn't mind, but I knew she would have . . .'

'Go on.'

'I know I shouldn't have, but I gave in to temptation. I couldn't stop myself. I scalded his cock. With tea. It's probably gone all brown and wrinkled. Tea stains, doesn't it? Mind you, it was really posh tea . . .' I start giggling in that false maniacal way, hoping she'll come round this side of the desk and take hold of my wrists like she used to in the good old bad old days when I needed placating.

She doesn't. She says in that ultra-cool voice that cuts right through me, 'Take some deep breaths. Compose yourself.'

'Perhaps you could prescribe me something, Doc. How about some beta blockers? I haven't tried those in ages. Might be amusing to see what little side effects they throw up. Let's see, I've had palpitations, high blood pressure, jaundice, hairy tongue . . . it's a full moon on Sunday. Maybe I'll turn into the wolfman.'

She says gently, 'If you want my opinion, you would be better off staying somewhere else, if this man is going to exploit your vulnerability. Didn't they sort something out for you before you left?'

'Yeah . . . a bloody hostel. They can poke it.'

She looks at me with an air of regret. 'I'm awfully sorry, Jes, but you'll have to go now. I'm expecting somebody.'

I try one more time to engage her. 'Cameron McGill . . . he plays this guy Jed Leith on TV. Honestly. I'm not making it up. It's him. Maybe I could sell my story to the *News of the World* for an absolute bloody fortune.'

'Yes,' she says. 'I've seen his programme a couple of times. Maverick ex-detective . . . scantily-clad girls running around toting revolvers . . . all the usual clichés. Very seventies.'

'I'll tell him you're a fan.'

'You mean, he's still talking to you?'

'He's away filming. I didn't get back until late last night and he was up at the crack of dawn. As a matter of fact, he's probably up the Crack of Dawn, as we speak, God help the poor girl. Can I bypass the Rottweiler?'

'Sorry?'

'For an appointment. I really need to talk some more. There's tons I need to get off my chest.'

She stands up and walks across the room to the window, then turns and meets my gaze. 'Jes, I can't see you. Not as your therapist. It's too personal. You need someone who can start over with you . . . someone who can analyze you objectively. That isn't me. I know plenty of good therapists.'

'You *are* a good therapist. The best.'

'But I'm not good for *you*.'

'But you just said we were OK.'

'We *are* OK.' She returns to her chair and opens that blasted laptop again.

'So . . .'

'Look I've got a colleague you can see. Jeff Daniels. He's a young Australian . . . enthusiastic . . . passionate about making a difference. He's really impressive, so they tell me.' Her painted fingers dance across the keyboard.

'That's what they said when you arrived on the wing. Not the bit about being from Oz.' I'm disappointed when she doesn't laugh.

'You're in luck,' she says. 'I can fix you up for the morning. He's had a cancellation.'

'Not *that* impressive then. But *I* want *you*, Pash.' I can't help stamping my foot like a petulant child.

She smiles a little too pityingly so that I am made to feel patronized.

33

'Wants and needs are two entirely differently things. Tough love, Jes, that's what you need right now. Trust me on this. Ten o'clock tomorrow, don't be late. Do me a favour. Apologize to Dora on your way out.'

Lizzy peers round the door. Her face tightens in disappointment when she clocks me.

'Not from Camelot, sorry.'

'And I'm sorry too, but we're closed to visitors. This isn't the National Trust – turn up, flash your membership card and in you come. I said one night, it's already been two.' Lizzy's got such a hard look about her when she doesn't smile. All mean and thin-lipped. 'No room at the inn.'

Ha, ha. 'I know it's a cheek, but come on, Sis. Just until Cameron gets back. It'll be company for you.'

'That's right, pretend you're doing me a favour, instead of the other way round. You were always good at that.'

'Have a heart.'

'You're confusing me with someone who cares.'

'Lizz – '

'I'm not shutting you out of my life entirely, Jesamine, I'm just not ready to have you hanging around me all time, snapping at my ankles like an irritating little terrier. It's all too intense. I can't handle it. I can't breathe.'

'What if I stay in my room? You can lock me in if you want. I won't even come out to eat. You can carve a little hatch in the door . . . shove a tray through at mealtimes.'

'And it's not that I don't feel sorry for you after the ordeal you've gone through. I'd hate for you to think that.'

'Really?'

'But you can't stay. It's simply not workable.' She dives into her bag and pulls out a postcard with a painting of the bistro on it. 'Give me a call at the weekend when Mum's up. Come over for lunch, or something.'

'Maybe the real reason you don't want me here is in case your husband of three years makes a pass at me.'

'Don't be silly.'

'Do you trust him, Lizzy?'

34

'More than I trust you.'

'Or maybe it's just, I'm impossible to resist? That's what you think isn't it?'

She shakes her head. 'You really don't seem to have learned anything from the last time around. They do say we go on repeating our mistakes, over and over again.'

'Yeah, Sis, they do, don't they?'

7

'Enid Bean,' the woman says, holding out her hand. I'm tempted to reply that never in my wildest dreams did I expect it to be Blyton. Pity though. I'm always up for a nice picnic. Marmite sandwiches washed down with lashings of ginger beer. Or was it Paddington Bear that like Marmite? 'We spoke on the phone. Come through. It's not exactly Buckingham Palace, but it's clean and quiet.'

I wondered what sort of person would lend herself to the name "Enid Bean" and now I know. She's thin and lanky, with cheeks like glowing coals and she's decked out in an ensemble of red checked shirt and brown cords. She looks like she might, in a more youthful existence, have walked the entire landscape of the Lake District in a fortnight. Or, more aptly, line-danced it. I'm slightly concerned I might accidentally resort to calling her Beanpole to her face.

'I've put you in an ensuite,' she says. 'I hope that's OK. And you have a pretty view overlooking the courtyard.'

I sigh. 'Courtyards – I've seen enough of the darned things to scar me for life.'

Beanpole looks at me like I'm slightly off limits. 'I've left a tea tray for you in your room. You know we don't take DSS?'

'I'm here on business. Don't mind me, I always dress casual. It tends to make people more relaxed.'

'I think it's better to be up front about these things. We don't want any bad feeling later.'

'I'll get the deposit for you this afternoon. Cash.'

'Don't think I'm being picky my dear, but I would prefer a credit card. That way, you know who you're dealing with. And it's all too easy to lose cash, isn't it? For it to get mislaid?'

'Is it? OK, fine. I'll sort it out with you this afternoon.'

'Much appreciated, Miss . . .' she glances at the booking sheet, 'Khan,' she says, looking at me in a slightly concerned way.

'My married name. We're not together anymore.'

'Mixed marriages – tricky business,' she says, patting my arm consolingly.

'And it's Doctor Khan actually.' It feels unbelievably thrilling to say those words. I can feel a stirring in the pit of my stomach.

'Oh, I say. A doctor in our midst. How marvellous,' she trills. 'You couldn't have a pop at my bunions, could you possibly?'

*

The guy turns out to be an imposing six-foot-three, with a covering of chin stubble and blue-black curly locks. He looks like he ought to be in a student band. He's younger than me, definitely. He holds out one hairy-backed hand and squeezes mine. Overly-hairy men always give me the creeps. And overly-hairy dames for that matter. I've encountered a few of those in my time.

'Jeff Daniels. Pleased to meet you.' He's got a smiley face and teeth so abnormally white they look like they've been coated with emulsion. I can't imagine him having to work too hard to get a woman into bed. A straight woman, obviously.

'Jesamine Vale.'

'I've got the right client then,' he says. 'Promising start. Grab a seat. Tea? Coffee?'

'I'm not a patient then? Client, eh? Like it. Coffee. Black.' He swivels round, slots a sachet in the coffee machine and presses a button. Then he wraps a cardboard holder around the cup and hands it to me. 'Be careful, it's hot.' I suppress a sudden urge to giggle.

'What has Doctor Khan told you about me?'

'Absolutely Jack Shit. We're starting afresh. So tell me all about yourself, Jesamine Vale. Pretty name by the way.'

'What would you like to know?'

'I understand you've just come out of clink.'

'Yep. I did away with my sister's first husband evidently.' His face doesn't change. I'm kind of disappointed not to get the shocked reaction I was hoping for.

'You don't seem certain?'

'They banged me up for eight years, so it must be true, mustn't it? You don't get a sentence like that for nicking a tube of Rolos from the corner shop.'

'Must have been a tough gig?'

'Whatever doesn't kill you . . . isn't that what they say? My brief swore blind they'd never convict a pregnant woman . . . fed me the biggest load of bollocks ever and I swallowed it.' I punch my head. 'How dumb is that?'

'Pashindra mentioned you had a child.'

'Yeah. They took her off me.' I rub my eyes. I'm damned if I'm going to let myself go in front of some stranger. 'They thought I might harm her – my baby. Fucking twats.'

'I'm sorry.'

'They should be fucking sorry.'

'You're here to sort out your anger?'

'I don't know why I'm here. Doctor Khan seemed to think it would be good for me. Everything changed after she left.'

'You two knew one another before, I understand.'

'She was Head of Mental Health at Whytemoor. After she left there were three suicides in as many months. What does that tell you?'

'That it was a shit place to be.'

'There was no-one to talk to. No-one who would listen anyhow. The place needs bulldozing and rebuilding with Lego bricks. I'll redesign it for them if they want. I'm a whizzo with CAD. Just one of my many underrated skills.'

'How best can I help you today?'

'Yesterday, I poured boiling water on my brother-in-law's penis.'

Daniels crosses his legs. And uncrosses them again. Unconscious reaction, I assume. 'Any particular reason?'

'He wanted me to have intercourse with him. Sexual, I mean, not social. I'd hardly punish someone for wanting to chat with me.'

'And you didn't want to have sex with him?'

'Bloody right, I didn't. After I'd done it, I felt elated. Orgasmic. Better than orgasmic. No, really. On a total bloody high. There's something wrong with me.'

'That's what we're here to find out. If you don't mind me asking, how are you supposed to have killed your sister's husband?'

38

'Miss Scarlet, in the kitchen, with the dagger. In this case it was a Sabatier, but let's not split hairs. I'd love to be able to romanticize it. Say like, he lost his life in a duel. Pistols at dawn and all that jazz, but unfortunately . . . and by the way, in case you're interested, I'm not sorry. He needed teaching a lesson. Want to see my press cuttings?'

'Harsh lesson . . . death. Couldn't you have paid someone to rough him up a bit? Knee-cap him, even.'

'Hindsight's a miraculous thing, Doctor Daniels.'

'Jeff, please.'

'Like I said, Jeff, I don't remember. I don't think I planned it. No I definitely didn't.'

'Tell me about your relationship with your father.'

'My father? Bit of a therapy cliché, isn't it? Before all this shit we had a brilliant relationship. We were as close as any dad and daughter could be.'

'So what's changed?'

'What's changed is that I haven't seen him in almost two years because all of a sudden he stopped visiting me and I don't know now if we can bridge the gap. In the beginning he used to come every fortnight, but I think he found the whole scene too upsetting. I intend to put things right, starting this afternoon. Make up for lost time. Go places. Do things. Like we used to.'

'Tell me about growing up with him.'

'I was the sporty one – rather Lizzy wasn't. She hated getting messy while I couldn't get enough of it. Dad used to kick a ball around the garden with me, while Lizzy and Octavia – that's my mother – baked scones and bread and went shopping. Lizzy had ballet lessons for a while – not that you'd know it now, she's turned into a right old porker. My world was football, rock climbing, building a den. It didn't occur to me then that Dad might have preferred a boy. It does though now. All the time. We spent our days out fishing. Camping. Making fires. My idea of heaven. Well, it was then.'

'Was your father demonstrative to you as a child? I mean physically.'

'We weren't deprived of cuddles. Dad wasn't a cold fish, unlike *her*. Oh I see where this is going. He didn't abuse us if that's what you're getting at.'

'No I wasn't. Are you always this defensive?'

'Only when I'm not sure what the agenda is.'

'Doctor Khan said you want me to hypnotize you.'

'So she *did* talk about me? She's bloody gorgeous, isn't she? A beautiful person inside and out. And so intelligent. And not the slightest bit arrogant. It's like she doesn't know what she's got. You know, like in that Liberty X song . . . they played it all the time on the landing when I first got sent down. Got bloody pig sick of it in the end.'

'If we could concentrate on you for the time being.'

'How long have you two been business partners?'

'Just over a year. We're still in the honeymoon period.'

'Sounds idyllic. It is *just* business, is it, Jeff?'

'Strictly.'

'How did the two of you meet?'

'We were introduced by a mutual friend at a dinner party. Forgive me, Jesamine, if I skip the small-talk, but we are here to talk about you. Why don't you hop up on the couch, we'll see what we can do.'

'It's too soon. Don't rush me. I don't know you well enough to let you hypnotize me. We haven't bonded.'

'There's really nothing to worry about. It doesn't happen the way stage hypnotists would have you believe. You'll be completely conscious throughout the process. You won't do anything you don't want to.' He stands up and goes across to the couch. The place where vulnerable people like me come to have their innermost secrets prised out of them. He pats the leather invitingly. 'Come on, babe, it'll be OK.'

I get up slowly and go across to him. There's a glint in his eye like he's got me exactly where he wants me.

'Really, there's nothing to be alarmed about. Put the cup down now, Jesamine . . .'

8

The woman at the Job Centre looks bored silly and it's barely eleven o'clock. She flips through a wad of forms the size of a telephone directory and asks if I've brought my CV with me. Yeah right, love, I've never had a CV in my life.

I mention that I've got eight GCSEs and I dropped out of college because I made the wrong choice of course. I was yawning my way through the Archaeology of Roman Baths syllabus when I had a Eureka moment and realized my calling was brain surgery. So I guess I missed my vocation.

Right at the end I casually drop in that I've just done eight years at Her Majesty's pleasure. Her indifferent face doesn't change. I fold my arms defiantly.

'I think it would all look a little sparse on a CV, don't you, love?'

She looks displeased, like she doesn't know what to do with me. No neat little box to file me away in.

'Look,' I say hopefully, 'let's do us both a favour, love. Whip out your calculator and do a quick calculation. Let me know how much my fortnightly giro will be and I'll sign on the dotted. Sorted.' I pick up her pen.

'It doesn't work like that,' she says sternly, snatching the pen back. 'We are required by the government to produce a written contract between ourselves and the jobseeker.'

'Contract? This isn't ruddy ICI. The world's gone bloody mental.'

'Could you please not swear.'

'You're a bundle of laughs, aren't you? What do you get up to in your spare time? Working the comedy circuit no doubt. I expect you'll be wowing the punters at the Edinburgh Fringe. With you at the helm it's bound to be a sell out. They'll be queuing all the way to John O'Groats.'

I glimpse her name badge.

'So it's Maureen, eh? I can just see it now . . . up in lights . . . Maureen Morose from the job centre. Heard the one about the ex-con who came in off the street looking for a hand out? Come on then, Maureen Morose, what's the punchline? Are you afraid your face will crack?'

'Look,' she says, 'my next customer is due in five minutes.'

'Customers, is it now. My God. I preferred it back in the days of the good old DSS, with its dingy waiting rooms and reinforced glass screens. We were claimants then – now we've been promoted to bloody customers. Well I don't feel like a bloody customer. If I was a bloody customer you'd be serving me frothy cappuccino and fois gras sandwiches with the crusts cut off.'

'If you continue to behave in this manner, I shall have no option but to call security.'

'OK, what do you want from me?' I hold out my wrists. 'Go on, take some. Drain my arm. Just give me a flaming giro, love. It's not rocket science.'

'Are you sure you can be bothered to do this, Miss Vale? This isn't a quick fix you know, it's all rather time consuming. This is only the beginning. At fortnightly intervals you will be required to produce documentary evidence to show that you have been actively seeking work. That means you'll need to produce copies of letters of application, records of telephone calls made to potential employers . . . details of interviews attended. If we don't think you're making enough effort to find work, we can review your claim at any time.'

'Review?'

'Yes.'

'That means cancel, yeah?'

'It means, *review*.'

'You're damn right, Maureen Morose, scrap it. I can't waste my precious time hanging around this dump. After all, my mother's filthy rich. I'll nab a few quid off her. And Cameron McGill – yes him off the telly – that gorgeous hunk Jed Leith – there I go name-dropping again. He's offered me a job helping him learn his lines and in between script-reading sessions, I get to suck his cock. Perk of the job, love.' People are laughing at me and even more so at Maureen Morose's purple face.

I fumble around in my pocket, pull out a fifty-pence piece and toss it at her. 'For the swear box. Have a nice day, love.'

*

42

She glances up from behind her desk and does a double-take.

'So you're Sandra Thomas now? Full marks for inventiveness. I love the wig. Makes you look twenty years older.'

'It's one of Octavia's. Hideous, isn't it?' I peel it off and rub my head vigorously in case there's anything nasty crawling in it. 'Horrible scratchy thing. I found it in Lizzy's wardrobe. Still it got me past your minder. I knew those elocution lessons would stand me in good stead one day.'

'I'm impressed you went to all that trouble.' She beckons at me to sit down. 'Or maybe you're into high drama.'

'I leave all that stuff to Mother. She once played a psychiatrist, you know, Doctor Uma J King in *Relatively Normal*. The starring role and she thought she was God. Used to swan around the set in her purple velour housecoat and chiffon head scarf. She had a whole bloody wardrobe of headscarves as I recall – all in lurid patterns that could trigger a migraine at thirty paces. I can't ever remember her wearing the same one twice.

'Course my mother wanted our family to be like the bloody Redgraves. Like, *Relatively Normal* just about sums our family up. Ha! Some joke, that. She went fucking mental when it got axed after two series. Never did find out what the "J" stood for. Mental – that's ironic, isn't it? Any chance of a coffee from your shiny new machine, Doc? Black, no sugar.'

'Of course. Where are my manners?' She's formal, almost curt with me today. Can't exactly say I blame her. She swivels her chair to face the coffee machine, pulls a plastic cup, presses a button. My eyes follow her exceptionally svelte legs as she strides across the room and pours herself a cone of filtered water. I've never thought of myself as a leg-woman, but right now I could be tempted. I'm drawn to her coral-glossed lips, as she sips the water thoughtfully, like she's working out what to say next. Unlike the self-contained Doctor Khan, I've always felt a compounding need to fill a silence.

I blurt out, 'Did Doctor Daniels tell you I'm mad as well as bad? There really is no hope.'

'What happened, Jes?' She says flatly, like she's tired of my company already.

'Didn't you ask *him*?'

'I'm rather keen to hear your version.' She fetches the coffee cup round to my side of the table and places it carefully on a metallic coaster.

'Are you thinking I might do the same thing to you, Doctor Khan?'

43

'Let's get one thing clear,' she says, perching on the edge on the desk in a way that makes her skirt rise above her knees, 'I'm not your doctor, I'm never going to be your doctor, so you had better call me Pash.'

'Really?' I feel my mouth break into a grin. She crosses her legs. Yet another provocative pose sent to try me.

She says: 'You thought I wouldn't give you the coffee, right? Considering you've scalded two people in three days. That's pretty good going. It was a test. Did I pass?'

'You're the one with the degree. Beauty and brains. It's a pretty combustible combination if you ask me.'

'You're excited at having that power over people. The power to shock and the power to hurt. It's like a potent aphrodisiac to you. Do you think I'm scared of you? Does it turn you on?'

'You're not, are you?'

'Do you want me to be? Is that what you want, to see me cowed in the corner?'

'No, no. That would be the worst thing.'

She puts her hands up like she's surrendering. 'See, that's why I'm sitting here like this. No protection. If you wanted to throw that cup of coffee in my face . . . in my lap . . .'

I pick it up. She doesn't flinch. Her eyes lock into mine in that intensely focused way that always makes me feel flustered.

'So why did you attack Doctor Daniels?'

'It just came over me like a wave. An impulse. An itch I had to scratch.'

'An itch you had to scratch? Jes, come on. This is me.'

'He was asking dumb questions about my father. Why not my mother? He was hassling me. He wanted to get me on the couch. He called me *babe*. Fucking *babe*.'

'Not as a term of endearment I assure you. It's the way he speaks. Jeff's a friendly guy. Most patients respond to it in a positive way.'

'I thought I was meant to be a client, not a patient.'

'Let's not sweat over the minor detail.'

'Does he call you, *babe*?'

'Probably. It's not something I've analyzed.'

'Is he shagging you?'

44

'Listen, we should go for a drink sometime. Out of hours. I don't think your coming here is doing either of us any good.'

'Are you letting him screw you?'

She looks at me like I'm some pathetic idiot.

My head drops automatically. 'Sorry for being crude. You're the only person I can trust, Pash . . . the only one who understands me. You're my rock . . .don't take away my lifeline or . . .'

'You'll play the 'emotional blackmail' card. You know I care about you, Jes, I can't help *that* much, but I'm *not* your lifeline. You have to start acting responsibly now or you'll end up in trouble again. The last thing I want to see is you going back inside. That would be too cruel. Despite recent evidence to the contrary, I don't think it's what you want either.'

'Did Doctor Daniels report me?'

'No. But somebody will, if you continue to lash out the moment someone utters a word that upsets you. Personally, I don't think some stranger calling you "babe" has got any bearing whatsoever. I've never held you in the raving feminist mould. It was simply a means to an end.'

'Clever aren't you, Doc?'

'You had already closed your mind to the possibility that therapy with anyone other than me could work. Probably I was wrong to suggest it.'

'Hypnotize me.'

'We both know that can't happen.'

'You're the only one who can unlock my mind. If nothing else, it'll be a case study you can write up in *Psychotics' Weekly*, or whatever journal it is you write for.'

I get up, walk across the room, kick off my shoes and slide onto her couch. It feels every bit as good as I knew it would. The cool hard leather against my skin. The sour expression on her face tells me I've fucked up again.

'Make yourself comfortable, why don't you,' she says, without looking at me. 'And you're not psychotic.'

'No I'm completely normal. It's what normal people do – go around scalding one another.'

'That you've recognized the fact proves my point. If you were psychotic, you'd already have convinced yourself your actions were entirely reasonable.'

'Unless I'm an ultra-smart psychotic who's into reverse psychology. Want to swap seats with me, Doc?' She doesn't answer. I shut my eyes. 'OK, what happens now? Put me under your spell.'

'This isn't some tacky porn flick, where I get to ravish you on the couch – some soulless Hollywood bonkbuster, for God's sake.'

'Surely that ought to be Bollywood?'

'Either way, I don't intend indulging your fantasies about me, so unless you'd care to take a nap while I'm out to lunch . . .'

I sit up. 'Fancy yourself, don't you?'

She opens her desk drawer, takes out a file and pops it into her briefcase.

'While you can't resist turning everything into a joke,' she says.

'What does that indicate?'

'Mmmm, let me see now . . .' she extracts a large tome off her bookshelf and flips through the contents. 'Here we are . . . maybe I should sign you up with Jongleurs.'

I jump off the couch and seize her hand, falling on my knees in front of her.

'Don't give up on me, Pash. I'm sorry. Tell your boyfriend I'm sorry. Tell Jeff – '

'He's not my boyfriend.'

'No?'

'No. And I really *do* have to go.'

'Already?'

She helps me to my feet, holding my fingertips and gazing at me with those cavernous eyes. 'Let me tell you something about therapy.'

'It's the new Rock 'n' Roll?'

She sighs. 'If you could be serious for one minute I'd really appreciated it. In the main, it's useful. It works. It helps you get problems into perspective and identify possible paths forward. But for some people, letting go of their therapist is traumatic – an emotional wrench. And that's why I can't be your therapist, Jes. I don't want to add to your hurt.'

46

9

Dad is sitting in his favourite green recliner exactly as he was the last time
we were both here. The fabric under his feet is threadbare now, but
otherwise the order of everything is pretty much the same. He always
said he'd die in that chair. It would go when he went and not a second
before.

He doesn't get up when I enter the room. He nods and smiles vaguely,
like we're casual acquaintances doffing our hats at one another at the
train station. I run to him and throw my arms around his neck.

'My, my, that's some welcome. I wasn't expecting anyone until later. I
think we're going to get along just fine and dandy, young lady.'

'Oh God, it's so fantastic to see you. I didn't know whether – '

'Have you come to give me a bath?'

'Dad?'

'Call me Eric, my dear. I don't see any need for formality. By the way,
what happened to the other young lassie? The one in the blue uniform.
She had fantastic legs . . . went all the way up her skirt and disappeared
up her arse.'

'It's Jesamine.'

He takes off his glasses and peers at me.

'Well now, that is a coincidence, my dear. I've got a daughter called
Jesamine. She's doing bird.'

I look into his eyes and nothing comes back. 'You're not mucking
about, are you? Not pretending?'

'I see no need. We're both adults.' He taps the side of his nose. 'Don't
let that dreadful matron in on our bit of banter. She doesn't much care
for laughter. You know the sort, iron fist in an iron glove. At least we all
know where we stand. To attention usually, if we know what's good for
us.' He chuckles.

I go across to the window and stare out into the garden where we
once played, my ears straining to hear faint echoes of laughter. The grass
has been concreted over, like no-one could be bothered to tend to it any

more. There's a few odd tubs containing half-strangled plants, struggling for life. A single tear squeezes out the corner of my eye and I swipe it away forlornly. My own father doesn't recognize me. What's worse, the twisted bastards didn't even tell me.

I snatch up a newspaper and pretend to be interested. 'Would you like me to read to you, Eric?'

I turn round and he's dropping his pants.

'I'd prefer a bath first, m'dear. If that's all right with you.'

*

The bistro is heaving. Mainly shiny-faced businessmen wearing off-the-peg suits and fancy ties that don't go with their shirts, stuffing their puffy cheeks with langoustines and knocking back wines with exotic-sounding names that I imagine cost several tens of pounds a bottle.

I watch from the patio as Lizzy scurries in and out of the kitchen in her navy skirt suit and kitten heels, ruthlessly efficient as ever. A chef in one of those black and white check pill-box hats leans against the fire escape door, smoking a cigarette.

'Yer all right, love?' he says.

I nod at him, suck in a deep breath and push the glass door that leads into the restaurant.

A girl in a black T-shirt dress, with, as my father would delicately put it, "legs that disappear all the way up her arse," whips across the floor and asks me if I have a reservation.

'Friend of the management,' I say, whispering into her triply-studded ear that Lizzy McGill is my sister. She says she had no idea Lizzy had a sister, before weaving me through rows of tightly-packed tables and into the calm seclusion of the conservatory, with the quiet aplomb of a Royal bodyguard.

'The VIP suite,' she announces, easing out a chair for me. 'Can I get you something to drink?'

'Champagne.'

'Glass?'

'Better make it a bottle. I'm thirsty.' I pick up the menu card. Before I have the chance to study it properly the girl is back, flashing the yellow

48

label of the champagne bottle at me. I nod appreciatively, even though I don't have the faintest idea whether it's any good or not.

'Today's specials are on the blackboard,' she says. 'Like me to run through it with you?'

I shake my head. 'There's something else I'd like to know though. What's it like working here? Is it like being in a concentration camp?'

'I'm hardly going to say anything terrible when you've just told me the boss is your sister.'

'Go on, say something terrible, I won't tell. Say something bloody awful. OK, I'll say it for you. She's a dragon isn't she?'

The girl extracts the cork expertly. She glugs half a glass of liquid into the flute and hands it to me.

'Yeah, she's a dragon sometimes. But a cuddly one. Enjoy your drink. I'll be back to take your order.'

Before I have time to shield my face with the menu, Lizzy comes round the corner. She looks at me, then at the champagne bottle and her face contorts.

'What the hell do you think you're playing at, Jesamine?'

'I could ask you the same thing. Sit down and chill out.'

She whips the bottle from the ice bucket. 'I take it you've somehow got the wherewithal to pay for this?'

'Yeah, like you can't afford it. This place is rocking, Sis. You got off lightly. I did consider ordering a magnum.'

'Now look here, I work bloody hard to scrape an existence. I've built this place up from nothing. The last people that had it let it go the wall. When was the last time you did a sixteen hour day?'

'Those mailbags don't sew themselves, you know, love. I'm not like you, born with my fingers welded to a Bernina.'

'Oh, so it's not all trips to shopping centres and afternoons at the cinema then?'

'Don't believe everything you read in the redtops. The last new release I saw was in black and white. And it was a silent movie. Pour me another one of those, I've got a proposition for you.'

'I'm not having you working here, Jes. No way on God's earth.'

'That's ridiculous. You need help. You're running around like a headless . . . dragon.'

49

'You don't have any people skills. You're a mess.' Lizzy taps her head. 'Up here.'

'People skills? What sort of shit-speak is that? I've just survived eight years in bloody Spandau – locked up with society's dregs – women society has given up on. Don't you go telling me I haven't got any fucking people skills.'

Lizzy snatches up my menu and puts it under her arm as if to say don't you dare try ordering anything else. 'I've got things to do. Cameron's due back tonight. The place is a tip.'

'Mustn't neglect your wifely duties. Make sure he's got his favourite single malt on the side, while you're laid back on the sofa with your legs prised apart, ready and waiting for him to give you a good pumping out.'

'Vulgar as ever. What a waste of a private education. Mother said we'd have to be prepared to bite our tongues.'

'You two old witches, true to form, stirring it up as per usual. Don't you realize, you ungrateful cow, I did it for you?' She stares at me blankly, but I know it's registered. I pick up the glass. 'Cheers.' She doesn't say anything. I snarl, 'Whatever you think of me, I've bloody earned this. I've just been to see Dad. He looks really well – a little pale perhaps – not that different to when I last saw him . . . except . . . I *mean*, he looks really well, but he isn't is he? A great bear of a man in an empty shell. I mistook the nanny for a housekeeper. Made a right twat of myself.'

'She's not a nanny, she's a qualified nurse. Mother and I pay for round the clock care.'

'Well, just as soon as my benefits come through, I'll chip in a few quid.'

She scowls at me. 'We'll manage.'

'Why the hell didn't one of you say something?'

She shrugs. 'And what would you have done about it in that place? It would have added to your nightmares.'

'What about when I got out? When I first came to see you, you should have told me then. He took his clothes off in front of me, Lizzy. For the one and only time in twenty-nine years, I was forced to look at my dad's prick. That's some bloody welcome home gesture, that is.'

She pulls out a chair and sits down. 'Look if you're serious about a job, I might have something. But don't piss me around else you're out on

50

your ear. No second chances. This is a hard game. It's not for wimps. I need players I can rely on.'

'Ever thought of applying to manage the England footie team, Sis? God, with an attitude like that they'd snap you up. Enter the Dragon! Least it makes a nice change from a turnip or a Swede.'

'Look I'm sticking my neck out for you. I hoped you might be the tiniest bit grateful.'

'Don't do me any bloody favours. And I'm not wearing one of those skimpy dresses that leave nothing to the imagination. That poor little girl you've got on reception looks like she ought to be propped up outside King's Cross, touting for trade.'

'Sex sells. Especially in an industry like this. Fact of life. Get over it, or cut and run like you always do when the going gets tough.'

'I never had you down as a pimp.'

'OK, you don't have to wear a dress if you don't want to.'

'Ta, Sis. I knew you'd see reason. You're not as hard-nosed as they like to make out.'

'You can wear whatever you like for doing the washing up.' She picks up my glass and drains the bottle into it. 'Cheers!'

*

My Probation Officer, Andrew Marsden, isn't amused.

'You're twenty-four hours late,' he says grimly, pushing a pile of paperwork to the edge of his desk. 'I've had to file a report. Hardly the best start we could have hoped for.'

'Better late than never,' I offer cheerily.

'The hostel said you didn't check-in either.'

'Well, as the lovely Katie Melua once said, you can call off the search, 'cos the girl's back, bigger and badder. She didn't mention that last bit – poetic licence.'

'I don't think you appreciate the seriousness of this matter, Jesamine,' Marsden says.

'Oh I do, mate. Thing is, I've found somewhere to stay so I'll let someone else have my suite at the hostel. Consider it my good deed for the day.'

'I see.'

'And I've got a job.' Come on Mr Pork Belly, act the weeniest bit impressed, why don't you.

'So soon. It's almost unheard of.'

'I'm a devilishly fast worker once I make up my mind about something.'

He frowns. 'I'll need the details of where you're residing and who your employer is.'

I can hardly tell him it's my sister, can I? The one I've been bound over not to go within fifty yards of.

'They're one in the same actually. I'm working for Doctor Pashindra Khan at the psychiatric practice in King's Charlton. I'm her PA. There's accommodation thrown in. It's only a bedsit, but we all have to start somewhere.'

He looks startled as you might expect. 'You do appear to have landed on your feet.'

'So you see, you really don't need to worry about me.'

'May I ask where the job was advertised.'

'It was kind of an informal process. A friend of a friend recommended me. Don't they say sixty per cent of jobs aren't advertised? It's a case of being in the right place at the right time. And I'm pretty good at that.'

'As long as it's all above board,' he says guardedly. He opens the desk draw, takes out a form and slides it in front of me.

'Kindly fill that out please.'

10

I sidle up to the desk and slide the plastic card in front of her. 'Whatever it costs, charge it. Money no object.'

Pash looks at me, concerned. 'Whose is this?'

'My sister's.'

'Does she know?'

'It's an advance on my wages. She's letting me work at the bistro as a scrubber. At least that's how it feels. Like being a prozzie.'

'I'm not putting anything on your sister's Visa. It's illegal for one thing, not to mention downright unethical. I don't want your money.'

'I'm not some charity case. Tell you what, Doc, I'll pay you in kind.'

She looks at me like she might have considered bursting out laughing, then changed her mind.

'Tell me about your mother, Jes,' she says, pen poised over a blank notepad.

'You think I'm funny, Doc, you ought to have a tête-à-tête with Octavia. Her one-liners are legendary. "I'd have got my ruddy dame-hood by now, had it not been for the dreadful misfortune of having a murderess in the family. What jolly wretched luck."'

'I meant, tell me about your relationship with your mother.'

'Ouch. Got a spare sweater? It's suddenly got mighty chilly in here. Cold as the arctic. Oppressive as an underground tomb. Up until the age of five I used to call our housekeeper, Ursula, "Mum." I'm afraid I was a Daddy's Girl. Our Lady of Grandeur, was never at home. She was always away . . . touring . . . filming . . . basking in the limelight. On the hunt for a new casting couch to straddle those mighty long pins over.'

'Is that why you insist on calling her by name? Because she doesn't act the way you think a mother should. Is it some kind of chastisement on your part?'

'I honestly can't remember how it started. Probably I was trying to annoy her. I did that a lot. Gave me a real buzz, that did.'

'You couldn't win your mother's approval?'

'Sod the approval bit. It's no big deal. Can we drop it, before I succumb to hyperthermia?'

'And you've never felt the slightest pang of envy about the relationship your sister has with your mother?'

'My mother's expectations are a burden for any mere mortal to live up to – Lizzy's welcome to them. Every single last bloody one of them. You know what I'd love? To get her on that jungle thing – that, *I'm a Celebrity . . . Get Me Out of Here*. It'd make interesting viewing to see how those poor innocent little anacondas and tarantulas coped with having a giant blood-sucking leech in their midst. They're the ones that'd need the bloody therapy, let me tell you. Now can we please talk about something else? Something altogether more pleasant. What are you doing tonight?'

'I need to ask you this, Jes. When you were inside, did you ever self-harm?'

'Once or twice. It's no big deal.'

'When was the last time?'

'Don't remember. Not recently.' I pull up my top. 'Want to check me over?'

'Happy to take your word. Did you ever hurt anyone else?'

'Nope.'

'You never felt like it?'

'One time. Only trouble is, if I'd given in to temptation, I'd be a vegetable now.'

'Eva Rowe.'

'Sorry I can't award any marks for effort.'

'But in the main, it's only men you feel the need to inflict pain on?'

'Well don't make it sound like an everyday occurrence. It's only an occasional impulse.'

'Because you can't hack it that you were born without a penis?'

I can't stop myself from laughing. 'Now that's way too simplistic, Doc. You can do better than that. I know you can.'

'Because you think all men have an ugly side – like Ewan Stafford?'

'You're getting warmer.'

'Guilty until proven innocent.'

'Why shouldn't it be like that?'

'Not really fair though, is it? That's not how the law works.'

'That's how Jes's Law works. I don't give a fuck for any other kind.'

'Sometimes you have to let your guard down and trust people. Not everyone is out to shaft you.'

'Some people I wouldn't mind being shafted by. For instance – '

'Shut up,' she says.

'Can I see you tomorrow?'

'Not tomorrow. I'm going away for a couple of days.'

'Where?'

'To a conference in London.'

'Can I come?'

'No.'

'Go on – let your hair down. It'll be a giggle.'

'That's what I'm afraid of.' She opens a drawer and takes out a CD in a plastic case. 'I'd like you to listen to it twice a day. When you wake up in the morning and before you go to sleep. It'll help you relax.'

'Relax? I don't have time to relax – it's all go, go, go, out here in the big wide world.'

'It'll help you focus then. Help you sort out your priorities.'

'I tried that crap once. Didn't do anything for me then.' She looks at me, unimpressed, like I ought to be trying harder. 'Is it your voice?'

'Yes.' She nudges the case in my direction and I pick it up.

'OK, I'll give it a whirl. Cheers.'

'If . . . when I get back next week, you've kept your nose clean and out of any trouble, I might think about taking things a step further.'

'You'll hypnotize me?'

'No promises. We'll see. We need to take things slowly.'

'Thank you, oh thank you, Pash.' I shoot round to the other side of the desk and throw my arms around her neck, immersing myself in the sweet, sensual fragrance of her skin. I want to stay here forever like this, just holding onto her.

When I drag my head away from her shoulder, she looks startled by my sudden outpouring of affection.

'I hope it helps,' she says. 'The CD.'

'Can I call you when you're in London?'

'Might be difficult. If your mobile goes off in the conference hall you're likely to get expelled. At least, it feels like it. The profession might come across like we're a bunch of trendy lefties, but I'm afraid we're an old-fashioned lot at heart.'

'But you won't be in there all night.'

'There's lots of social things we have to do – networking and stuff.'

'What if I have a crisis?'

'It's two days. You've just come out the other side of a hefty sentence at one of the toughest institutions there is. That proves you're resilient. You're a survivor. There won't be any crisis.'

'Lizzy says I'm a mess.'

'Well I don't happen to agree with her. People say all sorts of things for all sorts of reasons. Your sister might be working to another agenda. Who knows? If you really do have an emergency phone Dora and she'll get a message to me. But only if it's genuinely urgent.'

'Is Jeff going?'

'No. Jes, honestly, you have far more important things to concern yourself with than my love life.'

'So he *could* be boyfriend material?'

'That's highly unlikely. Besides, I don't think his wife would be too impressed.'

'His wife? I'm such a prat sometimes. My hang-ups – they're just leftovers from before. Sorry.'

'Everyone has them – even psychiatrists. Don't apologize.'

'Tell me about your hang-ups.'

'Over that drink sometime.'

'I'll listen to the CD.'

'Good girl.' She zips up her case. 'I'll see you around.'

'Not if I see you first.'

*

Lizzy's got that frazzled look about her today. The one that never fails to lighten my heart.

'You look stressed, love,' I coo. 'I've got a relaxation CD you can borrow.' I chuck my jacket at the coat stand and miss. Lizzy hooks it up on the toe of her shoe and hoofs it back in my direction.

'That stand is for our clientele,' she says. 'You'll find a spare staff locker out the back. We're a bit short on keys, so don't go stashing your diamonds in there.'

'Aye aye, boss. Very funny. So what's with the gurning?'

Lizzy sweeps her hand through her hair. 'Sian walked out after service like night. She's been poached by that new wine bar across the road. She didn't say it to my face, I just know it. I'll pop over there later and surprise her. There's no bloody loyalty in this trade.'

'How can you say that? I'm here. I'm loyal. And I just adore washing up. I think I must have had one huge crush on Nanette Newman as a child to like it this much. It's almost an obsession with me. Bring it on, baby. Pile it up. High as the ceiling if you like. I can handle it. Am I overdoing this bloody enthusiasm lark?'

'I don't want you doing the washing up tonight. You've just been promoted to front of house.'

I curtsy at her. 'But I don't think I'm worthy, Mistress.'

'Get changed. You're meeting and greeting in half an hour. We're fully booked tonight and as I'll be in and out of the kitchen I'm relying on you to be your usual charming self. You can manage that for six hours, can you? Before the façade slips.'

'I'm not wearing that bloody cheap tart's get-up.'

'It's clean, it's pressed, it's got your name on it. So get yourself upstairs, put it on and get on with it. One sniff of rebellion and you're on your toes. And I don't give a flying fuck if I have to get some acne-ridden teenager in from the agency to bail me out.'

'That's what I love about you, Sis, your constant witticisms in the face of adversity.'

She waves me towards the stairs.

Repeat after me, Jesamine Vale: I am not wearing a fucking dress. I am *not* wearing a fucking dress. I suppose I could customize it – make the look my own with a slash here and there. One across the tits, one across the arse, like some age-defying punk.

When did I last force this temple of a body into a bloody dress? Lizzy's wedding. That was some God-awful miserable occasion. She chose Wonderful Life by Black for their first dance. Some *Wonderful-bloody-Life*. She should have gone in for that one, Ever Fallen In Love

57

With Someone You Shouldn't Have Fallen In Love With . . . that's more bloody like it. That ought to be our Lizzy's theme tune, that did.

I whip off my clothes, grab the fastest shower ever and step into the hideous object of ridicule, catching sight of my reflection in the mirror. If some lecherous bastard dares to make one single derogatory comment, he's going to get his nuts flambéed. Don't say you weren't warned.

Lizzy is waiting for me at the bottom of the stairs.

I wag my finger at her. 'One word about it suiting me and you've got a strike on your hands. It's too tight. You can't expect me to wiggle my arse around all night without busting the seam.'

'It's called figure-hugging.'

'It's called a straitjacket.'

'I must say, you *do* scrub up well.'

'For a con. That's what you meant, isn't it? And there's no need to sound so surprised. Yours truly here *was Miss Whytemoor Hall*, two Christmases running. Back in the days when I had curves instead of protruding bones.'

'Lipstick.'

'What? No way. No. These lips ain't tasting no whale blubber, sister.'

'You've got exactly twelve minutes. Get yourself down the chemist.' She gives me ten pounds. 'Consider it an advance on your wages.'

'Lizzy, I can't. I'll feel like a prozzie in a blokes' prison.' I stamp my foot. 'Don't make me do it.'

'It'll make you feel good. All our staff wear lipstick, even the chefs. Especially the chefs. Come on, get moving. You're down to nine minutes and counting.'

'Want me to buy some condoms while I'm at it? Any particular flavour?'

'Shoo,' she says. 'I'm timing you.'

She's got the same crazy sense of humour as me. And it's clear underneath that spiky exterior, she still loves me in spite of what I did. What other choice do I have?

At the chemist, I smear five testers on the back of my hand and pocket the one I find least offensive, along with Lizzy's tenner.

On duty behind the front desk, I can't believe I feel so nervous. Nauseous actually. Sweaty-palmed and pukey. This isn't the best time to start reminding myself it's my first proper job in over ten years. Can it

58

really be that long? I run through the booking sheets, at the same time wiping my hands down the side panels of the dress. This isn't a dinner date with Pash Khan, so why am I bothering to get so worked up? How hard can it be showing a few diners to their tables and scribbling down food orders? Piece of piss. At least I don't have to cook the bloody stuff, which, let's face it, would really give the punters something to worry about.

Lizzy bustles out of the kitchen with a tray of glasses.

'Give these a wipe round,' she says, swirling a cloth at me.

'Sorry, I'm meeting and greeting.'

'There's no-one here. Apparitions don't count.'

'There will be any second.'

'And when there is you can stop wiping. It's murder in the kitchen,' she says, not realising what she's said. 'Jes – '

'Not something else you want me to do? Tap dance on the tables perhaps? Do a few handstands for the clientele?'

'Like the lippy. Suits you.'

'Fuck off.'

11

Glass wipe, stack, glass wipe, stack, glass wipe, stack. Glass . . . I catch sight of a man's broad reflection in the mirror and almost drop the sherry schooner I'm polishing.

'Got a table for one?'

'Cameron – you scared me.'

'And you scared me the other day. And scarred me. Poor old Jed. He's going to need skin grafts. You're lucky I decided not to sue. Mainly because you're flat broke.'

'Do you hate me?' I say, pretending to care.

He grins. 'I love the dress.'

'Do you? So do I. But don't let on to our Lizzy. She thinks I'm wearing it under duress.'

'Dress under duress, eh?' He peers over the top of the counter. 'You haven't by any chance decided to go commando for your debut performance?'

'As if I'd tell *you*, Casanova.'

'Give us a peek.'

'If I were you I'd tread extremely carefully. Let me show you to your table.'

'You don't have to. I want this one. Right here. Where I can keep a close eye on you . . . all night long.'

'Has Lizzy put you up to this?'

'Definitely not. In fact, if she could see inside my head right this second, she'd have steam coming out of her ears.'

'No change there then.'

We both start laughing. Lizzy emerges through the double doors of the kitchen with a face like a wet weekend in Morecambe.

'What are you two giggling about?'

'I couldn't possibly say, darling,' Cameron says, kissing her cheek.

'Well I'd be grateful if you could stop distracting my staff. I need all those glasses polished in five minutes.'

'I can do better than that,' Cameron says. 'I'll do them for you.'

The door opens. A man in a sports jacket and open-necked shirt comes in with a female half his age. And that's being kind. Cameron nudges me in the back. 'Get to it girl.'

'Good evening, sir. Madam.'

'We have a reservation, name of Kendrick.'

I run my finger down the booking sheet. 'Yes, here we are, table twelve. If you'd like to follow me.'

When I return from seating them, Cameron is grinning at me. 'What are they having? An affair I'll bet. Medallion Man meets Dolly Daydream for mutual flirting and multiple orgasms – jammy old fucker.'

'Stop making assumptions. It might be his daughter.'

'Bollocks. If it is, it's called incest and I'm calling the police. Trust me, she's not his wife. Do these plebs know no moderation? A little tip for you, Jes. Never assume any couple that comes in here is married. This place isn't known as Swinger City because of its monthly jazz nights.'

I can't help laughing.

'Lizzy used to laugh at my jokes when we first got together,' he says wistfully. 'The more pathetic they were the more endearing I became.'

'Yeah, our Lizzy used to have a cracking sense of humour before life wore her down . . . though not quite as razor sharp as mine, I should add – but then again, who has?'

'She's always so tense these days. And tired. If you called her panda-eyed the pandas would sue. That's why when I'm not working I like to take some of the weight off. It's a bloody hard life running a restaurant.' He prods me in the side. 'Laughter is the most potent aphrodisiac don't you agree? That and oysters. They do great oysters here. In fact, I might order some.'

'Oysters make me puke.'

'No, really? Pity. We'll have to see what we can do about that.'

'You don't give up, do you?'

Come midnight, we're sitting in the conservatory, the three of us, supping coffee and brandy, while the chefs are on the upstairs balcony

61

working on their lung disease. I kick my shoes off under the table. The balls of my feet feel like they've danced Swan Lake.

'Did you see those girls, in those wee costumes?' Cameron chirps, ever so slightly tipsy. 'It's enough to send any sane man over the edge.'

'Yeah our Mr Celebrity Hunk here was well in demand for autographs.' I nudge Lizzy. 'You should have seen where he was sticking his nib.'

'Spare me,' Lizzy says, rubbing her red-rimmed eyes and yawning.

'Happens all the time I'm afraid,' Cameron says. 'If they want to get their breasts out in public, who am I to refuse them? That girl with tits the size of the Eden Project said she's going to get my signature tattooed on.'

'I'm sure her future boyfriends will be ever grateful,' Lizzy says sourly, stifling another yawn. 'You did well tonight, Jes. Eighty covers. Not one slip up. Dare I say, I'm impressed. I probably shouldn't tempt fate so openly.'

'She was supreme,' Cameron says, winking at me. 'Miss Unflappable.'

'Carry on like this and – '

'I'll have a job for life – God help me.'

'By the way,' Lizzy says, opening her palm to reveal my tester lipstick, 'I found this on the window ledge in the loo.'

When I finally get in it's gone two. I'm not too bladdered to clock the note propped up on the dressing table. Unfortunately. It's from the line-dancing champ saying she'll collect a week's rent in the morning. Obviously the kind of woman who sees the proverbial glass as being half full, is our Enid Bean.

She says she hopes I had a nice evening. It's called working, dear. Slaving away to earn an honest crust. Hardly living it up. Frolicking around in a hayloft with the sisters from the Corrs – now that really would be something to get the juices flowing.

Anyway, given the choice, I'd rather do the washing up than front of house. At least you can have a bit of a daydream, whilst elbow-deep in soap suds. Still, I've decided appeasing our Lizzy should be my first priority in life. If she ordered me to lick her boots until my tongue fell off I couldn't afford to reject it out of hand.

I top up the jug kettle with water from the bathroom sink and open a packet of three crumbly digestive biscuits, making a mess on the duvet. Then I fix myself a black coffee, because I never could bear the acrid taste of UHT milk, and sit with my nose pressed against the window, staring out across the gravelled courtyard and marvelling that there's not one single murmur to be heard. Strangely eerie, that.

I gaze into the black still night until I can't keep my eyes open any longer.

12

This is the bit I've been dreading ever since they told me my release date. Being reacquainted with MOTHER. Ugh. It fills me with the same sense of panic I experienced just before I was about to be sentenced. When I was standing manacled in that cage before the baying court. That same giddy breathlessness that whirled up inside me like a tornado, as they whizzed me through the gates of Holloway prison.

I check my hands. Not surprisingly, the eczema's flared up on my fingers again. I examine the raised red bumps the size of pinheads, that itch like fuck.

Just as I'm considering making a dash for freedom, a taxi pulls into the lay-by. The door opens and those familiar stockinged legs extend onto the pavement. In almost thirty years, I've never seen my mother in trousers. Mind you if I had legs like hers I'd be loathe to hide them away.

Years ago, they used to rave on about Angela Rippon's pins. That woman's got nothing on Octavia Vickers.

She hugs me – not warmly – but accepting of our sealed fate.

'Excellent choice of venue,' she says, as if it was my decision to come here, rather than hers. She winks at me. Completely unnecessary, that. Or maybe she's got fluff in her eye.

She takes off her ridiculously over-the-top diamante encrusted velveteen hat and sets it on the spare chair like a Siamese cat. I make a mental note to order a milkshake to feed it with.

'It is just the two of us, yes?' I say, in the vague hope she might have thought to drag a couple of strangers off the street to act as witnesses.

'Of course.'

'Terrific.'

A spiky-haired girl in a tartan miniskirt fetches us leather-bound menus. Something to hide behind. The menus – not the miniskirt, unfortunately.

'I'm Leila, your waitress for today,' she says. 'Just let me know if there's anything you need.'

Can't wait. I watch Leila wiggle her way to one of the outside tables. For a woman who purports to being a breast-devotee, I have to admit she's got the most fantastic arse, that bumps from side to side as she walks. Perhaps I shouldn't view myself so much of a one-trick pony in future. Mother gives me an intense glare like she's just read my mind. I feel my face flush furnace-hot, as I scan the menu for inspiration.

'Think I'll have the antipasti to start,' she says, waving to some bloke at the back of the restaurant.

Think I'll just opt for a hundred aspirin and get my head down. 'I'll just go straight for the main,' I mumble.

'Nonsense. You need building up. Up to you,' she adds quickly, as if she might have come across as the control freak she unquestionably is.

'Yeah, I'll have the pork loin.'

'I'll have the poached salmon. You pick the wine.'

'Did you want red or . . .' We're like two strangers on a blind date. Ruthlessly polite. Uncomfortably edgy. 'We ought to have white really. What about the Orvieto?'

'Good choice,' she says, as Miss Fantastic Arse wriggles her way back to us. It occurs to me she must have practised that walk a zillion times to achieve that effect. Or maybe I'm just a sucker for a cute bum in a miniskirt.

'What can I get you, ladies?' she says in an Eastern European accent. My guess is she's from Poland. I've become somewhat adept at guessing people's accents these past few years.

Honestly? Don't go there, Jes. Don't. After we've placed our order, mother excuses herself and troops to the loo to powder her nose. I borrow a pen off Miss FA and scribble some prompts on my napkin for future reference.

By the time mother reappears I am happily supping my second glass of wine and picking away at her Parma ham.

'You don't mind?'

'Help yourself.'

'Our waitress is from Prague,' I gush. 'She was telling me about it. Ever been?'

'No. I'd like to though.' She pats my hand. 'Perhaps we could take ourselves off there for a long weekend.'

'Me and you? You and me? No matter how they tossed the dice . . .'

'I sense you're not keen.'

'Bloody right.'

'Jes, I realize this isn't easy. For either of us, but you have my utter admiration for trying.'

Why do I get the impression that every line she speaks has been scripted?

I glance at my napkin. 'So what jobs have you got in the pipeline? Anything nice?'

'I'm looking over a couple of TV scripts. And I'm meeting Trevor Nunn next week to discuss a possible West End project. I haven't done that scene in a while.'

'Pleased for you.'

'I'm still as incredibly fussy as ever. It's no bad thing.' Her eyes home in on the rapidly emptying wine bottle. 'Are you drinking for two?'

'Octavia, my liver's had eight straight years of being clean. Frankly, the thought of all that evil pinkness freaks me out.'

She smiles. After all these years I've managed to make the Grande Old Dame smile. Hallelujah. She says, 'I can't knock it back like I used to. A shared bottle of wine on a Saturday night is about my limit now. When I think of the after-show parties we used to attend when I was in my heyday. The merriment . . . the dancing . . . the booze on tap we used to knock back. And it wasn't all Snowballs and Babycham amongst our set, oh no. Far from it. There were several fine actresses of my generation who wouldn't get out of bed in the morning until they had downed a bottle of vodka.' She pats my hand again, ignoring the raging eczema. 'We shouldn't expect too much. Early days. These things take time.'

'Yeah.' I plunge my fork into a piece of her melon. 'Let's not rush anything.' It crosses my mind that it might be an idea to meet up every five years like the freed inmates did in *Tenko*. I don't voice it.

'You know, Jes, I have this friend, Marjorie Samuels. Capable woman. Stalwart of the WI. Up until a few months ago, she and her daughter, Eleanor, couldn't bear to be in the same room for more than five minutes. Now they're inseparable. They rowed the Atlantic together. Charity thing. Spent six months in a little craft not much bigger than a bath, enduring the elements . . . laughing together . . . crying together . . . sleeping under the stars . . .'

Does she honestly expect me to reply to that? I take a large gulp of wine. 'The thought of you and me in some lurid yellow bucket being tossed around on the high seas . . . you know I get sick on the Isle of Wight ferry. And I threw up over someone's waterbed once, though I'm not sure it had anything to do with motion sickness.' I've got this solid lump in my throat that won't go, no matter how many mouthfuls of wine I swallow. A mixture of anxiety and melancholy. 'Why didn't you tell me you and Dad had split?'

'What good would it have done with you being stuck in that place? You would only have fretted. You're as skinny as a whippet as it is.'

'You could have told me how ill he was.'

'It happened so gradually. You have to understand that. For ages we didn't think anything was really wrong. He may have gotten a bit forgetful from time to time. Then he suddenly started going downhill. The truth is, Jesamine, we hadn't been close as a couple for years. We'd even discussed divorcing. And when I met Leo – '

I raise my hand. 'Who the fuck is Leo?'

'Kindly keep your voice down. Leo is a good friend of mine. For a long time he was my financial advisor. Have you heard of hedge funds?'

'What's that, money that grows on trees?'

'It's damned risky business if you don't know what you're doing. Luckily Leo is adept at that sort of thing.'

'Oh yeah? And what else is he adept at? Fanny-licking?'

'I'm not rising to the bait, Jes. Leo and me . . . we're an item. There, I'm not going to deny it. In fact, I'd rather like you to meet him.'

'There's no hurry, is there? Not pregnant are you?'

'Don't be silly.'

'Unless you're rubbing your hands together, waiting for Dad to shuffle off this mortal coil so you can waltz husband number three up the aisle. In that case you needn't bother taking your wedding ring off between marriages.'

'She sighs. 'Even though your unfortunate experienced has hardened you, maybe you will, in time, come to realize I don't see Eric as often as I should because it's simply too painful.'

'You can't dump Dad like a puppy that's got fleas. A marriage is for life . . . not just for Christmas.'

'Your father is well taken care of I can assure you.'

'By some stranger.'

'Let's face it, we're all strangers to him. Lizzy and I have invested a small fortune in his welfare, so he can have round the clock care. He really does have the best of everything. I only wish I could afford the same for myself.'

'Says she who languishes in four star luxury on bloody Sark eight months of the year. And then there's your hedge funds to consider. Dad needs company. Stimulation. You can't just farm him out and forget about him, it's not right.'

'You've got a darn sight more time on your hands than I have, my girl.'

'I've sat with him every day since I found out.'

'It's not good to break his routine. You'll confuse him.'

'I don't care, I'm not abandoning him.'

'You needn't look at me like that. I'm not abandoning him either, but seeing him like that . . . ' she takes out a silk handkerchief and dabs her nostrils, theatrically. 'It breaks my heart.'

'You're an actor. You can cover up your emotions, easy as winking.'

'That's just it, I can't. Your feelings for a person don't die completely just because you've fallen in love with someone else. That connection that builds up over years . . . decades sometimes . . . that never goes away. I'm not the emotional coward you think I am, Jes. I spent nearly three hours with your father yesterday. Helped him finish that jigsaw you started. We've started another one: the Eiffel Tower. That will take some doing. Every darn piece looks the same.'

The lovely Leila arrives with our main courses and I ask her for another bottle of wine, fully expecting mother to chirp up: *"haven't you had quite enough, dear?"* Instead she says: 'I've arranged a get together at Lizzy's for Sunday lunchtime. Will you be there? We'd all be thrilled if you were.'

'We? Is Dad coming?'

'Don't make this any more difficult than it already is, Jesamine.'

'OK, I'll come.'

'Thank you.'

'Pleasure.' I can't resist stroking Mother's hat and at the same time, letting out a shrill, 'mee-ow.'

'So?' Lizzy says, easing me into a chair. 'Tell me all about it. I want chapter and verse. How much did you have to drink?'

'Two bottles. Not nearly enough. Give me childbirth any day.' I realize I shouldn't have said that. I slink down over the table. 'She's got someone else. Leo. Le-o. What kind of soppy name is that? Or is it his birth sign?'

'I didn't want to be the bearer . . . thought it best if she told you herself.'

'So what's the slimy old bastard like then? Mother said he's a financial advisor. That's another name for a bent crook, isn't it. Marginally worse than an estate agent.'

'Give it a rest.' Lizzy says. 'He's a property developer actually.'

'Greedy then. I knew it. A greedy, money-grabbing C-U-N-T.'

'Jes!'

'I only spelt it out, so don't go getting on your high horse.'

'Leo is a smart guy. Attractive for a man in his sixties. He looks after himself. Works out regularly.'

'I'll bet he does. Is he funny? I don't mean to look at.'

'Not particularly.'

'Then we won't have anything in common. I can't stand prats that take themselves too seriously.'

'Except Mummy.'

'What? Since when did you start calling Octavia, "Mummy?" That stinks. That utterly stinks, Sis.'

'Perhaps I'm regressing back to my childhood.'

I run my hands through my hair. It's become straggly – shapeless. In need of a decent cut. 'It was OK then, wasn't it? We got on.'

'We still do,' Lizzy says. 'Blood is thicker than water.'

'I've never believed in all that crap.'

'Mother does . . . and I do.'

'Which means you forgive me . . . '

'I've come to terms with it.'

'Did you have therapy, Lizzy? Afterwards.'

69

She shakes her head. 'All that psychobabble crap can really mess with your mind. What's the point in keeping talking about the same stuff, droning on and on . . .'

'Not if you get the right person – then it can really help you. There's nothing wrong with admitting you need something to prop you up.'

'You can get medicine for that.'

'I've been there, done that, got the T-shirt and I'm not going back. You can't numb yourself forever.'

'What's going on, Jes?'

'Nothing. I'm in therapy. Sort of. She's a friend. She was in Whytemoor with me for a while. As a therapist, I mean . . . not a prisoner.'

'Thank God for that. You're friends with your therapist? Weirdo.'

'She's wonderful. She can really get through to me in a way no-one else can.'

'I see.'

'She's got this silky voice that makes me go all shivery. What?'

'You said that like you've got a crush on her.'

'Don't be stupid, I'm almost thirty.'

'Your face goes all animated when you talk about her. And your cheeks flush.'

'Shut up.'

'Ooh and you get all agitated because I've sussed you out.'

'Give over.'

'Admit it.'

'OK, I give in. What d'you want to know?'

'Her name, for starters.'

'Pashindra Khan.'

'Oh, she's foreign.'

'She's from Croydon. That's in South London.'

'Yes, I know where Croydon is, thank you. It's where Kate Moss hails from.'

'Ooh, get you, Sis, name-dropping again. I remember on about our fourth meeting I asked Pash where she was from. Here's me thinking . . . Karachi . . Kashmir. And when she said she was born in Croydon, well I split my sides. It was a bit of a "Luton Airport" moment. I think she might have thought I was racist. From that moment I was smitten.'

'Oh my God, my sister's bi,' Lizzy squeals. 'Did they convert you inside?'

'For God's sake, don't tell me you never twigged before. When have you ever known me have a boyfriend?'

'I just thought you were choosy. Or else you didn't talk about it because they were *married*,' she says pointedly.

'I didn't realize I had to spell it out in bloody Scrabble letters. It was so bloody obvious. Doh! What about when I kept having Trudy Haines round for a sleepover? Six weekends in a row, doh!'

'So? You were two fourteen-year-old girls who enjoyed one another's company.'

'Enjoyed playing Doctors and Nurses more like. Nurses and Nurses.'

'Don't,' she says raising her hand. 'It makes me go all queasy hearing you talk like that.'

'Nothing happened. It was all pretty innocent.'

'So you like men and women? Would that be equally, or . . .'

'Just women. Always.'

She shakes her head, disbelievingly. 'So how on earth did you end up pregnant?'

'Don't know. I got careless.'

'What were you doing, experimenting?'

'It was an error of judgement. I won't be repeating it.'

'But . . . you don't look like a lesbian.'

'Christ, you're so naïve, Lizzy. Just because I agree to put on that pervy dress of yours and a bit of lippy . . . these days you can't tell a dyke in the street by whether she's wearing make-up or not. Not everyone goes in for the nylon vest and braces look. That's so last decade.'

'So you don't fancy Cameron then?'

'Don't be ridiculous.'

'All the young girls do. He's got kids half his age throwing themselves at him and all because of the way Jed Leith behaves. Why don't you invite this Pashindra to the party on Sunday?'

'Don't be ridiculous.'

'Stop repeating yourself. Why the hell not?'

'She's in London – at some conference.'

'Another time then.'

'I'll work on it.'

13

I poke my head round the door. 'Jeff Daniels, *This Is Your Life.*'

'How the hell did you – '

'Gave Dora the slip. You want to beef up your security. I learned a lot of tricks inside. If you want any help in that department, I'm your girl.'

'I'll bear it in mind. Doctor Khan isn't here.'

'I know. She's in London. It's you I've come to see.'

'Forgive me if I don't offer you a drink.' He switches the coffee machine off at the wall.

'I wanted to apologize. Sort of. Sorry if I scorched your nuts. Nothing personal.'

'Yeah, well . . . it's pretty personal to me. What do you want?'

'To ask you something.'

'Make it snappy, I'm in a rush.'

'Are you screwing Pashindra?'

'Woah-wo, lady. Hold it right there. My missus is due in here any second.'

'So?'

'You are way off the mark.'

'But she is seeing someone, right?'

'You'd have to ask her.'

'Come on, Jeff, just give me one itsy-bitsy little clue and I swear I'll never darken your doorstep again.'

'Doctor Khan is a very private person. We don't let our personal lives interfere with our work. House rule.'

'Why should I believe it's not you?'

'Because it's none of your bloody business, Jesamine. And if you want my opinion you'd do well to find another therapist. It would be better for both of you. I've told Pashindra that she's in too deep. You both need some space. Why else would she pretend to run off to a conference in London?'

'I don't believe you. Pash wouldn't lie to me. Why are you saying that?'

The intercom buzzes. It makes us both jump.

Dora says, 'Your wife is here, Doctor Daniels.'

'Thanks. I'll be out in one minute. And if I'm not, call for back-up.'

'A slight overreaction if I might say so, Jeffrey. I might need a word with your wife.'

'It's not me, OK? My relationship with Pashindra is entirely on the level. As far as I am aware she is in a long-term association with somebody. I don't know the details. I haven't asked and I'm not interested. Now, we're off for a pregnancy scan, so if you'd be so kind as to leave my office . . .'

I screw my face up at him. 'If there's one thing that pisses me off, it's blokes who say, *we're* off for a pregnancy scan; *we're* having a baby, like it's a fifty-fifty effort, when we all know it's more like eighty-twenty. And then, I'm being generous. So you donated ten cubic centimetres of your precious sperm – big deal. It's just sex to you, isn't it? Psychoprick.'

He picks up his bag. 'Look, I'd love to hang around and discuss the obligations of modern parenting with you, Jesamine. Perhaps another time.

As I go to leave, she's propped against the front desk nattering with Dora. A slight bird of a woman, with wispy golden hair and pale eyes, who looks like she belongs in a *Flake* commercial. She looks at me and smiles. As I pass by, I duck my face in front of hers.

'Tell hubby, best of luck with his preggy pics.'

*

'I'm not coming down,' I wail. 'Don't make me. I thought I could do it but I can't. It seems such a betrayal. I'm going to see Dad. I've got a lot of ground to make up.'

Lizzy takes my arm. 'Don't be an idiot, Jes. They're here now. You can deny it all you want but you're going to have to face up to it sooner or later.'

'Later it is then.' I grab my jacket.

'What would your therapist-friend say?'

'Oh I dunno, she'd probably say, go with the flow. Trust you to bring her up when I'm feeling vulnerable. Make me feel even worse, why don't you.'

'Well then, she's right. And you look terrific. So come downstairs with me now and knock 'em dead.'

'I don't want to be all precious about this, Lizzy. I just wish someone had told me earlier about Dad – about Octavia having some new beau in tow – given me a chance to get my piggy head around it.'

'I should have come to see you,' she says, a little artificially. 'The months turned into years all too quickly . . . I feel terrible that I abandoned you, Jes. It's like I left you to rot in that awful place.' She looks like she's about to burst into tears. 'Please,' she says.

I grab her hand. 'Fuck it. Let's do it.'

Mother greets me at the bottom of the stairs. She offers me her cheek and I peck it obligingly, even though she reeks of Youth Dew from every orifice. She beckons across a strapping six-foot, bald-headed man in a black polo-neck jumper. She's always had a thing for baldies ever since she crossed paths with Sean Connery on the set of *Never Say Never Again*. Pretty bloody apt that.

'May I present my youngest daughter, Jesamine,' she says in her ultra-posh accent. 'This is Leo Hendry.'

My mother's got three classic tones she uses in everyday life: semi-posh – for when she's speaking to people she considers of a lower class than her. Her talking down voice *I* call it. Superior-posh – for WI meetings, cutting ribbons at fetes and the like and ultra-posh – for occasions like this when she doesn't intend for anyone to challenge her authority.

He goes to shake my hand, then leans across and kisses me on the side of my mouth. I can only assume he was aiming for my cheek.

'Delighted. How are you, Jesamine?'

I know what I'd like to say, only I can hear Pash's sultry whisperings in my ear: stay calm . . . breathe deeply. And so I do. And you know what? She's right, it helps.

'Yeah, I'm fine, thanks. Call me Jes.' Bloody wife-snatcher.

'I'll go and fetch some drinks,' Octavia says. 'Leave you two to get acquainted.'

'So you're a property magnate?' How fucking tedious is that?

74

'Yes. It's fascinating work. No two projects are the same. I can be planning a high-rise city centre project one week and a New England-style river development the next. Plus there's a lot of money to be made in offshore investments.'

'I guess that makes you a millionaire?' Lend us a fiver, tightwad.

'I'm not one of these people who thinks that money is a vulgar commodity. I'm exceedingly proud of what I've achieved and I don't intend to rest on my laurels just yet. Retirement isn't an option. That's when people go downhill, don't they?'

'Meaning Dad?'

'Certainly not.'

'So how did you meet my mother?'

'In a bar in Soho. I got invited by a friend of a friend. I wasn't intending to go. I'd been invited out to a freemasons' do, but something made me cancel at the last minute. I suppose you might say fate intervened.'

'How fortuitous.'

'You don't approve of me, do you, Jes? Can't say I blame you. Lizzy didn't exactly welcome me with open arms at first. All I would say to you is please give me a chance to prove myself. I'm not trying to take the place of your father. That would be an impossibility. This is a difficult situation for all of us.'

'Do you love my mother?'

'Of course I do.'

'Then you deserve my utmost sympathy. Have you been married before?'

'Many, many moons ago. We separated twenty years ago. I'm afraid I was unfaithful. She booted me out. Quite rightly too. I was an arrogant rotter then. I've learned my lesson.'

'The world is full of married men.'

'Jackie Collins.'

'Don't tell me you're a fan?'

'As a matter of fact I am. Your mother was reading *Lovers and Gamblers* on our last European cruise. When she crept off to her Pilates class I picked it up for a bit of light entertainment. I've never looked back. Fair to say, it's been a right good education – better than any sex manual.' He winks at me.

Lizzy slinks over with two glasses of pink champagne. She eyes me nervously.

'Everything OK?'

I pull her to one side. 'You lied to me.'

'What?'

'You said Leo wasn't funny – but he is.'

14

I intercept her in the car park, as she's getting her Burberry bag out the boot.

'Never had you down as a chav, Pash.'

She laughs. 'Present from my mother.'

'If my mother gave me that I'd divorce her. There's a thought. So how was the conference?'

'Illuminating.' She's got dark rings under her eyes like she's been awake half the night. 'Yeah, pretty interesting on the whole.'

'But where did you really go? A dirty weekend in the smoke? Yeah I can just picture it. You and some aristocratic banker staked out in some penthouse apartment – the champagne on ice – while his dutiful wife is minding the four kids.'

'You think that much of me, huh?'

'Daniels told me you were only pretending to be at a conference to get away from me.'

'Well he's a naughty little tinker. He'll be getting a slap-wrist. You don't think maybe he was trying to put you off me?' She opens her bag. 'Would you care to see the agenda? Would you like to see my notes?'

'No. That doesn't prove you went. It sounds to me like you're trying too hard.'

She sighs. 'If you don't trust what I tell you, then maybe Jeff's right. You should shop around.'

'Jeff said you're in a relationship. Was that a lie as well? To put me off.'

'Look it's complicated. And It's something I'd rather not go into. I've got a heavy schedule this morning so . . .'

'Dad's got Alzheimer's.'

'Jes, I'm sorry. Truly.' She puts her hand on my arm. 'Look, I can spare five minutes. Let's go inside.'

She ushers me through the empty corridor and into that familiar room, where the resident aroma of her scent has been replaced by furniture polish. I plonk myself on the sofa underneath the window and hug my knees to my chest, protectively.

'Don't suppose you've got any booze tucked away?'

She takes out a compact and checks her make-up. 'Talking's better. Believe me.'

'Don't know where to start. It's gut-wrenching, seeing him plopped there in that miserable old chair that looks like it's on its last legs, filling out the crossword with random answers that don't relate to the questions. When we were kids, he always used to finish The Times Crossword, now any word will do so long as it fits in the gaps. Even then he struggles. And the worst thing is, no-one told me. They're all pretending like it's happened overnight. Octavia's taken up with this property-developer bloke. I wanted to hate the bones of him, but he's really sweet. He bloody would be like that, wouldn't he? To spite me.'

'And dare I ask, how's the job going?'

'Sheer bloody hard graft. I had no idea serving up overpriced grub to overpaid Hooray Henries could be so arduous. I'm knackered by the time the shift is over. My knees creak from all that up and down stairs to the basement lark. You'd think she'd get a dumb waiter installed, wouldn't you? I honestly don't know how Lizzy keeps going on five hours sleep. Then there's the fruit and veg market, four days a week. Think I'll become a consultant like you. Easy money just to sit and listen to twats like me prattling on about nothing in particular.'

'Yeah, easy money, except . . . and I hate to bring this up . . . you're not paying me anything. Did you check out the CD?'

'All the time. I've probably worn it out.'

'Twice a day, I said.'

'Wasn't enough.'

'Did it help you?'

'It made me wet. That always helps. All that murmuring about cavorting on a tropical beach . . . the waves lapping at your feet . . . sand between your toes . . . I'll bet you knew it would have that effect. You don't want it back, do you?'

She shakes her head. 'Actually, Jes, I'm not at all convinced it's wise for us to go on meeting like this. I've got this nagging doubt eating away at my brain telling me I'm not healthy for you.'

'Bollocks. Ignore it. That's what I do when I don't like what the nasty little voice inside is telling me. I'm not seeing anyone else. I flatly refuse. Look, all joking aside, Pash, I trust you more than anyone I've ever met in my entire life. I trust your judgement and I respect your integrity and . . .'

She looks at me seriously. 'If you really mean *that* . . .'

'I do. Please don't do this to me. I need you.'

'It's all too easy for the boundaries to get blurred between therapist and patient. If you want to keep on coming here then we're going to have to draw up a contract.'

'I'll sign whatever you want.'

'Not literally. We just have to agree it between ourselves. Verbally. Starting with the no physical contact rule. I don't touch you and you don't touch me. It's nothing personal. It's not because I don't welcome your hugs or anything like that. We need to keep things professional.'

'Shit. OK. I agree.' I hold my hand out. 'Shake on it?'

'And the second thing . . . no jokes.'

'Fuck. You don't like my jokes now?'

'I need to break down your defences. Strip away your protection.'

'Talk dirty to me, why don't you.'

Her eyes blaze into mine like she's some fuddy-duddy headmistress I've just sworn at in Assembly.

My head drops automatically. 'I'm sorry.'

'Let's get into the head of the real Jesamine Vale – find out what makes her tick – get her life back on track. How does that sound to you?'

'Good. Yeah, good. No jokes.'

∗

I watch her from the gateway in the alley. Unable to move my limbs or take my eyes off her. She's like a little urchin, dressed in yellow cropped trousers and a blue smock, with a mop of strawberry blonde hair that dances on her shoulders as she moves.

79

It's something of a relief to me that she doesn't look like him. She doesn't resemble either of us in any obvious way. She's putting a bridle on a plastic horse. She walks a brunette doll towards the horse and sits her in the saddle, carefully fitting the doll's feet in the tiny stirrups, chattering away to herself – in a private little world of her own.

So she was here all the time. My baby Lola was here all the time and they never told me. So that's why Lizzy didn't want me hanging around. It makes perfect sense now.

I accidentally lean against the gate and it squeaks. She looks up at me, startled. I hold my hands up. 'It's OK. Don't be frightened.' To my delight, she puts down the doll and horse and comes bounding across to me. Up close I notice she has the most striking blue eyes.

'Who are *you*?' she says boldly. From what Lizzy told me I expected her to be more timid.

'I'm Jes – Lizzy's sister. I know who you are.'

'Do you?' she says, 'I don't think so.' It makes me want to laugh out loud.

'You're Lola.'

'My name is Freya.'

'Of course, of course. Freya. Such a lovely name. A pretty name for a pretty girl.'

'Thanks,' she says. She opens the gate. 'Are you coming in?'

'Where's Auntie Lizzy and Uncle Cameron?'

'Upstairs I think. In the bedroom. And he's not my uncle – he's my Daddy.'

Impetuously, I clutch her little hand. She doesn't seem to mind. 'Well I'm delighted to meet you in person, Freya. I've seen loads of photographs of you. You're even lovelier in reality.' She leads me over to the groundsheet where she's been playing.

'I haven't seen any pictures of you. And how come I've never heard of you?'

'Do you know about black sheep?'

'I've never seen one. Not one that's completely black. Daddy took me to a farm once in Scotland and I fed a lamb that had a black face. Is that the same thing?'

'A black sheep – it's like – the person in your family you don't talk about because they're a bit of an outcast.'

80

'Like Granddad Eric – because he's lost his marbles.'

'Yes.' I swallow. 'It's very sad isn't it?'

'I suppose,' she says, picking up the horse and combing its mane with her fingers. 'I'd be sad if I lost my marbles. Will you play with me?'

'I can't stay long. Your mum and dad might not like it.'

'They'll be ages. They've got a lot of banging to do.'

I stifle a laugh. 'What?'

'They've got a new wardrobe for my room – for when I come and stay weekends. I chose it. It's white with pink ponies on it. Daddy says it takes forever to put together. He's crap at anything like that.'

'And how come you know a naughty word like "crap"?'

'Because Mummy uses it all the time. She's always saying how crap Daddy is.'

'Lizzy?'

'Lizzy's not my mummy, silly. My mum is called Suzy. Don't you know anything?'

'Clearly not as much as you.' I ache for her. I want to pull her to me and smother her in my love.

'Jes, are you coming riding with us later?'

'I don't know. I'd like to. I used to ride – years ago – when I wasn't much older than you. I wasn't what you'd term a natural. Kept falling off.'

'I never ever fall off. Well, hardly ever. And Mummy's brilliant at it. She's got cups and rosettes and everything. And she's got her own horse called Palazzo and she's going to buy me a pony for my birthday.'

'That's soon, isn't it?'

'Not really. Seven months. That's ages.'

'Seven months?'

'January the tenth. I'm a Capricorn. What star sign are you?'

'Scorpio.'

'They're meant to be dangerous, aren't they?'

'Some people might say so.'

'Have you got a sting in your tail?'

'That's reserved for people I don't like. Nothing for you to worry your pretty little head about.'

She hands me the toy horse. 'Will you help me plait Romeo's tail?'

. 'Romeo, eh? Love to. Tell me all about your favourite pony at the stables.'

'He's called Muffin. He's a Palomino – that's like, an orangey colour, with a cream mane and tale. His mane is so-o-o silky. Do you think Mummy will buy Muffin for me?'

'I would if I was your . . . does your dad ride?'

'Of course. Haven't you seen him on TV? He does all his own stunts. Well apart from the ones that are on big buildings because he goes all dizzy and he says his legs turn to marshmallow. Do you mind heights?'

'I used to, but I'm better at it now. I stayed at this place once where the landing was really high up and at first it used to make me go all shaky. I used to clutch on to the handrail at the top of the stairs and my hands used to go all sweaty. But after I'd been there a few months, the anxiety sort of went away.'

She beams at me. 'I'm not frightened of anything.'

'Then you're a very brave and confident young lady. But surely, everyone's frightened of something.'

'Well . . . I suppose . . . Mrs Farnham – that's my headmistress – she can be pretty scary if you don't do your homework on time.'

'Is it funny seeing your dad on the telly?'

'It was at first. Mummy doesn't always let me watch, because she says his parts are too rude.'

I put my hand to my mouth. My eyes are watering. I blink the tears away. She looks at me quizzically.

'What's wrong?'

'Nothing – I – I was just remembering something that's all.'

'Something horrible?'

'No, something nice. Do you ever have this feeling when something really nice happens to you that it makes you want to cry?'

'Not really. I suppose when Mummy buys me my pony I might cry.'

'And how do you get along with Lizzy?'

'She's strange isn't she? Mummy says she's got a hormone imbalance that makes her ratty. Mummy's really horrible to Lizzy sometimes, that's why I try to be extra nice to her, so she won't be sad.'

'You really are a sweet girl.'

'What *are* hormones exactly?'

82

'They're the things inside us that affect the way we feel and behave. You'll know all about them in a few years, once you hit your teens.'

'That's not for ages yet. Do you get ratty as well?'

'Sometimes I get impatient about things. If I want something, then I have to have it immediately.'

'My form teacher, Miss Carter, is always ratty. She's got dozens more hormones than Lizzy. Dad says it's because she's not getting any action in the bedroom department. I've got loads of friends at school, Jes.'

'I'll bet you have.'

'I'm not like Verity Stuart who has to buy her friends with bags of sweets, and they still talk about her behind her back. It's not worth losing your sweets over.'

'You've got a fantastic sense of humour, Freya. Could you do me a favour?'

'What?'

'Don't tell anyone I was here. Not your mum, or dad, or Lizzy.'

'Don't they like you?'

'It's not that. It's just . . . well . . . I'm doing some detective work. Undercover. Like your dad does on his TV programme.'

She says, 'Will you come back and see me again? Undercover, I mean.'

'You try stopping me.' I caress her cheek with my fingertips. 'Love you,' I whisper.

'Wicked,' she says.

15

Back at the B and B, I'm perched on a rock in a corner of the courtyard, under the shade of a lolloping yew tree, gazing lovingly at the pictures of Lola Lizzy sent me in jail and hiding from Enid. The last photo is dated just over a year ago. It's the same cutesy face, those huge, inquisitive blue eyes. But stature-wise, she's shot up. They do, don't they?

I don't notice her flip-flopped feet approaching until it's too late.

'Afternoon, Doctor Khan,' she says, a little sarcastically I thought.

'Enid.'

She's got a clipboard under her arm. I don't suppose she's wanting me for a customer survey. She says, 'I wondered how long you were planning on staying. It's just that I've had an enquiry about a rather large booking for the week after next. Party of eight. Professionals,' she adds cuttingly.

'And you want my room?'

'I'm not turfing you out, you understand.' She squats down beside me. 'Is everything all right?'

'It's fine. What with the marital split and everything. Just thought I'd take some time out to be by myself. That's what they say you should do.'

Her eyes narrow. 'Do you by any chance have your credit card to hand? We can complete the formalities.' Before I can find an answer she spies the photographs.

'My daughter.'

'Really? Let me see.' I hand over the pictures. Ought to distract her from her mission for all of two minutes. 'Gosh, you must be so proud. She's beautiful.'

'I can't describe it. Fit to burst.'

'What's her name?'

'Lola.'

'She's not with you then?'

'No. She will be soon though. Then I'll never let her out of my sight again.'

'Her father . . . not giving you trouble is he?'

'No, he's well off the scene. A distant memory.' I stand up. 'I'll get your money.'

'No rush,' she says kindly, patting my hand. 'I'm nipping down to the village. Shouldn't be too long. We'll sort it out when I get back.'

As she pads away, I kiss the photo. 'Lola, my darling, you're my lucky charm.'

'Look at the state of you,' Lizzy says, as I dismount. 'Whose rusty old cycle is that?'

'It belongs to my landlady. Whoever said you never forget how to ride a bike was talking through their arse. I fell off twice. Once in a ditch.

'So I see. You've got spots of mud all over your . . .' she puts her hand over her mouth.

'Don't you dare start laughing. It's a wonder I didn't break anything.'

'I assume there's a point to this . . . so . . . are you training for the Tour de France, or what? I can't see you in a yellow jersey somehow.'

'Lizzy, I'm in a tearing hurry. Can you lend me some money? Call it an advance on my wages.'

She looks at me with a pinched expression. 'How much exactly?'

'A hundred. It's for my lodgings, not to buy a Prada watch or anything.'

'Just as well, because a hundred wouldn't even pay for the holes in the strap. Anyway you've always come across as more Primark than Prada.'

'Cheers, Sis.'

'I'm due at a meeting, but Cameron's inside. Tell him I OK'd it. Catch you later. And don't be late for evening service,' she says, wagging her finger at me.

'You're the best,' I say, crossing my fingers behind my back.

Cameron comes to the door bare-chested. He looks like Tarzan and smells of aftershave. Nice aftershave – not inferior crap like Mr Moron's.

'Oh . . .' he says, looking startled.

'Expecting someone else, were we? While the cat's away . . .'

'Well if it isn't Little Miss Ragamuffin. What can I do for you?'

'Lizzy said she'd give me an advance on my wages. Two hundred. Give.'

'Manners.'

'Please.'

'And what exactly do I get in return?'

'My silence. I won't tell our Lizzy about the other day. Your proposition.'

He laughs. 'I wasn't being serious. Just my little ruse.' He pulls a wad of notes from his back pocket and peels off four fifty's. 'I'll need to keep the Penny Farthing as insurance.'

'Piss off.'

He lays the notes in my hand.

'So you're entertaining?'

'The former Mrs McGill. Suzy Sniper. She's bleeding me dry too. Child maintenance. Want a drink?'

'Best not. People might get the wrong idea.'

'I was about to put a shirt on. Why don't you go through to the garden and I'll fetch some wine.'

I go and sit on the child's swing at the top of the garden and wonder how many times my daughter has sat here before me. I want to tell him I know. That the game is up and I want her back with me. He emerges in a cream silk shirt, carrying an ice bucket and two bottles of white wine. It occurs to me if I was straight I could fancy him rotten.

'Listen,' he says. 'I think I might have made a bit of an idiot of myself. Lizzy mentioned you bat for the other side. Jed got that one wrong. Appearances can be deceptive.' He pats his crotch. 'Losing your touch, mate.'

'So how come you're wearing aftershave for your ex?'

'I'm the kind of guy who likes to make an effort.' He smiles. 'Are you really a dyke, or are you pretending?'

'And what would be the point of that?'

'To make your sister think you're not a threat to her marriage.'

'What made you marry Lizzy, Cameron?'

He shrugs. 'Rangers were playing away, there was nothing much on the box . . . the promo tapes for the new series hadn't turned up, it was a fine Saturday afternoon, so I thought, why on earth not. There are worse ways to spend your time.'

'Nothing better to do then.'

'Something like that.' He gives me that boyish grin – the one that renders me unable to tell whether he's being serious.

'But you were in love with her, yes?'

'Head over heels.'

'And now?'

'Of course I still love the old girl. But you know how it is once the honeymoon's worn off.'

'Not really. I've never been in a relationship that lasted more than three months.'

'That long, eh? I can't help being a serial flirt, Jes. It's in the genes. Liz knows I'd never leave her, but monogamy . . . it doesn't come naturally to a man. It's like being given a train set for Christmas and told you can admire it in its box, but you can't switch it on.'

'How long were you married to Suzy?'

'Two years. Listen, I've got a copy of my autobiography upstairs if you're really *that* interested.'

'Two years? What's wrong with people? Nobody tries any more.'

'Don't point the finger at me, darlin', it was her that wanted out. She spent more time with her blasted horse than she did with me, then she complained I was never there for her. Mind you, they just about suited one another – a pair of old nags together.'

'You don't like women much, do you?'

'Of course I do. You'll realize that when you get to know me better. I adore the fairer sex. I'm not a man's man, like the guy I play on TV. But it's true what they say about the female of the species being deadlier than the male. You're surely not going to disagree with me on that one, Jesamine?'

*

She strides into the garden sporting the tightest breeches I've ever set eyes on. Not that I know much about the showjumping scene. The *Horse of the Year Show* wasn't exactly flavour of the month with the residents of Whytemoor Hall.

They might not be breeches in fact. For all I know, they might be jodhpurs. Or riding trousers. I've never understood the difference. For argument's sake we'll stick with breeches, it sounds more exciting

87

somehow. As I recall, dozens of the Whytemoor women were enormously appreciative of Mr Darcy in breeches.

'Afternoon,' she says, matter-of-factly, like we've already been introduced.

'Hi.' I get up and move in for a closer look. 'You're Suzy, right?'

'Yeah. Suzy . . . the ex-wife.'

'I'm Jes . . . the ex-con.'

She smiles. 'Everyone deserves a second chance. Cons, wives – even husbands.'

'You don't want him back?'

'God, no, sweetie, that's one chance too many. Lizzy's welcome. There's only room for one handsome hunk in my life. In my case he's a sixteen-hands Arabian stallion. He's an absolute honey – a pleaser. More than any man I've ever known. He'd jump over the moon if it would make me happy.'

I can't stop myself saying, 'Is your daughter with you?'

'Inside. We're going to look at a couple of ponies. She's hankering for an early Christmas present. It's called winding Mummy round her little finger. I keep reminding her I didn't get my first pony until I was fourteen. The kid's spoilt. It's always the way when the parents split – it's like a trade-off.'

'I saw her playing here earlier. She's a credit to you.'

'Sweet of you to say. Want to timeshare?'

'I'll look after her for you anytime,' I say impulsively. 'Be happy to. So was it a difficult birth?'

'What an odd thing to say.'

'Just curious.'

'Put it this way, it was marginally worse than period pain but not as bad as having a wisdom tooth pulled.'

No Suzy, you're wrong. It was sheer bloody torture. And the agony went on . . . and on . . .

'So what happened, with the marriage?'

'Direct, aren't you?'

'I'm interested.'

'He said I spent too much time in the saddle, instead of in the sack pleasuring him. Men can't do without their rations, can they?'

I shrug.

'I mean, they can take themselves off for a good wank . . .' She laughs. 'I must say, Cameron seems content enough with Lizzy though. Maybe she's tamed him finally, although in my experience, middle-aged men do appear to have this boundless capacity for young skin. Would you term thirty-eight, middle-aged these days? I guess one day, when the old equipment becomes rusty, they no longer feel the need to prove themselves in that department.'

I think of Dad. Poor Dad, with only his familiar chair and vague recollections for company .

'I wouldn't know about that.'

'Oh yes, you're a dyke – Cameron told me,' she says squarely.

It gives me a kick when people aren't instantly won over. I see it as a challenge.

'You don't approve?' Bring it on.

'No, no, I'm fascinated. I've always wondered, what's it like?'

'What?'

'Shagging another woman.'

'Don't tell me it's your fantasy. If I had a pound for every women who has said that.'

'Not particularly. I mean, I've seen a few movies. What does it consist of exactly?'

In the nick of time, my baby bounds into the garden. 'Mummy, Mummy, what time are we going to the stables?'

'Give me ten minutes to fix my face. You chat to Auntie Jesamine.'

I've never been called 'Auntie' before. My little girl grabs onto my arm. 'Sometimes Daddy pretends to be a horse and I ride him round the garden. Would you do that with me?'

'Well – I – '

'Please, Auntie Jes, pul-lease.' She stands on tip-toe and whispers in my ear. 'I never told . . . about before.'

'Come on then.' I kneel down and she climbs on my back. It's an effort to raise myself up again.

'We can like . . . trot . . . and canter,' she says, throwing her arms around my neck.

'I was thinking more of a plod. Can't I be an old carthorse? One that's retired.'

'Carthorses are extremely strong.' This kid's got an answer for everything.

'How much do you weigh?' I groan.

'Mummy says you never ask a lady her weight, or her age. Some man asked whether she was expecting a baby at one of their dinner parties and she slapped his face. Have you ever slapped anyone?'

'Once.'

'Was it a man or a woman?'

'A man. I wouldn't slap a woman.'

'Did he ask you about your weight?'

'I'll tell you when you're older.'

'Must be something to do with sex then,' she says. 'Grown-ups always go all funny like that when it's about sex. What's the big secret?' She squeezes her thighs into my sides and flaps her feet. 'Come along, Jezzy, trot on.'

Just as my stitch is about to render me to the knackers yard, Suzy appears with two bottles of lager.

'She hasn't got you on that one,' she says, laughing. 'Time to dismount Auntie Jes now. Daddy's pouring your favourite cloudy lemonade.'

'Thanks Mum,' Freya says, leaping off me and thumping my aching loins heartily. 'She's not as quick as Daddy . . . he's more of a thoroughbred.'

'And you're one cheeky little mare,' Suzy says. 'Now go inside and wash your face, we'll be heading off in a minute.' She hands me a beer. 'Thought you'd prefer that to wine.'

'You're a lifesaver. Your Freya – a bundle of energy. And a proper little charmer too.'

'That's McGill's genes for you. I rather tend to call a spade a spade.'

'At least you know where you stand.'

She clinks the bottle against mine. 'Didn't want a glass with that, did you?'

'An oxygen tank would come in handy. Freya's worn me out.' Suzy looks at me like she wants to say something. I decide to get in first. 'I'm assuming you know what I was in for.'

'Look it's none of my business,' she says. 'I didn't know the man. From what people say he was something of a rotter.'

'Putting it mildly.'

90

'You had your reasons . . . and you've paid for it. Who are we to judge?'

'People do. All the time.'

'Stuff them. You'll find out who your true friends are.'

'The invisible kind.'

'I like you, Jes. You've got spirit. Can't stand women with no backbone, who whine and wail about their lot. Must've been tough for you?'

'No picnic.'

'But you've come through. You're pretty, you're fit . . . still young enough to make a life for yourself.'

Freya's head bobs out of the kitchen window. 'Come on Mummy, we'll be late.'

'You and me should hit the town sometime,' Suzy says. 'Do you like nightclubs?'

'Don't recall. Aren't they places that split your eardrums?'

'See, you do remember.'

'Mummy!'

'Come out here and give Auntie Jes a kiss goodbye.'

'She doesn't have to,' I say, faintly embarrassed.

Freya skips out carrying her riding gloves and velvet cap. I whisk her up into my arms and swing her round, then her lips explode onto my cheek in one big noisy extravagant kiss. Children are so generous in their praise, lavish with their affections. I'm reminded of how, at the beginning of my incarceration, I used to cry when some of the women's kids used to visit. Before I got hardened to it.

'Thanks Jezzy,' she says, grinning. 'Can we do it again soon? Next time, I'll set up some jumps for you.'

'I'll start training.'

With that she skips away down the path. Suzy passes me her empty beer bottle. It's got her lipstick on the rim.

'Look I'm free on Friday,' she gushes. 'I'll get Cameron to baby-sit. We can go to a gay club if you like. Is it a date?'

'OK, why not.' Bloody hell, she's a bit keen, this one.

I watch her sexy arse wiggle away. She stops on the patio, turns and blows me a kiss off her gloved hand.

16

Back at Enid's, languishing chin-deep in Lizzy's hideously expensive bath crystals I had to pick the lock on her bathroom cabinet to get at, I contemplate my forthcoming date with Cameron's ex and try conveniently to forget that Octavia is due over here in twenty minutes.

That Suzy was coming on to me. She definitely was. She said I was fit. She blew me a kiss. When she handed me the beer bottle her fingers casually brushed against mine. Accidentally – or not. Maybe that's why she split with Cameron. She's a closet dyke waiting to be set free. A genie in a bottle waiting for Jesamine Vale to uncork her. Now there's a prospect.

She's a striking looking woman, that's for sure. Better looking than our Lizzy. Whatever was McGill playing at, letting that one slip through his fingers? I've always found women that ride horses rather attractive. They have muscular thighs, they have good posture, they have stamina. All in all, it equates to being a pretty dynamic prospect in the sack.

I slide my hand between my legs. Instantly an image of Mother strolling up my path comes into my head and extinguishes my ardour. I draw my hand away a little too quickly, inadvertently elbowing the crystals jar into the water.

'Mother, I'm a lesbian. Just thought you ought to know.' It's short and to the point. I've rehearsed it enough times in the mirror, still it sounds bloody peculiar when I say it aloud in front of her.

'That's nice, dear,' she says, bobbing her nose at me briefly over her copy of *Country Life* and helping herself to a slice of Enid's lemon drizzle cake.

'Did you hear what I just said? I'm a dyke . . . a diesel . . . a beaver bumper . . . a rug muncher.' God, I stink of crystals.

'Don't you want to go off to Speakers' Corner and get on your soapbox, or something? Rally the troops.' She stuffs the magazine back in her bag.

'I'm so glad you understand. Phew, that's a relief. We don't have to have any deep and meaningful conversations about my sexuality. You're not as shocked as Lizzy. She raved on and on at me over it.'

The thin lips round into a smile. 'Nothing much shocks me these days. Anyway, Lizzy's already told me about it and I told her it's called "prison bent." Still, whatever gets you through the night and let's face it, you've had rather a lot of nights to contend with.' She leans across and pats my hand in that condescending manner that makes me want to scream. 'As soon as you meet a nice man like Lizzy's Cameron, all those sorts of tendencies will disappear like an autumn morning's mist under the noonday sun. Don't you go worrying your head about it.'

'I'm not worried, Octavia. Not a bit. As a matter of fact, I've already been online and got tickets for Gay Pride. I should have done it years ago – in my teens. Maybe I should take acting lessons, then I can be a lesbian thespian. Something to aspire to.'

'There are plenty of those about and it isn't always the obvious ones. Like I say, once you meet the right man . . .' She gets up. 'Aren't you going to show me around?'

'I'm living in a bloody bed-sit, not Windsor Castle. There is no "*around*." Unless you want to have a poke around in my drawers.' Let's see what kind of a reaction that throws up.

She opens the blinds. 'Let's go outside and sit in that very pretty courtyard. Looks to me like your landlady knows how to get the best out of a restricted space.'

'Yeah, I gave her some hot tips as a matter of fact. OK, but I can't be long. I've got to see my probation officer.'

She stops me in the doorway. 'You know, Jesamine, I'd have you to stay with me like a shot, but it would be impractical, wouldn't it? The Channel Islands?'

'My tag would be out of range,' I say sarcastically.

For once, she's got this genuine look of concern on her face. 'You're not lonely, are you? I expect you made lots of friends inside.'

'Who me? Lonely? I've got a social life that makes Paris Hilton look like a recluse.'

'It would be so nice if you could meet someone special, particularly now Lizzy is settled. We're all so content. One big happy family.'

I want to shake her. I want to yell in her face, what about Dad? I feel like punching the smug bitch in her smug, 'lipstick-like-an-oil-slick,' crimson gob.

'Actually, I have met someone, Octavia. But then again, I expect my foghorn of a sister's already told you all about her. She's the most beautiful person I've ever met – inside and out. She's kind . . . gentle . . . she treats me with respect . . .'

'Sounds exactly like my Ukrainian cleaner, Mags. It's a crush. It'll pass.'

'I'm nearly thirty, not bloody thirteen. I'm too old for a crush. God knows I had enough of them through school and college to know the difference.'

She takes hold of my hand with her bare one. I wish at least she'd had the courtesy to don some gloves. Staring straight ahead she says, 'You know the best cure for all this nonsense is to refrain from seeing this woman. Go cold-turkey. Be a brave girl. You'll be over her in no time.'

'Cure? But I don't want to be cured, Octavia. It's the last thing I want. What I want, is for Pashindra to sweep me up in her arms, carry me off to her bed and fuck me senseless. That's what I want.'

She looks at me with pale cold eyes that betray not a flicker of emotion. Her lips unfurl into a wry smile. 'That's nice, dear.'

When she finally departs, I rush upstairs, grab up a pillow and press it against my face. 'Aggghhhh. Aggghhhhhhh. Aggghhhhhhhh!'

*

'Your dad's sleeping,' Sally says. 'Not the best of nights. He woke me up three times, shouting. Couldn't make out what it was about.'

'Sorry.'

'It's all right, I'm used to it. Anyway, I'm off duty for a couple of days from tomorrow. Recharge the batteries. Might go to the coast if the weather stays like this. If you come you'll probably see Rhianna. She's his favourite because she's rude to him and answers him back when he snaps his fingers at her.' She pats my arm lightly. 'Go and sit with him if you want, I'll bring you a cuppa.'

'Thank you Sally, for everything.'

His head is laying against the headrest, his mouth gaping. His breathing is laboured and erratic. It occurs to me I could dial mother's number on my mobile and put him on and she'd think it was a dirty phone call. I pull up a stool and sit down.

'Let me tell you about my friend, Pashindra. She's quite the most beautiful woman I've known since Miss Richardson. You remember Miss Richardson, don't you? Junior school. God, that was some years ago. About Pash – when I say beautiful, I mean inside as well as out. Not just physically but emotionally as well. I'm not shallow.

'If you'd made me a boy instead of a girl, I would have had Pash by now, do you know what I'm saying? She gets my juices flowing. She only has to walk in the room and my nipples go bullet-hard. I want to pull her against me and make her feel what she does to me. Is this turning you on?'

I lower my face close to his.

'Now listen to me you selfish old bastard. Don't you dare go and peg out on me. Not yet. Not when your successor has practically got his diamond-encrusted platinum ring on Octavia's mucky paw. It wouldn't surprise me one bit if she has the funeral one day and gets hitched to Mr Moneybags the next. Have you been introduced to Mr Moneybags? I don't suppose so. Let me tell you about Mr Moneybags. For a start, he's got bundles more cash than you, he's better looking than you and Mother reliably informs me his cock is twice the size of yours. Personally, I'm happy to take her word for it.' I whisper croakily, near to tears.

'Don't you dare give her the satisfaction of getting one over us, do you hear me? Let's keep her life on hold, as she so delicately puts it, a little bit longer shall we?'

I pick up his withered hand and squeeze it.

'We have a deal here, so don't you dare renege on it. Do you fucking hear me, you miserable old git?' I look up and to my horror, Sally's standing there with the tea tray. 'Octavia, Lizzy and Cameron send their love,' I quickly add.

'That's the spirit ,' Sally says, chirpily, setting the tray on the table and passing me a cup.

'How much did you hear?'

'Don't worry about it,' she says grinning. 'I wish I could do it, but I can't. It's not in my nature and Eric would sense that. Besides it's OK you saying stuff like that, you're his daughter, but if Mrs Gerritt caught me I'd be collecting my P45. Even Rhianna's not that near the mark.'

I take a sip of strong tea.

'You don't think I went too far? I wasn't nicknamed Eva Braun at school for nothing. Being horrid comes naturally to me.'

She smiles and shakes her head. 'Not with him it doesn't. You need to keep working at it.'

When I get back, Enid is waiting in the hallway, with my small holdall.

'Sorry,' she says, dangling it in front of me, 'but that party I told you about is arriving tomorrow. I took the liberty of packing for you.'

'Must've taken you all of two minutes. Still, saves me the bother.'

'If your rent had been up to date it would have been a different matter,' she says gazing at the floor.

'Yeah, I know. No excuses. I borrowed some money off my sister, but I need it for tonight. I will pay you back though. Promise. I'm grateful for your hospitality – really. I know it might not seem like it.'

'In your own time,' she says, like she's disappointed in me.

'Look I haven't been entirely straight with you.'

'And I suppose you're not a doctor then? Thought not.'

'Was it the bedside manner that let me down? Or just the lack of funds?'

'No hard feelings,' she says.

'I've been away. Prison. I was hoping for a fresh start.'

'I've always though it's best to be honest,' Enid says.

'And have you reject me outright. Couldn't risk that.'

She says nervously, 'Well, that rather depends on what you've done.'

I pick up the bag. 'Best you don't ask.'

17

'You've brought an overnighter,' Suzy says, prodding the car door towards me. 'Think you're going to score tonight do you?' She lifts her D&Gs and winks at me.

'This,' I say, handing the bag to her, 'is practically all I own in the world. I've had to quit my lodgings. I thought you weren't going to drive.'

'It won't be the first time I've driven home pissed. I drive better pissed. People show me more respect.' She gets out and stashes my bag in the boot.

'Suzy you can't do that.'

She jumps in beside me. 'Now I thought you of all people would appreciate living on the edge.'

'You have a child.'

'Oh yeah, I forgot,' she says. 'Lighten up, I'm kidding. We can leave the car in town. I'll pick it up in the morning.'

She flips the radio on and off again, like she's unsettled.

'Nice car,' I say, unable to think of anything intelligent to talk about. It occurs to that we're both more anxious about this than either of us is prepared to let on.

'Reliable,' she says. 'I've always preferred automatics. You don't have to concentrate. And they're smoother. Want to drive?'

'Trusting, aren't you?'

'I'm well covered insurance-wise. I'm assuming you've passed your test.'

'Yeah. Dad stumped up for lessons for my seventeenth birthday. He used to take me out in the old Astra. He said I drove too fast. "This isn't Brands Hatch you know. They'll never pass you driving like that." Poor old bugger.'

'Yes, I heard. Shame, isn't it? So, how do you fancy driving a Saab?'

'Maybe sometime. Not now. I'd rather admire the view.'

Suzy gives me a look like she doesn't know which way to take that last remark. 'Let me show you what she can do,' she says, kicking down on the accelerator.

Everyone in this place is young. Bloody young. I was about to say young enough to be my daughter, which in some cases is almost certainly true. The door policy is supposed to be eighteen, which is a load of bollocks. Or maybe I'm miffed because the 'suited and booted' heavy on the door, whose sex I'm still undecided about, didn't ask to see my ID.

Suzy struts her way through a group of teenage girls confidently, while I'm left hugging the sofa. The music pulsates all over my body and I realize I'm sitting too close to a giant speaker.

I move to a place of sanctuary – another small room where the music doesn't permeate. Two girls are laid out about four feet from me, cavorting around like they're giving a floor show. The androgynous one extracts her tongue from the pretty one's throat, checks me out then gets back to the task in hand, giving a seemingly exaggerated performance to her unappreciative audience of one.

'Oh there you are,' Suzy squeals, setting down her ice-bucketed wine on the table, unable to take her eyes off the amorous pair. 'Bloody hell, is that meant to be a girl, or what?'

'Ssshh.'

'Sorry. God it's a real eye-opener that's for sure. Is it always like this?'

'How would I know? I've been banged up for eight years. This place wasn't here when I was last in town. I think it was a tea shop or something.'

'Sorry.'

'Stop apologizing and pour the bloody wine. I'm gasping. And stop staring – we we're young once.'

'Maybe, but I never did it in public. Cameron always wanted to. In those days he was happy to show me off anywhere . . . trains . . . planes . . . that Mile High club . . . not all it's cracked up to be. It's a man thing.'

'You haven't?'

'We were flying first-class to New Zealand, so we had time on our side. It was bloody uncomfortable squashed up against the sink in the loo,

I didn't come. I remember I was too nervous to fake it in case someone heard us.' She laughs. 'It must be so much easier now what with flat beds.'

'I suppose . . .'

'For all my bluster and bravado, Jes, it's not really my scene – making a public show of yourself, but it was back in the days before Cameron was famous, so . . .'

'Live and let live.'

'I'll drink to that,' Suzy says. 'Wanna dance?'

'Might as well.'

The dance floor is the size of a postage stamp. What passes for music these days is loud enough to drown out a small nuclear explosion. No-one talks. Just jigs around, some swigging from bottles.

Everyone sweats within the claustrophobic confines of the restricted space. As each track merges seamlessly into the next, there is a mass exodus of young women flocking outside for their nicotine fix. Or something more addictive.

'Had it,' Suzy says, breathlessly, grabbing my hand and leading me back to the 'library' – which is my name for the quiet room. The pretty one and the androgynous one are sitting back to back, with their heads resting against the wall.

'Let's get another bottle,' Suzy says. 'I want to get rat-arsed.'

'I'll go.'

The woman behind the bar smiles like she knows me. She says she'll bring it across. When I get back, Suzy is on her mobile. She folds it up.

'Just checking everything is OK with Freya. Evidently she's keeping them up playing Monopoly – and she's winning – right little capitalist I've bred.'

'Does Cameron know you're here?'

'Does Lizzy?'

'No.'

'No.'

'Embarrassed?'

'At my age I'm beyond embarrassment. So why didn't you tell Lizzy?'

'Never came up.'

'Same here.'

'So where does he think you are?'

99

'School reunion. Frolicking amidst the nuns like *The Sound of Music*.'

'Suzy?'

'What?'

'Why are you here?'

The wine arrives. She looks at me like she might answer my question then doesn't. 'Are you complaining?'

'Course not.'

Her fingers inch over my thigh. 'Fancy a slow one?'

'OK.'

The last time I danced properly with anybody was two years ago at the Christmas party. It wasn't a particularly romantic encounter. My room mate, Tess, was missing her family something chronic and needed someone to hold on to.

We had this unspoken agreement with the screws, that they wouldn't play any melancholic reminders of the things we were missing, like Lonely This Christmas, or even, Last Christmas, so we were swaying along to ridiculously cheery songs like Shaking Stevens' Merry Xmas Everyone and Elton John's, Step Into Christmas – hardly your most obvious slow-dance material. Oh and that one by Wings: Simply Having a Wonderful Christmastime. Trying to convince ourselves it might still be possible . . . somewhat of a losing battle in a godforsaken hellhole like Whytemoor Hall. Funnily enough, I've always had something of an affinity with that tune that begins: 'Chestnuts roasting on an open fire.' You get where I'm coming from?

Suzy lays her head against my shoulder. I can feel her hot breath on my skin. She slides her hand all the way down my spine and onto my bum. Smooching with women is too damned easy. There ought to be a law against it.

She breathes in my ear, 'Is this OK?'

I can't believe she's this forward. She's more forward than me, definitely, and I am forced to remind myself that's it's me that's supposed to be doing what comes naturally.

It occurs to me I ought to be doing this with Pash. You're not a proper couple until you've slow-danced. Don't they say it's like making love standing up.

'It's fine. Really . . . fine.'

She seems pleased. I feel her hands tighten against the small of my back. So we go through the motions over and over until there's a break in the tracks. I follow her into the restroom and into the toilet cubicle. She looks startled. And rather put out.

'What do you think you're doing?'

'It's what you want, isn't it? To carry it on?'

'No.'

'You don't want me?'

'No.'

'Then what were you playing at just now? Rubbing yourself against my thigh, whispering in my ear, grinding your fanny into mine. What was all that about? Play acting?'

'It was a dance Jes. It's what I've done hundreds of times with hundreds of people. OK so the majority of them were men. It doesn't do it for me, Jes, the girl-on-girl thing. Sorry. It's not you.'

'For fuck's sake don't apologize. But you led me on deliberately. Why?'

'Don't act like a man would. Don't demean yourself. It doesn't become you. Next you'll be accusing me of being a finger-tease.'

I turn on the cold tap and splash my face.

'I thought it would be fun to do something different,' she says. 'Sorry if you misread the signals.'

'I misread? Babe, I didn't misread anything. What was all that running your nails down my back? And feeling me up. You were giving out all right.'

'I guess I got carried away with the rhythm of the music.'

'And adding one more tick to your *I-Spy Book of Lesbians*.'

'What?'

'Nothing. I'll get you a cab.'

'I'm a big girl. I'll be fine.'

'Promise me, Suzy, you won't drive.'

'There's a taxi rank opposite.'

'OK.'

'Nice night, Jes. Thanks. I would say we should do it again sometime, but . . . maybe . . .' She goes to peck my cheek. I turn away. She pats my shoulder. I don't intend giving her arse the once over as she struts away. Don't want to give her the satisfaction.

The androgynous one comes in looking flushed in the face, wiping her eyes on her shirt. She leans against the wall, hugging herself and looking at me helplessly. Is this my cue to reveal myself as a trained Samaritan?

She says, 'Was that your girlfriend?'

'No. That was actually a straight woman who thought she might have a bit of fun flirting with me until I took the bait and then backing off double-quick. Not worth getting in a lather over.'

I pull a paper towel, dab my face dry and a hand her one. 'What's up?'

'Women – you can't live with them, you can't live without 'em. It's a bastard.' She kicks the wall.

'Want to talk about it?'

Her head droops a little, but still her eyes peer at me. 'You don't want to listen to my shit. I don't want to listen to my shit.'

'I just offered, didn't I? Do you like Liebfraumilch? Only I've got three-quarters of a bottle sitting out there and I can't stick the stuff myself.'

The restroom door opens and my bag comes flying across the floor. 'I figured it wouldn't take you long,' Suzy says, grinning. 'Have a nice night.'

She's got her head wedged against my shoulder and one hand under my top, her hot body pressed against me in a state of semi-slumber. Occasionally she stirs and slurs something derogatory about her girlfriend.

Outside in the cold air, I push her up against the wall and feel for her keys. She acts helpless, like she's enjoying it. Like I'm the screw and she's the con. Eventually I find them in the side pocket of her combat pants. I feel around in the dark for the lock.

'Come up,' she says grabbing on to my belt. 'You're not going anywhere.'

'Honey, I've got a home of my own to go to.' OK, white lie. 'Look I'll see you up.'

'If you leave me I'll do myself in. I will.' She pulls up her sleeve. I can just make out the naked ridges in the half-light.

'Shit. How old are you?'

'Nineteen,' she says. 'How old are you?'

'Old enough to know better.'

102

She stirs, lifts the sheet and gazes at her body. 'Did we?'

In my experience, you're damned if you do and damned if you don't.

'No, honest, I just put you to bed.'

'Shame. Was I a pain?'

'You'd just had one too many. We've all been there. I stayed with you in case you started throwing up.'

'God, I'm a nightmare when I get in that mood. I thought I could handle it.'

'What?'

'Life. Love. Death.'

'Where are you from?'

'Bridlington.'

'Run away from home, have you?'

'You're not a social worker, are you?'

I shake my head. 'You couldn't be further from the truth. It's Jes by the way.'

'Cool,' she says, extending a hand. 'Pleased to meet you. Stella Mackenzie. Mack to my friends. Want a beer?' The bedside clock says nine-ten.

'Coffee would be nice. Tell you what, I'll go and make it, while you get some clothes on.'

Five minutes later she saunters into the kitchen wearing what I assume is her girlfriend's kaftan. It looks odd on her rakish body. Like a tent.

I wave the coffee jar at her. 'How do you take it?'

'Anyway you're offering she says,' hauling up the kaftan and thrusting her g-stringed crotch at me. A teenager in a g-string – that's a whole new experience for me. She looks at me like she's about to cry again. 'Guess if you haven't had me already, then I'm not your type.'

'It's not that I don't . . . it's just that . . . well I don't sleep around.' You bloody liar, Jesamine Vale, Patron Saint of Letting Lesbians Down Gently.

'Good for you,' she says, like she doesn't believe me.

'Besides, neither of us were in a fit state to do anything worthwhile. You'd have despised both of us in the morning.'

'I wouldn't.'

'Tell me about your girlfriend.'

'Fuck her.'

'OK don't then. I didn't mean to upset you.'

'On-off, on-off, she doesn't know what she wants.'

'What's her name?'

'Arthur. Or is it Martha? I never bloody know from one day to the next. What am I meant to be a bloody mind reader?' Her fist crashes against the worktop. Imogen Gale – she's a trainee nurse.'

'And Imogen doesn't know whether she wants a guy or a girl, right?'

'She's seeing this bloke Davy. She says he's just a friend but they're spending more and more time together. . . it's tearing me apart. Look at me, Jes. I'm a fucking wreck.'

Mack holds her trembling hands out. I go over to her, put my arms around her and stroke her shiny short hair while she sobs into my shoulder.

When she's calmer we sit at the kitchen table and drink strong coffee. She tells me how her parents never accepted her sexuality, that's why she ran off. At first she slept rough in London, then she hooked up with a mate in Bristol and eventually she found a job here, working in travel. I tell her about my life as a jailbird. And about my nightmare of a mother, making it in Tinseltown at the ripe old age of fifty-five.

She puts her cup down. 'I don't half fancy you, babe,' she says. I always think it sounds odd when someone much younger calls *you* "babe". Truth be told, it makes me feel a little uncomfortable.

'It's not me you fancy, it's the baggage that comes with it.'

'Nah. Doing it with someone that's streetwise – that knows the code – it's the ultimate. Have you ever been tagged?'

'No, love. Don't go there. Take it from me, it's not something to aspire to.'

She pulls down her top and shakes her boobs at me. 'Are you hungry? I could rustle up something?'

I bet you could, darlin'. 'Another time. I have to get back before they send out a search party.'

'Nice that you have people that care.'

'They'll probably be putting the flags out.' I squeeze her hand. 'And if what I'm about to say sounds at all patronizing, well it isn't meant to.'

104

'Uh-oh, a lecture.' She feigns a yawn.

'Not really. A different perspective, that's all. When you're only nineteen, everything seems magnified. Yeah, I know it's real to you all right, love, and I know how much everything hurts and I'm not trivialising it, but this is only the beginning. Give yourself a few more years and everything will fall into place, I guarantee it. You'll be settled down in some nice pad in the country with a dog, two cats and the woman of your dreams.'

'Says the voice of experience.'

'It's true.'

'So how come you're not?'

'Told you, I was inside for a long time. I've got some catching up to do.'

'And how come you ended up in Larkhall, or whatever it's called?'

'Because I did something bad. That's all you need to know.'

'What did you do?'

'Doesn't matter.'

'Don't treat me like a kid.'

'I murdered someone.'

Her eyes widen. 'Wow.'

'You shouldn't be impressed.'

'Who did you do over?'

'My sister's husband.'

'Why?'

'Because he was a total shit-head. Controlled her like she was some mechanical doll.'

'So you saved her from Mr Nasty. How is that wrong?'

'She didn't see it like that. Neither did the jury unfortunately.'

Mack puts her hand on top of mine. 'Do you want to come to a rave on Saturday?'

18

'My God,' Cameron says, opening the door to me, 'you look shit-rough. Rampaging night on the tiles was it? Come in and tell me all about it.'

'I need a shower. My landlady's booted me out. Is Lizzy here?'

'Fish market.'

'Poor cow.' I go into the living room and he follows.

'Hair of the dog?'

'No thanks. My head's a little too fragile for that.' I slump into the nearest chair. 'I'm getting too old for that discoing lark.'

'That's what burning the candle at both ends does for you. Keep you up all night, did she?'

'Who?'

'Well now . . . a little birdie tells me you got off with some wee strip of a schoolgirl.' He rubs his hands together. 'Hot stuff, was she? Did she wear you out?'

'She was nineteen – and for your information we didn't *get off.* Suzy didn't waste any time running to you telling tales then.'

'We often text one another. Exchange information. She said she had a good time with you, Jes. The experience was – how did she put it? Educational..'

'Well that makes two of us. I found it *"educational,"* as well. Yeah, I learned a lot actually.'

'So how come you didn't do the business with the wee girlie? School uniforms not do it for you, eh?' he chuckles.

'Like your ex-wife rightly said, the girl was too young for me. I could've had her, but I'm not that unscrupulous. Unlike some people I could mention, I'm not in the habit of using people for my own ends.'

'Now, who might you be referring to? Magnanimous of you, Jes. Particularly as you were licking your wounds. Such a blow to the ego when a woman knocks you back.'

'What else has that bloody spoilt bitch, Suzy, been telling you?'

'Suzy might be a lot of things, but she's not one of your gang. Impressive acting skills though. Fool you, did she? Or did she make a fool out of you? That's more like it.'

'Not my type actually,' I say, less than convincingly.

'Ahh now, your voice is saying one thing . . . your body language is telling me something entirely different. Suzy told me what happened. Isn't it just horrible when women do that? Give out signals then don't follow through. I do sympathize. It's happened to me on a couple of occasions. Many moons ago, obviously, when I was less experienced.'

'I never realized the pair of you were so close. So you knew where we were all along. Suzy lied to me.'

'Knew? I instigated it, darlin'. Thought I'd have a bit of fun. We had a right laugh scripting it – Suzy and me.'

'You sick prick.'

'You get one over on me – I pay you back. It's only fair. I believe that's fifteen all.'

'So it's payback time, is it? Well, you may as well know, Cameron, I intend contacting a solicitor.'

'Because some canny woman led you on? That's rather hasty of you, if you don't mind me saying so.'

'I don't give a fuck about Suzy. Or you and your stupid games. This is about me getting my baby girl back. Don't act all innocent. You know what I'm talking about.'

He shrugs. 'I don't have the first clue, Jesamine. Enlighten me.'

'Freya. She's my kid. The one I gave up for adoption because they forced me.'

'Are you feeling OK? Whatever did you take last night?'

'Look, don't think I'm ungrateful. I think you've done a wonderful job with her – all of you – but she's my baby Lola and I want her back.'

'I really don't think you ought to be turning up unannounced treating this place like a dosshouse, ' Lizzy says, crossly. 'Bloody market was a nightmare. There's some crates in the car need taking round the back.' She throws her car keys at Cameron. 'You can stack them next to the shed. You never know, Jes might even get off her arse and give you a hand.'

'I've had problems with my lodgings, Lizzy. Cameron says I can stay for a bit.'

'Well you can't. You know it's breaking the rules.' She scowls at him. 'We need to have a talk.'

I take out the photo and place it on the table. Her face pales instantly. 'What the devil . . .'

'Remember this? Just one of the many photos you sent me in jail, Lizzy – of my daughter. This *is* Lola . . . isn't it? This is my baby? *My* baby.'

'I can explain,' Lizzy says, getting flustered.

Cameron shakes his head. 'I wouldn't have believed it of you, Liz. I thought she was making it up.'

Lizzy goes across to the window. 'Mother said you were becoming increasingly depressed. She was quite concerned when she came home from seeing you . . . on a number of occasions . . .'

'I always got depressed when I knew Octavia was coming to visit. That was a normal mindset for me.'

'We did it for you, Jes. Honestly. You needed something to cheer you up. You gave your kid up.'

'I was in the hospital, Lizzy. Shackled to a fucking demon screw, while my legs were wedged apart for sixteen hours. They were pumping me with drugs to shut me up. I didn't have any control over what was happening to my body, let alone my baby. Why couldn't you have taken her in?'

'Bloody stupid question. You know why.' Her voice softens. 'We were worried you might do something silly. We thought if you had something to live for . . .'

'So you sent me photographs of someone else's kid to keep me going, because you let them take my baby away and now we don't know where she is.'

'This is all so unfair,' Lizzy says, bursting into tears. 'I need a shower. Crates, Cameron.'

'Sod the crates,' Cameron says, as Lizzy scurries away, 'it can bloody wait.'

I cup my head in my hands. 'You know I said I didn't want a drink . . . I've changed my mind.'

He fetches a bottle of expensive brandy from the cellar. 'I had no idea they were doing that or I'd have put a stop to it,' he says, expertly removing the foil and extracting the cork from the bottle at the same time. Ordinarily, I'd be impressed, if I wasn't so damned shaken up inside.

'You're off the hook, Cam. If the witches didn't even let on to you that I existed, how could you possibly have known about their little charade. I should've realized something wasn't right a long time ago. Put two and two together. I only started getting sent pictures of her the last three years. After Lizzy got with you. No-one mentioned that either.'

He hands me a glass. 'Here. Drink. Medicinal.'

'What are you, my doctor now?'

'Well, I do have a PHD as a matter of fact. A Pretty Huge . . . sorry, it's not helping, is it? The humour?'

I shake my head.

'Look,' he says. 'I'm a pretty flexible guy. I can be anything you want. I know we've been a bit up and down with one another, Jes, but I'm being serious now. If there's any way I can make any of this easier.'

'My friend. Can you do that? I could do with a friend.'

'I can be your friend. I can be a lot more besides.'

'Haven't you got a script to learn?'

'Fuck it. Some things are more important. Let's get pissed out of our heads. Kill off a few more brain cells. They're overrated . . . brain cells.' He knocks back his drink in one go and pours another.

'Shouldn't you go and check on Lizzy?'

'In a minute. She'll be OK. She'll get in a rage . . . cry for a bit . . . she'll calm down eventually.' He helps himself to more brandy. 'Is sex important to you Jes?'

'Give it a rest for five minutes, can't you? I'm thinking about my daughter.'

'Indulge me for a second.'

'It's more important than some things and less important than others.'

'Complete and utter crap. Sex is the most important thing in the world. It's off the radar.'

'You're off the bloody radar.'

'So tell me, is it breasts or legs?'

'Are we talking turkey?'

'We're talking women, as you damn well know. If you really are a genuine lesbian you'll know what I'm talking about.'

'Eyes.'

'Eyes?'

'Soft doe eyes, a gleaming smile and a great sense of humour.'

'Don't ask for much, do you?'

'And if she happens to have a great pair of knockers as well, I won't kick her out of bed. The prison dentist had fantastic knockers. Like great big water melons. Anika Horst, she was called. Long blonde hair like that bird out of Abba.'

He leans in my direction. 'Tell me more.'

'I hadn't appreciated quite how fantastic her knockers were until I got to see them in magnificent close up.' I realize I'm feeling fuzzy headed already. 'You know how it is, when they recline the chair so your head is practically resting in their lap. As she leans across to work on your teeth, you can't help but bump into her cleavage now and again. Safe to say I came out with better molars than I went in with. Not many jailbirds can boast that.'

He laughs. Then he leans towards me like he's about to kiss me.

'It's not going to work, Cam. You're not going to seduce me by plying me with brandy.'

'Relax,' he says, topping up my glass. 'We're friends, aren't we? Friends ought to be able to tell one another anything.'

'I feel half-cut already. What's in this?'

'Have another one,' he says, topping up my glass. 'Let's kill it.'

'Are you trying to poison me?'

'I'd rather like to proposition you.'

'Piss off.'

'How about if I offer you some fantastic incentive to make me the happiest man alive? An arrangement that suits us both. It can be our secret.'

'No secrets. Secrets are dangerous. Anyway, I don't need your money, Cameron. I'm perfectly content taking my sister's. Especially after today.'

'I'm talking about something money can't buy.' He empties the bottle into my glass. 'I'm talking about . . . a baby.'

19

I lurch towards the door and fall into her arms.

'Jes – what on earth . . .'

'God knows how I made it here in one piece. You look amazing by the way. The shrink in pink!' I giggle. 'So where's the party?'

'You had better come in,' she says, leaning me against her and guiding me towards the living room.

'What happened to the no touching rule?' I slur, as my bum hits the sofa.

'In cases of emergency,' Pash says, 'rules go out of the window. Sit here for a sec, while I pop to the kitchen.

As soon as she disappears, I haul myself up and stagger across to the sideboard to admire her array of photographs. There's one of her in her graduation gown. There's one of her on a trekking holiday, lugging a huge rucksack on her back that's almost as big as she is. She's standing with two older people that bear a family resemblance – her parents, I assume.

There's a collage of her with a group of medics and a framed picture of her wearing a bronze and orange bikini and looking like a Bond babe, alongside a woman who's the image of . . . no . . . it can't be. It bloody well can't be. Perched on a rock in the sea with their arms draped around one another. I blink hard, trying to focus on the image and the room goes all hazy. I hear Pash's footsteps in the hall and launch myself at the sofa, Superman-style, banging my chin against the arm rest in the process.

'Here,' she says, sitting me upright and putting a glass of mineral water in my cupped hands. I spill some in my lap.

'Do I seemed a teeny bit pissed to you?'

'Slightly, yes. Perhaps after you've had this you should lie down.'

'I thought you'd never ask. Lead me to your boudoir.'

'Sip it slowly. You don't feel nauseous, do you?'

Stupidly I shake my head from side to side. Not to be recommended when the room is spinning erratically.

'What's going on, Jes?'

'My bloody saintly sister sent me pictures of Cameron's daughter, Freya, and pretended they were of Lola. Now I don't even know what my little girl looks like, because all this time I've been worshipping images of someone else's kid. And then to top it all, Cameron said he'd have a baby with me. It's a really naff idea, yeah?'

'Utterly ridiculous,' she says. 'You know it is. Let's get you sobered up.'

'Anyway, how can I have a baby when I haven't had a period for four years? Still get the bloody mood swings though.'

'It's OK,' she says, stroking my back. 'Take it easy. Keep sipping the water.'

'I didn't mean to drink so much, it's just . . . he kept pouring. There was all this brandy, right. A whole bloody bottle . . .'

'He didn't touch you?'

'Lizzy was upstairs.'

'Maybe it's as well.'

'I used to have this daydream, Pash. Me . . . on Brighton Pier . . . with Lola . . . eating ice creams . . . crashing around on the dodgems . . . screaming our heads off on the Ghost Train. Do they still have the Ghost Train?'

'I think so.'

'All this time I was fantasizing about somebody else's kid. The girl with the blue eyes and the strawberry hair.' I rub my eyes, wearily. 'Why is there a picture of you and Strychnine on the sideboard?'

The door opens. I can just about make out the rotund form.

'Well hello there,' she says. 'Isn't this cosy?'

She looks less brutal with her hair down. Less *Hammer House of Horror* than I would ever have imagined possible, probably because her severe fringe hides the deep crevices on her forehead. And she's had her red curls highlighted with flaxen streaks. I'm not about to tell her it's taken ten years off her.

She touches Pash's shoulder lightly. 'Darling, what time are we due at the restaurant?'

'Seven-thirty, for eight,' Pash says. 'I've booked a taxi.'

'You look smart, Strychnine,' I say. 'KGB chic still in fashion, is it?'

112

Her shoulders go back like she's standing to attention. 'Best thing I ever did quitting the prison service. I expect you've heard, I got awarded a place on one of those fast-track schemes. I'm an inspector now.'

'Buses, or trains? Cos I'll make sure I've got a valid travel ticket in future.'

'Glad to see in spite of everything, you've still retained that offbeat sense of humour that served you so well inside. Well, I'll leave to your out-of-hours consultation,' she says. 'Nice seeing you again, Jesamine. I'm almost tempted to say I didn't recognize you with your clothes on. I must say you're looking ever so slightly more dignified without your legs thrashing about in the air.'

I lurch towards her, fists flailing. Pash throws her arms around my waist and hauls me back to the sofa.

'Just as I've always thought,' Geraldine says. 'Taxpayers' money spent on anger management classes does rather seem to be a waste of resources. What is it they say about leopards?'

The door clicks shut. I collapse against the cushion. Defeated.

'You . . . and that blasted woman? Tell me my head's all fucked up. Tell me I'm hallucinating. You know it's what Norman Bates used to poison his mother . . . strychnine. It's no wonder you kept it a secret from me.'

'It wasn't deliberate' Pash says. 'I like to keep my private life private. And what was all that about not recognizing you with your clothes on?'

'Because I was bloody chained to her, wasn't I? – the bloody sadist vampire – when I gave birth to Lola. If there's one single person on this earth, apart from Octavia, who winds me up something chronic it's Geraldine bloody Strickland. I never, ever thought I'd see her again, let alone, here . . . with you. I'm speechless.'

'We're not together anymore. Not technically. Not that it's anyone's business. I'm moving out next week.'

'Well you seemed pretty together just now. Seven-thirty for eight, wasn't it, *darling*? Don't let me hold you up.'

'Jes.'

'What?'

'Relax.' She lays a cushion on her lap and lowers my head on to it. 'Let yourself go.'

'Easy for you to say, when my worst nightmare's lurking next door.'

'Forget about her.' She strokes my hair, still damp from showering. 'Shall I fetch you some more water?'

'No. Don't go anywhere. But there is one thing you can do for me. The room's revolving like fuck.'

'Name it.'

'Hold my hand.'

Later, in the cab on the way home, I prop my head against my hand – the one she clutched in hers for the best part of a whole hour. I can smell her perfume on my skin. I'm not going to wash for a week. Not ever, in fact. Strange how a smack in the teeth can sober you up at a moment's notice. Like finding out the object of your affection's secret lover is your worst enemy. Well, almost. After Eva Rowe, naturally.

How ironic is that? Beautiful Pashindra getting it on with Strychnine – Geraldine bloody Strickland. The thought of them . . . now I am feeling peculiar.

I plan to sneak upstairs undetected and get my head down for a couple of hours. Lizzy doesn't know I know where she keeps her spare door key: under the third flower pot to the right of the garage.

When I get there, Lizzy's blessed tractor is nowhere to be seen. To have the place to myself, even for a little while, is more than I dare allow myself to hope for.

I thread the key in the door, turn it silently and creep inside. As I tiptoe towards the stairs something stops me in my tracks. I peer into the kitchen and he's slumped over the table, snorting white powder off a piece of foil through a twenty pound note.

'That'd better not be what I think it is. Powdering your nose, Cameron? Or are you practising for *What's My Line?*'

Without looking up, he says. 'It's a recreational thing. We all do it on the set. Cast . . . crew . . . a little pick-me-up, that's all.'

I pull up a chair and plop down opposite him. 'I saw it all the time, inside. Young women's bodies ravaged beyond recognition. You'll end up killing yourself. Then where will your precious daughter be? Does Lizzy know?'

'Of course she knows. Lizzy's not a complete prude. She's been known to dabble occasionally.'

'I don't believe you.'

'The odd bit of speed to give her a lift. The hours she works, you can't blame her. We all need something.'

'This is crazy.'

'Look at you taking the bloody moral high ground. As far as I am aware, there's only one of us been locked away. Seems to me you're only one step off the 'park bench and can of cider', routine yourself.'

'Ouch. What happened to being my friend?'

'Sorry,' he says. 'Anyway how did you get in?' Something of a delayed reaction.

I dangle the key at him. 'Lizzy's never been that imaginative. Or security conscious.'

'Full marks for ingenuity.'

'Yeah, and I found this on the front step. I pull Lizzy's credit card out of my pocket and hand it to him.

'She's got too much to think about. Her head's all over the place. Join me?'

'No thanks. I'm not that desperate.'

'You're telling me you've never tried anything? Come on.'

'I've been offered gear – loads of times – but I wouldn't let myself do it. I'd shut myself away in my cell with my pictures of Lola. Freya. Maybe you ought to try it. Take the photograph . . . look into your little girl's eyes . . .'

'Give it a rest, woman. You're not my blasted mother.'

'Yeah, I forgot. No point in trying to reason with someone that's taken a hit. If you were my fella, I'd pack you off to rehab. That would be the honest thing to do. Not turn a blind eye.'

'And if you were my wife, darlin', I'd get my kicks elsewhere.'

'Yeah, yeah, for all of five minutes. Then you'd be off chasing something younger and prettier. Why don't you buy some courage from somewhere and take yourself off to The Priory. You're an actor. You must be loaded.'

'Very funny. Where do you get your information, woman? I don't have a cosy little nest egg stashed away for a rainy day. I spend more than I earn – always have done. It's what every self-centred bloke of my generation does.'

'So what's this then, a cry for help? You want to get your rocks off with me . . . you've made it your mission.'

'I'm serious, Jes . . . about this baby project. Make up for the one you lost.'

'Yeah, like I'm going to make a baby with some druggie. There are plenty of blokes up for casual sex. I can afford to be choosy.'

'So you *do* want a baby, then?' He sweeps the foil off the table onto the floor. 'Be a sweetheart and clear that mess up for me.'

I can hear him moving about upstairs. I stoop down next to the spillage. A few white flakes – it all looks so innocent. I know plenty of women who would rip my arm off to get at it. Hoover it straight off the floor up their mutilated noses. Women who would have given up a month's privileges for an ounce of dust.

How good must it be to get out of your head for half an hour even? You could say, I've never been so tempted. That's what he wants, isn't it? For me to take a hit. One hit . . . and there's no going back. I rake the dustpan out from under the sink and sweep it up. Then I flush it down the bog.

20

'I must be bonkers,' Lizzy says. 'Doing this . . . with you . . . when I could be out enjoying myself. Sitting outside a pavement café on this fine Sunday morning with a pastry and a cappuccino, sifting through the morning papers. And if you tell me one more time I owe you, Jes, that's exactly what I'm going to do.'

'I won't, OK. It's finished. I think I'm beginning to understand why you did what you did. And no doubt, Mother played her part admirably. I'll get over it – eventually.'

'Right,' she says, pointing the key fob at the car. 'We'll just go round the block a few times, see how you get on.'

I open the door and the stale smell hits me. 'This tractor reeks of puff, Sis. Have you been having a few sneaky ciggies in here?'

'Once or twice.'

'Lizzy! You're not back on the fags. I'm so disappointed in you. When?'

'I only have one now and again when I'm stressed. And right now I'm stressed.'

I tut at her. She narrows her eyes at me.

'There's no-one as critical as a reformed smoker, Jes.'

'Difference is, I'd never go back. Filthy habit. Think about your lungs.'

'Think about your liver. I'll remind you of that next time you're on your third bottle of Chablis. And concentrate.'

'Relax, Sis. How hard can it be? Where's the choke? Only kidding. Key?'

'There isn't one. You stick this in there, like that.'

'The wonders of modern technology. Pretty soon these things will drive themselves.'

'Until then . . . first gear,' she prompts.

'I have driven before you know. I'm not a complete beginner.'

117

'Many moons ago,' she reminds me. 'Adjust the mirror. You can't possibly see anything as it is.' She makes a big drama over fastening her seat belt. I pull the clutch up too quickly and the car kangaroos forward. I hit the brake.

'Stupid thing. What did it do that for?'

'It's you, jerking. Stop rushing. Take your time. And don't forget it's Mirror, Signal, Manoeuvre. Not simply, first gear, pull out, whatever.'

'Whatever.'

We stall at a junction in front of a black BMW and the driver blasts his horn. I pull up the handbrake and open the door. Lizzy grabs my arm. 'Jes, no. Don't get out. People have been killed for less. Just put your hand up. Acknowledge you made a mistake.'

I'll do better than that. I clunk the door shut, make eye contact with Mr Impatient in the mirror and stick two fingers up.

Lizzy slams on the central locking and signals at him frantically. 'If he gets out we're in big trouble.'

'No sweat. I've dealt with bigger twats that him in my time.' I pat her hand. 'I never realized you were such a nervous passenger. Relax.'

'I'm not . . . usually. Cameron's a considerate driver.'

Before I get going again, Mr Twat pulls round us and speeds off, flying over umpteen humps in the road like they weren't there at all.

'Fucking idiot.'

'Thank God,' Lizzy says, rubbing her forehead. 'You don't realize how much things have changed since you were last on the road . . . haven't you heard of Road Rage?'

'Haven't you heard of Ex-con Rage? Anyway I'm better on faster roads. Let's go on the dual-carriageway, get some speed up. Then you'll see what I'm made of. They do still have those, don't they?'

'Let's take five minutes out,' she says, twitching around the glove compartment and removing a packet of menthol cigarettes. Despite my protestations, she lights up. I press my control pad and open her window all the way. 'You're not taking me out with you, Puff Queen.'

'I do intend kicking the habit,' she says. 'When life isn't quite so challenging.'

'There'll always be something getting in the way. You just have to be strong. Make your mind up and go for it. Have you tried the patches?'

118

'Yes, but my heart wasn't in it. I'm waiting for them to develop a willpower patch.' We giggle and I'm reminded of how much I've missed her company over the years.

She says, 'So, what made you stop? You always loved a beer and a smoke. Particularly at barbecues.'

'Unfortunately, the establishment where I was stationed didn't go a bundle on beer. Nor on barbecues, as it happens. Fire hazard.'

She puts her hand to her mouth. 'Sorry . . . sometimes I forget . . .'

'I quit for several reasons . . . the cost . . . the fact that my colds used to go on for weeks rather than days . . . the smell that lingered on my skin . . . clothes . . . hair. It's not attractive, is it? I've been stopped five years now. Lizzy?'

'What?'

'You don't use anything else to relieve stress, do you?'

She smiles. 'What – like a Rampant Rabbit?'

'Like . . . drugs . . .?'

'Whatever made you say that?'

'Because if you did, I'd be concerned about you.'

'Well don't be. Because there's no need.'

'You would tell me?'

She takes one last long drag on her cigarette and drops it out of the window. 'Engine on . . . first gear.'

'Lizzy . . .'

'I'm fine,' she says. 'Really. You do come out with the oddest things sometimes.'

After almost an hour of dodging idiots and Sunday drivers, Lizzy says, 'Pull over.'

'No way, I'm having the time of my life.' We screech across a roundabout. Someone leans on their horn.

'You should have given way,' Lizzy chides, rubbing her forehead.

'Give over. Colin Cloth Cap was at least fifteen feet away. Don't some people get in a tizz over nothing. You know what, Sis, I think I'd make a fantastic rally driver. This is such a huge buzz.'

'Just do what I tell you,' she says, 'pull over, into that lay-by coming up. Just here.'

'Fuck off, spoilsport.'

'Do it,' she says, urgently. 'I need to throw up. And then, once I've fully recovered from this experience – and most definitely before I let you take the wheel again – remind me to phone my broker. I need to increase my life cover. I thought my days of white-knuckle rides were long since behind me.'

21

Nervously, I ring the bell. What if it's not Pash that answers. What if it's
her? Bloody Strychnine. Just my luck. I dab my finger against the side of
my face and sniff it. Does Cameron's aftershave smell OK on me? Not
too manly, is it? I've never found a single women's fragrance that suits
me. They're always too flowery, or too musky. On the other hand, I don't
want to smell overly macho . . . like a hod carrier on heat.

I run my sweaty palms over the front of my jeans. I can feel the hairs
on the back of my neck prickling. Standing on tip-toe I can see her
outline through the glass, striding towards the door. She opens it a few
inches and I am greeted by her cocoa-coloured cleavage peering at me
seductively through a fluffy white robe.

'Jesamine.'

I say anxiously, 'By yourself?'

'Yeah, I was going to have an early night.'

'Suits me.'

'Catch up on some reading.'

'Ahh, pity.'

I give her a bottle of Lizzy's most expensive red wine. 'Housewarming
present.'

'I haven't actually moved.'

'So I see. Advance housewarming present.'

She half-smiles and I can't tell whether she's pleased or not.

'You are still going ahead? With the move?'

'Up to my eyes in cardboard boxes. You wouldn't believe how much
there is to sort out when you break up with someone. Do you want to
come in for a minute?'

A minute? Oh well, better than nothing. I step inside.

'You remember where the living room is,' she says, pointing. 'Make
yourself at home. I'll open the wine. You smell nice, by the way, what is
it?'

'Don't know . . . but I'll find out.' Definitely.

Immediately I notice the photos have been removed from the sideboard. Something of a relief not to have to be confronted by Pashindra in that intimate pose with Strychnine. What happens in situations like this? Break ups. Do people share out the memorabilia of their courtship? Their years together. Or does everything get buried under a mass of tissue paper, because it's simply too painful to confront?

Pash fetches in the uncorked bottle, puts a glass in my hand and pours.

'Looks strange eh?' she says, glancing around the room. 'Minus personal effects.'

I want to ask her who's laid claim to *that* photo. I'll wait until I've sunk a couple of glasses of wine at least. 'My next place is going to adopt a minimalist look,' she says, unconvincingly.

'So what's happening with the this place? Have you sold it?'

'I've rented it out. Jeff's friend, Mel – she's a student – recently qualified. She might be joining the practice.'

She? A rush rips through my stomach. 'Is she gay?'

Pash smiles in a non-committal way. 'Cheers.'

'So how did it go – last evening?'

'A little awkward as you might imagine. Telling people about the split. Gerry would prefer to keep things as they are for now. I suppose we'll have to share out the friends.'

'Bloody Gerry, is it now? Sadist bitch. What did she used to do in the bedroom? Leap from the chandelier sporting a chest wig and a strap-on.'

Pash gives me a sour look that tells me she doesn't appreciate my rant. I lower my eyes, feigning shame. 'I'm sorry. Sometimes I think out loud. One of my few faults.'

'Six years is a long time to be with someone, Jes.'

'And I thought I had a tough time inside. You chose to be with her all that time. You had free will and you chose to be with her. What does that say?'

'You only saw one side – Geraldine Strickland the prison officer. She wasn't one-dimensional. She was kind, loving, affectionate . . . generous to a fault. She was more romantic than I ever was. She would shower me with gifts. One weekend she hired a private jet to fly us to Venice, quite out of the blue. It wasn't my birthday or anything, she just wanted to surprise me.'

122

'Well there's no danger of me doing anything rash like that, so if you want to call it quits now.'

'And when we first started seeing one another, she used to send me little cryptic messages about where to meet up, or some special surprise she'd got planned. A kind of foreplay.' She giggles.

'What?'

'Just thinking about the time she booked us in for salsa lessons at this new studio that had just opened up in town.'

'You've got to be bloody kidding.'

'That's what I thought when she told me. I did my best, but I couldn't take it seriously. Cackled my way through two classes, mainly, I think, because everyone else was so studious, before coming to the conclusion I ought to do everybody a favour and quit. Gerry got quite miffed with me. Her heart was in the right place. She sticks her tongue out. 'And she paid for this.'

'Oh my God, that's indecent. I want one.' I move in for a closer look. 'So how come I didn't notice before?'

'I don't always wear it for work. Or if my parents come over. They wouldn't approve.'

'Not bloody daft is she? Our Gerry. Seeing as she was the one reaping the rewards. I'm surprised she hasn't asked for it back, so you won't get to use it on anyone else.'

'She wouldn't get it back – the piercing hurt like hell. I intend to make the most of it.'

'Ugh.'

'Never had you down as the squeamish type, Jes.'

'I'm not – normally. I just feel sick at the thought of you doing *that* – with *her.*'

'We all have a history,' she says, caressing my arm. 'You can't change that. The relationship dragged on longer than it should. That's the way it is with women. It's the nurturing instinct. We find it impossible to let go, even when we know it's the right thing to do. It's the kinder thing in the end. You have to force yourself to move on and hope they can do the same. She's met someone else. I'm pleased for her.'

'God, there's more weird people running around than you'd give credit for.'

'Don't.'

123

'Still protective of her then?'

'She's taking some time out – it's what she needs. She's gone to stay with her parents.'

'Must be nice this time of year – Transylvania.'

'You think you're so funny.'

'So what went wrong?'

'The relationship got too intense. The interrogation would start up. Where are you going? Who are you seeing? What time will you be home? She didn't like me seeing my female friends, so I started lying to her. Pretending I was at meetings when I was seeing someone she didn't approve of. Deviousness becomes the norm and that can never be conducive to maintaining a healthy relationship. Don't get me wrong, I wasn't cheating on her. I wouldn't do that, though I might as well have been for all the good it did me. Pleading my innocence all the time. It's unbelievably draining, living with that, day in, day out. Like most women, Jes, I like to be cherished. I don't like to be possessed.'

I say sarcastically, 'Couldn't you have referred her to someone?'

'Geraldine categorically didn't believe in therapy. "Therapy is for nutcases," she would say. A little while back her unit got caught up in a siege. A bank in Gloucester. Gerry took the place of a woman hostage who was becoming hysterical. When it was all over it was obvious to me she was traumatized. She wouldn't talk about it with me. She received a commendation.'

'Bravo! Gerry Strickland the hero!'

'They arranged for her to see someone, to get it all out of her system, but she refused point blank. She saw asking for help as a weakness. Quite wrong. The way you look at me sometimes . . .'

'What? What am I doing?'

'That intensity . . . like you want me. Right now, I'm just not suitable relationship material. Not for you, Jes – not for anyone.'

'Who's talking about a relationship? It's just, well – I could use some company. I thought maybe, if you felt the same way . . . I won't hassle you, Pash . . . if you want to be by yourself I'll knock back my drink and leave you in peace. But . . . this thing doesn't have to get complicated, does it?'

She sighs. 'It's so much easier for the boundaries to get blurred in relationships with women. With men, you know that there's a fine line you don't cross in case they get the wrong idea. With women, it's easy to get in too deep too quick and suddenly find yourself out of your depth.'

'I'm willing to take that chance with you. And if I end up drowning . . . well . . . what a way to go.'

'You think so?'

'And another thing, I'm not possessive. Whatever happens after tonight, I won't try to own you, OK.' I pick up the bottle of wine and walk towards the stairs.

'So . . . welcome to your consultation,' she says. 'Allow me to remove your clothing for you.' She lifts my top over my head, unfastens my bra and my nipples spring proudly to attention. 'Mmmm,' she says, licking her lips. 'Either you're feeling a little chilly, or you're pleased to see me. Shall I close the window?'

'I'm not cold. Not at all.'

'Excellent. What are your symptoms?'

'Well, Doc, I've been experiencing a lot of tension recently. Right here, here and . . .' I pull the zip on my denims, 'particularly here.'

'Let me reassure you, I'm exceptionally successful at treating this condition. If you'd care to step out of your jeans and lie down on the couch.' She pats the bed.

'You like . . . playing games?'

'I like . . . having fun. Don't you?' she says, discarding her robe to reveal the slinkiest black lace panties that leave almost nothing to the imagination. Now that's what I call a sight for sore eyes.

'So what do you prescribe for me, Doc?'

She goes to the wardrobe and whips out a red silk scarf.

'First, I prescribe a little restraint. Lie back against the pillow, raise your arms above your head. Cross your wrists.' She says, kneeling on the bed beside me.

'Are you suggesting what I think you're suggesting?' I'm trying to remain cool, but I'm all too aware my voice has developed an edge to it.

She binds my wrists together, fastening them to the bedstead a little too expertly. It's obvious she's done this loads of times before.

'You'll love it,' she says. 'You can simply lie back and relax. No effort required.'

125

'What are you going to do to me?'

'Well now. I'm going to tease you until you're begging for mercy.'

'You'll have a long wait.'

'We'll see. And then I'm going to . . . if I tell you, it won't be a surprise.'

She opens the bedside cabinet and takes out a small bottle. 'Let's see, what flavour goes with red wine? Wild Cherry, perfect. She drizzles the liquid in a zigzag all the way down my body, following the trail with her lips, from my breasts to my belly. Then back up again. Slowly, slowly. Circling each nipple in turn with the tip of her tongue before taking it into her mouth. As she sucks me harder, I feel my buttocks clenching automatically.

'Please, get my pants off,' I groan.

'There's no rush,' she whispers. 'It'll be so much better if we take our time.'

She puts her lips against mine and kisses me, softly. My tongue probes for hers, but she pins me down my the shoulders, then withdraws her mouth and looks at me for a moment before resuming. This time she lets me have her studded tongue to toy with while she fondles my breasts with those incredibly sensuous hands. She puts her mouth next to my ear and whispers, 'I've just realized it's late night shopping – I might have to pop out for a while. I won't be gone too long.'

'Pash! You're driving me crazy. For God's sake, fuck me.'

'Thought you weren't going to beg, eh? Your resolve didn't last too long.'

She plants little kisses in between my breasts as she snakes her way slowly southwards, nibbling at the skin all the way across my taut belly, which sends tingles down the nerve endings in my back. She rakes a fingernail over the rim of my pants.

'Maybe I've teased you enough.' She eases them down over my knees and allows them to fall. Then she crouches at the foot of the bed kissing my feet from my toes to my ankles and all the way up the inside of my legs. My body is fixed rigid. I can't move at all. And it's like she senses it. It's as if she's stunned her prey and now she's moving in for the kill.

She climbs back onto the bed and straddles me in the sixty-nine position.

'Pash, what are you doing?'

126

'Hold on tight, honey, I'm about to blow your brains out.'

As each caress of her tongue draws me closer to the edge, I find myself employing the most ridiculous tactics to keep myself from letting go: recalling chemical symbols from the periodic table, we learned at school; the books of the New Testament; post-war Prime Ministers – which I'm totally crap at.

She's inside me now . . . probing me with those exquisite fingers. . . thrusting . . . deep . . . deeper. I can't hold it in any longer. I've run out of things to concentrate my mind on. My tethered fist clutches the iron bedstead, as I surrender my body to the climax that rips through me.

Pash rolls onto the pillow beside me and looks to the heavens.

'Granny Rosa, if you're tuned in, sorry about that. Maybe you ought to go back to your knitting. She was a champion knitter, was Granny Rosa – that's my Dad's mother. Always had a shawl, or a pair of gloves on the go. She gave me a pair of bootees once. I think it must have been a hint for me to get a move on. I told her she was in for a long wait yet.' She frees my wrists and ties the scarf around her head like a bandanna. 'Funny, the things that come to you at a time like this.'

'My God,' I say, trying to regulate my breathing, 'I can't believe what you just did to me. You really are a whore. A fucking fantastic whore. You've obviously done that zillions of times.'

'All that matters is this time. Nothing else. Don't you think?' She leans back against the pillow and lets out a self-satisfied sigh. 'Pass me some wine, darling. My mouth is as parched as the Kalahari desert.'

I rest my naked body against the coolness of the iron bedstead, unable to take my eyes off her. Everything this woman does is a turn-on. Eating, talking, washing the dishes.

'What?' she says.

'No-one's ever made love to me like that before. That was the most erotic thing ever. You know how to press all the right buttons.'

'It was good sex, because you'd already let me in,' she taps her temple, 'up here. There were no barriers to overcome. It's easy to let yourself go with someone you trust.'

'I guess . . . I've never trusted anyone before. Not like that.'

She looks pleased. She strokes my damp hair, 'Making love like that mellows you. That's a good thing.'

'So, if you'd do something that intimate with me . . . maybe you would . . . hypnotize me?'

'Maybe,' she says, draining her wine glass. She hooks her hand around the nape of my neck and draws me in closer. 'Let's see what you can do to persuade me.'

22

I wake suddenly and reach into the empty space, thrashing about for her. Next door, I can hear the shower going – so she's scrubbing my telltale scent off her skin already. I lie there working myself into a state of anxious anticipation until I can hear her pottering about in the kitchen. Then I go downstairs, uncertain of the reception I'm about to get.

She's unloading the dishwasher, her wet hair bobbing against her shoulders. When she stands up, I slide my arms around her waist from behind, easing the tie-belt on her silk kimono so I can feel her naked belly.

I press my hands against her and kiss the nape of her neck. 'You are one incredibly sexy lady, Pash Khan, let's go back to bed.' When it's clear she isn't about to respond, I take my hands away. 'Did I do something wrong?'

She swivels to face me, re-tying her belt so the kimono doesn't gape.

'No, Jes, I did. I shouldn't have let you make love to me last night. I was weak. We were both vulnerable. It was unforgivable. And unprofessional on my part.' She reaches for a towel.

'But I wanted to. You can't know how much I needed to do that. How could you expect me to lie there like that and keep my hands off you? It was like being on fire and not throwing yourself into the ocean. It was meant to make us feel good, for God's sake.' I rub my head and try to think of something to placate her. 'I'm not your patient, if that's what's bothering you. You're not my doctor. You're my friend. And now you're my lover.'

'There's absolutely no need to sound so bloody smug about it.' The tone is indignant but underneath I can tell she's smiling.

'Can't help it. Sorry.'

'You're not sorry.'

'No. I lied about that. Sorry.'

'It's been such a long time,' she says. 'I thought I'd learned to live without it.'

'Sex?'

She flips the switch on the coffee machine. 'It's not just sex though is it? It never is "just sex" between women. There's all the baggage that accompanies it. Guilt. Commitment. Responsibility. Like you own a part of each other. You can't just walk away.'

'Life isn't some goddam penance, Pash, although it bloody feels like it at the best of times. What's wrong with us taking our pleasure while we can? We're not hurting anyone. And don't tell me you didn't enjoy it, because I saw that look on your face . . . and I felt you kick in . . . you rocked, babe.'

'I can't promise you anything, Jes.'

'I know, I know. I'm not expecting us to traipse up the aisle next week, clutching a bouquet of roses each. Or even the week after.'

'God knows what my parents would make of it all.'

'They don't know you're gay?'

'Of course they don't know. Where my family comes from I could be stoned to death. Or I might conveniently disappear. Get disposed of down some waste chute. It's not unheard of when you bring dishonour to the community. People get dragged away in the night – never heard of again. Never spoken of again."

'You mean to tell me they're really that bigoted in Croydon?'

'Be serious. It would bring shame on the family – they'd be outcasts. I'd be called all manner of names. The Whore of Lahore . . .'

'But all that time you were with Strychnine . . .'

'Two professional women sharing a house. What's wrong with that? We maintained separate bedrooms for whenever my family came to stay.'

'All that effort. I couldn't be arsed.'

'Worth every second, believe me.'

'Don't your parents think it's odd you've never married?'

'You'd have to ask them.'

'It's a wonder they never had someone lined up for you.' Her eyes flicker away from mine briefly. 'They have, haven't they? My God, Pash, why didn't you say something before?'

'A friend of my cousin. Nameesh. A nice man. A lawyer. Good looking too.'

'Don't say that.'

'If you're into men.'

'Which *you're* not.'

'You don't know everything about me. How do you know I'm not bisexual?'

'Because that's a bloody cop out. *"Bisexual,"* is what those TV reality show morons say about themselves in the press to make themselves sound more interesting. *"Bisexual,"* is what girlie pop duos put out to sell more bloody records, probably because their agents tell them to. It's called sitting on the fence, love. Go on then, name me one genuinely bisexual person. Someone who claims to have had long-term relations with men and women – one-night stands don't count. You can't, can you? Bi-bloody-sexual, I've never heard such crap.'

She strokes my hair tenderly. 'Have some breakfast.'

'Not hungry.'

She pours herself a heap of muesli and drowns it in lactose-free milk. 'Well I am. Ravenous.'

'I'll just have a palpitation-inducing double espresso and sit and watch you eat.'

'Voyeur.'

When she goes to work, I put her kimono on and sit staring out of the kitchen window, daydreaming about last night's pleasures and trying not to let my mind stray to the possibility of some pre-arranged husband dragging her away from me. She'll be sat at her desk now, in the building next door, expertly analysing someone with a problem.

Isn't it weird that I, Jesamine Vale, know every inch of her physically? Strange when you come to know someone like that, yet you can never get inside their head. You have to trust what they tell you is the truth. Maybe it's not a universal truth, but it is *their* truth. You have to accept the limitations of that and try not to analyze it too deeply.

Before I leave, I go into the bedroom and hunt down her discarded knickers from last night and stuff them in my jacket pocket.

*

131

Sally welcomes me with a cuppa and a chat as always. She tells me about helping Dad finish his jigsaw last evening and that he managed a whole T-bone to himself.

'What makes you want to do this?' I ask.

'Belief,' she says.

'What, like religion?'

'Belief that I can make a difference to people's lives. That I can enhance the quality of the time they have left. Make their passing easier.'

'But how would you feel if someone died on you?'

She smiles. 'They have. More times than I can recall. Mostly it's peaceful – sometimes it's painful – occasionally it's traumatic. Once I needed counselling for six weeks. I have to console myself with the fact I did the best I could for them. That their lives were somehow made better for my being there.'

'Of course that's true. God, you're so brave. I couldn't do it. When I was in prison, I had to mop up people's piss and sick and blood. I did it because I had to. I never got used to it. You did know? About me being inside?'

'I guessed. There's only so long one spends on a gap year. Yours had turned into like – half a decade – from the things they were saying. Are you OK?'

'Yeah. Do you know what I was in for?'

She pats my arm . 'Honestly, it doesn't matter to me. Wanna come and see the old fella?'

'Don't want to bring this up,' he says, taking hold of my hands. 'Sometimes it's unavoidable. Best be blunt. How was it?'

'What, Dad?'

'The war. The fighting.'

'I got through it.'

'I kept asking your mother when you were coming home. There was always one more mission. Not shell-shocked are you?'

'I'm OK.' I clench my hands in my pockets, trying to stop myself getting emotional.

'It's what we trained you for. Shot 'em down good and proper, I hear from above. You'll be decorated, my girl.'

'Thank you, Sir.'

I stop short of saluting. At least he doesn't think I'm a boy.

'I knew you'd make a better fighter pilot that than Stafford chap. Lilly-livered twerp. Don't know what Lizzy sees in him.'

'They're not together anymore, Dad.'

'Are they not? Good thing too. Lizzy can do much better for herself you know. You tell her that from me.'

'I have already. In a manner of speaking.'

'That's my girl.'

His head drops forward. I take the magazine off his lap and sit on the sofa opposite, reading the problem page for half a hour, then Sally gently suggests I leave him to it.

I hug her for no reason other than she has my utmost admiration.

At the restaurant, I find Lizzy in the cellar doing a stock count.

'Dad recognized me,' I say, triumphantly. 'I was there at the house half an hour ago and he called me his little girl.'

'Don't get your hopes up,' she says flatly. 'He calls everyone that. He called the woman from the Social Services, Octavia, the other day.'

'I'm sure the poor cow didn't deserve that. I'd have sued.'

'You're too hard on her, Jes. Give it up, can't you?'

'I'm telling you, if she leaves Dad rotting in that godforsaken chair and goes off and marries Leo, I'll never forgive her. Never. How can you be so cool about it?'

'I'm not cool – I'm resigned – there's a difference. Besides Jes, you were always Daddy's girl, it's no wonder you're fiercely protective of him. I never really had a chance to get close to him in the way you did. You were always off playing football on the common in your little England footie kit. Days out fishing, sharpening sticks with penknives and pretending to be Robin Hood to Dad's Friar Tuck. Robbing the rich to give to the poor – I can't say you've changed all that much really.

'Lizzy?'

'What?'

'Do you think after they'd had you they wanted a boy? One of each. Even the score.'

'Do you? Is that why you're pretending to be a lesbian?'

'I *am* a bloody lesbian. Why won't anyone around here take me seriously? When I said to Octavia the other day I had fantasies about

Pashindra fucking me senseless, she just said, "that's nice dear." Nice? *Nice?* It's not fucking nice at all . . . it's a fucking outrageous thing to say to your mother.' I can't stop myself from beaming.

Lizzy prods my arm. 'You've done it with her, haven't you?'

'Might have.'

'You have. I can see it in your face. You've done the dirty deed.'

'And let me tell you, Sis, it got very dirty indeed. She was amazing. Wicked. She's got this piercing in her tongue that – '

Lizzy holds her hand up. 'Stop right there, please. Kindly keep the gory details to yourself, I haven't had a chance to digest my lunch yet.'

'Fair enough. Don't you go running telling tales to Mother now,' I say, crossing my fingers behind my back and hoping for the best.

'One thing about Mother, you can't fault her stoicism in the face of adversity,' Lizzy says seriously.

'Actually, I do. I utterly resent it. It's completely unnatural. I can't tell where the stage actress, Octavia Vickers ends and Octavia Vale, the mother, begins.'

'Do you prefer being a 'Vale' to a 'Vickers'?'

'Yes, of course. I loathed being a bloody Vickers. Do you prefer being a McGill to a Stafford?'

'How dare you.'

'Lizzy, come on.'

'Course I do. I adore Cameron . . . the way you clearly adore Pashindra. By the way . . . and I don't mean to burst your bubble, Jes, but there's a mountain of washing up and the dishwasher's fucked.'

Just as my arm is about to drop off, Cameron strides through the door, carrying a pile of freshly laundered tea towels.

'Leith to the rescue!' He drops the towels on the nearest seat, puts his hands either side of his temples and makes a charging motion like a ram.

'I must be hallucinating. All of a sudden you've turned into a new man.'

'Jes, baby, I owe you one. Leave that lot. Get yourself off for an early bath.'

'I don't trust you, McGill. Where's the catch?'

134

'No catch. I've got an hour spare and I'm grateful to you. I took your advice. Went to see your shrink. See if she could sort me out.'

The dish I'm about to stack slips through my fingers, clatters onto the floor and smashes into a hundred pieces.

'Now look what you've made me do.'

'I had no idea you were so jittery.'

'Joke, right? About Pash. Another one of your wind-ups.'

'She's every bit as gorgeous as you led me to believe.'

'I don't believe you went.' My voice is shaky. 'So . . . what did she say?'

He gives me a soppy grin. 'That you're a sex maniac.'

'Cameron!'

'What goes on between patient and doctor – well it's confidential.'

'OK, you've had your fun. Let's call it quits.'

'My money's as good as anybody else's. If I want to spent time on the couch of an exceptionally good-looking psychiatrist . . . while she gazes into my eyes . . .'

'You're a liar, McGill. That's not how it happens.'

'You want me to describe her to you? Ooh, let's see now. Five-foot-nine, I'd say, that's not including those slinky heels she wears. Raven hair bobbing around just below her shoulders. Intensely brown eyes . . . you said eyes are the most important feature. Now I understand where you're coming from.'

'Anyone could have deduced that crap from what I've already told you.'

'And a tiny little scar dotted above her left brow. The result of a glassing in a nightclub when she was a teenager. Trying to break up a fight, wasn't it? I can tell by your face, you're impressed with my eye for detail.'

'Why did you have to go and do that?'

'It was you who told me to get help, Jes, remember? I was only taking your advice.'

'Did you ask her to refer you to a drugs clinic?'

'I told you, the drugs thing I can deal with myself. This is about my sex addiction.'

'Sex addiction? Where do you think you are? Fucking Hollywood?'

'Thanks again for the referral. She's everything you said and more.'

'Well consider it a one-off. You can't see her again.'

'It's fixed. Tuesday. Wanna come with me? Hold my hand. Or anything else that comes up. Jed's already getting himself worked up at the prospect of seeing sexy Pashindra again, let me tell you.'

I feel my throat tighten. I can barely get the words out. 'Listen to me. If you don't cancel that appointment, I'm going to tell Lizzy everything. About you coming on to me, about the coke. Everything.'

'I can't do that, Jes. Not even for you. Besides I'm looking forward to it. There's no much I need to relieve myself of.'

'I mean it . . .'

'And who do you think Lizzy will believe? Her devoted, hard-working charismatic husband, who can persuade her of anything, or a man-hating dyke who resents her sister's relationships with men because they remind her of her empty, sexless life. All she's got are her pathetic little fantasies about her therapist – a woman who can never return the feelings she puts on her – and if the truth be known, probably despises her.'

'Pash cares about me. We made love. We're an item.'

'Yeah, yeah, in your dreams, darlin'.'

'I'm warning you – '

'Face it, Jes, the only way you'll stop me doing exactly as I choose is to wipe me out like you did Ewan Stafford.'

'So Lizzy finally told you.'

'Not before time. Can you face another eight years behind bars?'

I pluck a knife out of the washing up tray.

'You're not nearly worth it.'

23

After an hour sitting in the park opposite the clinic in the searing heat, she emerges, briefcase in hand. I scurry across the road and seize her arm.

'Jes, you startled me. I was miles away.'

'Where are you heading?'

'Cirencester. To give a teaching class. If that's OK with you?'

'I thought we might have lunch. A picnic. I bought some stuff from the deli. I was going to get champagne, but then I thought . . .'

'You should have rung me.'

'I know. Well tonight then. I'll make us dinner. Or we could go out. I'll pay.'

'Can't do tonight, Jes. Sorry. I've arranged to go out with Mel and some of her student friends. Bowling.'

I give her my best bowling action. 'I used to be a bit of a demon for the old strikes. I'm probably a tad rusty.'

'Another time,' she says.

'I wasn't hankering for an invite.' She's like a different person. In her bed, she made me feel like the most special woman on earth . . . and now . . . now I could be anybody. The person come to read her gas meter.

I hang on to her jacket sleeve like a lost child. 'Can I see you for a consultation? It's important. I mean, when you have time.'

'Pop in and check with Dora. I'm pretty sure I've got a ten o'clock slot in the morning.'

'Did Cameron come and see you?'

She frowns. 'You know I can't discuss another patient.'

'So he did. Cheeky bastard.'

'It's no big deal. Nothing for you to fret about.'

'He's only doing it to get one over on me. He plays these silly little games. He set me up with his ex-wife. Got her to pretend she wanted to make out with me. It's pathetic. You don't resent me, do you?'

She checks her watch.

'Right now I'm finding this is a little irksome, because I'm a punctual person and I don't like keeping people waiting unless it's completely unavoidable.'

'OK, I'll go. Could you just do me one teeny-weeny favour?'

'Which is?'

'Refer Cameron to Jeff.'

'Jeff's on holiday. He's taken a few days leave. They've gone to Gozo. Helen's pregnant.'

'Sod it. He would do that wouldn't he? Talk about shit timing.'

'Don't take it personally. I'm quite sure he didn't do it to get back at you.'

'Pash, this sex-addiction thing, it's a load of crap. McGill's just using as an excuse to indulge his fantasies with you. I don't want you to be used like that – like a sex object. It's demeaning.' This is coming out all wrong. Like I'm desperate.

'People in therapy tend to do that, Jes,' she says. 'It goes with the territory.'

She bends forward and kisses my cheek lightly, then she gets in the car.

When I get to the restaurant, Lizzy is on the phone. 'Bloody call centres,' she says. 'I've been hanging on nineteen minutes.' She opens the desk drawer. 'This came for you. Brown envelope – looks official. I make it a rule never to open those until I've had a stiff drink.'

'Nah, probably fan mail. Used to get tons inside, being the undisputable babe magnet I am.' I slide my finger under the flap and it draws blood. 'Blasted paper cut.'

'I'll fetch a plaster,' Lizzy says, passing me the phone. 'Hold this.'

The note reads: **I know who you are. You have twenty-four hours.**

It's typed in the kind of bold font favoured by the tabloid newspapers and made to look as if the letters have been cut out and pasted on. Someone's spent time putting this together, which tells me I'm meant to be taking it seriously. I have twenty-four hours to what? To leave town? To live? Tulsa? Hastily, I fold it into quarters and shove it in my back pocket.

'What was it?' Lizzy says, peeling the back off a blue plaster. 'Final demand?'

138

'Junk mail. At least I got spared that inside.' I'm hoping my voice passes for normal.

'You've gone rather pasty, are you sure you're OK?'

'Yeah, don't fuss, Sis. Poxy paper cut. Makes me realize I could never self-harm. I'm not nearly brave enough.'

Lizzy pats my hand. 'Daft thing.'

I give her back the phone.

*

When I arrive at the B and B, Enid is sweeping the courtyard with one of those twig-brooms, I've never got the point of.

'Goodness,' she says, visibly jumping, 'I wasn't expecting visitors.'

'By yourself?'

'Uh-huh.'

'Guests gone out for the day, have they? That's if they ever checked in in the first place.'

She gives me a sideways glance. 'And who are you meant to be today? I'm not frightened of you, you know.' She holds the broom protectively across her small frame.

'Enid, I'm so sorry I lied to you. It was a senseless thing to do. My name's Jesamine Vale.' I hold out my hand. 'Can we start over?'

'Well, I – '

'Please . . . give me a chance. I want to explain.'

'Come inside,' she says, 'I'll put the kettle on.'

She settles me into her dolls house-sized lounge, cluttered with knick-knacks, while she potters around in the kitchen. After five minutes, she returns with a tea tray and a biscuit tin pressed under one arm.

'This is really kind. More than I deserve.'

'As a matter of fact,' she says, 'I'm rather glad you came back. It's been playing on my mind.'

'Really?'

She nods. 'I felt rotten chucking you out like that – I've never been one to listen to idle gossip. I ought to have taken your side into account. I felt bad about that.'

'Did somebody warn you off me?'

'Let's just say there was a lot of whispering in corners. Rooms falling silent when I entered. As a devout Christian woman for the best part of fifty-six years, I've not been used to being talked about in such a disrespectful way.'

'And, as a Christian woman, do you believe everyone should be given a second chance?'

'That all depends.'

'I killed someone.'

'Was it self-defence?'

'No.'

'I see.'

'I didn't plan it . . .'

'And no doubt you've regretted it ever since.'

'No. Regretted getting put away for it, that's all.'

'Jesamine, I'm sorry if this sounds a little wimpish on my part, but I'm finding this difficult to listen to. If you're looking for a Good Samaritan I could – '

'I'm not.' I reach into my pocket and pull out the note. 'Someone sent me this.'

She draws in a sharp breath.

'The blood's mine by the way. I caught my finger on the envelope.'

Colour rises in her cheeks. 'Well this nasty piece of work certainly isn't down to me.'

'I realize that, Enid. I'm not sure what it means. I wanted your advice. I don't really have anyone else to ask.'

'It means, you should deliver this into the hands of the police, post haste, young lady, that's what it means.'

'They won't take me seriously. A woman who's just come out of jail . . .'

'Course they will, it's their public duty. I'll come with you if you like, see fair play done.'

'I'll think about it.' I sip my tea. 'Enid?'

'Yes my dear.'

'Do you think it's OK to be gay, or do you consider it the path to eternal damnation?'

'It's not what I think that matters, although . . .'

'What?'

'Well, personally speaking, I've always believed you should be true to yourself – your nature. It seems pointless to me to put on an act all your life and be unhappy. That's the way I view it. I hope it's of some use.' She takes the lid off the biscuit tin. 'Do help yourself to a homemade ginger snap.'

24

The first thing I notice is her divine arse bobbing up and down. She's wearing the most fantastic painted jeans I've ever seen on anybody – supermodels included. And a cream silk top that shows off her magnificent cleavage every time she bends down. According to Jesamine Vale, Pash Khan is officially the coolest woman on the planet. I glance at the scoreboard. She's bang last. Fourth of four.

She steps up to the lane and releases the ball. It trickles along the runway and eventually makes contact with two skittles, before plopping pitifully into the gully. She turns and shrugs to a group of girls, who start mocking her playfully. That is, apart from the tall one with the curly locks who bears a striking resemblance to Katie Melua. I ought to have known that throw away remark to my bloody probation officer would come back to haunt me.

The KM lookalike steps forward and slaps *my* girlfriend on the back and it turns into a half-embrace. Pash picks a beer bottle off the table, raises it in her direction and takes a swig. It's now or never.

I stomp across and as she lowers the bottle, take hold of her face in my hands and crush my lips against hers. She doesn't resist immediately. When I try to force my tongue in her mouth, she shoves me away.

I hold my hands out. 'I can explain.'

'Not now, Jes,' she says firmly, her eyes blazing furiously at me. 'I thought I made it clear earlier, I'm busy tonight.' Her voice is controlled, but I can tell she's uncharacteristically rattled. She goes to turn away. I make a grab for her hand. She folds her arms defiantly. You'd hardly have to be a student of body language to know what that means.

I say helplessly, 'Listen, Pash, I might not be around much longer. I just had to remember what it felt like.'

'What do you mean, not around?'

I shrug. 'Nothing. Aren't you going to introduce me to your friends.'

'Don't push it,' she says.

I say to the KM lookalike, 'You must be Mel.'

'Yeah. How did you know?' she says, straightening her shirt.

'Lucky guess.'

She holds out her hand. 'Melissa Parris.'

'Jesamine Verona.' Ha bloody ha. Isn't this all so jolly?

'This is Anya and Nikki,' Mel booms, in a brash, confident tone of voice that goes right through me.

I mumble feebly, 'Nice meeting you all.' Well I could hardly expect them to ask me to join in, could I?

Pash takes out a paper tissue and dabs her lips delicately, trying to regain her composure.

'Don't wipe it away, love,' I say. 'You never know, it might change your luck.'

I look from one to the other. No-one laughs. When I accidentally catch sight of my reflection in the mirror on the way to the exit, I realize I've got her lip gloss smeared across my chin.

I can't get off to sleep. My body is weary, but my mind won't switch off. I toss and turn, fretting about the poison pen letter. And cursing myself for acting like a prize prick in front of Pash and her new student buddies. Then I start pondering when my twenty-fours hours will be up exactly and when it is, whether I will spontaneously combust.

I check the clock for the fifth time in twenty minutes. I've bloody had enough of this now. I get up, pull on my tracksuit trousers and a clean sweatshirt, creep downstairs and extract Lizzy's car fob from the peg in the hall.

When I get there, the drive is empty, so I park up on the far side of alley, with the two nearside wheels straddling the pavement. This car desperately needs valeting. The stench of smoke makes me want to puke.

I sit there for ten minutes with my head wedged against the cool glass of the window, then I rummage around the glove compartment for something to occupy me and stumble upon Lizzy's ipod. What gems will this little beauty throw up?

Just as I'm about to find out, the glare of headlights rounds the corner. I recognize the sound of Pash's motor instantly. I dim the lights and open the door. I'm about to dash over there, when Melissa emerges from the driver's seat. I duck my head down, peering over the rim of the window. Pash gets out and goes to the boot. She opens it and takes out a plastic carrier. I can hear bottles clunking together.

Mel throws her arm around Pash's waist and the two women stroll into the alley, like a pair of movie stars, with their big hair and 'toothpaste commercial' grins. Going to carry her over the threshold are you, Pashindra?

Anger whirls up inside me. I feel betrayed. Dumped. Thrown on the scrap heap after one bloody night of passion. What did I do wrong? Trust me to go after a woman everybody wants. I feel like banging on her door and saying "surprise!" Would that come across as too bunny boiler-ish? Bugger this.

My hand dips into my jacket pocket, fingering the mangled lace of her panties. I'm so horny for her I could scream. Fuck it. I start the engine, clunk Lizzy's trusty steed into reverse, drop the handbrake and the car shoots backwards. I don't notice the bollard until we connect.

*

Amazingly, come eight-thirty-five on this bright summer morning, I'm rather pleasantly surprised to find I'm still alive.

I'm even more pleasantly surprised when I arrive at the practice and Dora reliably informs me I haven't been blacklisted from seeing the good Doctor Khan.

I run through the brief in my head. Don't, whatever you do, mention Melissa Parris. And don't be accusing. Don't say you were spying on them. Give her a chance to come clean and admit something's going on. And . . . whatever happens, I tell myself, don't, for fuck's sake, act in any way like you want to possess her.

I dip my head round the door cautiously and am slightly disappointed to note that she's swapped her sexy painted strides for a red crepe skirt. Still fetching though, in its own way.

She purrs, 'Come in and sit down, Jes.' I can tell from her manner she's perfectly relaxed – not a bit cross with me. Bad sign that. Very bad. Must mean she enjoyed a spectacularly good sex session with the KM lookalike last night and she's feeling guilty for knocking me back. I plump for the sofa, hoping she'll take the hint and come and join me.

She says gently, 'You go first.'

Now it's come to the crunch, I find my bravado's deserted me totally. 'Last evening . . .' I begin tentatively. 'I thought I could explain it, but I can't. Tell you what I can do though.'

'Go on.'

'Give you some tips on brushing up your bowling technique. Shouldn't be too difficult to improve on.' I stand up and go through the motions. She doesn't laugh. Not even when I do that mime of inserting three fingers into an invisible ball. That always raises a chuckle. 'Something of a relief, actually,' I continue. 'I thought you might turn out to be one of those infuriating people who's good at everything. Did my snog change your luck after all?'

She stands up. Walks to the window. Turns to face me. 'What the hell did you think you were doing? Showing off?' This is more like it. Maybe sex with the student siren wasn't so red hot after all. Even if it means I'm in Pash's bad books, I can't help feeling chuffed.

'No.'

'What then? I really need you to help me out with some answers here. Did you know, Jes, you're easy to like, but you're not easy to help.'

'At least that proves you still like me. It's not the same as love though, is it?'

'Self-sabotage,' she says, firmly. 'I was hoping you might recognize it as such.'

'What?'

'You think you're not worthy of happiness, so when something good comes along, you have to destroy it. You're on a one-woman, self-destruct crusade.'

'Yeah, I mean, like, good things happen to me all the time, don't they, Pash? Only last week I won the rollover on the lottery. Must have forgotten to mention the seven-figure cheque I just banked. Yeah, and the week before, Cameron Diaz summoned me to be her sex slave on board her Caribbean yacht. God knows what's around the corner. Talk about counting your blessings.'

She looks at me seriously. Her voice lowers into that hypnotic lilt that makes me quiver inside. 'Think about the law of attraction. What you give out to the universe you get back many times over. Do you believe in that?'

'You mean I shovel out shit and I get back a shed load to boot.'

'I might not have put it as succinctly as that. Then again . . .'

I pull out the note and hand it to her. 'It got sent to the bistro yesterday. Freaked me out a bit. My ex-landlady thinks I ought to go to the police.'

She perches on the edge of the sofa and examines it thoughtfully. 'Some hoaxer . . . hopefully.'

'Yeah and I suppose it's down to the shit I'm putting out. It's the universe paying me back, or something.'

'This could be serious, Jes. Don't fuck about.'

It occurs to me that it's the first time I've heard her say that word. It's quite engaging. Like she really does care about me.

'Well whoever did it was must be local, because it wasn't franked, so someone must have delivered it by hand.'

'Unless it was sent by courier, but then they'd normally have some kind of label on the packet. Personally I agree. You ought to put it on record.' Her fingers brush my hand reassuringly. 'Just as a precautionary measure.'

Unlike Enid, she doesn't offer to go to the police with me, which irks me just a little.

'Could I stay with you for a bit? I mean, a while. Little while. A few days at the most.' Not for the first time, I sound pathetically desperate.

Pash smiles. 'I'm sorry Jes. I'd love to help, really I would, but I've got someone lodging with me for a week or so while the flat is being done up.'

'Mel?'

'Mmm,' she says, licking her lips, I assume unconsciously. 'Mel.'

*

At the top of Cleeve Hill, I rip the poisonous note into confetti-sized pieces and watch them drift away in the breeze.

'Come and get me!' I yell at the clouds. 'I'm not scared of you, you fucking faceless coward!'

A woman walking a Westie turns and scurries off in the opposite direction.

Bloody Mel Parris, the student shagging machine. What's she got that I haven't? Apart from brains, beauty and charm in abundance, that is.

And as for that fucking two-timing, psychoanalysing bitch, with all her bloody cranky 'universe' theories, well get this from me, darlin', two can play at that game.

25

In the space of a minute, the pair of us are butt naked — frolicking around on the bed. Biting. Sucking. Fucking. The sex is rough, hard and strangely satisfying, the product of my pent up anger.

'You bad girl, I'm going to fuck you so fucking hard,' I growl in her ear. 'You had better fucking do what you're told.'

She throws her head back and laughs abandonedly.

'Give it to me baby. Fuck me. Fuck meeeee. Harder. Do it. Do iiiitttt! Wow!' Mack says, crashing against the pillow. 'What's got into you? The Devil?'

I slump onto the bed beside her and turn my face away, so she can't see I'm biting my lip to stop myself from crying. Eventually I whisper, 'I'm sorry.'

'You twat,' she says propping herself up on her elbows. 'What the hell are you saying sorry for? It was the most exciting thing ever — being taken like that.' She grins. 'I never knew you felt that way about me. Wow, I'm gobsmacked.'

She cups my chin in her hand, pressing her lips against mine. When it becomes clear I'm not about to respond, she pulls away.

'You want to scrap the romantic bit? You only like it rough, right?' Before I can gather myself, she rolls me onto my stomach and straddles my legs. Face down, I bite into the pillow.

I get the feeling this is going to hurt. A lot.

*

At the bistro there's a bulky brown envelope poking out of my pigeon hole. I slide it out and hold it next to my ear. When I realize it's not ticking I shake it. I find a paper knife in Lizzy's desk drawer and gingerly run in down the side crease of the envelope in case it turns out to be booby-trapped.

I once shared a cell with a woman whose weapon of choice was the 'lobster pot' – where they staple razor blades to the envelope pocket, so that when you pull your fingers across the opening – well you can imagine the carnage. So much worse than a blasted paper cut. She'd used the technique to mash the sensitive fingers of her husband's mistress – a professional harpist.

I tip the contents onto the desk. A box of matches and a note:

You know what they do with witches. Burn in hell bitch.

Friendly.

I drop the note in the sink and strike a match, just as Lizzy marches in.

'What the hell are you doing? Razing my kitchen to the ground?'

I douse the match with water. 'Don't overreact, Sis.'

'Well?' Lizzy says.

I show her the sodden note. 'It's someone's idea of a joke, don't panic.'

'Oh my God. Who would do this?'

'No idea. I haven't exactly been around long enough to make any enemies. Well, one or two, perhaps.'

'Well you need to sort this out,' she says, 'because – and I don't mean this to sound heartless, but if someone's intent on getting to you, I'd rather it wasn't here.'

'Charming. Thanks for caring.'

'That did sound rather callous, didn't it? Sorry.'

'Not good for business, eh? Some hooded henchman taking out the owner's sister. Maybe you could write a little note on the blackboard asking whoever it is, not to make a mess. Scribble it right there, underneath the jam roly-poly. Hopefully they'll take the hint and comply.'

'I'm taking you off tonight's rota,' she says firmly. 'I'll get Cam to pitch in. He's at a loose end and a handsome man with too much time on his hands is never a good thing. You'll still get paid.'

'OK, OK, I'm sold on it. Being paid to do fuck-all is my idea of a good time. Sis?'

'What?'

'Nothing.'

'Go on. You've started now. Might as well say it.'

'You don't trust him, do you? It's happening again.'

'I don't know what you mean.'

149

'Lizzy, I can see it in your face. That pinched expression like you're struggling to control your emotions. Why can't we talk openly for once?'

Lizzy sighs. 'A man like Cameron is always in demand with women and some of them aren't shy in the way they go about things. They'll flirt with him, sit on his lap, coo in his ear. You'd think I was bloody invisible the way these harlots behave in front of me. But you know what, Jesamine – it's the ones that go about it behind your back . . . the ones who'll happily seduce your man under your very nose and make out that it's him that made all the running. They're the ones you have to be wary of.'

*

I'm sat on the wall scuffing my heels and counting silver saloons for a whole fifty minutes before she arrives. She glides into a "No Parking" bay, switches off the engine and takes out her mobile. She checks her make-up in the car mirror. At least she's not putting her face on in the outside lane the motorway like some women do.

She tweaks the mirror again and this time I know she's seen me. The window lowers. Her elbow pokes out at an angle.

Dora hurries across the car park and hands her a box file. They exchange a few words then the receptionist goes inside again.

Pash sticks her head out the window. 'I'm not stopping, Jes.'

I go across to the car, not knowing what to say to her.

She winds the window all the way down. 'Did you want something?'

'I don't know.'

'Can I give you a lift somewhere? I'm going to Burford.'

'That'll do.' I jump in, before she has the chance to change her mind.

As she puts her hand on the gear stick, I put mine over the top of hers and squeeze. 'It's OK, you know. It's not as if we're joined at the hip. We're both free agents.'

We drive out of the car park and onto the main road.

She glances at me with an odd expression. 'Jes, are you alright?'

'Yeah, yeah, fine. Haven't taken any mind-altering substances that I'm aware of. Love is the drug of choice these days. Had mind-blowing sex earlier as a matter of fact. You should see the scratches on my back. Pull over and I'll show you.'

150

'I'll take your word for it.'

'Suit yourself.'

She smiles. 'I've really tried to figure you out, but hey, you've got me stumped this time. You want me to be jealous, right? Because some female marked you. And would you like me to enquire as to her name, because I'm damned sure you want to tell me.'

'Melissa of course. She's playing us both.'

Large droplets of rain appear out of nowhere as if to match my filthy mood.

Pash throws back her head and laughs.

'What's so funny, Doc?'

She switches on the windscreen wipers and they squeak as if in protest.

'You are. Pretending you seduced Melissa. Think that gives you kudos, do you? Seducing a student.' She shakes her head. 'You're one strange cookie.'

'Let's get this straight, Pash, she seduced me. Couldn't get enough of it. The sex went on well into the next morning as I recall.'

'Yeah, well these students have such stamina,' she says, her mouth breaking into a huge grin.

'You're laughing at me.'

'I can't help it. It's hilarious. And seeing as you mentioned the word "straight," I feel duty bound to point out that Melissa Parris is straighter than a laser beam. She wouldn't get into your bed, Jes, if the entire male species ceased to exist. Sorry to spoil your little ego trip.'

'Well if that's true, how come *you* had her?'

'You make me sound like a sexual predator. Not sure I'm flattered. I'll have to think about that one. I just told you, Mel is a friend, that's all.' She jabs a finger in my direction. 'Can you get that through your thick skull?'

Inside the pit of my stomach I feel empty. On the verge of nausea.

'Don't worry,' she says, 'I won't let on to her that you fancy her. Your secret is safe with me.'

'I don't, *you* do.'

'Ah, now we're getting somewhere.'

'I was there the other night, when you came home from bowling.'

'What were you doing? Lurking in the bushes?'

'I borrowed Lizzy's car. I was over the road. I saw the two of you –
she had her arm around you.'

'Yeah, so? It's what women do, isn't it? If you must know we were
about to have a midnight celebration. Nat asked her to get engaged.
That's Nathan, by the way, not Natasha, or Natalie, in case you're still
harbouring any doubts. So you were spying on me.'

'I came to say sorry for being a prize prat at the bowling alley. Now
I'm an even bigger one.'

'No harm done.'

'I hope not. Pash?'

'Mmm.'

'Can you drop me here. I need to do something. I have to go back.'

'You'll get wet.' She touches my arm lightly. 'It looks like it might
storm.'

'It's no more than I deserve.'

26

She grabs hold of me by the lapels of my sodden jacket and hauls me inside.

'You're soaked through, babe. Let's get you out of those wet clothes. Twice in one day. Can't get enough of me, eh?' she squeals. She's high – like she's been sniffing glue or something.

'Hang, on, Mack. Slow down.'

'What's up?' she says, undoing her jeans. I take hold of her hands before she has the chance to get her top over her head.

'Slow down,' I repeat again, hoping it registers this time. 'I have to talk to you.'

'Let's save the talking for later, babe. I'm on fire.'

I step back from her. 'What happened earlier . . . I acted like a complete idiot. I forgot myself. Who I was. What I was doing.'

'You're not making sense. The rain's got to your brain. Come through to the kitchen.'

I pull up a chair.

She opens the cupboard. 'Want a brandy to warm you up?'

'Please.'

'You're trembling. What's happened? Have you had an accident?'

'I'm such a fucking twat sometimes.'

She hands me the tumbler and I drink. Lots of little sips, barely allowing the rim of the glass to lose contact with my mouth. She swivels a chair round, straddles it and grins at me.'

'You were like a woman possessed, babe. It's been a while since somebody's had that effect on me.'

'That wasn't the real me – I'm not like that.'

She runs her hands up and down her scored arms anxiously. She says, 'There's lots of ways we can do it. Doesn't have to be like that if you don't want.'

'I don't . . . want.'

'It's OK,' she says. 'Don't get upset.'

'Like I said, I'm the idiot here. Please accept my apology.'

She looks at me through narrow accusing eyes. 'You saying what happened with me was a mistake?'

'Not at the time, no.'

'But now, just a matter of a few hours later, it is. So what's happened to change your mind?'

I shrug, helplessly. 'I'm not good at this stuff.'

'Well, I don't believe what you're saying. You initiated it. You ambushed me at the door, ripped off my clothes and – '

'You're far too young for me, Mack. You're a baby.'

'And you're not exactly Grandma, rocking on the porch with your comfort blanket.'

'No . . . but . . . it was a crazy urge and I indulged myself with you. I'm sorry.'

'An urge? You forced yourself on me, Jes. Intimidated me. Made me do things I didn't want to.'

'Don't say it like that. What things?'

'You were beastly.'

'It was an act. Come on, Mack, you were practically dropping your knickers the second I walked through the door just now. It couldn't have been all that bad before.'

'Bad is the new good,' she says and laughs.

I lift my T-shirt and turn around. 'That's what you did to me. I've seen in the mirror and it's not pretty – it's like a bloody patchwork quilt. And as for the inside, well . . . I'm creeping around with a red hot poker up my arse. You probably think that's justice, Mack, and there's at least three blokes knocking about who would agree with you. If there's any way I can make things better between us . . .'

'Stop pissing around then,' she says. 'Get your kit off.'

'I didn't mean sexually.'

'Got a note from your mother, have you? To excuse you.'

'My mother wouldn't give me a note. She'd say I deserved everything I got. And then some.'

Mack gets up and snatches the glass from my hand. Brandy spills onto the floor. 'Go now please.'

'Can't I finish my drink?'

'I said, go please.

'Can't we talk about this?'

'What's left to say? I think you just said it all.'

'Will you be OK?'

'Get out.' She thrusts the glass at me. 'Get ouuuuuuttt!'

I walk the two miles to the restaurant in an attempt to clear my fuddled head.

As I sneak in through the back door, Lizzy's waiting to pounce. She gives me a sharp look and taps her watch. 'You're twenty minutes late.'

'Sorry, Sis. These shoes are giving me blisters. I might have to go shopping in the morning.'

'Fine,' she says, putting her arm across me and barring my path. 'Just as long as it's under your own steam – and *not* in my car.'

'Uh. Shit. I can explain.'

'You don't have any tax or insurance, Jes. So explain.'

'Yeah, sorry. It was an emergency, I wasn't thinking straight.'

'What if you'd hurt someone? Christ, you didn't did you? You haven't left a trail of destruction for me to find out about later? Tell me you didn't run someone over.'

'Stop panicking. Why must you always think the worst?'

'Don't even get me started, you bloody irresponsible twerp. Yet I was the dumb idiot who got pulled over by one of your friends in blue, with practically the whole village looking on like it was a spectator sport. "Madam, are you aware your offside rear lamp is broken?"'

'God, Sis, no. Bloody eagle-eyed plod.'

'No, Officer. It must have been my husband driving. Because it certainly couldn't have been my rebel of a sister who's recently left prison, because she isn't allowed to come within fifty yards of me and my family, let alone help herself to the keys to my pride and joy and drive it away without my consent.'

'How much was the fine? Take it out of my wages. You didn't get any points on your licence, did you?'

'He let me off with a caution, no thanks to you.'

'Good old PC Plod. Did you bat your eyelashes at him?'

'I don't think you're quite understanding me. We're not talking about your average rust bucket here. It's a Lexus – top of the range. That means replacement parts are very expensive, not to mention labour costs.'

'OK, I'll pay for it. I'll rob a bloody bank if I have to. Keep your thong on.'

'Luckily for you, the leasing company will take care of it this time. I'll say I did it. But don't you ever pull a stunt like that on me again. Got it?'

'Absolutely. Loud and clear.' I find myself saluting her, without meaning to. She raises her eyebrows at me in disgust.

'You'd better hurry up and get changed, we've got the local Chamber of Commerce in tonight. We're talking about prestigious business people who don't mind giving their gold cards a blast, so make sure you're on the ball.'

'Aye-aye, boss.'

'I want you hovering in the vicinity all night – no-one's glass is to run dry, understand?'

I nod. 'Sure. Piece of cake. Where's Cameron?'

'Why?'

'Just interested.'

'He had an appointment . . . with his agent I think. He said he might drop by later.'

'With his agent . . . I thought his agent was in Edinburgh?'

'He's quite mobile. He travels all over the place . . . even down South, it has been known.' She scans my face. 'Is there something you're not telling me?'

'No, no. Everything's fine.'

I scuttle upstairs. My uniform for this evening is hung up behind the door. One of Pashindra's business cards is poking out of the pocket. I turn it over and he's scrawled: *Enjoy the evening. I'm off to get some 'healing.' Have a good one – service I mean. I intend to*, followed by a single kiss.

I can feel my face reddening. My heart hammers furiously in my throat. I lean over the basin and splash my face with cold water. Now bloody Lizzy's calling me from the stairwell.

'Coming!'

I breathe in for a count of seven and out for a count of eleven, to help quell the panic, like Pash taught me to do and remind myself that Doctor

Khan is a grown woman. Professional. She can handle things. She's dealt with murderers, rapists . . . all manner of low-life . . . she can surely cope with Cameron McGill's unabashed flirting.

What if he tries it on with her? What if she succumbs to his dubious charms? What if she really is bisexual after all? I stare at my reflection in the mirror, watching as my hand stings my face, in the vague hope it will calm me down.

'You look flustered, Jes,' Lizzy says, as I enter the kitchen. 'Are you sure you're OK?'

'Yeah, yeah. I think I might be running a temperature.'

'Not tonight, *please*,' she says. 'I'll fetch you some paracetamol. The first of the Chamber's mob has arrived – party of eight – I've seated them in the conservatory, if you'd care to take their food orders. I've sorted the wine.'

'Cheers.'

'Jes?'

'Mmm.'

'You haven't had any more of those awful letters?'

'No. Stop worrying. I'm sure it's somebody's pathetic idea of a joke.'

'It's just that . . . your face appears to have broken out in a rash.'

I can hardly confess to slapping my own face, can I? Lizzy would really think I'd lost the plot this time.

'It's nothing.' I press my fingers against my cheek. It feels bruised. 'I'll disguise it with make-up.'

'Good idea,' she says.

I don't want to do this. I don't want to be here. I'd rather be a fly on the wall in Pash's office. Maybe they're not meeting at the office? Maybe he's arranged a home visit. That's what the dirty, cheating bastard's done, behind our backs – mine and Lizzy's.

I go into the back room and phone the number of the practice. When I get through, it's Dora's voice on the answerphone informing me the office is now closed and advising me to call back after nine tomorrow morning.

Lizzy throws open the door. 'What are you doing, Jes? Our guests are waiting. After what happened earlier, don't you dare think of letting me down tonight.'

'OK, OK, I'm right there.'

In between transmitting orders to the kitchen, I trot back to the office and ring Lizzy's home phone. Pick up, you bastard. I imagine the pair of them sitting on the sofa sharing a bottle of wine – their legs entwined.

When I return to the dining room, Lizzy thrusts a tray at me. 'Table six. I've just seated another five guests, so chop-chop.' She claps her hands at me in a condescending manner. If you want to know what it's like being a twenty-first century slave, just ask.

'Listen, is there any chance I could flit out for ten minutes. Not now, I mean, when their main courses arrive.'

'No chance. I'm sorry, Jes, but whatever it is will have to wait. Nothing's that urgent.'

Wanna bet? They're leaning towards one another. She's kicking off her shoes. He's unzipping her dress . . . sorry Lizzy, this can't wait. It simply can't. I pull off my pinny and make a dash for the taxi rank.

'Oi,' some woman says, shoving me out of the way. 'There's a queue. Are you blind?'

'No, but you will be if you don't get out of my way. This is an emergency.' I accidentally catch her foot. She yelps. She swears at me them mumbles something about Karma.

I jump in the back, give the taxi driver the address and tell him to put his foot down.

'Not something we tend to do in these parts, love,' he says.

Cameron's jeep is parked on the drive. I leap out.

The taxi driver says, 'Aren't you forgetting something? Seven pounds-fifty.'

'You've got to be kidding me. It's only a couple of miles. Look wait here. You can take me back in a minute.'

I scoot up the path and grab the key from under the flower pot. In my head, they're writhing around on the floor naked. They're throwing their heads back and laughing. Really laughing. I head straight for the kitchen.

As I pass the knife block I pluck out the one with the longest, thickest blade. 'Cameron . . . Cameron . . . Pash . . .'

158

'Where the hell did you disappear to?' Lizzy says. 'We finished service half an hour ago . . . '

'I can explain.'

'And you've cut yourself. You're dripping blood all over the floor.' She grabs a tea towel and binds it around my hand.

'Don't fuss.'

She raises her eyebrows. 'I'm concerned about the floor. Whatever's happened?'

'Accident.'

'You are a bloody accident. A bloody motorway pile-up waiting to happen. What's wrong with you?'

'I think it's the therapy. Maybe it's not agreeing with me. I'm sorry I left my post.'

'Yes, well, my girl, you're damn lucky that I was able to get a replacement at extremely short notice. Another time we might not be so fortunate.'

Cameron comes bustling through the double doors pushing a trolley laden with calorific desserts. 'Everything OK, Jes?' he says, handing over the trolley to one of the chefs and walking away from me. I corner him in the washroom.

'What the hell are you playing at?'

'Being the perfect host. The guests seem to appreciate it. Least I managed to smooth over your mistakes, which, how can we put it politely? There were rather too many of this evening. '

'Like?'

'The woman at table five asked for her steak well done, but you had put 'rare.' What happened? Did your concentration go AWOL?'

'That wasn't a mistake. I did that on purpose. I was hoping she might faint in the blood – jumped up little tart.'

'And you ordered the wrong sauce for the duck.'

'Shouldn't the chef have picked up on that? I'm new to this lark, not Gordon fucking Ramsey.'

'I'm not entirely convinced you're cut out for the customer service industry. You need charm . . . sophistication . . .'

'Bullshit.'

'And bullshit. Then there's the matter of an irate taxi driver.'

'Why did you leave me that card?'

He grins. 'I couldn't resist. You tease me, I tease you back. Your turn.'

'So, you didn't go to see her tonight then?'

'Who?'

'You know damn well. Right, you've had your chance, I'm off to tell Lizzy.'

'Grass. And to think I offered to make a baby with you.'

'I play fair, Cameron. If you want to play dirty you'll see another side to me.'

'Ooh sweetheart, I'm really shitting it now. Grow up Jes,' he says flinging the door open. The handle crashes against the wall and leaves a dent.

'Thank fuck that's all over,' Lizzy says, pulling off her apron and draping her arm around Cameron's neck. 'Thanks darling, for pitching in.'

'Always a pleasure. Your sister has something she wants to tell you.'

'Let's have a drink first,' Lizzy says. 'Brandies all round. Help us unwind.'

'I'll get them,' Cameron says.

Lizzy pats my hand. 'Sorry if I was a little hard on you earlier. It's a lot to adapt to. I hated it at first. I guess I wasn't used to being nice to people's faces all the time. The opening night was a ball, but after that I wondered what I'd let myself in for. It's not the sort of thing you can dabble in – we had to remortgage the cottage to get this place. That's one hell of an incentive to make things work. It's a lot like a marriage really. You have your ups and downs, but deep down you know you're in it for the long haul.'

'Here,' Cameron says, setting three enormous brandy balloons down in front of us.

Lizzy says, 'What are these, doubles?'

Cameron winks at me. 'Trebles.'

Lizzy takes his hand. 'Make damned certain I sleep soundly tonight. What was it you wanted to say to me, Jes?' She rubs her eyes. 'Nothing too deep and meaningful please, I'm exhausted.'

160

'Uh – thanks for putting up with me. I know I haven't exactly been Miss Reliable, but well – I'll aim to do better in future.'

'Perfect,' Cameron says, bumping his glass against mine. 'I'll drink to that.'

27

'You can't keep on doing this, Jes,' Pash says, running her hand through her hair. 'Turning up here whenever you feel like it. It's not fair on the staff and it's not fair on me either. It's like having a stalker. I find myself looking over my shoulder every five minutes, expecting you to be there. I can't relax.'

'I've got a CD you can borrow.'

'You're sapping my energy.'

'Didn't hear you complaining the other night.'

'Another thing, Jeff's back from holiday on Friday. We need to introduce some normality around here before he decides to find himself another partner. One whose mind is on the job. I've always erred on the side of radical, but this is farcical.'

'OK, OK, you've made your point, don't go on. I'm in trouble, Pash. There's this girl . . . ' I feel like I'm going to burst into tears if I carry on speaking.

She gives me some filtered water and I sip it gratefully in between deep breaths. She says gently, 'Tell me about the girl.'

'Mack. She's on the rebound from her girlfriend, who's two-timing her with some guy. I've been counselling her . . . trying to help her. Only I got this sudden crazy impulse and things went too far. We like . . . had sex.' I screw my fingers into a fist.

'This isn't another one of your pretences?'

'I'm deadly serious, Pash.'

'I see.'

'Do you think, like, I've betrayed you?'

She shrugs, nonchalantly. 'Depends. Sex is sex. Making love is making love. Fucking is fucking.'

'If that's meant to have some profound meaning, I'm afraid it's gone straight over my head.'

'It means, what were your intentions towards this girl? We're you making love with her?'

'No. It was just sex. Raw sex. Fucking. It hurt. Physically. I've never been into that scene. I can't bloody walk properly . . . and it burns when I go to the loo. Sorry – too much information.'

'And what about from her point of view? Is she in love with you?'

'She's infatuated. She's nineteen, Pash. When I was nineteen, I only left someone's bedroom to eat, or to pee and not always then. What were you like?'

'Studious. I was a late developer.'

'So do you think I've been unfaithful to you? Tell me. It's doing my head in.'

'I think . . . you should think more about this poor girl . . . and less about me and you.'

'There's another problem.'

'Oh.'

'Well, like I said, it was crazy. We went at it like animals. Am I offending you?'

'Don't be silly. What do you think people come here to talk about? The weather?'

'She was so up for it. I'm not exaggerating.'

'So you intimated.'

'Only now she's saying she wasn't. She's saying I made her do stuff, but I didn't , I swear. You know that's not my style. And another thing, she cuts up.'

She shakes her head. 'Whatever were you thinking of, Jes?'

'God, you sounded uncannily like my mother. Scary, that.'

'You've exploited a vulnerable young woman . . .'

'Shut up, I know.'

'I don't understand you.'

'I don't understand me. Help me make sense of it.'

How can I begin to explain to Pash that it was an act of revenge on my part? That I was getting her back, because I thought she had two-timed me with Melissa.

She says, 'I think if you're completely honest with yourself, you'll admit this isn't about her. Why do you have to take everything to extremes?'

163

'Because that's the way my life has been.'

'OK, I want you to think about this young girl. This incredibly helpless, damaged young girl, who's see-sawing between you and some other dodgy lover, who by all accounts has very little integrity. And as for you young lady . . .'

'Don't you dare tar me with the same brush as that Imogen bird. I didn't mean to hurt Mack. I thought I was back there in that hellhole. Look, against my better judgement, I'm going to come clean about my past. It's been bugging me for a while now.'

'Go on.'

'The last couple of years in Whytemoor – after you'd left – if a woman needed cheering up, I took care of it. Made her feel special.'

'I take it we're not talking Interflora.'

'I should have mentioned it before. Sorry.'

Her face registers a mixture of shock and disbelief.

'You mean before you slept with me? Before I . . . that's brilliant. Utterly brilliant, Jes.' She puts her hand to her mouth.

'I'm not carrying anything. I've been tested regularly and that.'

'Fantastic.'

'You think I'm a slut. Go on, say it. I'll say it for you, shall I? Jesamine Vale, you're a slut. I was providing a service, Pash. It was very popular.'

'You don't say.'

'The women liked it. The screws liked it, because, as we all know, the post-orgasmic woman is a creature of contentment.' I squeeze my thighs together. It still burns, dammit. 'And then again, Pash, some of the screws just loved to watch the action – eyes glued to the spy-hole and didn't make any bloody secret of it. Your ex, for example, the lovely Gerry. Lovely, generous Gerry Strickland. Rumour has it, Eva Rowe was knocking off a warder. It couldn't have been the fragrant Gerry, by any chance, could it?'

'That's enough now,' she says, firmly. 'I'll listen to your troubles and I'll help you out, Jes, if I possibly can, but don't make it personal, OK.'

'Well don't you expect me to get all hung up about me fingering a few fannies, because it wasn't a bit humiliating. Actually, if you can bear to hear the plain truth it was quite liberating. Besides I wasn't doing it out of the goodness of my heart. What it meant to me was nice soap, deodorant and unlimited phone cards. It was more of a little business venture really. Sir Alan Sugar would be proud of me.'

'I'm quite sure he would. Then stop trying to justify yourself to me. You don't need my approval for the way you behave, we're hardly what you'd call an item.'

'But I don't want to spoil anything.'

'What's to spoil? Like I said . . .'

'Fuck it. You know damn well, Pash. You're angry with me, aren't you? Yell at me if you want. Tell me what a fucking slut I've been. It isn't good for you to repress your emotions – that's what people like you tell people like me, isn't it?'

'I think . . .' she says in that irritatingly measured way of hers, 'you are angry with yourself, Jes.'

'Stop analysing everything and turning it on its head. And don't say, it's what you do. Tell me something I don't know, OK.'

*

Rhianna says, 'I've given him a sleeping tablet. He had a such a rough night, the poor fella's exhausted. I know Mrs Vickers doesn't approve but . . .'

'You did the right thing.'

'Please stay,' she adds, taking my arm. 'Just chatting away to him helps. I'm convinced some of it gets through. I'll fetch some tea.'

So I go and sit down opposite him, trying to dream up something meaningful to say. Something that will lift his spirits. Something that will ignite the passion for living again, even though I know deep down that the flame has long been extinguished.

I pluck a magazine out of the rack and thumb through it randomly, seeking inspiration. The advertisements are nearly all size zero models wearing ridiculously skimpy outfits and flaunting obscenely-priced accessories, where I can only conclude too many noughts have been stuck on the end – and a whole host of the latest perfumes with the dumbest names imaginable, launched by so-called 'celebs.'

It makes me wonder why Mother has never cashed in on this lucrative opportunity for blatant self-promotion. I drop the magazine on the table. There's nothing here to stimulate a man's dying brain.

I open my mouth and close it again. It must be like authors who suffer from the dreaded Writers' Block – unable to face the blank page. Can you get Talkers' Block, I wonder.

I'm just going to start with the first thing that comes into my head. I lean across the table, close enough so I can feel his faint breath against my cheek.

'Let me give you some sound advice, Dad. Never, ever, cross a woman. Don't even think about it. "Hell hath no fury" and all that. Well it's bloody true and I should know. I've crossed two women in as many days and I know I'm going to pay for it big time. Actually, I've crossed three if you count our Lizzy. I pranged her very expensive motor on a bollard and she got stopped by the cops. Stop laughing this minute, Dad, or I swear I'll tell her.

'The gorgeous Doctor Pash pretends she's not miffed with me, but then that's her way. Miss Uber-cool. She's not German, by the way, but you'd guessed that already, hadn't you? It's like, on a professional level, nothing phases her. But then there's this unbridled, intensely passionate side to her I never knew existed until the other night, and the truth is, I'll probably never experience again. Not now I've confessed my colourful past.'

I take out her panties and lay them across my thigh, fingering the delicate lace.

'Shall I tell you what she did to me? Shall I? OK then, Daddy, dearest. Are you sitting comfortably?

'The other night, Pash enticed me into her boudoir, plying me with Lizzy's expensive plonk – not that she needed to do that. She stripped me naked . . . she bound my wrists to the bed. She smeared me in this cherry potion . . . God, she got me so worked up with her antics, I thought I was going to have a massive coronary, before I ever got round to the orgasm bit.

'And as for the finale – well – she's got this little silver stud in her tongue – apparently it hurt like fuck when they put it in. Anyway, when she went down on me . . . ' I check myself. 'Shut the fuck up, Jes. What the hell is wrong with you?'

I lean across and whisper in his ear, 'I'll tell you when you're old enough, OK.' I take a deep breath. 'Did I mention, I've been getting these weird notes? Not very pretty. I'll spare you the gory details. At least

166

I can cross Mack off my list of suspects – that's Stella Mackenzie by the way – she calls herself Mack, though she's not a bit butch, or anything, or I wouldn't have done it with her. At the time of the first note I hadn't got under her skin. In either sense of the word.'

'What do you do when you upset a woman, Dad? How do you go about putting things right? Flowers? Chocolates? Sackcloth and ashes? You must have gotten yourself into Octavia's bad books a few times down the years. She was always a bloody impossible bitch to please.

'You ought to be knighted for putting up with her for the best part of four decades. Services to bitchkind. You were too easy-going with her and she took advantage of your gentleness every step of the way, like the Grande Old Dame tends to do. I've a feeling this Leo Hendry will be exactly the same. We're dealing with a shrewd old vixen here. She baits her trap, then she backs them into a corner, knowing they're too weak to resist. Before they know it, they're getting swallowed up alive. Poor-old-Leo.'

I pick up the magazine.

'I'd made up my mind I wasn't going to mention the L-word.' I pat his hand. 'Sorry, mate. Let's change the subject. So then, what do you think Mother's new scent ought to be called?'

28

Evening Standard

"Evil Eva" Judge's Wife Suffers Miscarriage

Two weeks after he sensationally freed paedophile ringleader, Eva Rowe, Judge Hedley Calderfield's wife, Sarah, 35, has suffered a miscarriage.

Considerable strain has been heaped on the couple's thirteen-year marriage and threats of violence have been made against the family, including the children, Annabelle,12 and Toby,10.

It is thought that a significant proportion of the blame will be attributed to the stress brought on by the aftermath of the Rowe case.

A spokesperson for the campaign group Women Against Pornography and Violence said: "Now Judge Calderfield knows what it's like to lose a child in the most tragic of circumstances. Whilst some people will undoubtedly say this is poetic justice, our hearts go out to his wife and children."

*

'Do you remember that perfume, *"Tramp?"*'

'Before my time,' Lizzy says, not looking up from her paperwork. She opens the desk drawer and pulls out a calculator.

'Don't give me that crap. You're two years older than me and I remember it like it was yesterday. Aunt Val used to drench herself in it on special occasions.'

'Bully for her.'

'Can't recall the smell though. I was thinking they'd never bring something with that sort of name out now. People wouldn't wear it.'

'Wear it. Funny.' She prods at the number keys and jots something on her pad. Then she frowns and recalculates. This time she looks altogether happier with the outcome. I perch on the edge of the desk.

'What?' she says.

'Was Aunt Val your favourite relative?'

'Not particularly. I liked them all.'

'She *was* mine. I wanted to trade Mum in for her. Don't suppose for one minute her kids would've agreed.'

'Jes!'

'I suppose the name had different connotations then. It was hip. I mean, they're hardly going to bring out something called *Lady of the Night*, or *Streetwalker*, are they? She's wearing *Streetwalker* . . . and she'll shag anything that moves. Or how about, *Eau de Jailbird*: combines the heady aroma of piss and bleach with the merest hint of skunk. Next time you get hit on by a sassy broad, make sure she's wearing nothing . . . but *Eau de Jailbird*.'

'What's brought all this on?' Lizzy says, doodling on a sheet of blotting paper. 'Are you thinking of working in media?'

'Ha bloody ha. If Octavia brought out a perfume, what do you think it would be called?'

'Have you been drinking, Jes?'

'Odd name for a scent, that. Not nearly catchy enough. Try again.'

She shakes her head. 'Is it the medication kicking in?'

'I'm not on anything. I'm high on life. Good old life. Remember that? I've got a lot of living to make up. I popped in to see Dad and guess what we've been up to?'

'Sorry, don't have time for guesses.' She taps her watch.

'We've been working on a list of potential perfumes to make the Grande Old Dame even wealthier than she is presently. You're nobody until you've had a scent named after you, don't you know. They're all at it: Kylie, Kate Moss . . . every bloody WAG in existence. Want to know what we came up with?'

'No thanks.'

'God you're so boring sometimes. Well you ought to take an interest, cos it might make a huge difference to the inheritance pot.' I rub my hands together. 'Not that I'll bloody see any of it. She can poke it.'

'Still no.'

'Your decision entirely. Trust me, you'll go to your grave curious.'

'Customs and Excise beckons. I can't afford to get behind.'

'Sod that, this is tons more fun. Come on, play the game, Sis. I'll announce the winning three in reverse order: 'In third place: *Mommie Dearest*. Shame Joan Crawford's kid got in there first. In second place: *The Bitch is Back*. Stone cold sober as a matter of fact and shouldn't we all be sodding grateful . . .'

'Jes, you're not being funny now.'

'You just said I was.'

'Hardly original either. Besides it's too cruel. She doesn't deserve your vilification.'

'OK, get this, Sis, you'll love this one. And it's all my own work, promise. In first place, trumpet fanfare please: *A Warped Sense of Uma*. A reference to Uma King – get it?' I take a bow. 'I think a polite ripple of applause is in order.'

She stares at me stony-faced.

'You do remember Uma King? Good old Oo-Ma. Oo-Ma, put the kettle on. Oo-Ma, what time's dinner? Oh, I almost forgot, it's fend for yourself around here. Never mind the bloody lifeboat drill, it's every man, woman and child for themselves.'

'Mummy's finest hour,' Lizzy says, wistfully. 'She said that part was written especially for her.'

'That figures. Remember how off-her-trolley *Mummy* went when they axed it? Naturally, on the outside she was her usual genial self amongst her adoring public, but inside she was a raging cauldron of seething bitterness. Her pride was mown down and we mustn't have that, must we?'

Lizzy frowns. 'And, dare I ask, how many on this *short-list* were Dad's idea?'

'Well put it this way, he didn't disagree with any of them. Which one do you prefer?'

'Well put it this way,' she says imitating my tone, 'I think it's you that's warped.'

170

29

I think about writing a note and posting it through her door but it seems too impersonal, considering. So I ring the bell three times and get no response. I guess she's out. Bit of a relief really. I step back and the upstairs curtain twitches. For some reason, my blood runs through me like frozen water. I flap the letterbox.

'Mack, it's Jes, are you in there? I need to talk to you. I've written my number down. Ring me, OK.' I walk away up the path and glance up at the window again. This time the curtain is closed. I go back, stoop down and peer through the letterbox. 'For fuck's sake open this door now, else I'm calling the police. I know you're in there . . . you've got exactly ten sec – '

The door opens. Imogen eyes me curiously. 'Can I help you?'

'I'm a friend of Mack's. Is she in?'

'I don't think I know you, do I? Though your face is familiar.'

'I was at the club the other night, when you walked out on her. We got chatting.'

'She didn't mention it.'

'She mentioned you, Imogen. Quite a lot actually.'

'Right. Well she's been a bit poorly. I'm taking care of her.'

'Can I see her?'

'She's resting. She's not up to visitors. I'll tell her you called.' She tries to close the door on me, but I wedge my foot in the gap.

'Is Davy inside?'

'I beg your pardon. Who *are* you?'

'Look I know about what's been going on. You are OK – you and Mack?'

She scowls at me. 'I'm sure it's none of your bloody business, so unless you've got a warrant to search the premises . . .'

'Yeah, darlin', I've been there, done that, all the while you were just a twinkle in your mother's eye, so don't fuck with me.' I move to restrain her. She kicks at my knee and misses. I grab her by the gullet and push her against the wall. 'Calm down, just calm it down, there's a good girl. There's not going to be any trouble. I'm not the law, I'm just here to make sure Mack is OK. I'm concerned for her wellbeing. Understand?' Her wild eyes flicker furiously at mine. 'I'm going to back off, but take it easy. I'm not looking for a fight.'

I release her and she doubles up.

'You're a head case,' she splutters eventually. 'A bloody nutter.'

As I make my way upstairs, the front door slams. Another emotional coward that can't face me, eh? In the bedroom, there's streaks of blood on the sheets and some on the wall. Her eyes are open, staring at the ceiling.

'I heard the commotion,' she says in monotone. 'You'd better not have hurt her, Jes.'

I whip a pillow case off and rip into strips to bind her wrists while she lies there passively.

'Your girlfriend might be a nurse, Mack, but she sure ain't no angel.'

'Come to savage me again? Want my body?' She stretches her arms out into the shape of a crucifix. 'Well take it. I'm all yours, babe.'

I plop on the bed next to her and begin patching her up. 'I'm really sorry if I hurt you. I mean emotionally as well as . . .'

'What do you care, anyway?'

'Aren't I allowed to even like you now? Can't you handle it? She starts to cry softly.

'I'm taking you to hospital.'

'Piss off and leave me alone. The cuts – they're not deep.'

'Do you want to get sectioned, or what? Is that what you want?'

'They won't do that.'

'They will if it's for your own good. I know a doctor who will section you this minute.'

'You need two doctors for that.'

'Fine. I'll ask her to bring along a colleague.'

'And a social worker.'

'Know it all, don't you? I'm just going to borrow your phone. Let me give her a quick buzz.'

'No, please,' she grapples with my hands. 'I'll do whatever you want, but no doctors, no hospitals. I can't hack it.'

172

'Then you're coming home with me. To my sister's. I've discovered which plant pot she keeps her spare key under.'

'Jes – '

'Not negotiable.'

She puts her bound wrists together like I've handcuffed her and issues me a look that is pure poison.

Back at Lizzy's I usher her inside and snap the mortise on.

'You're not locking me in this place?'

'Relax will you. You're quite safe here. Make yourself at home.'

'Imogen *will* get the note, won't she?'

'Of course she will. Just take it easy. You're in shock. I'll make us a brew.'

She sits in silence, working through stuff in her head and chewing on her nails relentlessly, until I sit down opposite her. I take her hand away from her mouth.

'OK, ground rules. We need to be able to trust one another, so if you have any inclination to hurt yourself again, we need to talk it through. I can't watch you every second of the day, but you let me down, just once and there'll be hell to pay.'

'You don't understand what it's like.'

'Listen matey, I've been left rotting in a place where there were more deaths than a turkey farm at Thanksgiving. We used to affectionately refer to it as the "*Hotel California*," cos you could check out any time you liked, but you could never leave. And boy did they check out. Pretty women . . . cutting themselves . . . stringing themselves up . . . burning themselves to death. Unless you've been in that hellhole, darlin', you wouldn't begin to comprehend the level of desperation, so don't you dare tell me I don't fucking know what it's like to hurt myself.'

Her eyes widen. 'You did it too?'

'When someone I was incredibly attached to left the prison. When they told me the job in the library had gone to Kathy Unwin, who was as thick as two short planks and then some. When my best friend, Tess, died of an overdose because she was kept in solitary too long and no-one realized she'd stashed away enough amphetamines to start her own pharmaceutical company. When I found out she was dead, I was too bloody numb with grief to feel anything much, so do you know what I did?' No reaction. I get up and shake her by the shoulders. 'Do . . . you . . . know . . . what . . I . . . did?'

She shrugs.

'I punctured my arms with a bulldog clip and poured bleach over them. It worked a treat. I could actually feel my skin burning – fizzing – like I'd dipped them in a vat of acid.'

'Stop it, stop it,' she says, clamping her hands over her ears.

The front door rattles. Lizzy's voice: 'Who's in there?'

'Let me do the talking, OK? Go upstairs and unpack your stuff. It's the second room on the right.'

'My God,' Lizzy says, as I open the door to her, 'I thought we had burglars. Whatever did you stick the lock on for?'

'To stop the burglars.'

'How did you get in?'

I flash the key.

'You're impossible.'

'But you love me.'

'Have you got someone here? Only there's a rather pungent smell.'

'Yeah, cheers. I'm fond of bringing the neighbourhood hobos home as you well know.'

She goes straight through to the kitchen and takes out a can of air-freshener. She points the nozzle above my head and sprays liberally. Why is it air-freshener always smells so repulsive?

'I thought I heard something upstairs,' Lizzy says, between bursts.

'That'll be my mate, Mack. I've invited her to stay for a couple of days.' I grab the can off her. 'For God's sake, Lizzy, give it a break. Any more and you'll single-handedly have demolished what's left of the ozone layer.'

'What you just said . . .'

'The ozone layer. What people don't realize – '

'Sod the bloody ozone layer, we don't have any room for "mates," Jes, let alone people you pick up off the street. Don't bother trying to talk me round.'

'Mack's a natural in the kitchen. Be perfect for the bistro. You'll wonder how you ever got by without her.'

'I don't care if she's Marco Pierre White's sister . . .'

'Niece, actually.'

'In that case, I'm sure she's got better places to stay. Honestly, what is wrong with you? You always have to take things one step too far.'

'Please. I'll do extra shifts for you when you're short-staffed and I won't expect a word of thanks.'

'One night Jes,' She says, her hands flailing helplessly in the air.

'Come up and meet her. You'll like her. She's just unpack – I mean, sorting out her stuff .'

Lizzy narrows her eyes at me the way she did when we were kids and I'd done something very wicked with one of her dollies – my favourite torment was drawing Nazi moustaches on them.

After I make the formal introductions, Lizzy seizes my arm. 'Jes – a word.'

She hauls me into the bathroom. 'This isn't fair. You didn't tell me about the bandages.'

'What's up? You scared she's going to bloody your very expensive duvet?'

'That sort of thing frightens me Jes, I don't understand it.'

'Well I do. I'll take care of it.'

'And another thing, if you're intent on sleeping in the same bed as that girl, then I'll have to insist on no hanky-panky. Remember, we're only the other side of a very thin wall. Whatever will mother say?'

'Yeah right, Octavia Vickers – the mother of all morality. What about when she had that fling with that bloody thirty-year-old set electrician? That was only a couple of years back.'

'Best Boy.'

'I'm sure he was. Best she could bed anyhow.'

'Malicious paper talk,' Lizzy says defensively. 'You shouldn't believe all you read.'

'Yeah well, when you're banged up you can't exactly get away from it. Let's face it, she could have bloody sued the rags if there wasn't a grain of truth in it. Look, don't stress yourself, Sis. Unlike some people I could mention, I don't particularly enjoy engaging in noisy sexual activity when there are sensitive ears in the next room.'

175

She opens the linen cupboard. 'Put these on the bed. They're old.'

'Listen, I can sleep on the sofa if you prefer.'

'You will not. Don't you dare leave that girl to her own devices. The last thing I need is to wake up and find a corpse next door.'

Sometimes you can't bloody win whatever you do.

'Sorry,' Mack says. 'It sounded a bit heated just now.'

'That's not heated, darlin'. Not for this family. That was only my hormonally-imbalanced sister telling me her version of the facts of life. Pretty bloody inaccurate – a five-year-old could have done better. How are you feeling?'

'A bit tired. A bit edgy.'

'We are cool though . . . me and you?'

'Yeah, I suppose.'

'Ever thought of talking this stuff over? Someone professional, I mean . . . like

a psychiatrist. It's just that I know somebody who could help you. I'm seeing her myself at the moment.'

'Straight up? What do you need counselling for?'

'Because I'm not the together broad I make out I am. It's all an act. I've got issues . . .'

'You're not still hurting yourself?'

'No. It's not that.'

'Detest therapy,' she says. 'I tried it once. It fucks you up. They stuck me in

this room with this posh bird in a posh suit and she comes across like, why are you cutting yourself you stupid little girl. So bloody patronizing. I went away and carved noughts and crosses into my thighs with a penknife just to spite her. Then she got me sectioned – just to spite me. She had the last laugh. I'm never going back there again.'

'My therapist isn't at all judgemental like that. She's sweet. Kind. And not at all up herself. You'd like her.'

'Not as much as you obviously. You had a twinkle in your eye when you said that. Nice looking is she?'

'Get off.'

'Are you getting it on with her?'

'We did one time. Not anymore.'

'You're too much,' she says, shaking her head, disapprovingly.

'That's enough about me,' I say breezily. 'The offer of help's there if you change your mind. I'll leave you to get some rest, Mack. I'll just be downstairs.'

'Lay with me for a while,' she says, reaching out her hand. 'I don't mean like . . . we can keep our clothes on. Just hold me.'

'OK.' I roll onto the bed and meet her in the middle, with both of us lying on our sides facing one another. I put my arm around her and she snuggles her face against my breasts. The ultimate comfort zone. What would Pashindra do in a situation like this? She'd empathize. She'd be tender. Compassionate. Like always.

If I try and touch Mack now, will it come across like a mixed message? Especially now I've told her about Pash. Is it possible to touch someone you've been intimate with, without it seeming like the intention is sexual?

Without knowing the right answers, I find myself stroking her back through her vest. Slow, rhythmic, sleep-inducing circles with the tips of my fingers. After a few minutes her body relaxes. I'm on the verge of dozing off myself, when Lizzy barges in. I put my finger to my lips. She raises her eyebrows at me, the mare. How dare she. That sister of mine has got sex on the brain. She puts a bowl of something on the dresser.

'Not hungry,' I whisper.

'Potpourri,' she says and bristles out again.

When I stir, Mack is sitting on the edge of the bed listening to my ipod. She pulls the plugs out of her ears. 'Like your music.'

'Most of it is from before you were born.'

'Missed out then,' she says.

'Lizzy had it made up for me. She didn't come and visit me in jail, but at least it shows she was thinking of me. It's better in a way than turning up every fortnight, sitting there in that hideous netball vest and pretending you've got nothing better to do with your time.'

She flips the cover on her mobile. 'I've got thirteen missed calls. All from Immo.'

'Did she leave a message?'

'Yeah. "Call me," thirteen times.'

'If you want some privacy I'll leave you to it.'

'No.' She grips my hand. 'It can wait. I've got you now.'

'Let's go downstairs. Get a beer. You don't have to be nervous of Lizzy. She's a pussycat wearing a striped jersey.'

Cameron and Lizzy are sitting at the kitchen table drinking wine.

'Och, you didn't tell me the kiddies were in,' he says, getting up and extending a hand.

'This is Mack.'

'Fine Scottish name. I'm Cameron. Delighted to make your acquaintance.'

'I've seen you on telly,' she says. 'Well . . . trailers . . . and magazines.'

'Fantastic,' he says. 'We've just opened a bottle of rosé. Care to join us?'

'Thanks,' she says.

He gets up and fetches two more glasses. 'Or would you prefer a whisky, Mack?'

We groan in unison. I pull up a chair for Mack and one for me next to her.

'So . . .' Cameron says, 'tell us your life history.'

Lizzy digs him with her elbow.

'I don't like talking about myself,' Mack says. 'I'm quite shy actually.'

Under the table, I take hold of her hand.

'Shyness can be an attractive trait,' he says, giving me a knowing glance. 'A very attractive trait.'

I could biff him one sometimes. I feel her fingers tighten against mine.

'Would you mind if I take this upstairs?' Mack says. 'I've got a call to make.'

'Be my guest, darlin',' Cameron says.

I release her hand and she gives me an apprehensive look, before disappearing upstairs with her wine glass.

'Did you have to do that?'

'What?' Cameron says. 'What did I do this time?'

'You zoomed in on her. You made her feel uncomfortable. She's a nervous wreck as it is.'

'My we are touchy today. Not intentional I can assure you. So what's with the bandages? Latest must-have fashion accessories, are they?'

'Don't be an arsehole all your life.'

'Will you two kindly pack it in.' Lizzy says.

When I get to the bedroom, she's bagging up her stuff .

'Ignore him downstairs. He's a tosser. I should have warned you. He doesn't know how to act around attractive young women.'

178

'It's not him – I have to go, Jes. Imogen says if I don't get back there in half an hour we're finished.'

I take hold of her shoulders. 'Sit.'

'I don't have time. Please . . .'

'I'm not letting you go anywhere while you're in this state.'

'You don't understand.'

'This hold she has over you. What's it all about?'

'She's always done everything for me. I was homeless. Jobless. Imogen was the one that pulled me out of the gutter and got me on my feet.'

'She made you dependent on her.'

'I fell in love with her,' she says, like she truly believes it.

'Tell me three things you love about her and I'll let you go.'

'She's strong . . . she's fearless . . . and she knows what she wants . . . most of the time.' She zips up the bag.

'And what does she do for you?'

'She takes care of me.'

'Does she make you feel good about yourself, Mack?'

'Why should I? She's better than me. That's not her fault.'

'Usually, when we love somebody we build them up, not kick them when they're down. If someone knocks them, we defend them to the death. It's called a protective instinct. Does she do that with you?'

'I have to go.'

'Out of love, or loyalty, or fear – which is it?'

She sinks on the bed and starts to cry.

'Are you frightened of her because she wants to control you? Wants to keep you in that miserable state of trying to please her all the time. That's not love. That's nothing like real love.' I resist the impulse to put my arms around her again. 'I can't stop you going back to her. Just know I care about you, Mack, and I'm scared for you. That's it. End of story.'

At the door, she turns and smiles at me. 'If you ever fancy getting it on, drop by anytime. No strings.'

30

After she leaves I go downstairs to the kitchen and find a note stuck to the fridge from Lizzy saying they've gone to the cinema. Fucking fantastic timing. If only they'd decided to piss off half an hour ago, I know I could have persuaded Mack to stay. Enjoy your fucking popcorn, cretins. I fling open the door and take out the nearest bottle of white wine. Fifteen minutes later and it doesn't even touch the sides. And it's not even a wine I go for.

Why am I doing this? Putting myself out for some damaged girl I've only known five minutes? Could it be because she reminds of someone? Me? No, I was always far too arrogant for my own good at that age. Lizzy? Ever since puberty, our Lizzy always had some unsuitable beau in tow. Larry was her first boyfriend. He was from a family of bankers – take that how you will – that lived in the next road to us. How can you get excited over a guy with a pathetically uninspiring name like Lar-ry?

Then it was layabout Jay, who spent so much time on his arse, I remember being surprised to find he did in fact have legs. The one time I ever saw him use them was to turn the TV over to the FA Cup Final, because someone had hidden the remote. Wonder who that could have been? Tee-hee.

Then came stockbroker Eamonn – who – on paper was the best prospect of the lot. Not exactly much to beat. He promised my sis a yacht and a home on each of the continents. Last heard of living as a bearded recluse in the Outer Hebrides.

Then there was a break of about a year, when Lizzy went though her disillusioned phase of trying out the reject shelf for size, because she thought she was in danger of being cast there permanently.

By the time the charming, but seriously flawed, Ewan Stafford, appeared on the scene, Lizzy was desperate to settle down. He wowed her with tales of his army heroics, even though for the majority of his service, he'd only been a bloody chef in the Territorials. Ewan swept her off her feet when she was at her most defenceless – easy as an aardvark sucking up a colony of ants.

No, the reason I feel so desperately responsible for Mack is not because she reminds me of anybody else, but because I'm on one huge guilt trip here. I owe her.

I open another bottle of wine and in my suitably anaesthetized state, impetuously call Pash's mobile. I hold my breath as it trills several times. I don't have a clue what I'm going to say to her.

'Hello . . . Doctor Khan's phone.'

Bloody Melissa Parris. That confident tone bordering on arrogance that gets right up my hooter. Miss *"Straighter Than A Laser Beam,"* right Pash?

'Can I help you?' Mel says. I can hear giggling in the background. It sounds like they're in a pub. 'Hello,' she says again.

I'm trying to make up my mind what to say when the line goes dead. Trust her to get in first and cut me off. I'm about to press redial when the doorbell goes. It's Mack – she's seen sense and come back. Thank God. I grab a bottle of Lizzy's best champagne from the fridge and scuttle to get her.

'Octavia.'

'Jesamine.' Her eyes fall on the bottle. 'Making ourselves at home, I see. Are you going to invite me in?'

'Lizzy and Cameron have gone out.'

'I know. I asked them to make themselves scarce. It's you I've come to see.'

She swans past me and into the hall.

'Were you about to open that?'

'Not now I've clocked the bloody price.'

'Well how about if I replace it? You do the honours.'

I shrug. 'If you insist. What are we celebrating?'

'Your home-coming. Isn't that sufficient? Now remember, twist the bottle darling, not the cork.' If she calls me "darling" just once more this evening, I swear I'll swing for her.

'You packed Lizzy off to the pictures?'

'You and me – we've never spent time on our own. Not even when you were little.'

181

'Oh I don't know. Visiting times we were on our own . . . as I recall we struggled to find something to talk about most of the time. It was the slowest hour of my week certainly . . . how was it for you?'

She dabs her brow. 'Those places, Jes – not for the faint-hearted. I didn't like the look of some of those women you were in with. On the whole they seemed quite an ugly bunch of delinquents.'

'And to think, they spoke so highly of you.'

'I was rather hoping we might be able start acting like grown-ups now. Stop all this futile sniping at one another. Hasn't our family been through enough these past few years? And now, what with your father . . .'

'Sorry Octavia, but I refuse to believe this is social call. Call me cynical.'

'You've always been cynical. It's part of your make-up. I hardly expected prison to change that. OK, cards on the table time, seeing as you appear so impatient. I've decided to move in with Leo. It makes sense to downsize. Sell off the house and put the money to better use.'

'Don't tell me you need the cash.'

'The term is, I believe, asset rich, penny poor.'

'Penny-pinching, more like.'

'Besides there are rather too many ghosts.'

'What does Dad think? You have asked?'

'Your father gave me power of attorney a year ago.'

'So he doesn't know?'

'His consultant at the hospital says it's important he doesn't get stressed or confused. He's better off in his own compact little world.'

'But the money will go to help Dad?'

'Partially.'

'What the hell does that mean?'

'Of course some of it will enable us to see out the remainder of Eric's life in comfort. Your father will continue to have everything he needs, I can assure you.'

'Everything, but not everyone . . . like a loyal wife by his side for instance. So what else do you want money for?'

'There are a number of investment opportunities I am considering . . . on Leo's advice.'

'It's *your* house, Octavia. You don't need my permission. I take it Lizzy knows?'

'I aired it to her on the telephone the other day.'

'I wouldn't have expected to be told before Saint Lizzy. I've always known I'm last in the pecking order. I'm not under any illusions.'

'Drink your champagne,' she says. 'You never know, it might placate you a little. So how have you been?'

'Terrific. Yeah, firing on all cylinders.'

'Still in therapy?'

'That was just a rumour.'

'Don't isolate yourself. I'm always here if you need to talk.'

'It takes more than a pair of ears, Octavia. When I was at Whytemoor, I got trained up as a Samaritan. The things I heard would make your flesh creep. Women who'd had things done to them . . . women who'd done to somebody else. What was it they used to say on Crimewatch? "Don't have nightmares." After listening to some of those terrifying recitals you were fucking begging the screws to leave the lights on.'

'Why didn't you tell me any of this when I came to see you?'

'What's the point? I've never exactly been one to spill my guts in public.'

'You're still my baby, Jes. You will always be that to me, however much you choose to deny it.'

'You have never once been there for me. Never.'

'You're wrong,' she says, 'I've always been there for you, but for some reason . . . be it independence . . . pride . . . whatever . . . you've never been able to acknowledge the fact.'

I get up.

'There's plenty more fizz in the bottle,' Octavia says.

'Fine. You have it. I'm getting a beer.'

'You'll give yourself heartburn.'

'Like you give a fuck.' I open the fridge door and grab the nearest brown bottle. As I pull the top off carelessly, the beer rises in the neck and froths over. I quell it with my mouth and Mother gives me the filthiest glare.

'Don't you want a glass with that?'

'There were times I thought I'd die in that shit-hole, Octavia. I'd be lying on my tummy on the top bunk, staring out through the small barred window and not being able to recall how it felt to be free. Even the simplest of life's pleasures . . . shopping . . . strolling by the river . . .

183

taking the bus into town to meet a friend . . . all the everyday things you and Lizzy and the rest of the liberated world take for granted when you have choices . . .

'Prison is a claustrophobic cauldron. You do whatever you can to get by. You lose your senses. Your values. You give in to instincts that would, in any other situation, crucify you. You give your body to people you wouldn't offer a light to in the street, in return for a phonecard or a deodorant. Hard to hear, that, isn't it, Octavia?'

'If you need psychiatric help, Jes, I'll foot the bill. I know a splendid man in Tewkesbury. He'll sort your head out.'

'Yeah, fine. Book me in for a frontal lobotomy a week next Tuesday. You can fund it out of the profits from the sale of the house.'

She sighs heavily. 'I was rather hoping we might have a civil conversation, but the prospect seems beyond you. Seeing as we've hit rock bottom, I may as well plough on. There's no easy way of saying this, but I promised myself I would, so here goes. Leo and I have set a date for the wedding. It's going to be in December. On my birthday.'

'Well you'll have to excuse me if I don't rush to offer the happy couple my congratulations. Dad's dying. Can't you hang on a bit?'

'His brain is dying. Physically he's not in bad shape. We could plod on like this for the next fifteen years. I shall very soon be sixty. . . .that's not old, I know. Not today. Sixty is the new forty and all that.'

'Plod on? You callous cow. You make him sound like some donkey that's outlived its usefulness. You're intent on marry Leo, while Dad's in this state. Think that's OK, do you? You think it's ethical?'

'If it's a question of ethics, Jesamine, I'm not sure you're qualified to judge me so readily. Unless you've suddenly discovered religion in prison. Found Jesus in your cornflakes, have you?'

*

'She always has to get one over on me, Enid. Always has to have the last word, no matter what the subject. I even tried to talk to her about Lola last night, but the wily old bitch wasn't leaking anything. She blanks me every time – when it suits.'

'Perhaps she doesn't know where your little girl is,' Enid says gently.

184

'Of course she knows. She knows everything. Mother is the puppeteer in this production. She'd want Lola to be somewhere she could keep an eye on her, particularly as the last thing they expected was for me to head back this way. That's why I call her the Grande Old Dame. G-O-D. That's the perfect acronym for her, cos that's who she thinks she is. '

Enid looks away from me.

'Sorry, was that offensive to you?'

'A little.'

'Sorry,' I offer again. 'Anyway, when I said to Mother that I considered sixteen hours in labour entitled me to some bragging rights, the mealy-mouthed old sow chirps up, "Paula Radcliffe was in labour for twenty-seven hours, you know."

'I was quick to point out that Paula Radcliffe regularly runs twenty-six-point-two miles in a little over two hours, without hardly breaking sweat. Then again, Paula sodding Radcliffe, thinks nothing of squatting in a tub of freezing cold water with only a mug of cocoa for company . . . we can therefore reliably conclude that her pain threshold is a damn sight higher than mine.

'And to cap it all, Paula fucking Radcliffe wasn't shackled to a bloody sadist screw when she dropped her sprog, was she? Get that, Mother. Wish I thought of that at the time. I ain't making out to be no fucking iron-woman, babe, I just want my daughter back. Sorry, Enid, for the swearing. And I didn't mean to call you, "babe," OK.'

'And you think that's right, do you, Jesamine? Taking a child away from a happy, loving home? People she's been with since she left you, perhaps?'

'Not if she's happy. Of course I wouldn't want that. I only want for my baby to be happy.'

'I don't know an awful lot about family law, but frankly speaking, I wouldn't imagine you'd get custody . . . happy or not.'

'OK. Fair enough. Thanks for cheering me up then. Mother hasn't been working on you as well, has she? Sticking matches down your fingernails.'

She laughs. 'I tell it like it is. Some people don't like it that way, but it's how I've always been. Maybe I can do something to help you though. I have a huge network of associates, particularly in this neck of the woods.'

'What are you, Interpol?'

She taps her nose. 'If your instincts are right and your mother is the control freak you insist she is, then it could work in our favour. And what with my contacts . . . I'd say we have a better than eighty per cent chance of locating your daughter.'

'Enid Bean, I could snog the face off you. Sorry.'

31

As Dora ushers me into the consulting room I feel an overwhelming sense of anticipation. Pash is standing by the window, staring into space. She turns and smiles at me. That strong, reassuring jaw-line.

'There's no-one else in this afternoon,' she says, 'so you can take as much time as you need.'

'I'll bet you say that to all the girls.' I decide against mentioning my impulsive phone call to her last night. The last thing I want to do now is to get into a confrontation with her. 'Do I get to lie on your couch, at long last?'

'Be my guest.'

I kick off my shoes and stretch out on the object of my fantasies. 'Should we put on some music? Get ourselves in the mood.'

Disappointingly, she settles herself in the chair opposite me. That's not nearly close enough for what I've got in mind.

'Make yourself comfortable, Jes,' she says quietly. 'As soon as you feel OK, you can close your eyes.'

'Ready when you are, Doc.' I feel like I'm about to get a fit of the giggles. I bite into my lip.

Pash says, 'Following a brief introduction, I will ask you, in your mind, to start counting backwards from two hundred.'

'Then I come and find you, right?'

'I intend taking this seriously. If you don't want to go through with it we can always scrap it.'

'I do, I do. You know what I'm like. It's just the nerves kicking in. What if I can't perform?'

'You will. It's a lot like sex – better if you don't try too hard. So relax. Not another word, OK?'

I mouth, 'O-K.'

'I am going to start off by making some suggestions that will aid the relaxation process. And you are not going to speak at all, from now until

I give you permission . . . because if you utter one single word, I will gag you.

'So, now, Jesamine, I want you to rest your hands lightly on your abdomen . . . so that you can feel the gentle rise and fall as you breathe in and out. Concentrate on your breathing . . . and allow yourself to relax deeply. Extend each out breath fully, and as you do so, let your shoulders soften a little more, until they feel perfectly loose. With every breath you are finding your body relaxes a little more . . . and more still, until all the tension in your muscles is released.

'As you focus your attention on your breathing, your only other awareness is the sound of my voice. Listen to my words, Jes . . . and let your mind ease off thinking and slow right down. You are feeling deeply calm now . . . content with just being in this moment.

'If, at any time during this process, you begin to feel uncomfortable . . . you will be able to return easily to this mindset and find a plateau of calmness and serenity. I want you to begin counting down now . . . from two-hundred.'

Two hundred . . . one-nine-nine . . . one-nine-eight . . .an image pops into my head from the other night: Pash with her head dipped between my legs . . . I censor it . . . focusing on my breathing like she told me. . . allowing that exquisite voice to take me over. One-nine-seven . . . one-nine-six . . . one-nine-five . . . one-nine-four . . .

I stretch my arms out, then my legs. I've got pins and needles in one foot. It feels as if I've been asleep for a hundred years, like Sleeping Beauty, when the reality is, I haven't slept at all.

'I feel shagged,' I say, yawning. 'Did you drug me?'

'Lie back,' she says. Don't be in a rush to get up. Most people feel groggy afterwards. I'll fetch you some water.'

'How long have I been under the influence?'

'Forty minutes.'

'I was spouting crap, wasn't I?'

'No, you made a promising start. Don't expect too much. Generally it takes a bit of time to make progress.'

I sit upright. 'And I'm wasting yours. You don't have to be so nice about it. Why can't I remember anything past toying with the knife? It's so fucking frustrating.'

'I don't know,' she says, taking her mobile phone out of her bag and passing it to me. 'But I *do* have a suggestion.'

When I introduce Lizzy to Pash, I'm even prouder than when Octavia and Dad first got to meet Miss Richards at Parents' Evening when I was seven. I try my best to hide my amazement that my sister actually showed up. Probably more out of curiosity than genuinely wanting to help. There I go again . . . Miss Cynical. Mother's right about that.

'Thanks for coming, Lizzy,' Pash says. 'I appreciate you taking time out of your busy schedule to help us with this. Particularly at short notice.'

'I don't see what help I can be,' Lizzy says, apologetically. 'It all happened such a long time ago now.' She looks at me guardedly. 'I think we'd all rather forget.'

Undeterred, Pash continues, 'I've had a session with Jesamine under hypnosis – and while she can recall certain details about the afternoon of your husband's death, we are a little sketchy in places and we're wondering whether you might be able to fill in some of the gaps.'

'You don't want to put me in a trance or anything?' Lizzy says, nervously, fiddling with her wedding band.

'That won't be necessary. If you can just relay what you remember from the moment Jes turned up at your house.'

'I let you in. You seemed a bit the worse for wear. You tripped up, remember?'

'Mmmm. I've still got the bruises.'

Pash gives a look as if to say shut up.

'You'd been shopping with Lisa. Ewan was in the kitchen, preparing dinner. We went through to the drawing room. I fetched you a glass of . . . Bordeaux I think. Well it was red anyway.'

'Shiraz.'

'You may be right. You seemed quite strange, Jes, as if you were locked in your own little world. We chatted for about ten minutes, mainly to do with the plans for New Year. Then you excused yourself. I

189

assumed you were going to the bathroom. The doorbell went and it was Mother. She said Dad had stopped off at cricket club for a drink and would be along in an hour or so. When I went to the kitchen to tell Ewan, Mother had arrived, the pair of you were locked in combat. Verbally I mean. Low-flying insults all over the place. You had a knife in your hand, waving it around like a baton, jabbing it in Ewan's direction.'

'We were messing about.'

'It got quite fiery. Mother tried to calm things down, Ewan went back to his cooking and we thought that was the end of it. The next thing we know, you're standing in the doorway of the living room with the knife in your hand. Dripping blood.' She cradles her face in her hands, like she might cry.

Pash fetches her a glass of water.

'But I was unconscious, Lizzy.'

'You passed out. You dropped the knife and your knees buckled and you kind of folded . . . I don't know what else to say. 'We picked you up and laid you on the settee.'

'Why did you move me? Why go to the bother of picking me up off the floor?'

'We were concerned for you. Mummy and me.'

'Mummy as well – that's a first. Didn't you think that by moving me you might be interfering with a crime scene?'

'You don't think when you're in shock . . . you just react.' She looks at Pash. 'Is that OK?'

'Thank you, Lizzy,' Pash says. 'That was brave of you.'

'Happy to do what I can,' she says, sipping at the water.

'Except,' I say, 'I know it didn't happen like that.'

'Well that's how I remember it, but like I said, I'd prefer not to dwell on it.'

'Fuck it, Lizzy.'

'So give us your version, Jes.' She puts the glass on the table and folds her arms defiantly. 'In your own time.'

'I can't. Because I can't damn well remember. You know I can't.'

'Well if you do remember anything concrete, call me in again,' she says, donning her gloves. 'I've got things to do now. I'm meant to be meeting a cutlery rep in half an hour.' She leans across and offers Pash her hand.

'It was really nice meeting you. And to put a name to the face. Sorry I couldn't be any more help.'

'You did well,' Pash says, rising out of her chair. 'We do appreciate it.'

The door clicks shut.

'Thought that went well, Doc.'

She looks at me and shakes her head. 'Have you never heard of the expression, "*playing it cool*"?'

'You expect me to sit there biting my tongue while my sister spews out a load of bollocks.'

'How do we know that, if you can't remember?'

'Instinct.'

'Not good enough. If I were you, I'd employ your instinct in choosing a nice, big, expensive bouquet of flowers and then go on a grovelling mission. Kiss her feet if you have to. You're not going to get anywhere by alienating people – especially the likes of Lizzy. She's done a lot for you these past weeks, if only you'd realize.'

'But Pash . . .'

She waves me away. 'Get out of my sight. Scram.'

'Can I see you later? For a drink. Or do you and Melissa have something planned this evening?'

'I'll see you the same time tomorrow and we'll have another shot at it. It's important to gain some momentum now we've started.'

'So you are busy later?'

'Yes – I'm busy.'

I hold the bouquet in front of my face and edge towards her. She looks up from her books.

'Is that meant to hide the shame?'

'You do still like Gerbera, don't you?'

'More than I like you. Calling me a liar in public like that. I was doing my best to help you and this is all the thanks I get.' She picks up a red pen.

'Pash told me not to be so ungrateful – in so many words.'

'And I suppose the flowers were her idea?'

'OK, let her have all the credit. I don't see why I deserve any.'

'At least you take notice of that woman. She's good for you, Jes. She seems nice. And so pretty. It's what you need, someone to keep you on the straight and narrow.'

'Could we not use the S-word? It's not appropriate for this situation. Uh, did I catch a glimmer of a smile there?'

'A faint one. Just cos I can't help laughing at your pathetic jokes doesn't mean you're off the hook. I'm still mad as hell at you. I need to get this figure work done, it's giving me a bloody migraine.' She lets out a heavy sigh. 'If you really insist on making yourself useful you can put those beautiful flowers in water – there's a vase in the cupboard above the new freezer – and fetch me a cup of ginger tea while you're at it. With a good hefty dose of honey in it.'

'Ugh, if you say so, boss. Coming right up boss.'

Her head slumps over her paperwork.

'Lizzy.'

'What is it now?'

'Love you.'

'Don't, Jes. I think on balance, I prefer it when you're being horrible.'

'I'll make the tea then.'

*

I've got an appointment with a man called Jenkins at the council.

I used to have a teacher called Mr Jenkins – used to teach RE when I was twelve. Miserable old sod. I detested him because he used to give the whole class detention if one person played up. Hardly fair, is it? He used to whistle through his teeth when he talked. And he had this infuriating habit of snapping his chalk in half and scraping his nails across the blackboard in a way that sent a chill down your spine. Probably one of the reasons I've never been fanatical about religion.

I go across to the 'Welcome' desk and someone yells at me because I've just barged in front of a line of people. I shout back that the twat should keep his hair on – words to that effect. He would turn out to be entirely hairless, wouldn't he? Mother would adore him.

My faux pas somehow gets me fast-tracked to the front of the queue, probably because security sensed a storm brewing. I can't believe they employ 'uniforms' in council offices these days. Have things really gotten that bad?

Rodney Jenkins turns out to be someone quite important – the Deputy Head of Housing and Social Services, no less.

'How can I help?' he says, settling himself opposite me, without any formal introduction.

'Eight years ago, I gave birth to a baby daughter – in Holloway prison. *They* put her up for adoption.' I'm careful not to say 'I,' like it had anything to do with me. 'I've just got out and I'd like to find her.'

'There are agencies that may be able to help with that sort of thing. There's one in Bristol, hang on, I've got a card somewhere. We're extremely limited on the resources we can provide to someone in your situation unfortunately. Do you have any identification with you?'

I show him the dog-eared driving licence.

'Presumably you need ID for breathing now?'

'We have to be cautious, Miss Vickers. Identity theft is a major problem nowadays.'

'Well, if anyone desperately wants to be me, they're more than welcome to give it a whirl. They'd need their head examined though. And my name's Vale. I mean, it used to be Vickers – that's the family name.'

'Then you'll need to inform the DVLA. They'll issue you a new licence. Looks like you could do with one.'

Ha, ha. 'I was going to.'

'Naturally, if your daughter should wish to contact you later on . . . when she's older . . . the law gives her the right to obtain the details of her birth parents . . .'

'What, in ten years time? Do me favour. She's got a right to know I'm her mother. Whoever she's with is probably making out I don't exist.'

'You put your daughter up for adoption, Miss Vale.'

'Not willingly. Not because I didn't want her. Because I wasn't allowed to have her with me and I had no-one to look after her.'

'I see . . .'

'Do you? The meagre wage I got for working in the laundry didn't extend to paying for a child minder.'

'Why not speak to the agency. It can't hurt . . . and you never know, they may be able to put you in touch with other people that are in the same boat as you. That, in itself, can offer some comfort.'

'Yeah, great, we can all wallow in one another's misery – I don't think so, mate. There must be something else you can do.'

'There really isn't,' he says brusquely.

'Would you accept a bribe? How much?'

'I'm sorry,' he says, getting up quickly and banging his leg on the table. 'Please don't think I'm unsympathetic to your situation, Miss Vale, but you must appreciate my position. I'm afraid our hands are tied. Good day.'

I'm more than a little relieved there isn't a hot cup of coffee in the vicinity.

32

On my way in to the clinic I nip into the newsagents and pick up a paper. That same bloody photo stares out at me, the evilness airbrushed from her vile face, making her appear almost normal. How they can take a mug shot of a paedophile granny and turn it into something resembling a glamour feature for a lads' mag is beyond my comprehension. It's bloody immoral, I know that much.

I toss the paper onto the desk in front of her.

'So where do you think she is?'

Pash shrugs. 'Could be anywhere. My guess is she's hopped it abroad. Somewhere like Thailand.'

'Where whatever kind of sex you're into, it's as easy as popping into your local for a pint. So she's still at it. Sick bitch.'

'I wasn't implying that.'

'These cranky messages I've been getting. What if it's her?'

'Why on earth should it be Eva Rowe?'

'I don't know. You've met her.'

'Five years ago.'

'Didn't it make your skin crawl being in the same room with her? Course it did.'

'Want me to be truthful? No, not really. There are people who have got to me more. You don't seriously think it's Eva Rowe doing this, Jes?'

'Well who else . . .? I'm crapping myself at the thought.'

'Then whatever it is that's going on in your mind, best you get it out in the open.'

'I can't.'

'Because it's obvious to me she's got some kind of hold over you. You were servicing her . . . is that it? She was one of your clientele?'

'What do you think, Pash? I'm sick in the head as well?'

'You brought it up.'

'Well now I wish I hadn't. Are you going to hypnotize me, or what?'

'If you think you're in the right frame of mind.'

'Meaning?'

'You seem angry today. Angrier than normal.'

'Because that woman makes me boiling mad. And you make me fucking madder because you don't react to her like you should. Even though you're not a mum, it's not normal to be this calm. You know what she did to those innocent kids.'

'You mean, I'm not normal? Is that what you're saying? Before I set up here, most of my work was based around one institution or another. Prisons . . . psychiatric units. Tell me this, Jes, in your *expert* opinion, what sort of therapist would I make if I got overly-emotional every time I came face-to-face with a rapist, a wife-beater, or a murderer? The obvious answer is, not a very good one. It wouldn't earn me much kudos amongst my peers. I need to maintain objectivity. And I need to be rational. It's the only way.

'During the course of my work I've met a lot of people who have committed deeply disturbing acts. When you're in their presence it affects you. Even as a trained professional, it can make you intensely uncomfortable. These people have what I call an *aura of evil*. It seeps out of every pore like a bad odour. You can smell it, you can feel it, you can taste it. You come out of the encounter contaminated – like you'd need to scrub every inch of your skin under the shower for a whole week to rid your body of the stench. Eva Rowe didn't have that *aura*. So you're right about one thing – that makes her potentially very dangerous indeed.'

'And if she came to you tomorrow and asked you for help . . .'

'Then I'd see her of course.'

'You can't change what's inside scum like that.'

'I beg to differ. If someone asks for my help – '

'Idealist.'

'Probably.'

'OK, off the record then. Forget being a therapist. You must hate the bones of the vile bitch like every normal human being does. Well? If it's true what they say, that only the good die young, that she-devil will live to be two hundred. They should have executed her.'

'Many people would agree with you. So you believe in the death penalty?'

'For scum like her, yes I bloody do.'

'And some people will undoubtedly say you don't deserve to be walking around free.'

'Well I think that's different altogether. Yes I killed someone. But I'm not some cold, calculating, sadistic bitch like her. I've paid the price. I lost my liberty . . . my daughter . . . my family . . . all the things that mattered to me. My poor dad's turned into an empty shell of a man. Now I have trouble remembering what he was like before he got ill.'

'So, Eva Rowe – '

'Will you stop repeating that bloody name over and over. You're doing my head in, woman.'

'Because it triggers something in you. I don't mean to gnaw away at you, but perhaps, if you'd just let it out . . .'

'Typical shrink mentality.'

'You know I'm not the enemy.' She gets up, comes and stands directly in front of me, plants her delicate hands on my shoulders and says softly, 'Tell me what happened. I promise you'll feel better.'

'But I've never told anybody.'

'And it's eating you up . . . so try me.'

She makes us tea and sits with me on the sofa, holding my hand.

'Take your time.'

'Eighteen months ago. Must be, although I remember it like it was yesterday. I'd been having a series of run-ins with a woman called Angie Stone – AKA Hatchet-face. God, she was an ugly cow. The sort of woman you wouldn't want to bump into in the daytime, let alone a dark alley.'

Pash says, 'I remember the case. It was all over the news. She hired a hit man to bump off her husband . . . only the guy she hired turned out to be an undercover detective.'

'Ace memory, Doc. Plan was that Stone and her girlfriend, Maudy, would rake in the insurance and head for the Caribbean. Once they got put away they weren't nearly as close – what with the idyllic dream scuppered – Maudy was keen to break ties. Course the first thing the screws did was bung them in separate cells which was great for Maudy, but it drove Stone nuts. Maudy, being half Stone's age and stunningly attractive, decided she'd do well to shop around.

197

'She came to see me, when I was doing my Samaritan bit. Well, in this case, I was more like a Relate counsellor. She confided in me about the problems they were having. Said she didn't fancy Stone any more. More or less implied she never had – she was in it for the money. Some of the other girls warned me to keep my distance, but me, being good old me, I thought I could handle it. I didn't do anything with her, Pash, just listened to her tales of woe and sometimes they turned into fantasies about some of the women we were in with, which alternated between being quite amusing and sometimes dark, depending on Maudy's mood.

'Maudy Maughn wasn't a dyke. Come to think of it, Angie Stone had more testosterone in her than most blokes I've met. We're you on the scene when that rumour went round about Eva Rowe getting sent in a gold-plated vibrator?'

'No,' she says, almost laughing.

'Which was just as well, because she was that toxic, no self-respecting woman would have gone near her without the protection of an industrial suit. Evidently the top brass threatened to fit a silencer on the bloody thing after receiving a record number of complaints – she was buzzing away at all hours allegedly. That woman had no bloody consideration. Down at inmate-level, we figured either she'd end up burning it out, or she'd get white finger. Knowing Rowe's reputation, if she'd stayed inside much longer, she'd probably have ended up suing the prison service.'

'Probably.' She squeezes my hand. 'Want to go on?'

'One morning, in the shower block, when I was still half asleep, I got hit on by Stone and two of her henchwomen. It was a Saturday. I remember it like it was yesterday. One was armed with a bottle, one had a home-made blade. They got me down on the floor and were about to rape me, when in she walks – Eva Rowe – wearing nothing but a fake tan and an Armani towel, draped casually over her shoulder. Nothing else, apart from her bling, that is. Never seen without her bling was our Eva. She had this chain arrangement that was so bloody chunky it would have made your average mayor feel under-dressed.

'So Stone's positioned behind my head, with her steel fingers clamped round my neck – I could hardly breathe, let alone scream for help. She says to Rowe: "Come to watch? Or to play?"

'Rowe struts across, stands over me, one leg either side of my ankles, smirking. And it's all I can do to keep my eyes off her pussy. There's this jumble of crazy thoughts buzzing around my head. I'm thinking any second she's going to squat down and take her turn with me.

'The next thing I know, she's peeling off her bling: her ruby earrings, white-gold chain, charm bracelet. She says in this low, husky drawl: "That's enough now, ladies," like she's in some bloody movie. Then she turns and walks away from me.

'Without so much as a glance at Stone, the women jump up and rush to Eva to claim their booty. Eva Rowe did something far worse than gang-raping me, Pash. She saved my skin. And now I owe her.'

Pash shrugs. 'I don't see it like that. Look at it logically. Eva Rowe had eighteen months to get what she wanted from you – and now – unexpectedly, she's been granted her freedom. I hardly think she'd risk losing her liberty to take a pop at you. If you want my opinion, I'd say you're pretty low on her list of priorities. Maybe she got her kicks from rescuing you. Perhaps that was reward enough. People can change, you know.'

'Not her. You don't really believe in that shit?'

'I've seen it happen. If I didn't believe, I wouldn't be in this field. I'd give it all up and become a documentary filmmaker. That's what I wanted to do as a kid.'

'You never said.'

'Yeah, I used to terrorize the life out of my family with my father's camcorder. I used to sneak up on them at the most inopportune moments – like my parents would be in the middle of this blazing row and they'd have this irritating six-year-old kid poking a camera in their faces and asking dumb questions like, "if you're still yelling at one another by tea time, do we still get to eat?"'

'And you're still asking dumb questions.'

'Yeah, yeah.' She smiles. 'So what did you want to be?'

'You mean, when I grow up? I always thought I'd end up doing something glamorous and daring, like be a pilot in the SAS. Or a firefighter. I think I must have always had an unconscious thing for uniforms. Bet you looked a sight for sore eyes in your doctor's coat. You did have one of those white coats . . . as a student?'

'Of course. Think I've got it tucked away in a box somewhere, along with my name badge and my certificates.'

'You should have worn it the other night . . . for my consultation. With sod-all underneath. You'd have driven me crazy.'

'Thought I did.' Her eyes tell me she's flirting with me again. It would be rude not to flirt back.

'Did I give you that impression?'

She smiles knowingly. 'If I were you, I would put Eva Rowe to the very back of your mind, along with all the other negative stuff. Don't waste your energy dwelling on her a second longer.'

'I'll try . . . if that's what you honestly think.'

'I do.'

'Getting back to the other night.'

'What about it?'

'Was it a one-off for you? Because I want it to happen again. And again.'

She lets go of my hand. 'I can't be sexual with you right now, Jes. It wouldn't be right. Not while I'm treating you.'

'I won't tell.'

'Doesn't matter. I couldn't live with myself.'

'Kiss me.'

'Stop it. You're making this worse for both of us.'

'You don't fancy me anymore, do you? Now you know where I've been.'

'I'll see you tomorrow,' she says firmly, ignoring the question. 'We'll try another session under hypnosis.'

'What's the point? It doesn't bloody work. Anyway I only come here to flirt with you.'

*

I pick up my second helping of freshly baked carrot cake and bite into it, peering over Enid's shoulder while she taps away on her ancient computer, writing multiple e-mails to her magnitude of friends and acquaintances all over the world.

I've never known anyone have such a wide network of associates as Enid Bean. I find there's nothing quite like a good old comfort binge when you're feeling unloved. She's great around the home, her baking is legendary and she's an exceptionally good listener. She'd make somebody a great wife that's for sure. When she finishes tapping away I'm going to ask her what's been on my mind. I might even ask her to marry me, if only she was twenty years younger and of my persuasion.

'What?' she says, glancing over her shoulder.

'Enid, I've been wondering. Have you ever been in love?'

'Twice,' she says, without hesitation. 'The last time was fifteen years ago.'

'Ahhh, sweet.'

She swivels her seat round to face me.

'The first chap was married, so naturally nothing came of it. I'm not a marriage-wrecker. We sort of, gazed longingly at one another over the rhubarb patch. I used to have an allotment, you see. Our gardens were side by side. A year or so later, I fell for my bank manager, Richard Reeves. I think I was on the rebound from Ernie.'

'Rhubarb man?'

'That's the one. Richard was newly divorced. I went in to see him about a home improvement loan and he asked me out on a date. Most improper conduct. I told him so.'

'You didn't go? Oh Enid.'

'Of course I went. And he leant me five thousand pounds more than I asked for.'

'You still had to pay it back though.'

Her eyes brighten. 'Yes, but he gave me a fantastic rate of interest.'

'You devil you. Aren't bankers boring though?'

'This one wasn't. Richard was into the arts, theatre . . . museums.'

'That's what I meant.'

'You're a proper little minx.' She moves her chair closer to me. 'Now then, you might as well tell me all about her, before I start on this next batch of mailings.'

'Who?' I say unconvincingly.

'This young woman you've set your cap at.'

'There isn't anyone.' I can feel myself getting hot.

'Up to you entirely,' Enid says, reaching in her pocket for her address list.

I suck in a shallow breath and gabble, 'OK, she's my therapist. The real Doctor Khan. Pashindra Khan. Pash. We've like . . . taken things quite far . . . in the bedroom department.' I can feel myself squirming.

'You mean, you've made love with her.'

'Yeah. Yes we have.' It comes out defiantly, like I'm expecting Enid's condemnation.

She smiles. 'I may be almost thirty years older than you, Jes, but I do understand, really I do. I was young once.'

'The thing is, Pash says we have to cool things – while I'm her patient.'

'That sounds perfectly ethical to me, as well as logical.'

'I'd rather skip the hypnosis bit and go back to being lovers.'

'I *do* think you ought to give the treatment a fair chance.'

'Do you? I'd wait for her, Enid, honest I would, but I think she's giving me the brush off. There's this psychology student – Melissa – she's brash and cocky – I didn't take to her. Pash has moved her into her new place – one of the new townhouses in Charlton Kings – must've cost a bomb. She says it just a temporary arrangement while this Melissa's flat is being done up, but I'm not so sure.' I sigh. 'Anyway, what happened with you and Rich?'

'We broke up. Lasted all of three months.'

'Don't tell me, he couldn't hold your interest.' I laugh. 'Sorry Enid.'

'We rowed a lot. Turns out he was two-timing me, with Chloe from Iceland.'

'That's a long way to go to find a date.'

'The shop, Iceland. She was a part-time shelf-stacker. She was younger and trimmer than me. And far prettier.'

'It's exactly the same with me and that bloody cocky Melissa. She's the image of Katie Melua, and let's face it, who wouldn't want a girlfriend like that on her arm? I wonder if she can sing. Bet she can. She's the sort of girl who reckons herself at everything. Probably serenades Pashindra while she's undressing her.' Automatically, I find my fingers scrunching up. My knuckles protrude like I'm up for a fight.

'Men!' Enid says, raising her eyebrows and shaking her head from side to side. 'There's no satisfying them sometimes.'

I imitate her actions. 'Women!'

33

I can just about make out Lizzy's silhouette as I fall into the restaurant.

'Jes? What on earth? You're drunk.'

'Ditch the accusing tone, Sis, I might have had one or two glasses of Enid's home-made raspberry wine, OK. I'll grab a quick shower.'

'Quick shower, no good,' she says, like she's auditioning to be Tonto in the umpteenth remake of The Lone Ranger. 'I've got no other help this lunchtime – Cameron's out on the town with his film crew cronies – it's just me and you, so if you can't hack it, kid, you'd better go and crash out somewhere.'

She hasn't called me 'kid' in a long time. 'No way. Give us a sec.'

I sprint upstairs and turn the shower onto cold. Full blast, willing my body to burst into life as the azure tiles loom in at me from all directions like I'm on that fairground ride where you stick to the walls and the bottom falls away.

When I can't bear the cold a second longer, I stagger out and wind a towel round my hair. Come on babe, you can do this. I dry myself off in double-quick time and squeeze my bloated body into the little black number and it seems tighter than ever. God only knows how women with periods manage.

As I trot downstairs,. Lizzy is escorting a party of four blokes in suits to the table in the corner. She hands me a pile of menus.

'Good girl. I knew you'd come through.' Now she sounds reassuringly like Dad. 'Don't forget to plug the specials.'

I saunter across, awkward in my body, feeling like my bandy legs don't belong to me and wondering whether, in my floaty state, I look the least bit normal.

'Afternoon, gents, what can I get you?'

'Now that depends,' one of them says, adjusting his tie. Mr Pinstripe.

'Like some drinks?'

'Do you do cocktails?' the bloke with the plummy voice chimes up. Bloody Hooray Henry – that's all I need.

'Sure. What would you like?'

'We were rather hoping you could recommend something,' Hooray Henry says.

'A slow comfortable screw,' his gruff mate says, smirking. Caveman, or what?

'Four of those, is it?'

'Only joking, love. We'll have four lagers to start,' Caveman grunts.

Hooray Henry extracts a pair of round spectacles from a leather case. 'Can we get a gander at the wine list?'

'Certainly, sir.' I run into Lizzy outside the kitchen. 'Who are those obnoxious blokes?'

'Don't know,' she says. 'Never seen them before. But it looks from their clothes like it's money no object, so please feel free to flirt with them. Any of them. All of them. In the line of duty, naturally.'

'Talking of which, I popped in to see Dad earlier. He was in fine form, if you're interested.'

'Of course I'm bloody interested,' Lizzy says. 'It's just that I'm up to my eyeballs in shit. Marketing, accounts, final demands. I don't neglect him on purpose whatever you think. I just don't know what to talk to him about, that's all. We sit there like ships passing in the night, starring idly at one another and not connecting. Maybe, one day, when you feel like taking on more responsibility you can hold the fort here and I'll go and spend some quality time with him.'

'Cameron will do that for you.'

'Leave him to take centre stage while I'm out of earshot – no thanks. Might as well treat him to a season ticket to the local brothel and be done with it.'

'You just told *me* to flirt. It's harmless enough. They can't touch you for it.'

'Cameron doesn't just flirt, as you well know. He gets young women to pull their tops down so he can write something salacious on their breasts. He gets suspenders left with calling cards, as tips. These hussies are devious. They'll stop at nothing to get their legs wrapped around somebody famous.'

'What do you expect, Lizzy? You knew he was an actor before you married him. Never mind animals and children, never get hooked up with bloody actors, I say. You know, while I was banged up, I read Octavia's biography. It was in the prison library. Defaced with expletives – some of which were mine, granted – but still legible nonetheless. The way she bangs on about family life, you'd think we were the bleeding Waltons, instead of the Dysfunctionals. Talk about keeping up appearances.'

From the other side of the restaurant, Mr Pinstripe clicks his fingers at me.

'Any chance of them beers, love?'

'Just coming.'

'Remember to flirt,' Lizzy says. 'It won't make me start to question your sexuality, if that's what's bothering you.'

'Fuck off.'

'About time,' Mr Pinstripe says. 'A fellow could die of thirst.'

'Here's hoping.' I plonk their beers in front of them, not caring that I've spilt some on the table.

'Charming,' Hooray Henry says, when he realizes I've splashed his tie. 'Not exactly what you'd call Silver Service.'

'What are you doing later, darlin'?' Mr Pinstripe says.

'Washing my wig.'

He gives me his card. Royston Bell, Financial Advisor.

'So what do you do, Mr Bell? Swindle old ladies out of their pensions?'

'Funny aren't you?' he says. 'In a caustic sort of way.' I feel the flesh on my bum pinch.

I clench my teeth, willing myself not to react. As I turn to go, he does it again – to the other cheek. So I wallop him across the face.

'I'm glad you're back early,' Enid says. 'I've got something to tell you.'

I flop on the sofa. 'Enid, I'm not really in the mood to be sociable. Lizzy's just given me the bullet.'

'That's good,' Enid says.

'What?'

'Because it means you'll have some spare time on your hands. Sit down.'

'Got any more wine?'

She disappears into the kitchen and returns with a huge jug of liquid and two tumblers.

'Fantastic. Let's get rat-arsed.' I pour us both one. 'Cheers!' I take a big swig. 'Doesn't taste very alcoholic.'

'That's because it isn't. It's elderflower cordial.'

'Ugh, you trying to poison me, or what?'

'I want you sober.'

'Enid Bean, you're not about to proposition me.'

'I've had some feedback . . . one of my contacts in Stow. It's promising news.'

'You've discovered where Lola is?'

'In a village . . . not very far from here, there's a little girl that's rarely glimpsed in public.'

'Some opening line, that, Enid. You ought to take up novel writing. What, she doesn't go out?'

'Hardly ever.'

'She's agoraphobic, or what? What village? Where?'

'Patience, my dear . . . all will be revealed. Apparently, people expressed considerable surprise when the wife first appeared in public with a baby – she hadn't said anything to anyone about being pregnant. Now I must confess I find that most odd.'

'Odd? It's more than ruddy odd. It's downright sinister.'

'They educate her at home evidently. She's very serious. Studious. My friend, Hazel, says she's seen her a couple of times, reading a book in the back garden. Not a kid's book neither.'

'But she must have friends though?'

'I suppose. It can't be healthy to keep a child locked up like that without any company. But then, if you don't go to a conventional school and you don't go out and socialize . . . the opportunities for friendship must be somewhat limited. Hazel tells me they call the girl, Lorna.'

'Lorna? What sort of fucking old-fashioned name is that? It's her. My Lola. Got to be.' I swallow my drink down. 'So come on, Enid, chum, cut to the chase. I'm itching to get over there.'

'We could hang about for hours and you might not catch so much as a glimpse.'

'I don't care. Quit stalling. Get Morris fired up and let's go.'

'I think this kind of thing requires careful planning.'

'Well, I beg to differ. I've always been a 'fly-by-the-seat-of-your-pants,' kind of girl.'

'Why does that not surprise me?'

*

'You didn't say it was a bloody vicarage, Enid.'

'Sorry. Neglected to mention. He's called Reverend Massey. Raymond Massey. His parishioners say he's a good man.'

'They would, wouldn't they? He's probably brainwashed them all, like some bloody sect.' I think of Mr Jenkins – the teacher – not the arse from Social Services. 'Religion has always made me uneasy to the point of queasy. So how do we get to meet Reverend Massey?'

'Sunday Service.'

'It's Tuesday, Enid. You can't expect me to wait that long. Let's go round the back.'

On the far side of the fence, there's a lean woman pegging a sweater on to one of those triangular washing line contraptions.

'Can I help you?' she says, visibly startled.

Enid nudges me forward.

'Mrs Massey?'

'Who's asking?'

'My name's Jesamine Vale. My surname used to be Vickers.'

'Can I help you?' she says again, through a vacant mask.

Enid says, 'Does that name mean anything to you, Mrs Massey?'

'Look, please state your business.'

'You have a daughter . . .' I venture.

'My friend here thinks she might have some connection with your little girl,' Enid says.

The woman's face pales. 'You'd need to speak with my husband. Can you come back another time?'

'Is your daughter here?'

'No.'

I put my foot on a tree stump and straddle the fence. Enid reaches to grab me but I'm already beyond the point of return. The woman reaches for a hanging pendant around her neck.

'This is linked to the police. All I need to do is pull this cord . . . you take one step closer and I'll . . .'

'OK, I'm backing off. I didn't mean to frighten you. I only wanted to talk.'

'You can talk with my husband. I told you.'

'Is he here?'

'He's gone into town.'

'We can wait,' I say a little too keenly.

She says curtly, 'I'm very busy. I don't need people getting under my feet. Come back at four-thirty.'

'OK. Thanks.'

Vaulting the fence the other way isn't nearly so easy. I snag my foot in a thorn and nose-dive onto the ground. Enid picks me up and brushes me down. The woman picks up her washing bowl, still half-full, and scurries inside.

'What d'you reckon?' Enid says.

'Nervous as a calf that's just sniffed the slaughterhouse.'

'We need a chemist,' Enid says, passing me a pristinely-pressed cotton handkerchief. 'Your nose is bleeding. And we need a coffee shop . . . for some refreshment.'

After some effort I persuade her that the Lygon Arms is a better prospect for "refreshment" than the local coffee shop. Enid settles for a sedate port and lemon, while I amble my way through a bottle of Soave. She trawls through the daily newspapers, seemingly reading every page, every sentence, every bloody word, while I randomly scan the pages of some organic magazine. Boring. From time to time she lowers her broadsheet and checks on me.

'Go easy with that,' Enid says, nodding at the rapidly emptying wine bottle. 'You need to keep a clear head.'

'What I need is Dutch courage, woman – and plenty of it – never mind the sodding clarity.'

*

Reverend Massey is waiting for us at the front door. We introduce ourselves and he shakes our hands warmly. I catch sight of my reflection in the hall mirror. My face is still flushed from the wine. The woman with the washing brings us tea and biscuits I recognize from my childhood.

'What else would you expect from a man of the cloth?' I say. 'Abbey Crunch.'

'Very good,' he says.

The woman looks at him in a pleading way, as if she doesn't know whether to hang around or make herself scarce.

'This is my wife, Carolyn,' Massey says.

When I shake her limp hand, it's like an icicle. My girl is here, in this place. I feel her presence around me vividly, as only a mother could.

'So . . .' Reverend Massey says. 'How can I be of assistance?'

Enid nods at me encouragingly.

'Eight . . . almost nine years ago, I gave birth to a child – a baby daughter. Circumstances dictated that I gave her up for adoption. I think she may be here. With you.'

'What makes you think that?'

'Is she . . . here?'

'Really, I'd like to help,' he says.

I say boldly, 'The child – is she yours by natural means?' Thank God for Soave.

'You have a damn cheek coming here like this,' Carolyn blurts out suddenly then leaves the room.

'My wife is upset,' Massey says, as if it weren't obvious.

'She's my baby Lola. Please let me see her.'

'Our child is called Lorna.'

'Look, I don't care what she's called, only that she's well cared for.'

'I can assure you of that, Miss Vale. We have been down all the proper channels. We are her legal guardians.'

'Please – five minutes, that's all.'

'Then we'll leave you in peace,' Enid says.

'I'm afraid she isn't here. She's visiting my brother's family in Anglesey.'

'You've done this deliberately. You knew I was coming. Well I'll be back, you can bloody count on it.'

Enid puts her hand on my arm.

'Do you mind not being quite so rude,' Massey says.

'And next time I'll bring a social worker.'

209

'Carolyn and I have nothing to hide. This is perfectly above board. In fact, I'd prefer it if you did have some official with you. It might make this process easier.'

'Do you perhaps have a photo of Lorna?' Enid says gently.

'Of course we do. We have hundreds. Our child is extremely photogenic.'

'I wonder if we might . . .'

Massey ignores her and turns to me. 'You gave your child up for adoption, Miss Vale, because you were not deemed to be a suitable mother. Don't think I'm judging you – only God can do that.'

'I gave her up, Reverend Massey, because I had no other option. There's not been one single day when I haven't thought about her. Wondered where she was, who she was with, what she looked like, if she was happy. Is she happy?'

'This is a happy home, Miss Vale. Exceedingly so. A disciplined home is always a happy home.'

'I've heard Lorna doesn't go out much.'

'Wherever did you hear such nonsense? Like I said, she's having a break in Anglesey. A well-deserved holiday.'

'For how long?'

'For as long as she wants. As long as she's enjoying herself. Rest assured, if Lorna is your daughter – and I use the phrase guardedly – then she's had the best start in life any young girl could want. You should be proud of that fact.'

'Tell me about her.'

'I've a sermon to prepare. Many demands on my time.'

'Sixty seconds. That's all.'

'Lorna is a kind, conscientious, meditative human being.'

'What about sports? What about larking about? What about danger? I was always kicking a football at her age.'

'And that has no doubt made you the role model you are today.'

Sarky bastard. I chew my lip.

'She plays backgammon and chess to an impressive level,' he says pompously.

'What about the physical stuff? Climbing trees, riding horses . . . getting bumps and bruises. Scraping her knees to buggery. It's what I did at her age.'

210

'And you would consider yourself a suitable role model for an impressionable young girl?'

'Don't you dare patronize me.'

'The world can be a dangerous place, Miss Vale, as I'm sure you – more than most – can appreciate.' He stands up. 'Now if you'll excuse me.'

As we go to leave, Enid puts one of her business cards on the hall table.

Outside, I lean against the wall and take a deep breath. '"The world can be a dangerous place," what the fuck is that meant to mean?'

'You were good,' Enid says. 'you did well. You kept your sangfroid in a tricky situation.'

'My what? So what the hell do we do now?'

'We do something to take our minds off the situation.'

I jump up and down, clapping my hands together. 'Brilliant! Let's go to Anglesey. Do you think your trusty steed, Morris, could get us there in one piece?'

She pats my shoulder. 'Jes, be sensible. I thought we might go the theatre.'

Sitting in Enid's front room with its knick-knacks, relics and general clutteredness reminds me of Pashindra's organised chaos.

'Have you always been restrained, Enid?'

'Only in my choice of men,' she says. 'I wish I'd been more adventurous. I used to dream of the rugged types who would drag me off to some hidden idyll and have their wicked way with me. That only happens in films, doesn't it?'

'Enid!'

'You know, I think Mr Rhubarb might have been the one. I gave up on the idea of romance far too easily. Thought I was destined to be on my own. Always the bridesmaid, that's me. My elder sister, Eunice, she's been wed twice. Can't tell you if she's happy though. She's got a rather plain, expressionless face that belies little.'

'Eunice and Enid . . .'

'Mmmm. Both of us used to detest the names we were born with. As youngsters, we swore when we got to twenty-one we'd change them.'

211

'So . . .'

'I suppose I mellowed. Can't speak for Eunice. We're not that close actually. It's a good job I've got a lot of friends.'

'Enid, if you were any more mellow they'd be carrying you out in a wooden box.'

'What a charming thought.'

'So what's the plan?'

'I thought we might go and see *An Inspector Calls* – it's an amateur production at the village hall – then how about a spot of supper?'

'Fine, whatever. But I meant about the Masseys.'

'You are aware that you have no legal right over this child even if she does turn out to be your daughter.'

'Not sure about that. What if she was taken away while the balance of my mind was disturbed? That's what they call it officially, don't they? I wouldn't be able to give my consent then. Not properly.'

'Is that what happened?'

'I don't know. All I know is I was drugged up to the eyeballs. Yeah I scribbled my signature on a manky scrap of paper because they stuck it in front of my face and told me to. But frankly, when you're in that place, your options are limited. Let's face it, if the prats that had the say-so thought I was in danger of harming Lola, they'd have had her off me one way or the other. If the law won't help me I'll have to do things my own way.'

Enid fixes me with a look that starts off as a reprimand then relents into something more gentle. 'Why don't you run yourself a soothing bath? Relax for an hour. Meanwhile I'll get on to the theatre and see what they've got available.'

'You're a very kind woman, Enid Bean.'

34

You're going to have to play this extremely carefully Jesamine Vale. Swallow a mountain of humble pie and hope it's enough to win her round.

Dora waves me through reception, without a second glance, almost like I'm part of the furniture now. I even manage to check myself from barging straight in to her consulting room like I usually do, remembering to knock politely and wait until she says 'come,' before entering.

She raises her expressive eyebrows at me. 'Am I expecting you?'

I pull up a chair and plop down opposite her. 'OK, Doc, you win. I'm sold on the hypnosis.' I'm not brazen enough to go straight for the couch.

'You mean you haven't come here simply to flirt with me?'

'Enid, my landlady – she's got these contacts. Reams of them. And she doesn't even have a profile on Facebook or Spacebook, or whatever it's called. We think we've found Lola, but the sneaky devils that have got her packed her off to Anglesey. Enid doesn't reckon I'll get her back . . . but I had this thought . . . what if I gave her up while the balance of my mind was disturbed? While I was freaked out . . . drugged up. You have to help me find out what happened.'

'Jes, slow down. It's terrific if you've found her – I'm genuinely pleased for you. I can't do anything for you right now. I've got a meeting with Jeff and the other directors in five minutes. To discuss my future.'

'What's up, Doc? I've always wanted to say that.' I clap my hands together.

'Who did you tell that we had sex? Because I haven't told a soul and unfortunately for us – correction, unfortunately for me – Jeff knows about it.'

'And I'll bet he's right turned on.'

'So, who, in your questionable wisdom, did you decide to share it with?'

'Let's see . . . I might have mentioned it in passing to my sister – but she wouldn't say anything . . . unless . . . well I'm guessing she's probably

213

enlightened Mother. Cameron – but only to get him back cos he was teasing me. Mack – the one with the two-timing girlfriend . . . oh and Enid – my landlady – but she wouldn't breathe a word. She's good as gold.'

'Just those few lucky chosen ones then. You didn't by any chance take out a full page advertisement in The Observer while you were at it?'

'Too pricy. No big deal is it?'

'Not for you, no.'

'Are you in trouble? Smack wrist, don't do it again, Doc.'

'Yeah, yeah, something like that. Don't you give it a second thought.'

I lean across and put my hand on her arm. 'I didn't mean to be flippant. And I am worried for you. Really.'

'Me too.'

'Can I like see you . . . like, lunchtime?'

'I'm not sure it's a good idea, considering. '

'Please. Even if it's just for ten minutes. I need to know you're OK.'

'Everyone reckons that new place across the road is pretty cool. I'll let you buy me a drink if you want. Shall we say one o'clock?'

'Great. It's a date then.' She opens the door for me and I sneak a quick kiss on her lips.

At precisely the same moment, Jeff comes round the corner.

I arrive twenty minutes early, the way I always do when I want to impress somebody. I'm not sure I can afford more than one round, so I'll wait until she turns up. I nip to the loo and check my face for spots and general blemishes. Then I liberally apply the mascara I nicked on the way here, from the same chemist as I took the tester lipstick. Mmm, not bad. My eyelashes have never looked so hot.

Pash strolls in on the dot of one, with her jacket over her arm. Miss Punctuality.

I casually drop my magazine back in the rack. 'What are you drinking?'

'I'll have a white wine spritzer please. Actually, forget the watering down. Just a glass of wine. Dry. I never usually drink at lunchtime, but sod it.'

'Be right back.'

214

'I'll grab a table, she says, fanning her face with a paper napkin. 'Mind if we sit on the patio? It's rather stuffy in here.'

'Honey, I don't mind if we sit in quicksand as long as it's together.'

She doesn't laugh at my jokes these days. I don't know why I still expect it.

When the barman asks who's next, I wave a ten pound note frantically at him though the crowd. No-one objects. By my reckoning that's saved me a good fifteen minutes. If anyone tried pushing in the dinner queue at Whytemoor Hall, they'd soon as likely find themselves on the following night's menu.

When I get outside with the drinks she's checking her BlackBerry – scrolling down the messages, of which there seem to be zillions. Miss Popular.

'Anything important?'

'Nothing that can't wait.' She glances up at me. Her mouth spreads into a slow smile and I'm hoping it's not because I look like a drag queen, or something. 'You're wearing make-up.'

'Just making an effort.' At least she noticed.

'Suits you.' She raises her glass and I chink mine against it.

'Meeting didn't turn out so well, huh?'

She drops the BlackBerry into her bag. 'Let's not talk about it.'

'Go on, unburden yourself. Give me the chance to play therapist.'

She takes a sip of wine and seems impressed. She ought to be. It bloody cost enough. I don't tell her my wine is an inferior version of the same grape variety, because I didn't have enough for two glasses.

'I tried to explain to Jeff and Celia – that's the other senior partner – she's based at our Cirencester branch – that I've been working with you as a favour. And that no money has exchanged hands. That seemed to make things worse in their eyes. The upshot is, the management team has requested I don't see you again at the practice.'

'And I suppose you agreed? Just like that.'

'I had no choice, Jes. When I say, 'requested,' I mean, it was an official order from on high. They said I'd be in breach of contract if I continued with, now how did Jeff delicately put it? "This act of divine madness."'

'Could the leak have anything to do with Melissa?' I say hopefully. 'She's almost one of the gang now, isn't she? Maybe she's put the boot in.'

215

'No way. Mel doesn't know about us. Like I said, I didn't tell anyone. Either one of the "select" people you confided in, has confided in someone else and it's become a game of Chinese Whispers, or . . . you give me an alternative.'

'I don't have one. But you'd better believe I'm working on it. If I find out it was one of my lot, I'll swing for whoever it was.'

'Please don't,' she says. 'Honestly, Jes, I'd rather you kept your liberty.'

'Give us a cuddle,' I say impetuously. I'm not expecting a result, but hey, nothing ventured.

She comes to my side of the table and sits down next to me. I lay my head on her shoulder. Her sleek, raven hair smells of lemongrass. Her body is all warm and soft.

'Feels good,' she says, pulling me against her.

'I'm sorry if I got you in trouble Pash.'

'I'm a big girl – I can handle it.'

'I'm sure you can. So we can go back to being lovers now.' My lips find her neck.

'Jes, take it easy.'

I slide my hands inside her top and undo her bra.

'Not here. Anyone could see.'

'That's what makes it so exciting. The lure of the wild outdoors. Relax.'

'I can't – I have other priorities.'

'Such as?'

'I'm meeting Mel in an hour. Said I do her a favour.'

Bloody Mel. It's always bloody Mel lately. 'A favour, eh? Sexual?' I let go of her.

She smiles. 'Not even worthy of a reply. Drink your wine. It's nice by the way.' She does up her bra. Adjusts her clothes.

'Indulge me . . . the favour?'

'OK, I said I'd lend her my car for a day or so. She's just passed her driving test and she wants to go and hunt for a new one. So much easier than going round on the bus, or taking taxis everywhere.'

'She's just passed her test and you're lending her your car. Must be serious.'

'She hasn't had time to develop bad habits. I'm willing to lay good money she's a better driver than you.'

216

'She's probably better at loads of things. No doubt you'll let me know in time. Still time to fit in a quickie.'

'I don't do, "*quickies.*"'

'Why didn't you say you were busy just now when I . . .?'

'You asked for a cuddle.'

'Bollocks. So when do I get to see you properly?'

'I'll call you.'

'Like being in control, don't you? Typical bloody Gemini.'

'It'll be worth the wait,' she says, getting up. 'My round.'

I'm about to stuff my fist in my mouth and scream my head off, when Enid phones me with the best news ever.

35

The little girl is standing there in the doorway, with Carolyn's arm draped across her slender shoulders protectively. Reverend Massey nods at his wife like they're about to surrender a hostage. Carolyn takes her arm away and the girl steps forward.

My girl. With me. At long last.

Carolyn says, 'This is our Lorna.' She's wearing a pink cotton dress – her brunette hair cut into a smart bob.

'Hi babe,' I say brightly, then curse myself. Probably not the best opening gambit I could have come out with. That's what trying to act cool does for you, when inside you're a gibbering wreck.

'This is Miss Vale,' Reverend Massey says. 'She's a family . . . acquaintance.' He might at least have said friend. Meanie.

'Hello,' Lola says, extending her small hand at me. 'Pleased to meet you.'

'Pleased to meet you too.' I take her hand and squeeze it, forgetting momentarily to give it back.

'Why don't you show Miss Vale your room?' Carolyn says. 'I'm sure she'd be interested. Show her your project on the rainforests.'

'OK, Mum,' she says. The word goes through me like a bullet piercing my gut. 'This way, Miss.'

When we're out of earshot I whisper, 'Please, call me Jes. At least when it's just the two of us on our own.'

'You sure?' she says, strolling sedately upstairs, like the lady of the manor. At her age, I always got so excited at the prospect of having someone come visit, I would have bombed up the stairs two at a time dragging our poor unsuspecting guest after me.

In total contrast to my wreck of a bedroom at her age, Lola's room is implicitly tidy. There's a pine bedstead standing alongside a matching chest of drawers and in the corner a wooden desk and chair painted crimson. There's a pin board with handwritten notes stuck on it and a calendar. The walls are bare except for a map of the world and one of the Solar System. No pop stars. No movie stars. No sporting heroes. No-one to indulge your emotions on. This whole thing makes me feel unbelievably miserable. When I think of the fabulously well-rounded life Freya has, compared to this, I'm so disappointed for my poor baby. I plop down on the bed and she sits on the floor cross-legged like I'm some Sunday School teacher about to read the day's lesson.

I beam at her. 'So, what do you like to do?'

'Study. Learn new things. Broaden my horizons.'

Broaden my horizons . . . in a hothouse environment like this? It sounds altogether contrived – like they've brainwashed her.

'Where are your toys?'

She stares at me like I'm quite mad.

'You do, have toys?'

'Toys are for babies,' she says. 'When I was little I had dolls. And some furry animals. A donkey and a camel. And a teddy bear. Dad put them in the Christmas bazaar at his church. But I didn't really mind because it meant I was being grown up. And because he said the money they raised would help the poor and needy.'

Her little cherub face is so resolutely accepting of everything it makes me want to weep. I swallow hard several times, trying to compose myself.

'So, what do you do to relax?'

'Read. And I watch TV.'

'*Tweenies* . . . *Teletubbies* . . . *Ninja Turtles* . . . *Bratz* . . . *Dora the Explorer* . . . I'm big on it all. Ask me anything.'

She focuses on my face intently. 'Tonight there's a programme on global warming on the Documentary Channel. Dad says I can stay up and watch it. It's vitally important we all do our bit for the planet. No excuses.'

'Absolutely. No excuses.'

'Will you be watching?'

'Would you like me to?'

'Everybody should. Too many people don't want to take responsibility for what happens to our environment. If we all did a little bit more, the world would be a better place.'

'Then I'll watch. And I'll think of you watching it along with me.'

She switches on the computer and shows me her essays on pollution and endangered wildlife species, which run to tens of pages each.

'Wow. You're a bright kid. And your dad marks these does he?'

'Yeah,' she says. 'he's my harshest critic.'

'I know how you feel. My mother's exactly the same.'

She adds, 'But also my greatest supporter.'

'Ah, no. Can't say the same for Mother, unfortunately.'

'What was your favourite subject at school, Jes?'

'Games,' I say a little too quickly. Only because I had a massive crush on Miss Mellor, who took us for hockey and netball in the winter and tennis and lacrosse in the summer. Posh eh? Not everyone plays gets to play lacrosse. Jammy sods.

And as for the gorgeous Miss Mellor . . . there's something about a young woman in an electric-blue tracksuit, sloshing around a hockey pitch, knee-deep in mud. Well, there was back in those days. I decide against telling Lola all this stuff. Instead I gabble, 'I was quite good at English. And Art. Do you draw? Paint? My *Play-Doh* sculptures are legendary.'

She looks at me like I'm from another planet. 'Occasionally I do drawings . . . and watercolours. I'm better at writing though.'

'Maybe one day you'll become a famous author. Like JK Rowling. She's incredible. Are you into *Harry Potter*? I was thinking we might watch a video together.'

'Dad doesn't like me watching things like that. He says it's a bit dark.'

He would be like that. Spoilsport. This is so hard. It ought to be the most natural thing in the world, engaging with your daughter.

'Listen, do you have an e-mail address? I could write to you. You wouldn't have to show it to anyone. It could be our secret.'

'Dad says, perhaps when I'm older. I am allowed online now, but only when I'm being supervised. He says there are nasty people out there that prey on children.'

'He's right. That's the sensible thing to do – wait until you're older. Lol-Lorna?'

'Yes.'

'Don't you want to ask me anything? Go ahead. Anything . . . I'll be completely open and honest with you.'

220

She smiles, thoughtfully like she's got a mass of possibilities running through her mind. 'Do you recycle?'

Shit. It would be that, wouldn't it? Of all the bloody things she could have come out with and it's that. Recycling – my specialist subject. 'You know what?' I tell her, 'I'm always hanging around the bottle bank of a Friday evening. It's like my second home.'

She rubs her hands together. 'Excellent.'

'Anything else?'

'Do you go to church?'

'Not for a while. I'm thinking of starting up again though. I'm a bit rusty.'

'But you do believe in God?'

'I've had a bit of a crisis of faith these past few years, but if you're asking me today, then yes, I do. Especially today.'

'I could lend you my Gideon bible.'

'No, I couldn't.'

'Go on. It's no trouble.' She opens the desk drawer and takes it out. 'It's OK I've got another one. A bigger version.'

'I used to have one of these when I was your age. I remember these people coming to the school to talk to us and we all took it in turns to go on stage and be presented with one. I remember it had my name inscribed on the inside page. That's so kind of you. You don't even know me.' I put in my pocket. 'I will give it back you know.'

'Dad says we should extend the hand of friendship to strangers. Anyway, you seem like a nice person.'

'Lorna?'

'Yep.'

'You do like . . . get to go out to places and stuff, don't you? I mean, you're not cooped up here all the time.'

She nods. 'My parents don't like me going out by myself, but they sometimes take me places. Like to the Forest of Dean. Or to relatives. My Auntie Veronica and Uncle Robin live in Anglesey. Do you know it?'

I shake my head. 'But you would be allowed to go as far as the corner shop say? Down to the village?' I have images of me sneaking off for clandestine meetings with her between library bookshelves.

'Not by myself, no. A girl got taken from outside the bakers last year. They still haven't found her. Mummy says she's most probably dead.'

'I could take you out if you want? Anywhere you like. The zoo . . . theme park . . . you'd love The Eden Project.' I have this sudden vision of Cameron scribbling his autograph on the big girl's boobs. 'You'd be quite safe with me.'

'You'd have to ask my parents.'

'Well of course I would do that.'

She looks at me thoughtfully. 'So how do you know my mum and dad?' At last she's asking the right questions.

The door opens. He's standing there. Hands in pockets. He looks a yard taller than when I last saw him. 'What have you two been chatting about?' he says accusingly.

Talk about crap bloody timing.

'Global warming,' Lola says. 'Jes — I meant, Miss Vale — is into recycling. That's good, isn't it? She's going to watch the documentary tonight. And she said she'd take me to The Eden Project, if that's OK?'

'We'll see. Mother's made us some tea downstairs. Shall we?'

After he makes a point of Saying Grace, we sit there stiffly in rigid-backed chairs eating Carolyn's superb homemade wares, while barely making eye contact with one another. I can only manage one scone, even though they are utterly delicious. I can feel the rumblings of an onslaught of heartburn.

'Go on,' Carolyn says, waving the plate under my chin. 'You can't tell me with a figure like that you're watching your weight.' She seems composed now.

'It's the excitement.'

'More tea then,' she says topping up my cup.

I stare out the window at the immaculate lawn. 'Do you want to show me around the garden, Lorna?'

'I'm afraid Lorna has revision to do,' Reverend Massey says, dabbing his chin on a pristinely-ironed napkin. 'Algebra. For a test this evening.'

'But she's only eight,' I protest. 'Couldn't you leave it for today?'

'We have our routines,' Massey says firmly. Carolyn nods at the child. 'Go and run your bath, Lorna. And say goodbye to Miss Vale.'

'Surely not already.'

She holds her little hand out at me. 'It was very nice meeting you.'

'You too. See you again very soon.' I manage the briefest of hugs before she skips away.

'Our child is very bright,' Massey says. 'It's both a privilege and a curse – like beauty.'

'Why doesn't she go to a proper school?'

'What advantage would it be? My wife and I both trained as primary school teachers. We may discuss sending her somewhere in a few years time, but right now we think it would drag her down. You see, Lorna is far more intelligent than the average eight-year-old. In my experience it's all too easy to become distracted . . . to deviate from the true path. Our daughter needs to remain focussed.'

Your daughter? Give me some credit why don't you. 'But what about friends? I protest. When does she get to mix with kids her own age?'

'My sister has children a little older than Lorna and so does Carolyn's brother. Let me reassure you, Lorna is self-contained, but not lonely. Never lonely.'

I get up from the table. My legs feel wobbly. I need a drink. A proper stiff drink. Maybe Reverend Massey has some communion wine knocking about. 'Thanks, Carolyn, for the tea, it was totally delicious. And you, Reverend Massey, for allowing me to come over.'

Carolyn smiles briefly. 'I could give you the recipe if you like . . . for the scones.'

'You could, love, but it would be wasted on me. I've been known to cremate beans on toast.'

Massey holds out his hand. 'I believe you have something of my daughter's.'

'No, I – oh you mean the bible? She's lending it to me.'

'I don't mean to be disrespectful, Miss Vale, it's just that the item has sentimental value. On occasions when property has left this house it hasn't always been returned. I'm quite sure you understand.'

I delve into my pocket and hand it over shamefully, like some errant schoolgirl caught pilfering sweets from the local shopkeeper.

The words come out before I can censor them. 'So you were listening at the door? Snooping on us.'

His face tightens. 'We have to be extremely careful about the sort of influences our daughter is exposed to. She's at an impressionable age. I'm sure you understand.'

36

I pace Pashindra's newly-decorated living room like an irate tiger, while she eyes me, patiently, from the comfort of her recliner.

'And another thing,' I growl, 'he finishes every other ruddy sentence with: "I'm sure you understand." Well I'm not sure I *do* bloody *"understand."*

'It's early days, Jes. You can't expect to stroll into your daughter's life after eight long years and expect everything to be perfect. This isn't *Little House on the Prairie*. Happy endings not guaranteed, I'm afraid.'

'Oh it's far from ruddy perfect. And don't I know it? All this time I've been harbouring this stupid fantasy that my daughter would turn out to be like Cameron's Freya. Inquisitive, adventurous . . . downright fearless, just like I was at that age. A devilish glint in her eye as she plants the whoopee cushion under the Bishop's seat.

'Instead, I've given birth to a ruddy Stepford Child. Unfailingly obedient. Subservient. Polite to the point of making you want to curse. The complete bloody opposite of me. In a couple of years they'll be signing her up for fucking Question Time, you mark my words. She's eight, going on fifty-eight, with all the weight of the world on her slender shoulders.

'Of course it's good she's aware of global warming and all that crap, but it's not the be all and end all. She doesn't even do girly things. The poor kid's had her toys confiscated – permanently. Her make-believe father made her sell them off to boost his church coffers. She doesn't have any friends her own age. She can't even sneak off to the corner shop and buy a copy of *Viz* to smuggle under the duvet, for fuck's sake. And she's not allowed to read *Harry Potter*, because he will condemn her to a life of eternal damnation. What kind of artificial fish-bowl existence is my baby, dare I use the term, "living," in? That's not what I want for her. The hell it is!'

'What *you* want? You've made huge strides in just getting to see her at all. I don't think you realize nearly how much you've achieved in such a short time.'

'All thanks to Enid.'

'You're not going to change her whole world overnight, Jes. That's not how these things work. You need patience. Persistence . . .' Pash makes gentle swirling movements with her hands like she's charming a cobra. 'And calm reasoning.'

'And what sort of fuddy-duddy name is Lorna? Lor-na. Sounds like a granny in a woollen shawl with a hot water bottle stuffed down her thermal long johns. No wonder the poor kid's old before her time. Don't you dare laugh at me, Pash, I'm serious. This is doing my head in.'

'It's hard not to laugh when you behave so appallingly ungratefully.'

'Bollocks.'

'You, my friend, may think you're being fair, but let me tell you some of your views are downright one-sided. The reverend and his wife – they sound like a decent couple to me.'

'Don't fall into that trap. Just because he wears a dog collar . . .'

'Think of it this way. Would you prefer Lola was hanging around on street corners, or slumped under a tree in the local park, stoned out of her brain on dope and cider with a bunch of delinquents? Because that's what some kids, not much older than Lola get up to. Next stop, the detention centre, then . . . who knows where they'll end up? Prison? Dead in some alleyway?'

'Of course that's not what I want. I love her.'

'Well then – be reasonable.'

'All I'm saying is there has to be a balance.' I stop pacing. 'Pash, I've had an epiphany. Just now – it came to me like a bolt from the sky.'

'Do us both a favour, darling, and keep it to yourself.'

'You don't mean that.' I plant myself on a chair opposite her and lose myself in those sultry eyes. 'We get her a fake passport – you can get them for a couple of hundred quid if you know the right people – and I do. We drive to the Costa del Sol and start a new life, me, you and Lola. It's perfect. Let's face it, armed with bogus documents, you could set up anywhere under an assumed name. We can hire a car and dump it once we get across the border.'

'Thelma and Louise with a kid in tow . . .'

'It doesn't have to be Spain. Maybe Greece would be better. Or Turkey . . . Xanthos . . . I went there once when I was eighteen. They'd never track us down there. I'll share the driving.'

'No thanks. I value my life. Cameron told me how you subjected poor Lizzy to a white-knuckle ride. Poor woman.'

'OK we'll take it in stages. Overnight stops. Doesn't matter how long it takes.'

'Get a grip, Jes.'

'I mean it.'

'You're not thinking straight. You're acting like Lola's unhappy, but that's just you, dumping your feelings onto her. You don't know anything for a fact.'

'If Octavia had kept me tied to her apron strings like that Massey-bloke does with Lola, I'd have bloody well rebelled. I'd have run away – you wouldn't have seen my heels for dust. Wouldn't you?'

'Not if it's the only thing I'd ever known. The truth is Jes, she probably feels secure in that environment. Protected. Cherished. Dare I say, a little spoilt. I know it's not what you want to hear.'

'Damn right. Don't you want me to get her back? Not jealous are you?'

'Go for a walk. You need to clear your head.'

I reach for her hand across the coffee table.

'I can't expect you to feel like I feel. She's my baby – my own flesh and blood. When we're in the same room I can feel the electricity between us. It draws me to her like a needle in the middle of a magnetic field. '

'I'm on your side, whatever you think,' Pash says. 'I'm scared for you. Terrified you'll blow it.' She thumps her chest. 'In here, I'm rooting for you. You'd better believe it.' We get up at the same time.

I put my arms around her neck. She kisses my forehead, then my lips. I press myself against her – wanting her like never before.

*

I'm helping Dad lay out the pieces to a kit model of a spitfire, when Rhianna comes in with two blokes in suits. The first man identifies himself as DS Large, which makes me giggle because he's leaner than Amy Winehouse, sideways-on.

'Something amusing you?' he says.

I shrug. 'Irony. Not something you people would understand.'

'My colleague, DC Osman,' he says.

'I'd like to say I've got all your records, Donny, but I'm more of a Whitesnake fan myself.'

'Os-MAN.'

'Bet you two witty hunks have got the WPCs queuing round the block for a date.'

'We'd like to ask you a few questions,' Large says.

'Ah and here's me thinking you've come with my pizza delivery. Come to harass me, have you? The girls said it would be like this. It always is when you've been done before. Easy pickings. How the hell did you know where to find me?'

'Mrs McGill tipped us off.'

'Cheers, Sis. Still the same old goody-two-shoes she always was. Well, as you can see, I'm busy. This kit won't do itself.'

'Either we can do this here, or down at the station, whichever you prefer,' Large says.

'Hear that, Dad? The boys in blue want my company again. Nice to be popular.'

'In view of your father's condition, perhaps we might pop next door . . .' Osman says.

'My pleasure officer.'

Dad's frail hand reaches for mine. 'Don't you tell them anything unless the blighters torture you, right?'

I wink at him. 'Course I won't tell. Never.'

'That's my girl.'

I glare at DC Twat. 'He might be ill, but he's not stupid.'

They escort me to the lounge, one flanking me on either side like you see on cop shows.

'Yesterday afternoon,' Osman says. 'Run through your movements from four-thirty, would you?'

'My bowel movements? Well seeing as I'd had beans on toast for lunch they were pretty loose as you'd expect.'

'Want us to make this formal?'

227

There's no way I'm telling them about Lola. Having the police turn up at the vicarage would almost certainly scupper any chance I've got of seeing her again. Keep it neutral. So they can't prove things one way or the other.

'I went for a walk at around half-past four. Got a take-out coffee from the bakers in the village about five . . . got home around six. Poured myself a nice large glass of wine and had a bath. Then I watched TV until Lizzy came home around ten-thirty. Not exactly a jet-setting lifestyle. Are you going to tell me what this is about?'

'Can anyone verify your whereabouts?'

'Big Brother. I'm sure you've got CCTV swarming all over the place. Someone forget to put the film in, did they?'

'What about the person who served you in the bakers?'

'It wasn't Keira Knightly, so unfortunately I don't remember.'

'Did you get a till receipt perhaps?'

'Perhaps. Then again, perhaps I chucked it away. Though not on the ground, officer. In a bona fide waste receptacle, obviously. I'm pretty certain it was green. I might be able to pick it out of a line-up, if it's that crucial.'

'On your walk, did you happen to venture anywhere near the psychiatric clinic?'

'This is to do with Pash Khan, isn't it?'

'Answer the question.'

'I saw her earlier today – she is OK, isn't she?'

'Were you around the area of the clinic yesterday? Large says.

'No I wasn't.'

'What about last night?'

'No. I told you.'

'We're investigating a wilful act of vandalism against Doctor Khan's motor vehicle.' Osman says.

'Well it wasn't me. The last thing I'd want is for Pash to be hurt.'

'I didn't mention anyone was hurt.'

'No, but you'd hardly have taken the trouble to hunt me down if someone had keyed the door. '

Osman says, 'Somebody tampered with the brake fluid.'

I jump up. 'Tell me she's OK. I've got to see her.'

He steps across my path. 'Sit down, Miss Vale.'

228

Large says, 'We've been making enquiries and we've discovered that you fancy yourself as a bit of a mechanic.'

'Rubbish.'

'You did a course at Whytemoor Hall.'

'A very basic course. It wasn't exactly Formula One stuff.'

'But nevertheless the course covered the subject of maintaining and disabling brakes, did it not?'

'Anyone could do it.'

'Your probation officer informs us that you are an employee of Doctor Khan's – her PA, no less. That comes as news to Doctor Khan's receptionist.'

'I made it up, OK.'

'For what purpose?'

'To impress people. And to get my bloody probation officer off my back. Arsehole. Is Pash alright?'

Osman tucks his notepad in his pocket. 'I'm not obliged to say any more. I suggest you keep out of the vicinity of the practice and Doctor Khan's home. In fact, I must insist that you do. I strongly advise you to comply, Miss Vale. If you do not, I am advising you now that you may be liable to arrest.'

'Stay away . . . for how long?'

'Couldn't say,' Osman says. 'For as long as it takes us to conclude our enquiries. Sit tight, keep your legs crossed and we'll keep you posted.'

'I could report you for that.'

He winks at me.

'I heard what happened. The accident,' I say breathlessly, hovering over the reception desk.

'You shouldn't be here,' Dora says. 'The police said if you were to turn up I am to ring them.' She puts her hand on the phone.

'Dora no – wait – I haven't done anything wrong. Please – is she OK? Tell me she's OK.' I can feel my armpits sweating.

'It's serious,' Dora says. 'She might not pull through. Something about a blood clot on the brain.'

'Oh God, no. But I was with her . . . earlier . . .'

229

'Last we heard they're planning to operate, but they don't know whether . . .' Dora puts her hand to her mouth.

'I have to be there. Where is she?'

'She's at the General. It's family only, I think.'

'Sod that, I need to see her. I have to tell her that I . . . can you get me a taxi?'

'You'll get yourself in more trouble. Stay away, Miss Vale,' she says firmly.

'I can't. Please . . . help me . . .'

'Doctor Khan went up there an hour ago. She'll ring me if there's any change.'

'What did you say? But Pash – she's not . . .'

'You thought it was Doctor Khan in the crash?'

'Of course I did. So . . .'

'It was her friend Melissa that was driving.'

*

I'm just about to nip into town on a pilfering jaunt, when the squad car pulls up. Thank God Lizzy isn't about. She'd be having a cardiac at the prospect of all those twitching curtains. DS Large again. This time with a busty blonde bird in a uniform that looks like it belongs on someone two sizes smaller.

I open the front door. 'Not you lot again.'

'This is DC French,' he says, inviting himself in.

'Ooh la la. Well I must say, she's a bit of an improvement on the last one. Donny tied up at the recording studio this afternoon, is he?'

Reluctantly I take them through to the kitchen.

'Forgive me if I don't offer you a drink, guys, it's just that I'm pushed for time. Don't want to turn it into a social occasion. You know how it is.'

'We'll make it snappy then,' Large says. 'During the course of our investigations we've taken away a number of Doctor Khan's files for examination. We've also paid a visit to Whytemoor Hall . . .'

'You guys have been busying yourselves. I sincerely hope you didn't have the spag bol. It's only good for cleaning the drains. Is Melissa OK?'

230

He gives me a look like I've just said something I shouldn't.

'We're awaiting an update on Miss Parris's condition.'

'Why did you let me think it was Pash that got hurt?'

'To see how much you knew. You'd be surprised how much some people reveal when they're trying to be clever.'

'Meaning?'

'Amongst Doctor Khan's personal effects, we found several undated notes we believe to have originated from you. Expressions of affection. Love letters, mostly.'

He hands me a photocopy. 'Is this your handwriting?'

'Yes, it is.'

'As I say, mostly affectionate, but this one for instance. "If I can't have you, no-one else will."'

'That was from ages ago. When she left Whytemoor, I was wound up. I felt she'd led me on. I never posted it.'

'So it was written in anger.'

'I can't remember. Probably.'

'Are you suggesting Doctor Khan acted less than professionally in her capacity at the prison?'

'Don't twist things. I was in a state of confusion. Got things out of proportion as people often do when emotions run high. What you blokes call "time of the month," only it lasted all year. Several years.' I turn to the WPC. 'You'll back me up on this one won't you, love?' Not a flicker from the impressively made up face. 'Just as I thought – a numbskull inside a blow-up doll.'

'Behave yourself,' Large says. *"If I can't have you, no-one else will –"* a somewhat sinister message wouldn't you agree, Miss Vale?'

'I told you, I was emotional. It's from years ago. Get the ink tested, or something. You must have the technology.'

'Doctor Khan received a copy of this particular message in yesterday morning's post, around an hour before Melissa Parris lost control of her vehicle. How do you explain that?'

'It wasn't me. I didn't send it.'

'And you don't have an alibi for the time we estimate the vehicle was being tampered with. Do you know Miss Parris?'

'We met once. Briefly. At the bowling alley. You're going to ask whether I liked her and you expect me to say yes, right? Well I didn't particularly. Too cocky by half. Really fancies herself, that one.'

'So you disliked her? Was that an intense dislike, would you say?'

'I didn't like her, I didn't not like her. I was indifferent.'

'Whoever sent this note wasn't *"indifferent."* Whoever interfered with Doctor Khan's motor vehicle certainly wasn't *"indifferent."* You weren't at all jealous when you heard Melissa Parris was moving in with Doctor Khan?'

'OK, a bit, but there's nothing going on between them. Pash already told me Melissa's got a fiancé. And I didn't send that note. Listen, I've had weird letters sent to me too. Threatening letters.'

'Can we see?'

'I got rid of them. Someone's idea of a sick joke. There's some bloody sick specimens walking about.'

'Were you and Doctor Khan conducting an intimate relationship?'

'Not at Whytemoor.'

'And since you left prison? Did your relationship become sexual?'

'What does Pash say?'

'I'm asking you, Miss Vale. Have you slept with her?'

'Well now, Detective Sergeant Large, as I recall, on the night in question, I don't remember either of us doing much sleeping.'

'And Melissa Parris . . . were you sleeping with her, as well?'

'Not very well informed are you? Mel Parris is straight,' I say, with an air of smugness. 'You lot are fucking useless.'

'I suggest, Miss Vale, it's you that isn't very well informed – we know for a fact that up until the time of her accident, Miss Parris was having a liaison with at least one woman.'

'No, no. You're wrong.'

'We just don't know who that woman is yet. But rest assured, we *will* find out. That's all for now.' He gets up, goes to the door, then stops, like he's remembered something. It reminds me of the style of some rough-looking American cop from many years ago, whose name escapes me. 'One more thing. Do you ever keep trophies of your sexual conquests, Miss Vale?'

37

'Enid! Enid!'

She comes flying out of the kitchen. 'Thank heavens you're all right, my dear. I was worried.'

'Have the police been here?' I rub my sweaty palms on my jeans. The second and third fingers of my right hand have broken out in ugly red welts again.

'An hour ago. They had a warrant to search the premises. They took your denim jacket.'

'Fuck.'

'Are you in trouble, Jes?'

'I haven't done anything wrong. You do believe me, don't you?'

'Of course I do.' She sits me down. 'What you need is a nice cup of strong tea.'

'Bugger the tea. Give me a brandy.'

'Not sure I have any. I'll look.'

'OK, anything. Bloody cooking sherry. Anything. You don't know me very well do you?' I say accusingly, then feel guilty for taking it out on her.

I get up and go across to the window. I can hear her ferreting around the kitchen. Cupboard doors opening and closing. The kettle going on. 'It's all right,' she calls, as if reading my mind, 'the tea's for me.'

Two minutes later, she fetches in a steaming mug of tea and a large tumbler of neat brandy for me. 'I won this one Christmas at the village hall. Can't think when.'

'Enid you're a saint. My lifesaver.' I take a gulp and it burns my throat.

'It's probably almost as old as you,' she says. 'Do you want to tell me what's going on?'

'Poisonous notes. You know like the ones I got. Pash got one yesterday. It said, *"If I can't have you, nobody will."* Then her car crashed. She wasn't driving. She'd leant it to Melissa – the girl who looks like Katie Melua. She's in a bad way.'

Enid sips her tea thoughtfully. 'And the police think you wrote the note?'

'I did write the bloody note, that's the problem.'

'I don't understand.'

'I wrote bundles of notes when I was inside. It was my way of coping. Some people would cut up – some people refused to eat – I wrote masses of scribblings. It kept me sane. Just. Only they got taken from my cell. It's Eva Rowe, she's after me . . .'

'Eva Rowe? Eva Rowe! My goodness, but why?'

'It's complicated, Enid. Basically, I snubbed her after she'd rescued me from this pack of she-wolves. No-one snubs Eva Rowe and gets away with it. She's had me set up.'

'You think she's here? This village? My goodness,' she says again. 'I'll have to alert my contacts.'

'Knickers.'

'That's tame for you.'

'The police knew I had Pash's underwear – her knickers – and where to find them. But how could they know? The only person who knew I had them was Dad – and he's not exactly compos mentis.'

Enid shrugs. 'Now I'm afraid you really have lost me.'

*

'My goodness, the old fella's popular today,' Rhianna says. 'He's in the garden. Your mum and sister are with him.'

Just when I was starting to think today couldn't get any bloody worse. She walks with me to the back door. I try to sound casual.

'Have the police been here?'

'Not since the last time. When they spoke to you.'

'Are you sure?'

'Positive,' Rhianna says. 'I've been on duty all the time. On call twenty-four hours. Don't want anyone to think I've deserted my post. I adore your father. He can be the most amusing company.'

I feel like hugging her.

Lizzy is pointing out something in a magazine. Dad appears uninterested. He flicks at the pages impatiently.

234

Mother's face shrivels when she sees me. 'Jesamine . . . what a lovely surprise.' Her mouth hardly moved when she said that. 'Look, Eric. Look who's here . . .' She's always had this ability to make her face do one thing while her voice does the complete opposite. That's what RADA does for you, I guess.

'I'm glad we're all together,' I say, pulling up a chair for myself, as neither of the two witches seemed keen to do it for me. 'Now then, which of you three has been crowing to the cops?'

Dad says, 'Not us. You did my dear. The other day. When they were here.'

'Since then. Lizzy? Octavia?'

'Well don't look at me,' Octavia says. 'I've hardly had a second to myself these past few days. I certainly haven't spoken to anyone official.'

'So that's a denial?'

'It most certainly is. May I ask what's going on?'

'Lizzy?'

'They asked me where you were – that's all – and I told them.'

'Dad, are you sure nobody's been here asking about me?' He stares at me blankly. 'Look you two, would you mind giving me and Dad some time on our own?'

'Why?' Lizzy says suspiciously.

'Because I want to discuss something with him. In private.'

'Don't you go upsetting him now,' Octavia says.

'Because you're perfectly capable of doing that all by yourself.'

Octavia takes Lizzy's arm. 'Let's leave them to it, dear. We've been here over an hour and I've got things to see to in town.' Lizzy rises from her seat reluctantly. She puts her arms round Dad's neck and pecks his cheek.

'See you soon, Daddy.'

Octavia takes hold of his hands theatrically. 'I shall pop by on Thursday, Eric, with the documents. We must get together soon, Jesamine,' she adds, like it's an obligation. Dad salutes her. Her brow creases disapprovingly.

As they walk towards the house, Dad screws the newspaper into a ball, cups it behind his head with both hands, like he's about to launch it at her.

'Bloody women – nag, nag, nag. Best let them get on with it. They'll nag themselves to death eventually.'

He lets the paper ball drop onto the table and nudges it towards me. I unpeel it. 'What's this?' Two red biro rings circle the photographs. There's a pencilled note in Lizzy's scrawl I can't make out.

'They want to move me, Jes. Bulldoze this place for development. They seem to think I'd be better off in a nursing home. They say I'll have company. The pair of them did their damnedest to convince me, but if you want to know what I think . . . I think this is all about filthy lucre. Not sure I'm going to comply. I'm happy here. I like all the girls but particularly that Rhianna. She loves having her arse slapped, you know. Now then, what's troubling you, m'dear.'

'The other day, when I was here . . . you were asleep and I was rambling . . . utter bullshit really.'

'Oh yes,' I remember.

'You don't really remember though, do you? You're just saying that. You were asleep.'

'Remind me.'

'I was talking about a woman called Pashindra Khan. She's my friend. She's a doctor.'

'Ahhh, yes.' He taps his temple. 'Now I remember.'

'I was saying stuff – I might have got a bit near the knuckle. Rude, even.'

He leans forward and pats my knee. 'It's always a pleasure to see you, Jes. I probably shouldn't say this, but you always were my favourite girl. You and me, we think alike. The others used to gang up on us, didn't they? Particularly when we were late back from fishing.'

I can feel the tears welling up behind my sunglasses. I find an old tissue in my pocket and blow my nose.

'You remember? Honestly?'

'Of course I do.'

I sniff loudly. 'I'm not having them move you, Dad. I don't care if I have to chain us both to the radiators.'

'Could get a bit warm in the winter,' he says chuckling.

I rub his hands. 'I think you're a canny old codger on the sly.'

'M'dear, it's an essential requirement when you're dealing with the likes of Octavia Vickers. And another thing,' he says, winking at me. 'I've found out you learn an awful lot more by pretending to be asleep.'

*

When I get to the restaurant, the new sommelier, who introduces himself as Thomas, informs me my sister isn't feeling too bright and won't be in until this evening. I've never known Lizzy throw a sickie without good reason. I sprint to the taxi rank – the invalid can pay.

When I get there the front door is open. Lizzy is crouched in the hallway with a dustpan and brush, sweeping up remnants of china. She stares up at me accusingly.

'If you've come looking for a row you're about twenty minutes too late,' she says dourly.

'Well as a matter of fact I did, but if someone's beaten me to it.'

She rattles the dustpan. 'Mother's favourite vase. She entrusted it to me as a wedding present. Obscenely expensive.'

I put my hand to my mouth. 'Dare I suggest superglue . . .'

'That's not funny.'

'What happened?'

'*Leith's Country* is no more. They've shelved the next series.'

'Put it on hold?'

'Axed.'

'Oh . . . but I . . .'

'They're saying they want to go out on a high. They're doing that all right. It's not as if the programme is sliding in the ratings. It's been in the top five since it began.' She blinks several times and swallows hard like she's trying to stop herself from crying.

I cup her chin in my hand. 'Lizzy, look at me. He doesn't hurt you, does he?'

'You don't have to defend me now. We're not in the school playground. Why are we still playing this game?' she says bitterly.

'But he does get violent, yeah? How often does he break things? How often does he ruin your beautiful home?'

'Jes, stop it. This is our home, not mine.' She ferries the remnants of the vase to the kitchen and I follow.

'You mean you want me to put a stop to it? Is that what you're saying?'

'No. Don't go there. Don't you ever go back there. Promise me.' She opens a drawer and presses two tablets out of a foil sheet. She looks at me. 'Nothing to worry about.'

'What are they?'

'Mood stabilizers. I've got a bloody fiftieth birthday bash at the bistro tonight. I've got to be on the ball.'

'I drank a whole bottle of that Rescue Remedy stuff the morning I got out of jail, before I read the label. It said: put four drops on your tongue. Do not exceed the stated dose. I'm still here to tell the tale.'

She smiles a little sadly.

I knit my fingers through hers, then wish I hadn't.

'Where do you think he's gone?'

'To get pissed out of his brain of course. His male pride is wounded, so he'll have retreated to his cave. It's what men do. He won't let on of course. He'll be giving the regulars in the pub a load of old spiel about how he was the one that declined to make another series although they begged him on bended knee. Didn't want to get typecast. Bet you anything he'll be on the phone to mother before the week's out, getting referrals. Hollywood is where it's at, Jes, don't you know.'

One thing I don't know, is why I persist in holding her hand when clearly she's uncomfortable with it, but hey, I am a trained Samaritan. 'Is that what you want? To up sticks to the other side of the ruddy pond?'

'Not really. I'm settled here. I'm the first to admit we don't exactly get to socialize much, but this is home to me. All the locals know me well enough to stop and chat in the marketplace. Business at the restaurant isn't exactly booming, but it's ticking over nicely, even if I do have to give away the odd free meal to a disgruntled diner because my rogue of a sister thinks she's Mike Tyson.'

'Don't think I'm about to apologize. That prat grabbed my arse — twice — that's assault.'

She extracts her hand from mine. 'In my book that's a compliment, but that's where we differ. I suppose if a woman had done it, you wouldn't have objected.'

'Depends on the woman.'

'Right,' she says, studying me.

238

'What?'

'When did you know that you were gay?'

'Way back in junior school when spotty Paul Summers got down on one knee on Sports Day, just after he'd won the Egg and Spoon race, and proposed to me with a beaded ring he nicked off his sister. I'd never been so panic-stricken. Now if only his sister had asked me . . .'

'He's done ever so well for himself. He's a headmaster now. And not spotty at all.'

'Great.'

'He's got four kids and a wife that looks like a supermodel.'

'Well that was never going to be me, was it? I don't have the legs for it.'

She removes her fingers from mine. 'Mother thinks you're just playing at it – this, being gay lark.'

'Yeah she said, bloody cheek. And I suppose you're not convinced either? I'll prove it to you. Go on, give us a snog, Sis. Let me stick my tongue down your throat.'

'Don't you dare come near me,' she says, her bottom lip curling. 'There are women that do that you know, when it's all that's on offer.' Her face creases. 'I don't think I could.'

'Some of them aren't even in prison.'

'Meaning?'

'Suzy Wong.'

'Suzy? Cameron's Suzy?'

'Bloody Schizoid Suzy. That school reunion thing. It was all a ruse. She was with me. At a gay club in town.'

'No way.'

'Holding my hand. Stroking my arse with her acrylic nails . . . rubbing her tits against me.'

'Jes, you're not serious.'

'Doing her level best to pull my strings, just so she could turn me down, sick bitch.'

Lizzy says, 'Fancy a scotch?'

'Yeah, go on. I could bloody murder one.' I really must delete that word from my vocabulary.

Lizzy fetches the bottle over and two tumblers.

'But why would Suzy do that?'

239

'For kicks. And because that husband of yours egged her on. She said they planned it together.'

'I'm afraid he's a terrible practical joker.' She knocks her scotch back in one hit and pours herself another.

'Easy, girl.'

'Some of the things Cameron does drive me to distraction. He thinks he's being funny. Like the time he made out our housekeeper was after him. Just turned twenty-one, she had . . . the age you were when . . .' she looks away from me momentarily. 'I wasn't laughing I can assure you.'

'You had a housekeeper. Whatever did you need a housekeeper for? Rich bitch.'

'Isn't that what they say . . . every woman needs a wife. Have another drink,' she slurs.

I'm on the verge of telling Lizzy about Lola, when her head slumps on to the table. She cradles it in her arms and starts to snore contentedly.

'Lizzy?' I shake her arm. 'Lizzy, wake up. I haven't finished with you yet.' I press two fingers against her neck and feel her pulse. Slow and steady. Then I go to the drawer and take out the packet of pills. It says in bold letters: **Avoid Alcohol**. Fantastic. I go back and shake her again.

I grab her flannel from the bathroom and douse it under the cold tap. 'Come on, Lizzy, wake up. Your clientele needs you.' I dab the back of her neck with it, then her face. The water streams off her cheeks like she's crying. She bloody will be if this party bombs. She groans, half opens her eyes and closes them again.

The front door opens as I'm trying to perform a fireman's lift on my lifeless sister.

'What on earth are you playing at?' Cameron says.

'You're sober, thank God. We thought you'd gone to the pub.'

'Went for a walk,' he says.

'Breathe on me.'

'No ta, you reek of booze. I'm keeping my distance.'

'Great, you really are sober then. Help me drag Lizzy upstairs.'

He picks up the empty scotch bottle. 'What the hell's been going on?'

'I'll fill you in later. This one needs her bed. And we need to get ourselves showered and over to the restaurant. Me and you have got a party to organize.'

*

Cameron pushes a CD into the player, sticks his feet up on a chair and lights a self-congratulatory cigar.

'What a fucking night. We did it, Jes.'

'You can't smoke in here.'

'Fuck it, we're closed. Have one. Let your hair down.'

'Pass. And if we get busted you're coughing up the fine.'

'Relax. Have some more champagne. We've bloody well earned it. At the beginning of the evening I thought you must have been bonkers merely for suggesting it. Now I know you were.'

'If only the bloody lawyers had agreed with you, I'd have had my freedom a long time ago. Got through it though, didn't we?' I want to tell him about finding Lola, but it would be unfair to mention it before I tell Lizzy.

'I suppose I should be impressed that you actually managed to make it through a whole evening without insulting anybody, or slapping someone's face. Or pouring an Irish coffee over their head.'

'I did it for Lizzy. We owe her. Can't you see she's totally exhausted? This business is driving her into the ground.'

'Remind me to increase the life cover.'

I slap his knee.

'Ouch. You just assaulted me again. Thought I spoke too soon.'

'You smashed Octavia's favourite vase. Lizzy was livid. That's why we started on the scotch – to calm things down.'

'Fuck off. The hell I did, darlin'. Since when does someone use alcohol to calm things down? Only an idiot would think like that.'

'You're saying you didn't break the vase?'

'Course I bloody didn't.'

'So it leapt off the table, or what?'

'You're being silly now.'

'So if you didn't do it . . .'

'I promised her a holiday of a lifetime, didn't I . . . Caribbean . . . Indian Ocean . . . her choice entirely. And now thanks to the wisdom of the production team bailing out on me . . . fill in the blanks darlin'.'

'You're saying Lizzy broke the vase.'

'She chucked a paperweight at me and missed.'

'And instead, took out Mother's very expensive vase. Priceless.'

'Your sister needs to see a doctor – get that medication looked at. Maybe you can persuade her. I don't seem to be able to get through to her.'

'But you still love her, don't you?'

'That's not the point, Jes. There's so much help out there. You two are like chalk and cheese. There's you practically living in your therapist's lap and her, won't go within a ten-mile radius of the doctor's surgery. But then I guess that rather depends on the therapist.'

'Don't start.'

'Lizzy gets irrational sometimes. I mean – completely off the wall – imagines things are going on when they're not. Take me and you. Do you want to snog me first, or shall we just get down to it? The act, I mean. Copulation. Fucking.'

'There you go again. You always have to spoil it.' I get up to go. 'Leave me alone. I'm not interested.'

He seizes my arm. 'Neither am I.'

'What?'

'Sit down. Please, Jes. Two minutes. It's all I'm asking.'

'It's all you're getting.'

'The first time we met. When you came to the house to find Lizzy. Did I behave at all improperly towards you?'

'Probably. It's in your nature after all.'

'No, it isn't.'

'As I recall, you tried to get me to take my top off.'

'Because I was genuinely trying to help you with your stupid security tag. I flirt around women. I have a bit of fun. Sure, I'll be the first to admit it. But I don't proposition them. I don't offer them money to give me head and I don't beg them to jump in the sack with me. I don't need to. I've got a queue of nubile young women longer than a Rangers' season ticket waiting list . . . all I have to do is snap my fingers.'

'OK, so you don't do that stuff, it's all down to that sick prick, Jed, right?' I jab a digit in the direction of his crotch. 'That's what you call it.'

'Forget Jed. It was a joke that started on the set and got out of hand. I'm serious. I don't muck about. I'm faithful to Lizzy.'

'Are you saying you don't fancy me, Cameron?' .

242

'I'm saying, while I'm married to your sister, I'm not going to go chasing anybody else. Particularly if she bats for the other side. Joke.'

'I'm too tired for this . . .'

'Then have some water.' He picks up the jug and fills my glass. 'Come on, drink. Splash some on your face. This is important. It might just save our lives. The reason I came on to you, Jes, was because Lizzy wanted me to.'

38

When I get downstairs, Enid is in the breakfast room serving eggs and bacon to a couple of pensioners. The smell makes me heave, even though Enid is one of the best cooks I've ever met. I realize that's not saying much, particularly in recent years.

I go through to the kitchen and help myself to a chunk of her homemade bread, pulling off miniscule pieces and stuffing them into my ungrateful mouth that doesn't want to be fed. Enid bustles in carrying four empty side plates.

'Oh, so you've surfaced,' she says. 'Make yourself useful and stack the dishwasher for me. I'll knock you up a fry-up if you like.'

'Ugh, no. No offence, mate, but I don't feel the best. Pash wasn't answering her mobile just now, so I phoned the practice and Dora said Melissa's rigged up to a life-support machine. It's fifty-fifty. Touch and go.'

'That poor girl. And only young too. Her poor family. Whatever must they be going through.'

'Poor me, you mean. Jesamine Vale – bloody public enemy number one. What about, what I'm going through?' She gives me a look like she can't believe I've just said that. I shrug at her. 'I didn't mean it, E.' Even when someone's name is only four letters long, I have a propensity to shorten it. Like at Whytemoor, Isla was 'I,' Emily was 'M,' Belinda was 'B,' Casey was 'K..'

'I'm sick to the stomach. And I really need to talk to Pash. I need her professional opinion on something. She's probably at the hospital, that's why she isn't answering.'

'Anything I can help with? I'm not a doctor, but I've always thought of myself as being on the practical side. And as you know, I'm fairly non-judgemental.'

'Yesterday, Lizzy and Cameron had a blazing row. They've axed his show and it all got a bit fraught. A vase got smashed. Mother's favourite piece as it turned out, so not all doom and gloom. Lizzy made out to me it was Cam's fault the vase got broken and I was worried he was knocking her about, but then he told me it was her that chucked it at him. And d'you know what? I believe him over my sister.'

'Does it matter who was to blame?'

'Yes it does. Because he told me something else. Something freaky. He told me Lizzy wanted him to come on to me. No not so much wanted – she made him do it. Like, to test me out.'

'She doesn't know you are of the alternative leaning?'

'Never heard it put quite like that before. You're a delicate flower, Enid. Yes, she knows. I bedded her first husband. Was she testing me then, too? Was she testing him? Was that how things ended up the way they did? There's so much I don't understand.'

She looks at me earnestly. 'I hope this doesn't come across as too dense, Jes, but might I enquire, seeing as you insist you've always been this way, why did you sleep with your sister's husband?'

'That's not dense at all, Enid. That's right on cue. I thought I knew the answer. Honestly I did. But now I'm not so sure.'

I prod the start button on the dishwasher and Enid gives me a peculiar look.

'What? I can work a dishwasher, E.'

'You forgot the soap tablet.'

When Enid goes to the cash and carry, I decide to give the kitchen a blitz. So I spruce up the oven with a substance that gets all the way down into my throat and makes my eyes sting. Then I clear out the cupboards, making room for the new stock. Then I have this great idea about making dinner for us both. Enid's been so kind to me, I feel I owe her something. I decide to pick some herbs from the garden, even though I won't have the faintest clue what they are. All herbs smell nice, don't they?

As I open the side gate, they're waiting for me.

'Not you lot again. Three of you this time. My God, must be serious. Want me to come and identify the litter bin?'

Osman steps forward. 'Jesamine Vale, I'm arresting you on suspicion of the murder of Melissa Parris. You do not have to say anything, but it may harm your defence if you do not mention now, something which you later rely on in court. Anything you do say may be given in evidence.'

'Murder? Melissa's dead? But she can't be. You stupid wankers.'

Before I can fight them off, my arms are wrenched behind me. Cuffs snapped carelessly around my wrists so they burn my skin.

'You're hurting me.'

'Shut up and get in the car,' Osman says.

All the way to the station I have to witness Osman's not so subtle flirting with WPC Mute Blow-up Doll – his baggy eyes darting in and out of the rear view mirror intermittently – not once in my estimation, to check on the traffic, while Large flips through a tome of notes to rival War and Peace. Wonder if Osman's missus has any idea that he's carrying on. I make a mental note to look up the Osmans in the phone directory later.

At the station, they remove the handcuffs and chuck me a cell, to cool off, so they tell me. How anyone is supposed to remain cool on a scorching day like today beats me. Someone brings me a cup of lukewarm tea, with what tastes like half a bag of sugar in it.

The sparse compactness of my surroundings reminds me of our caravan in Bognor in the mid-eighties, when Octavia was between jobs and Dad had been laid off from the docks. All winter Lizzy and I had been excitedly making plans, while they scrimped and saved for the trip. As it turned out, I loved roughing it. Collecting sticks for the camp fire, going off on day-long fishing expeditions with Dad. But Lizzy wailed practically every day the whole holiday. She said if this was what holidays consisted of, she never wanted another one as long as she lived. She couldn't comprehend why her classmates sent postcards saying what a lovely time they were having. She swore their parents must have stood over them with a cane and made them write those things.

The following year, Dad was back at work as a clerk for an insurance firm and Octavia had *Hello Dolly* in the offing and they flew us off to Jersey. This time it was luxury all the way. Lizzy was in her element, swanning around the hotel in orange sunglasses and Octavia's lurid kaftans, like a princess, while I got bored out of my brain. There's only so much fun you can have collecting crabs in a bucket. I guess I was built for slumming it. Funny really, how Lizzy and I, born two years apart, turned out like chalk and cheese.

I lie prone on the bench practising the breathing exercises Pash taught me in what seems like another lifetime. Breathe in for a count of seven, hold; then let slowly out for a count of eleven.

The person in the next cell is yelling obscenities and banging his fists against the door, which has a strangely soporific effect on me. It's like the madder he gets, the calmer I feel. How weird is that? It occurs to me that I'm far better at confined spaces than I used to be. If I can manage eight years in a dump like Whytemoor Hall – don't let the fact that it sounds like a ladies finishing college fool you – I figure I can muster the will to see off a few hours here.

Eventually my cell door opens and Osman is standing there with a leggy, olive-skinned, sharp-suited brunette. I pinch the skin on my arm.

She says in a cut-glass accent that would rival Octavia's, 'Harriet Bryher, duty solicitor. I take it you don't have your own?'

'Even if I did, love, consider them sacked. Can I phone a friend?'

'Of course,' she says. 'Who would you like to call?'

'Pashindra Khan.'

'That won't be possible,' Osman says. He turns to Bryher. 'Doctor Khan is a potential witness for the prosecution.'

'Anyone else?' Bryher says.

'My landlady, Enid Bean.'

'Do you have the number?' Osman says.

'She runs a B&B on the edge of town – "Bean My Guest" – yeah, I know it's corny, but you can't hold that against her. She's a smashing lady.'

'I'm sure she must be, if she's a friend of yours,' Osman says. 'Interview room two is available Miss Bryher, if you'd care to show your client the way.'

'Sarky bastard.'

'Ignore it,' she says, ushering me into a side room and motioning at me to sit down. She snaps open her briefcase. 'I'll need to ask you some questions.'

'I'm free tomorrow night. Least I will be if you do your job properly. I prefer Indian to Chinese, but I'm happy to go Dutch. How about you?'

'How about, we dispense with the wisecracks and get down to business,' she says officiously. 'Did you tamper with Doctor Khan's car, with the intention of injuring either Doctor Khan, or Melissa Parris?'

'You don't pull any punches, do you? I haven't been near the bloody car. You won't find my prints on it.'

'Forensics don't appear to have discovered anyone else's prints on it either, unfortunately.'

'Well they'll have to look harder. They've got nothing on me. It's all circumstantial.'

'Tell me about your relationship with Doctor Khan.'

'She was my psychiatrist for a while. When I was in Whytemoor. Group therapy – not one-to-one, unfortunately. When I got out – that's two weeks' ago – I looked her up.'

'Would you say you looked upon Doctor Khan as more of a friend, than a counsellor?'

'Yeah, I did. It's hardly a crime.'

'More than a friend?'

'Well . . .'

'Lovers?'

'She could get in trouble.'

'So could you, if you lie about something important.'

'We slept together once. Then she went cool on me.'

'How did that leave you feeling?'

'Unbearably horny. Listen, babe, the woman's got a tongue stud that can do incredible things for a girl like me. You haven't by any chance – '

'No. Would you say then, that you and Doctor Khan parted on bad terms?'

'We're still friendly, as far as I'm concerned. Unless she says different.'

'Did you know Melissa Parris well?'

'Hardly at all. I met her once in person. We shook hands. Oh – and once she answered Pash's mobile phone – but I didn't speak, because before I could think of what to say, she cut me off.'

'There wasn't any animosity between the two of you? You didn't see her as a rival for Doctor Khan's affections?'

'At first I thought she might be. Then Pash told me I was being silly. She said Mel had a boyfriend – Nat. He'd proposed to her evidently. Hey, maybe they argued. Maybe they weren't as happy as people thought. Perhaps Nat realized he'd been too rash in proposing and wanted out . . .'

She raises her hand. 'Baseless theories are all very well, but I want to get you out of here as soon as possible.'

'I'm all for that. There's a cracking little boozer not half a mile from here.'

'Doctor Khan received a note: *"If I can't have you, no-one will."*' She produces a photocopy and slides it in front of me.

'My writing, I know. But I didn't send it. It's an excerpt from a journal I kept in jail.'

The door opens. 'We're ready to proceed,' Osman says.

'Well I'm not,' Harriet Bryher says firmly. 'The matter of my client's phone call . . .'

'Your, Enid Bean, doesn't appear to be answering her phone.'

'Then keep trying, Sergeant Osman,' she says. 'I'm sure we'd appreciate it.' He pulls the door shut a little too quickly, as if in temper.

'Can I ask you something?'

'Go ahead.'

'Do you ever smile?'

'Only when my bank statement arrives.'

'Incredibly sexy though . . . the sulky look. I bet you look sensational in a dress.'

'Must look one out for my next visit,' she says. 'Client satisfaction is my number one priority. Now, do you have any ideas as to who might have sent the note?'

So I tell her all about my connection with Evil Eva. How she intervened when I was about to get raped in the shower block. About her summoning me to her 'suite' to take afternoon tea with her and me passing up her invitation. How, a short time later, I returned from one of my Samaritan sessions in the chapel to find my cell had been turned over. Barbie Fisher, one of Rowe's henchwomen, standing outside smirking at me as I crossed the landing. My personal possessions gone. My photos. My musings.

'I'm paying a debt, Miss Bryher. Eva Rowe, or one of her head honchos, is keeping tabs on me. Watching my every move. She knows when I sleep, eat, piss. She knows where I am this very second. She's had me set up and there's not a damn thing I can do about it.'

'Let's not be so negative,' she says, dipping into her briefcase and taking out a voice-recorder. 'You've got me on your side for one thing. Congratulations. Smart move. Because, luckily for you, Jesamine Vale, I'm very, very good.'

After two hours of firing questions at me, they let me go. Disappointingly, Miss Bryher declines my invitation to the watering hole round the corner, citing her immense workload as an excuse. At least she understands the wisdom of letting a girl down gently. She shakes my hand firmly and says she'll be in touch. She doesn't smile. For all I know she might be toothless. I don't allow myself to dwell on the prospect.

As she heads towards the underground car park, I'm just on the verge of running after her on the pretext of cadging a lift, when I turn a corner and bump into Leo, closely followed by MOTHER.

'Octavia. Fancy seeing you here. You haven't been cautioned, have you? They didn't nab your dabs instead of an autograph.'

'Hardly a social visit,' she snarls. 'Who do you think stumped up your bail? Expensive business.'

'O Fairy Godmother, I can't thank you enough for granting my wish. I only hope it didn't make too much of a dent in your hedge funds.'

Leo smiles at me. 'Are you all right, Jes?'

'A bit mashed up. A young woman died . . . they think I . . .'

'We know,' he says, patting my shoulder.

Mother seizes my elbow, as if I'm about to take flight. 'You're coming with me young lady. We need to get a few things straightened out. Leo, fetch the car round to the back. Inspector Gilchrist has arranged for us to depart from the rear exit.'

'Ouch.' My rear exit still stings from my encounter with Mack.

She tuts at me. 'You're out of prison not five minutes and already you're causing us trouble.'

'Not me, Octavia. It's Eva Rowe. Evil Eva. She's watching us.'

Mother presses the palm of her hand flat against my forehead. 'You need to see a doctor.'

We get outside just as Leo draws up in the car.

'Got a blanket for my head? Want me to get in the boot?'

'Get a hold of yourself, Jesamine,' Mother barks, as Leo gets out and opens the rear door for me.

'Proper gent, aren't you? Mummy's Husband Number Three in the making.' I get in and worryingly, she climbs in next to me. 'You don't have to act like we're joined at the hip,' I say, scowling. 'I'm not going to abscond.'

'If you do you're on your own. I'll tell you that for nothing. Frankly we have better things to do with our time. And money, for that matter,' she adds, solemnly.

'Ease off her, Octavia,' Leo says. 'Can't you see your daughter's in shock?'

I slap the back of his seat. 'Did I detect a whiff of attitude there, Mr Hendry? You two might just stand a chance.'

We spend the remainder of the fifteen minute journey in silence, apart from Leo whistling off-key occasionally, which is really fucking irritating, but still preferable to having to listen to the Grande Old Dame prattling on about how she's down to her last half million bucks.

As our chauffeur pulls into the gated driveway, I can't resist. 'Aren't we going round the back? I know there's no neighbours for a mile or so, but you can't be too careful. The paparazzi might be camped behind the rhododendrons.'

'Leo, I want you to brief Damien Locke,' Mother instructs. 'We'll get him on the case. His number's in my book.'

'We don't know yet that there's a case to answer,' Leo says. 'They haven't charged Jes with anything.'

'Sorry to spoil the party,' I interject, 'but I've got my own solicitor thanks all the same. That numpty you got me last time, Octavia, was fucking clueless. And frankly, I'd be worried stiff having a prick called 'Damien' represent me.'

'Damien Locke happens to be a first class defence lawyer. Phone him please, Leo.'

I get out of the car and Mother hovers over me like she's marking me in a netball match. She reaches for my arm again.

'Don't touch me, OK. I'll do what you want, but I can't do the tactile stuff – I'm tired.'

'Stop behaving like a petulant teenager,' she chides.

Inside, Mother ushers me through to the open-plan kitchen-diner.

'Nice décor.'

'Leo is extremely talented . . . in many fields,' Mother says, smiling adoringly at him. I can't ever remember her fawning like that around Dad.'

'I'll make that call,' he says, businesslike.

251

'Do what the fuck you like, the pair of you. I know I'd rather be staring at the lovely Harriet Bryher from the dock than some pleb called Damien. You'd like her Leo. She's got the look of a Greek Goddess about her . . . olive skin . . . sultry eyes . . . hair down to her waist. Maybe that's why Octavia would rather you got a man on the job.'

Mother issues me a stern glance. 'Really, dear, you're completely overdoing the *Sisters of Sappho* act now. I was going to make tea. Do you want a beer, or something?'

'Yeah, cheers.' I'm getting to the stage of cynical-ness where I'm immediately suspicious when she offers to do something nice for me.

Mother insists on prattling on all the time Leo is on the phone, so I can't overhear his conversation. Occasionally I glimpse the bottom half of his legs pacing up and down the hall.

Two minutes later he comes back in, looking jolly pleased with himself.

'That was quick,' Mother says. 'Tea?'

'I rather think I'll join Jes in a beer,' he says, opening the fridge door. 'Upshot is, my love, that this Harriet Bryher has more about her than simply being eye candy.'

'What a revolting term,' Mother says.

'That Locke fellow says she's top notch. Acutely bright. One of the most promising young lawyers he's come across in years. Couldn't recommend her highly enough.'

She frowns. 'Very well the pair of you. I know when I being ganged-up on.'

'Unless she's *too* good,' I say. 'We can't get anyone too good on the case, they might get me off.'

'Really,' Mother says, getting up from the table. 'I've never heard such nonsense. I'm going to call Lizzy. She asked to be kept in the loop.' She picks up her cup and saucer and marches into the hall.

Leo smiles. 'Can't have you being unhappy, can we? Do you have Miss Bryher's number? Unless you'd rather . . .'

I pull the crumpled card out of my pocket and hand it to him. 'Can you fix it?'

'My pleasure.'

'Generous of that Damien bloke to be so complimentary. Fancy him passing up work.'

252

Leo gives me a sideways glance. 'I'm afraid he didn't say anything of the sort.' He puts a finger to his lips. 'Ssshh, don't let on.'

'Don't understand.'

'Well he might have said nice things about your Miss Bryher had I given him the chance . . . only . . . I didn't call him. Another beer?'

'Leo Hendry, I could kiss you.'

Mother does her utmost to persuade me to stay the night. If only, I suspect, to protect her investment in me a little longer. Leo offers to drive me to Enid's, but the Grande Old Dame pointedly reminds him he's sunk two beers, so he rings me a cab and bungs me twenty quid.

When I march through the door, Enid is perched in front of the television with the sound on mute.

'I've been worried sick about you,' she says, shakily, getting up and throwing her skinny arms around me. 'Where on earth did you get to?'

So I tell her about getting picked up by the cops and about being interrogated for three hours in the company of the lovely Harriet Bryher and about Leo's blatant act of deception in front of Mother.

'Anyway, don't blame me, I tried to call you. You were my nominated phone-a-friend at the police station. So where were you in my hour of need? Treading raspberries in the courtyard?'

'I was here all day. Washing, ironing. Another guest booked in this afternoon. American. He didn't know what time he was arriving, so I could hardly go out. The phone didn't ring once.'

'Fucking Osman. He'll swing for this.'

She takes hold of my hands. 'Don't stress, love.'

'Just don't offer to make me tea.'

'Brandy,' she says, sitting me down. 'I'll put the water on for a bath.'

I try Pash's phone again. It diverts straight to answerphone. I don't bother leaving a message.

It's like me and her never happened. I can't remember how she looked that night. Can't remember the smell of her scent. The feel of her mouth on my genitals. Her fingers inside me. The unrelenting climax. Nothing. It's all gone. I'm like an empty void.

Enid brings me my drink. I sit clutching the brandy bowl, sipping at it intermittently and rocking my body into a state of exquisite drowsiness.

39

With Harriet Bryher sitting beside me I feel I could conquer the world. Everest, at least, even though on this occasion she's decided not to indulge my slinky dress fantasy and has turned up in a black hunting jacket with a plain white camisole underneath and a flowing grey skirt. Not to mention the black leather boots that hug those firm calves. More than meeting me halfway, I'd say.

Osman appears with dark rings around his sunken eyes like he hasn't had enough sleep.

Large hovers in the doorway. 'Coffee?'

'No thanks,' Bryher says, checking her watch. It's like she's speaking for both of us. I don't bother saying I'd like one.

'Well now,' Osman says, smirking. 'We have received information from a witness who says you were acting in a sexually aggressive manner with Doctor Khan on the fourth of June. The incident in question took place at the Multiplex.'

'What did you do – hold a séance?'

'Is it true?'

'I kissed her on the mouth. If that's classed as sexually aggressive behaviour these days – well. It's not as if I wrestled her to the ground.'

'Did she welcome your kiss? Did she invite it?'

'Ask her.'

'We shall,' Osman says. 'Our witness says you drew blood.'

'Yeah, I'm a vampire by night. *Vale the Vamp*. Not true – about the blood. At least, if I did, it wasn't intentional. That's not how I get my kicks.'

Large says, 'We have reason to believe you knew Melissa Parris would be driving Doctor Khan's motor vehicle that particular morning of the crash.'

'Pash told me she was lending it to Mel. And I said she was an idiot, cos the kid had just passed her test.'

'You told her she was an idiot?'

254

'I didn't say it, I thought it. Because that car has a powerful engine.'

'Clearly you've studied it up close, Miss Vale.'

'Pash has given me a lift once or twice. I know it's a goer.'

'So you were concerned for Melissa's safety?'

'Don't be ridiculous. You're making out I had some connection with this girl I met once for all of two minutes.'

'Did you think Melissa Parris and Doctor Khan were close? A meeting of minds, perhaps. Close enough to engage in a sexual relationship?'

'Pash told me Mel was getting engaged to Nat. That's Nathan by the way, not Natalie or Natasha.'

Osman smirks again. 'And you swallowed that?'

'I trust her. She wouldn't lie to me. Are you saying it's not true?'

'I can see the doubt creeping in.'

'You fucking two-timing dwarf. At least have the sense to take your wedding band off before you start flirting with the likes of WPC Plastic Knockers.'

'Five minutes out, please,' Bryher says, gripping my elbow and anchoring it to the table.

'I don't think we can permit a break so soon,' Osman says.

'DI Large . . .' Bryher says. 'I'd appreciate it.'

'Very well,' Large says, gathering his files. 'Five minutes.'

Osman gives his colleague a sharp look, like Harriet Bryher has got him under her spell, then he turns to me. 'Would you like a glass of water, Miss Vale?'

I shake my head.

The door closes behind them. I get up and pace the floor.

'This is where I get a spanking, right? Want me across your knee?'

'I've dealt with Osman before. He's ambitious. He plays mind games. He makes it his job to get under your skin. He'll be relishing the fact you're such a pushover.'

'Don't you start on me. You're meant to be on my side.' I scuff the wall with my trainer.

'Sit down,' she says firmly.

'I like a woman who takes control.'

'And I like a client who can keep her temper in check. I don't take hotheads into court with me no matter how much they pay me. There are times when it's OK to get emotional – this isn't one of them. When

255

Osman comes back into this room you're going to act so implicitly cool with him, he'll think he's run into an iceberg.'

'Easier said than done.'

'Let me help you out then. What's the one thing men universally fear? Being cursed with a tiny penis. Osman has a penis the size of a hazelnut. He's an insignificant little man with a gigantic ego. Every time he makes eye contact with you from now on, you're going to think of him as DS Hazelnut.'

'DS Hazelnut?'

'But don't you dare think of making any quips about it, OK. This is just between ourselves. It always works for me in court, when some misogynist in a curly wig is doing his best to rile me. And keep your answers short, you don't have to elaborate. You can rely on me to step in if anyone says anything out of order. Just keep your cool, OK?'

'DS Hazelnut. Got it.'

Just as I'm beginning to enjoy Harriet Bryher's company, the pair of them stride back in. Large switches on the tape recorder. 'For the benefit of the tape, DI Large and DS Osman are re-entering the room.'

'I trust you're feeling calmer,' Osman says.

I think of the hazelnut. Small, round, insignificant. 'Much. Thank you.'

He pushes a plastic bag across the table. 'I'm showing Miss Vale item 'C2.' It's the note received by Doctor Khan on the morning of Melissa Parris's accident. It reads: "If I can't have you, no-one else will." You have already admitted that the note originated from you, some years previously. How many years exactly?'

'Three. Four. I can't be exact. It got nicked from my cell.'

'When was this?'

'July. Two years' ago. Eva Rowe had my cell turned over. Anything of value to me got taken. Photos of my kid. A diary of my time inside.'

Osman smirks. 'Fancy ourselves as a female Jeffery Archer, do we?'

'So Eva Rowe stole your things,' Large says. 'Did you report it? Did you tell your PO?'

'Do I seem like I've got a death wish?'

'You were frightened to say anything?'

'I figured it wasn't worth the hassle. *Snitches end up in ditches*. It's one of the first things they tell you when you arrive on the wing. Anyway my PO would of laughed in my face. She was a sadist.'

'Pity. We might have been able to verify your story,' Osman says. 'Why would Eva Rowe be sending your note to Doctor Khan?'

'I snubbed her when we were inside – she wants revenge.'

'So Eva Rowe had Doctor Khan's brakes tampered with, did she?'

'I know it sounds far-fetched.'

'What if I tell you, Eva Rowe is ten thousand miles away. Sunning herself in Brazil.'

'Nobody knows where she is. You don't. The press don't. Anyway, it wouldn't be her doing it, would it, you tosser. Rowe never liked getting her hands grubby.'

'I'm afraid your theory is pie in the sky,' Large says.

'Look at it another way,' Harriet Bryher says. 'Why would my client incriminate herself by sending a threatening note in her own handwriting? It's a pretty dumb thing to do.'

'Not if your client has convinced herself she's being persecuted by Eva Rowe,' Osman says. 'Maybe it's sent her a little . . .' He makes a swirling motion with his finger.

Bryher gives me a stern look, at the same time curling her finger and thumb into an oval shape. It's all I can do not to burst out laughing.

'Something amusing you?' Osman says.

'Just some nutty quip I heard earlier.'

'Can we wrap this up?' Bryher says. 'Unless you have anything else of significance to ask my client.'

'One more thing,' Large says. 'Did Doctor Khan accuse you of acting like a stalker?'

'No.'

'Would she have had a reason to suggest that?'

I shrug. 'You'd have to ask her.'

Osman says, 'We most certainly shall.'

Large reaches for the 'stop' button on the tape recorder. 'Interview terminated at fourteen-twenty.'

Outside, Harriet Bryher dons an expensive-looking mac. As she pulls up the collar it begins to drizzle. She strikes me as the sort of person who's well prepared in advance of everything.

'You look like the detective now' I say. 'Fetching.'

'I'm parked round the corner,' she says, breaking into a jog. 'Come on, I'll give you a lift.'

257

In the next street, she takes out an electronic key fob and points it at a red Alfa Romeo.

'Hop in.'

The smell of new leather hits me as soon as I open the door. Makes a refreshing change from stale smoke. She stashes her bag behind the front seat and pulls the seat belt across her narrow chest.

'Red for passion, eh?' I say hopefully.

'That's what my husband said when he bought it for me.'

Ouch, no. There is no God. I look at her empty fingers. 'Did he buy it instead of a ring?'

'Jewellery brings me out in a rash. Even the expensive stuff.'

It pains me to ask. 'So what does your husband do?'

'He's a lawyer. For a different firm. We met at work, but when it started getting serious one of us had to move, so Claude did.'

'Chivalrous Claude, eh? Is he French?'

She laughs. 'No, he isn't.'

'Gotcha! I was beginning to wonder whether you had a full set of teeth in that pretty head. Aren't you going to ask me?'

'What?'

'Whether I did it?'

'Did you?'

'If you need to ask then . . .'

'Don't keep anything back from me, Jesamine. If there's something I should know, then I'd rather hear it now. I don't like surprises.'

'Except for thirty grand motors.'

'Forty,' she says, with an air of smugness, that reminds me of Melissa.

'I can see how Pash might have thought I was stalking her. I was waiting for her at the house after I snogged her at the bowling alley. I wanted to say sorry for embarrassing her. Melissa was driving that time as well. They didn't see me. I thought they were about to get it on . . . so I left. When I told Pash I'd seen them, she accused me of spying on her. It was a bit of playful banter really. If I did unnerve her, she isn't the type to show it.'

'I wouldn't worry too much about it,' she says as we hit a steady stream of traffic.

'Got any kids?'

'Not yet,' she says.

258

'I've got one. Lola. She's eight. I had to give her up for adoption. Could you help me get her back?'

'Not my bag, I'm afraid. I can put you in touch with someone good though. Someone on a par with me.'

'That good, eh? Does she have legs like yours?'

'I'm not qualified to answer that. You'll have to judge for yourself.'

'Can't wait.'

'His name's Donaldson.'

'Do you want to stop for a drink?'

'Sorry,' she says. 'I don't – drink.'

*

When I get in, Enid is fiddling with the radio tuner.

'Enid, do you think when somebody doesn't touch alcohol, it's because they've had a problem with it?'

'Not necessarily. It doesn't agree with everyone. Me, for instance. I can take it or leave it. It's nice on occasions. A glass of champagne at a wedding reception.'

'We had some right old boozy concoctions at Whytemoor,' I say wistfully. 'Seventy per cent proof.'

'Then you're lucky you've still got some brain cells left.'

'If I get put back inside, will you come and see me?'

'You mustn't think like that.'

'Cos I'll send you the VOs in future, instead of the Grande Old Dame. I wouldn't expect you to come every fortnight.'

'In your room,' she says. 'There's someone to see you.'

I feel the colour drain from my face. 'It's not Mother, is it?'

Enid's face illuminates. 'I think you'll find it's someone a lot more welcome.'

I race to the stairs, like a stampeding elephant, almost tripping on the rug and just managing to save myself on the banister.

When I open the door, she's sitting by the window, like some glorious manifestation. An artist's muse.

'Oh . . . my . . . God . . . I . . . I . . . are you OK?'

She gets up and comes to me.

259

'Just about,' Pash says. She looks like she hasn't slept in days. 'Are the uniforms giving you a hard time?'

'A bit. Mind you, I've got a red-hot brief. Kinky boots, flowing skirts. Straighter than a laser beam, sadly.' Wish I hadn't said that.

She smiles, wearily. 'Glad to hear the trauma isn't wreaking havoc with your libido.'

'Sorry if I'm gabbling. It's because I'm so bloody nervous. I can't believe you're here. I thought I might never see you again. When I heard about the accident, I thought you were . . . you're not wearing a wire, are you?'

She takes off her jacket and throws it at me. 'You think I'd set you up. I thought you thought more of me, Jes.'

'I do. Of course I do. And I feel terrible over Melissa. I wished dreadful things and they happened. I feel wretched. And it's true, I was jealous. Poor kid. Have you seen the family?'

'We were all together at her bedside. When she was on that ghastly contraption. We speak on the phone once a day. I feel incredibly guilty just for breathing. It should have been me that got it.'

'Don't say that.'

'It's true.'

'How do you know?'

'Because you were the only person who knew I wouldn't be using the car that day. And because I'm going out on a limb in making the assumption you had nothing to do with this.'

'Bloody right. You couldn't put in a good word for me with DS Hazelnut.'

'What?'

'Nothing. What about Nathan?'

'Devastated. He and Melissa had a tempestuous relationship.'

'But he'd asked her to marry him.'

'Yes. He begged her. All the time. Sometimes phoned her fifteen times a day. I know what that's like and it's hell to live with. Once I heard him yelling down the phone at her.'

'You're going to tell me he's a mechanic aren't you? Please, God, get me off the hook.'

'He works for his father's removals company. They've been doing a week-long job in Hull. His alibi ties up apparently.'

'Thought so. Just my luck.'

'Mel liked to think of herself as a free agent. She saw other people when Nat was off the scene.' Pash takes hold of my hands. 'And when I told you she was straight, that wasn't strictly true. She boasted of being bisexual as lots of girls her age do. And yes, she did flirt with me sometimes . . .'

'Fuck it, Pash, you lied to me.'

'White lie. Mel and I shared a bit of harmless fun that never went any further. Made us both feel good.'

'You sound like Cameron.'

'It's a drop in the ocean compared to your conquests.'

'And that's why you haven't come near me since that night,' I say accusingly. 'Because I'm a whore. You try being in prison for eight fucking years and not having anyone comfort you.'

'Don't be like this. Not now.' She pulls me against her. I run my hands over the contours of her body. There's less of her than before. She says, 'I don't want to stay away from you, but I can't rationalize things right now. And if whoever it was that tampered with my brakes, meant it to be me lying in the morgue, instead of Melissa, which it is only right and proper to assume, then they won't stop until they finish the job. That's why I'm running scared.'

'I'll look after you,' I say, sliding my hands under her top. That bloody vulnerability thing again. It gets me every time. 'Don't make me resist you, Pash, because I'm helpless.'

We cast off our clothes and dive onto the bed and at first it's as if she's fighting me. We roll over and over, jostling for top position, like two competitors in a naked wrestling contest. Eventually I manage to straddle her. I seize her wrists and pin them above her head. Immediately she stops struggling, like she's been given the signal to submit.

I crush my mouth against her sensuous lips. As my hands cup her breasts she writhes appreciatively beneath me. When I suck her nipples, she groans. She takes my fingers and shoves them between her legs, moving against me harder . . . stronger . . . an unbreakable rhythm. It's all so easy this time. And she's beautiful. More beautiful than ever.

She comes with the half light shadowing her face. She doesn't scream, or cry out, or make any noise at all. I feel her body tighten then release, like a kind of prolonged shudder and then it's over.

She sinks back against the pillow and expels a lavish contented sigh. Then she turns onto her side facing the window, away from me, like a man would do. Like *Him*. Not like *Him*. For one panicky second I think she's about to nod off on me.

'You OK?' I venture, croakily.

'Mmmm,' she says, stretching out, with all the grace of an exotic feline. 'I needed that.' She kisses the top of my head, then settles on her back, with her hands behind her head. She looks like she should be on the front cover of some glamour magazine. Or stapled between the centre pages.

She reaches out and pulls me to her. 'I've missed you so much,' she purrs.

40

At breakfast, Enid brings us coffee and croissants and pastries and a selection of home-made preserves in little pots with hand-written labels.

'This is fantastic,' Pash says. 'Thank you.'

'You're welcome to stay if you want, Doctor Khan,' Enid says. 'We have the room.'

'She's only saying that so you'll take care of her bunions.'

'Jesamine!' Enid chides.

'A most kind offer,' Pash says. 'I might take you up on that, Enid. For now I intend to keep things as normal as possible. It's what the police have advised.'

'It's OK for them to say that,' I say sharply. 'I'll bet they haven't offered you round the clock protection.'

She shrugs. 'We have to get on with things. I'm meant to be back at work this morning. I'll buzz them – say I'm going to be a little late. No I'll send a text. That way I don't have to get drawn into a conversation.' She pulls out her mobile phone, flips the lid and taps away.

'I'll fetch more coffee,' Enid says. She really is the most thoughtful person I've ever come across.

When Pash puts the phone away, I say casually, 'I've had an idea,' as if it's just this second come to me.

'Not Xanthos, *please*.'

'No, I've shelved that. Why don't I move in with you? Just until all this mess is sorted out.'

She reaches across the table and takes my hand, seemingly not caring if the other guests are watching.

'There's nothing I'd like more, Jes.'

'Great.'

'Only, I don't think it's very practical. For one thing I don't think the police will like it.'

'Bugger them. I can protect you. I can be at your side twenty-four-seven. They ought to be grateful, seeing as they're doing sod-all.'

'It's a lovely thought, but also . . . I can't put your life in danger . . . it's not fair on you or your family.'

'But I don't care and my family certainly doesn't care much about me. And anyway,' I say rashly, 'I love you, Pash Khan. Promise me you'll think about it.'

She looks startled. She says, 'I never tell anyone I love them until at least the fourth date. But thank you. And, I'll think about it.'

When she heads off to work, I join Enid in the courtyard. Weeding duty. I've been offering my help for days now without actually getting down to doing anything.

'Choose your weapon,' Enid says, nudging a box of assorted trowels and forks in my direction. 'Not a very tactful choice of words. It's that old, "mustn't mention the war in front of the Germans," thing.'

We giggle. She says, 'I've only got one set of kneelers, but you're welcome to grab a padded seat cover from the shed.'

'I'll be fine,' I say, squatting down and rattling around the box to seek out the most trusty trowel. Or at least, one that doesn't look like the handle's about to drop off.

'We weren't too noisy last night, were we?'

'Well,' Enid says, without looking at me, 'I didn't hear anything untoward. And I haven't had any complaints from your neighbours. Mind you, both the Parsons are a bit on the deaf side. And as for Mrs Franklin . . . she's been known to sleep through an earthquake.'

'Aren't you going to ask how it went?'

'I think you just told me. And what with the pair of you trotting down to breakfast wearing soppy grins and very little else . . . one can only presume . . .' Enid smiles at me. She really is the sweetest-natured person.

'The strange thing is, how Pash gave it up so easily last night, when she hasn't wanted to come near me for days. She was rampant. Horny as hell. I'm sorry, Enid, no-one in their right minds wants to hear about someone else's sex life, do they? Particularly when they're not getting any themselves.'

'Charming,' Enid says, indignantly.

264

'God, me and you – what are we like? We're both so tactless this morning. Must be something in the coffee.' I plough my rusty, rather than trusty, fork between the cobbles and proudly extract a nettle. 'Actually that's not true. What I just said about listening to the details of somebody else's sex life. Men love it, don't they? Cameron's insatiable like that. He goes crazy when I talk about various women's knockers I've encountered.'

'It's that whole imagery thing,' Enid agrees. 'They love to build up a picture. Mr Rhubarb was like that. He invited me to his potting shed once on the pretext of talking propagation. And as for Richard. As a matter of fact I think we might have invented phone sex.'

'Enid!'

'It seemed to me he got more aroused talking to me on the phone, than he ever did when I was actually there in person. All he wanted to do then was read the FT.'

'And then he took up with Chloe from Iceland.'

'Yes. Thanks for reminding me,' she says, cuttingly. We burst out laughing.

'Enid, can I talk to you about last night? Properly, I mean.'

She visibly winces.

'Not graphic detail, nothing like that. I wouldn't do that to you. It's just, well it's really bugging me. It's like Pash was acting. I don't mean the orgasm bit. That was obviously the real deal. If she'd been faking she'd have screamed the place down. That's what most women do, isn't it? That, or lots of pathetic sighing and moaning . . . gets on your nerves.'

'Thank heaven for small mercies,' Enid says, dropping her trowel.

'She was really turning it on. Making out like I was some goddess. I can't say it didn't make me feel amazing at the time. It's only now I come to think . . .'

'You ought to take a long look at yourself, Jes. You don't realize what a splendid catch you are. You're a pretty girl, you're articulate, you're fun to be around. There's a lot of women who'd be chuffed to be with someone like you.'

'Stop that silly talk at once, woman. You're making me blush, Enid Bean. Not on the turn, are you?'

'This has nothing whatsoever to do with my sexuality, young lady, thanks all the same for enquiring.'

265

'It was like everything changed this morning, when I told her I loved her and then I offered to move in with her. It was as if the bubble had suddenly burst. It makes me think she's using me.'

'If you want my advice it would be this, don't pressurize Pashindra into anything. She's had an horrendous agenda to cope with these past few days. I'm not meaning to sound flippant here, but she probably could do with some therapy herself.'

'There's no-one else I could say this to and I know it sounds crazy, but . . . do you think it's possible that if you work around psychopaths long enough, you could develop those sorts of tendencies yourself?'

'Possibly, in exceptional cases. Surely the majority of Doctor Khan's clients are simply ordinary people with exaggerated problems. Plus it's been several years since she was in a hard core environment like the one you're suggesting. And if you think she's been acting a little out of character, then, I'd be inclined to say it is only to be expected, given the circumstances.'

'Enid, you're so together. How'd you get to be so rational?'

'Years of experience, my dear.'

'Another thing, Pash admitted to me that Melissa flirted with her. She said that's all that happened, but what if it went further? What if they were having a full-on affair?'

'Well, if that was the case, so what? They were both single.'

'Melissa was on the verge of getting engaged to some bloke called Nat. That's if he exists at all. What if Mel was blackmailing Pash? What if she'd found out Pash was sleeping with one of her clients and it threatened to end her career. Pash likes to be in control. In everything. What if she bumped off Mel and put me in the frame for it? How easy is that?'

At least she doesn't laugh at me for being a fool. Part of me wishes she had.

'Enid, say something. Your lack of response is making me nervous.'

'Rather extreme suggestion isn't it? I thought you were of the opinion it was Eva Rowe doing this?'

'I was. But then this copper told me she's in bloody Brazil. I don't know what to think. Don't take any notice of me. I talk complete shit most of the time. It's me that's got a bloody persecution complex, Enid. And it's me that needs the bloody therapy.'

Just as I'm beginning to think my back is about to snap in half, Pash phones and offers to buy me lunch. Obviously the woman can't get enough of me.

*

'Hope you didn't mind me suggesting here. It's not that I'm deliberately ploughing money into the family's coffers, it's just that I promised Lizzy I'd help her out for a couple of hours this afternoon.'

Pash smiles. 'Here's as good a place as any. If not better. What do you recommend?'

'Do you like oysters?'

'Of course. Don't you?'

'Willing to try. The oysters here are legendary, so I'm told.'

'Then that's what we'll have.'

When Thomas casually recommends a ninety quid Chablis I look at Pash and giggle. When she nods and says we'll take it I almost slide off my seat and under the table.

'You don't have to impress me,' I say, fanning myself with the menu.

'No?'

'Because you already do. In every way possible. That bloody sommelier bloke must be on commission.'

'Any news? The police?' she says a little anxiously, dipping into her bag and flicking away at some device I assume is her BlackBerry.

I run through my last conversation with Enid in my head.

'Are you OK?' Pash says, giving me a concerned look.

'Yes. Why?'

'Because you just shivered.'

'Did I? I wasn't aware. No. No further developments on the legal front.'

'The car's a write-off,' she says, hugging herself. 'Completely mangled. They showed me a photo. No-one could have walked away.'

'Sorry,' I say automatically. 'You'll be getting another one I suppose.'

'Not for the time being.'

'Oh.'

'I wanted to talk to you, Jes. About us . . .'

Us. At last.

Just as proceedings are starting to get interesting, Thomas trots across with the wine and we have to endure his mini-speech about the region it came from, like we're christening a baby, then we both have to taste it and honestly, I'm on the verge of spitting it at him, when finally he takes the hint and buggers off.

Then Lizzy's new kid on the block, Ginny, arrives and she's really dithery over the order, going through everything twice to make sure it's all correct.

The nanosecond we find ourselves alone, I say urgently, 'About us . . .'

'Nice wine,' Pash says.

'I should fucking think so at that price. It's a wonder my sis isn't swanning around in a gold-plated roller. And I must have a word with her about flaming Oz Clarke over there. You were saying . . . about us . . .'

'Last night was wonderful by the way.'

'But?'

'Why should there be a but?'

'Because you said that about last night with an air of regret.'

'I don't do regrets,' she says, flicking her hair over her shoulder. 'It's just . . . I don't want to hurt you.'

'So you're ending it now. Last night was our last fling – is that it? I'm not good enough for you.'

'Nonsense, of course you are.'

'Then what's wrong?'

'It's not you, it's me. When I'm ready to make a fresh start, then it'll be with someone who values exclusivity in a relationship. I don't get the impression monogamy is your thing, Jes. I feel like I'd be stifling your creativity.'

'My creativity? It's no big deal, Doc. I can do monogamy . . . course I can do monogamy. When I'm fiddling with myself – which is a lot – there's only one woman I'm thinking about.'

She looks as though she might spill her wine. Her eyebrows arch expressively. 'Dare I say I'm flattered.'

'Pash, if we were together, I'd never so much as look at another girl. Trust me on this. I'm telling you, Keira Knightley would be history. D-U-M-P-E-D. It's no good begging me, Keira, love, my mind's made up, so best you get over it soonest. There. Done.'

'There's something else I need to tell you. I'm taking extended leave from the practice.'

'For the honeymoon? I was kind of thinking Mauritius, but I'd settle for the Isle of Wight, as long as it's the Freshwater side. It's more exclusive, isn't it?'

The waitress brings our oysters, setting the platter on the table between us.

'You go first,' I say, chewing my lip and not letting myself acknowledge how disgusting they look.

Pash plucks out a shell, gracefully dispenses the oyster into her mouth and swallows. I'm not at all sure I can do this.

'Go on,' she says. 'Take the plunge.'

'In a minute. Finish what you were saying.'

'I've been offered a job. Setting up a women's refuge. It'll be a brand new challenge. One I hope I'm up to. My bosses seem to think so.'

'Course you will. You'll be terrific. Will we have to move, or . . . because I don't mind – '

'It's in Karachi.'

'Shit. Didn't they have anything in Croydon?'

'Not this time around. What with everything that's happened recently, I think it's probably for the best. Only thing is, they want me to leave as early as Thursday.

'This Thursday?'

'Yeah.'

I snatch up the nearest oyster shell and tip the contents down my throat. I don't manage to make it as far as the loo before it comes back up again.

So she's going. Doing what they all do. Leaving me. It's only to be expected after all, so why didn't I see it coming? Here's me, going on about the fucking honeymoon, while all the time, she's planning her escape.

So then, Jesamine Vale, it's about time you started developing a new life for yourself. Get yourself a Plan B, girl – and pronto – cos Plan A's fucked.

269

41

Leaning against a conifer on the green opposite the vicarage, I'm watching intently – waiting for them to make a move. One of them. Any of them.

A perfect summer's day and I suspect they've got her cooped-up indoors again. This is worse than solitary confinement, because at least in solitary you knew you weren't missing much. Here there are villages and fields and orchards to explore. There are streams and bridges and shops and people to mingle with. Life is for living – especially when you're Lola's age.

After an hour, Reverend Massey emerges with a folder tucked under his arm. He goes to the garage and wheels out a bicycle. He tucks the folder in the rear pannier, straddles the bike and heads off towards the village.

I sidle up to the bell and prod it.

'Miss Vale,' Carolyn says nervously. 'I thought my husband had forgotten something.'

'I've come to see my daughter.'

She reaches for her neck and realizes she's minus the pendant. She doesn't resist as I brush past her.

'Please don't make a noise,' she says anxiously. 'Lorna is sleeping.'

I follow her through to the kitchen. 'I won't even raise my voice. Milk, no sugar,' I whisper.

'What?'

'For the tea.'

She closes the kitchen door. 'You shouldn't have come. If Raymond finds out you've been here . . .' She flips the switch on the kettle.

'Carolyn, sit down. There's really no need to be so jumpy around me. Is it because I've done time?'

'It's because I don't trust you.'

'Charming.'

'You want Lorna back, at all costs. Doesn't matter how many lives you ruin, including our little girl's. Raymond's gone to the village to see a solicitor. He won't be away long.'

'Are you frightened of him?'

'No. You've got this all wrong.'

'Can I see my daughter? Just let me see her. Five minutes, then I'll go.'

'I can't do that.'

'It must be really important being a vicar in a place like this. So many people rely on you – turn to you in their hour of need. And in that role you'd have to be seen to be a paragon of virtue. Above reproach.'

'Miss Vale . . .'

'Jes, please.'

'Honestly, you'll be the loser in all this, if you start something.'

'Let me see her.'

'I told you, she's asleep. Why are you hell bent on causing all this destruction?'

'Let me take her out for half an hour. Please. At a time to suit you. Just say the word. I promise I'll take care of her.'

'If I let you take Lorna out, it means you're asking me to go behind my husband's back. We've never had any secrets in our marriage. And you do realize you'd be asking Lorna to lie as well.'

'I just want to see her. You can understand that surely. It's a mother's instinct to want to be close to her child.'

'I'd convinced myself you wouldn't come looking. Didn't think you'd have the nerve somehow.'

'There wasn't a day went by when I didn't think about her.'

She looks at me with contempt. 'So you expected to waltz in here after all this time, pick up the reins and carry on like nothing's happened? Well I'm sorry . . . it doesn't work like that.'

'If you don't let me see her, I'll get my own solicitor on the case and we'll see you in court.'

She looks as if she might burst into tears.

'Carolyn, why do you wear that pendant?'

'Ten years ago, I was attacked on my doorstep in broad daylight. Assaulted. I wasn't raped. I screamed and a passer by stopped. The man ran off. I was lucky. After that I couldn't leave the house. For two years I didn't set foot outside.'

271

'How did you get better?'

'Time. Raymond was so patient with me. He used to walk me round the block, counting the trees and lamp posts to see if I'd made any progress.'

'Did they catch the bloke?'

'Not that I know of. I didn't report it.' She shrugs her shoulders, dismissively. 'Lorna's got a dental appointment at nine tomorrow. Be at the bridge at ten-fifteen. You can see her for half an hour. No more.'

I move to hug her. She turns her back on me, gets up and opens the kitchen door. I don't dare push my luck over the tea.

*

'Lizzy, if I share something with you, do you think you could bring it upon yourself not to enlighten Mother?'

'Not if you don't want me to.'

'I've traced Lola. I knew all the time she was around here, then one of Enid's contacts gave us a lead.'

Her mouth gapes.

'I've been to the Masseys . . . for tea. You do know them?'

'Yes,' she says.

'And Carolyn's letting me see Lola tomorrow for half an hour.'

'Oh Jes, do you think it's wise?'

'I'd be mad to pass up the opportunity. Besides, Pash is going back to Pakistan. She's got a job in a women's refuge.'

'I'm sorry,' Lizzy says. 'I thought it was going so well for you.'

'So did I, Sis. So did I.'

'We're nipping off for a while too. LA. Saturday. I'm sure you're not surprised. Mummy's managed to pull a few strings. Cam's got a couple of movies in the offing – not definite – but hopeful. Definitely hopeful.'

'Bravo, Mummy! What with Pash in Karachi and you in Hollywood, I'm going to need something to occupy me. All it needs now is for Enid's Mr Rhubarb to scoot back onto the scene, hoe in hand and pledge his undying love and I might as well be back in Solitary.'

'Jes, it's only three weeks. As for, "something to occupy you," you can't talk about Lola like she's some school project.'

'You know I didn't mean it like that.'

'Besides, Mother's only a short flight away.'

'That's what scares me the most.'

*

I've treated myself to a Fairtrade T-shirt in organic cotton. I mean bought, not pilfered. Really I wanted the dusky blue one, but I've opted for black, because past experience has taught me it doesn't show the sweat marks nearly as readily.

I stand on the bridge, arms folded, mouth dry as a budgie's cage. What can we do in half an hour? Sod-all really, but I keep telling myself I mustn't be so bloody ungrateful. Carolyn's risking her neck for me. Her marriage anyway. Think I'll take Lola to the teashop in the village. Treat her to a cake. Or scones and clotted cream. I could murder that myself.

I check my watch again. They're five minutes late. Perhaps she's had to have a filling. Maybe her mouth will be numb and she won't be able to eat cake. I'll buy her one for later. I wonder if her dentist is anything like Anika Horst, and if so, whether she is taking on new NHS patients.

They're coming at me from all the points of the compass – four of them this time – including Large and Osman. It's suddenly become a crime to take your daughter out for a cream tea. Nothing would surprise me.

'You can hardly blame me if I develop a prosecution complex,' I say, making the sign of the cross at them as they close in on me.

'Persecution,' Osman says, grinning.

'I know what I mean. You're trying to pin something on me. Anything.'

'Jesamine Vale,' Osman says. 'I'm arresting you on suspicion of conspiracy to abduct a minor. Get her in the car.'

At the nick, they take my snapshot, record my fingerprints and a woman with a crew cut swabs my mouth with a cotton bud. Then she – at least I'm assuming it's a she – tells me to take my clothes off. I tell her she's not my type, but I do it anyway. I've never been one to begrudge anybody a cheap thrill. Besides, no point in not doing as you're told because you've got zilch chance of getting out otherwise.

273

I don't take my eyes off her as she picks over my stuff. How easy would it be for them to plant something on me. Dead easy. Call me cynical.

When I'm dressed again, they whisk me off to an interview room. A different one from before, yet the interior is strikingly similar, as you would expect.

The man already sitting there introduces himself as David Wallace, a colleague of Harriet Bryher's. He tells me she is in court this morning, but he will "*bring her up to speed,*" on her return.

'Well now,' Osman says. 'Do you know why you're here?'

'Not the foggiest. But it can't be that serious because you haven't switched the tape on. Brushing up on our speedwriting skills, are we?'

'A little bird tells us you had plans to abduct a young girl called Lorna Massey.'

'Crap. I had an arrangement . . . with Carolyn Massey. I was going to spend some time with Lorna – half an hour, that's all. Her husband must have found out about it. Maybe Carolyn panicked and made something up. I don't know. I've been set up.'

'Again. This is becoming something of a habit. Are we still looking for Eva Rowe on this one?'

I glance at Wallace. 'Aren't you going to say something? He's being flippant.'

'Because she's a long way from here,' Osman says, breaking into his trademark smirk. He really is the most irritating bastard I've come across in a long while.

'If you'd done your homework on Rowe, you'd know she never liked getting her hands dirty. Check out Barbie Fisher. She was one of Rowe's most trusted accomplices. See, I'm doing your job for you.'

Osman's brow creases.

I grin at him. 'Ever considered Botox?'

An officer in a pristine uniform enters the room. 'DI Gregan,' he says, vaguely in my direction and sits down.

'Let me speak to Carolyn Massey,' I plead with Osman. 'Let me call her. This is just a stupid misunderstanding.'

'No.'

Gregan glances at his notes. 'Miss Vale, have you ever mentioned anything to anyone about snatching a child and taking her abroad?'

274

'Oh my God, Pash. Is she here?'

Gregan looks blankly at me.

'Sir, she's referring to Doctor Pashindra Khan – a psychiatrist,' Osman says.

'OK, so she's dobbed me in, but I wasn't being serious.'

'What's that?' Gregan says, as my phone goes off.

'It's my mobile.'

'She's not supposed to have that back until she leaves,' Gregan reprimands.

I press the button.

```
Can your daughter
come out and play?
```

There's a photo of the vicarage. Blurred. Like the person who took the picture was moving at speed. Before I can show them, another text comes through.

```
Let's knock and see
shall we . . .
```

I slide the phone across the table. 'Get a trace on it,' Gregan says.

'Never mind that, we don't have time.' I jump up from the table. 'What are you waiting for?'

'Sit down, Jesamine,' Gregan says.

'What about Lola? Lorna?'

'We despatched someone to the vicarage as soon as we got word of a possible abduction,' Gregan says. 'Your daughter is quite safe.'

I sink back down again. A WPC enters the room and Osman gives her my phone. Without making eye contact, he says, 'Run a check on where the last text was sent from, would you.'

This one's the complete opposite of what Osman would go for. No make up, no outstanding features to speak of. WPC Plain. Not worthy of eye contact from the would-be superstud that is DS Hazelnut.

The silly little ring tone starts up again. We all peer at the dial in silence. It's as if everyone in the room is holding their breath at the same time.

```
You should have
done what I wanted
when I asked nicely
```

'Give it to me,' I say, holding my hand out. 'I want to reply.'

Gregan nods. 'Ask her what she wants. We're assuming it's a woman.'

```
What do you want,
Eva?
```

```
Not Eva.
Try again.
Three guesses.
```

```
That you Barb?
```

```
Not even warm.
Don't have time
for games.
You don't have
time for guesses.
```

There's a photo of Lola sucking a lollipop, strapped into the rear seat of what looks like a station wagon.

```
Looks happy,
doesn't she?
For how long . . .?
```

'I thought you said she was safe. Is that what you call fucking safe? One of Rowe's henchwomen has got her.'

'If you don't calm down,' Gregan says, 'you can wait in a cell.'

I turn to Wallace. 'How am I meant to keep calm, when these imbeciles have let my daughter get snatched by some paedophile? Has someone turned your fucking sound onto mute?'

'This isn't helping,' Wallace says, patting an invisible dog with the flat of his hand, the way people do when they're trying to quieten a situation.

```
Would Lola like
to be in a movie?
She's very
photogenic . . .
like her mother
ha ha ha . . .
```

'What does that mean?' Gregan says.
'How do I know? I'm not the one with the stripes.'
'Have you had any photographs taken recently?'
'Yeah, here, fifteen minutes ago. For fuck's sake . . .'
'Apart from that.'
'No, I haven't.'

```
Maybe an X
cert . . .
like mother,
like daughter,
eh Jes?
```

Before they take my phone away to get it analyzed I call Pash, but she doesn't answer so I leave a message telling her to call me urgently.

'That's who you want to get on the case – Doctor Khan – she's brilliant at reading people. Profiling and all that stuff.'

'Well maybe we will,' Gregan says, 'If she decides to answer her phone.'

Sarcasm is clearly a prerequisite to getting ahead in today's police force.

WPC Plain returns with my phone.

'You've had another message,' she says handing it to me.'

```
Bit of a crisis
will explain
later
P x
```

'It's from Pash.' I show Gregan. 'She's very understated. She plays things down.'

'So it should read, she's in the middle of a war zone.'

'Very good. You're catching on.'

'How did the trace go, WPC Bender?' Gregan says.

I blurt out, 'You've got to be kidding me.' The woman's plain cheeks flush crimson.

She says, 'We've managed to establish that the texts were made in the region of Snowdonia.'

'Snowdonia? I don't know anyone in Snowdonia.'

'Evidently you do,' Osman says.

Bender says, 'Interestingly, this last text, which was sent from a different phone, was made from roughly the same area.'

'What are you idiots telling me? That it's Pash Khan doing this?'

Gregan says, 'It may be a coincidence. Ring her.'

'Why? What would I say?'

'Just say you're in a bit of a state. Tell her about the texts. Tell her you're worried. Don't say you're here.'

'OK.' I punch the number in from memory. I have to stand up because my heart's beating so ferociously in my throat I fear I am about to suffocate.

'What is it?' she says curtly.

'Pash, it's me.'

'Yes, I know. What do you want?'

'Where are you?'

'Busy,' she says. 'I'm in the middle of something.' For once she sounds flustered.

'Only I've had these weird texts sent to my phone. About Lola . . .'

'Can't talk now,' she says, a little breathlessly.

'Pash, what the fuck's going on?'

She says something inaudible then her voice breaks up. I just catch the end part, before the line goes dead.

'What did she say?' Gregan says.

'I didn't catch it all,' I say shakily. 'But her last words were: "don't involve the police."'

'Rather too late for that,' Osman says.

278

42

Everything happens in a blur. They put me a car, whisk me out to an airfield and stick me in a helicopter, sandwiched between two burly male officers wearing full body armour, which is something of a cramped experience to say the least.

I'm thinking I must have suddenly become invisible, because whenever I try to ask anything, they both ignore me. Or maybe it's because it's so bloody noisy in here they can't hear me. It occurs to me, this could be a scene out of the now defunct Leith's Country, if only I could trade the burly hunks for a couple of – as Pash put it – scantily-clad women.

Pash wouldn't hurt me. Or Lola. Why would she? My vision is starting to get impaired with little crystal stars like I'm about to get a migraine. Don't suppose either of my minders has a spare Anadin in their Taser pouch.

After twenty minutes in the air, one of them answers a radio call and relays something inaudible to my ears to the pilot. The helicopter starts to circle. Below us I can a castle. Lots of people in pretty clothes. As we descend, my eyes focus on a woman in a flowing white dress. We're about to gatecrash a bloody wedding.

'Sick bag,' I say aloud to myself.

'Sit tight,' the one on my left says. 'Coming in now.' So, it speaks. I screw my eyes shut. When I open them again we're on the ground. The twin burlies help me out onto the grass. I spit out the sick just risen from my throat.

'Where are we?' I croak, a little disorientated.

'Anglesey. Your little girl was taken from her adoptive mother by a woman who showed them police ID. She told them the authorities had reason to believe the child was in imminent danger and that she had arranged for her to be taken to a safe house.'

'The woman was posing as a police officer?'

'She *is* a police officer.'

We walk towards the bridge. Beyond the police cordon I can see Pash, her hair flowing in the breeze, her arms outstretched like a sleepwalker. I manage to give my minders the slip, when they stop to chat to a commander, by diverting into the middle of the rapidly gathering crowd. As I get nearer to the bridge, my old feelings of vertigo resurface. Maybe they never really left me. I just buried them under a mass of other emotional stuff.

Now I can see them . . . Pash . . . and . . . Lola . . . and . . . Strychnine. A policewoman stops me at the cordon, so I tell her I am Doctor Khan's colleague and to my amazement she lifts the tape.

I've got this awful sickening thud in my gut like some heavyweight's punched me, but I force myself to go onto the bridge anyway. Pash is saying in that low, measured voice, that never seems to change no matter how stressful the situation, 'Let the girl go, Gerry. We can talk. Just the two of us. Just us. Nobody else.'

As I draw parallel, Pash senses my presence. She puts her hand on my arm. 'Remain perfectly calm, or back off now.'

Strychnine walks Lola to the barrier. Pash tightens her grip on me, but her voice stays even.

'Tell me what this is about.'

'It's about respect. You don't respect me anymore.'

'Yes I do,' Pash says, gently.

'Else you wouldn't go flaunting her in front of me.'

'Shall I send her away?'

'No. I want her here. I want you to know what it's like to feel pain, Jesamine,' Strychnine says. 'Intense pain. Like giving birth,' she cackles, coldly. 'What a riotous occasion that was. Pashindra, you had better keep a hold of your new girlfriend, because she might not like what's coming next.'

Pash squeezes my fingers. 'For Lola's sake, keep it together, OK.'

'I want her to suffer, the way she's made me suffer,' Strychnine says, her voice shaking. 'I saw you.'

'What do you mean?' Pash says.

'You know full well, you pair of conniving bitches.'

Lola's little face is fixed – like she's too scared to move. Too scared to cry out. Hovering on this vertiginous monstrosity, where many others have found beauty, I feel almost overwhelming bouts of dread and panic in equal measure. My mouth is so dry I can't utter one word of encouragement, or pleading, or condemnation towards Geraldine Strickland.

'I'll tell you what is going to happen,' Pash says, as matter-of-factly as if she is a tourist guide discussing the itinerary for some city visit. 'You're going to release the child. Allow her to walk to safety. I will come to you and we can talk. For as long as you want.'

'Think you can still control me, do you?' Strychnine says flatly. Then a little more animatedly, 'Well I'm damn sure you won't. I'll tell you what is going to happen if you take one step closer to us either of you. One more step . . . and we're gone . . .' she makes a plunging motion with her arm. Lola screams.

Pash slides her arms around my waist. 'Perfectly still,' she says in almost a whisper. 'Gerry, I'm here for you. I'll do whatever you want. Get you whatever you need. Talk to me.'

Lola starts to struggle. 'Keep still you brat,' Strychnine says.

'Stay calm, Gerry, it's OK.'

For a second, Lola appears to wriggle free. I break to get her. Strychnine lunges at her and misses. She climbs over the safety barrier. 'Talking's done.' She leans off the side and releases her grip. She lets out a squeal as she plummets. There's an almighty splash.

It's uncanny how the defining events in your life happen as if in slow motion. Pash casts off her coat. It's as if I have all the time in the world to stop her, yet I don't have any time at all. She steps out of her shoes – kisses my mouth. 'I love you, Jes.' Then she plunges into the water. I lurch towards the edge, then haul myself back just as quickly. My mind won't allow me to go any further.

'She said we were going puffin-watching,' Lola says, burying her face against me and crying softly. I bend down and gather her up in my arms. 'It's OK, darling, Mummy's here.' Finally, I get to say it.

Paramedics and police gather round us in a frenzy of activity. Lola clings to my hand. Someone steadies my elbow from the other side. They escort us off the bridge, to an ambulance where Ray and Carolyn are waiting.

'Thank God,' Carolyn says, sniffing into a paper tissue. She throws her arms around Lola. 'Lorna . . . my baby. You're safe.'

281

A paramedic says, 'We'll take her to hospital, get her checked out.' He turns to me. 'You too, Miss.'

I shake my head. 'I'm not going anywhere.'

Reverend Massey turns to me. 'I can't thank you enough,' he says, trying to shake my hand. 'As a gesture of our appreciation for what you did, Carolyn and I would like to extend an invitation for you to take Lorna out sometime. Whenever you wish.'

I can't say anything to them. I open my mouth, but no words come. I find myself hurtling towards the riverbank. There's all manner of emergency workers: police, paramedics, fire crew. A rubber dinghy with some frogmen, who don't appear to be doing anything much except gazing into the murky water.

Further out a wet-suited head bobs out of the water. An arm goes up. They're pulling someone out. Please let it her. Please. Please. I jog alongside the river, as the men in the water edge closer to the dinghy.

The first thing I see is the flattened red mass of her curls. Bastard. The rescuers bypass the dinghy and propel her straight towards the bank, where she is helped ashore by at least six people. Her sodden clothes cling to her. As they drape a blanket around her shoulders, she makes eye contact with me.

The dinghy is being brought in – a body slumped carelessly across it. Emergency personnel wade into the water carrying a stretcher and slide her on to it, before bringing it ashore. The person doesn't look like Pash. It resembles a blow-up doll that's had some of the air sucked out of it. Flimsy. Lifeless. My head feels like it's about to explode. I want to scream.

Strychnine shakes her head at me. 'This is all your fault. We would have made it work. Why couldn't you have stayed away?'

Two policewomen escort Strychnine to an ambulance, while the medics lay Pash on a groundsheet and erect a makeshift screen around her – the sort of thing they use at racecourses when a thoroughbred has broken its leg and they have to shoot it. Through the canvas I see them roll her onto her side. There's a lot of nodding and whispering, but not much action.

'Do something!' I yell into the mass of bodies.

Some male voice booms, 'Get her away, somebody.'

My mind goes back to *that* night. The first night we made love. *"If I drown . . . what a way to go."* What made me say that? Careless words, issued

282

without a thought for their real meaning. *"Honey, I don't care if we sit in quicksand as long as it's together."*

If only this had been a movie instead of real life. My heart hurts so much I can't even cry. I fall on my knees, facing the opposite direction from them so I don't have to see. Eyes tightly shut, I clasp my hands together. 'Please God, do something for her. Pash doesn't deserve this. She's a nice person. Caring. Compassionate. She saves people. She's not selfish like me. I don't give a shit if she goes to Karachi. I don't care if she's on the other side of this world as long as she's still in it.

'Please do something. Please God . . . I'm begging you . . . please . . . please . . . I'll never ask for anything else . . .' My fists thump the ground in desperation. 'Please . . .'

Behind me, there's a polite ripple of applause. A gurgling sound. The expunging of water from Pash's gullet. I turn to see. She's writhing around on the groundsheet coughing and spluttering. A male medic is kneeling beside her, plucking debris out of her hair.

'Oh God, thank you, thank you.'

I stumble to my feet. It feels as if I've aged sixty years in as many minutes. As well as having a hatchet embedded in my forehead.

At the makeshift barrier, an officer stops me. 'Stay back please, Madam. Are you a relative?'

I feel like saying, "Er, excuse me? Look at her – look at me, you idiot." That's what bloody political correctness does for you. I start to laugh, harder and harder, until my ribs throb.

Eventually the tears overwhelm me. I crouch on the ground, hardly daring to look as they fold away the screen. Pash is sitting up now. She sees me and extends a thumb, as some kind of belated reassurance.

I'm that bloody furious with her, if it weren't for the fact that the medics are over there now, fastening a surgical collar to her slender neck, I'd have whipped across there myself, picked her up by the throat and shaken her to within an inch of her life.

I get up and wander around in small circles in a daze until some female paramedic comes to me. 'Are you OK, my love?' she says, putting her arm round my shoulder. 'It's the shock, is it?'

I nod at Pash. 'She's my girlfriend,' I say. 'My other half. My better half.' That's for sure.

'They're taking her to the hospital now. She's a very lucky lady to survive an ordeal like that. Would you like me to pass on a message to her?'

'Yeah,' I say, through the tears streaming down my face, 'just tell her, Keira's cool about us. She'll know what I mean. And . . . can you give me something for a headache?'

The next thing I know, Lizzy and Cameron are coming towards me.

'Got a ride in a police copter,' Cameron says. 'What a buzz. Out of this world.'

'What's going on?' Lizzy shouts at me, trying to jog through the mud and getting her heels stuck in the ground. Fancy turning up in bloody heels.

'This crazy woman – Geraldine Strickland – she used to be a prison officer, now she's a police inspector – she kidnapped Lola, but Lola got away. Strychnine jumped off the bridge and Pash went in after her. She's Pash's ex-girlfriend.'

'Bloody hell,' Lizzy says, brushing grass off her shoe, 'you couldn't make it up.'

Cameron puts his arm round me. 'My God, are you OK, darlin'?'

Three star-struck firemen and a male nurse come charging across to get Cameron's autograph – for their girlfriends, they insist. Ha ha.

'Let's get out of this mayhem,' Lizzy says. 'Before Cam gets mobbed.'

'Really, it's no problem,' Cameron says.

Lizzy gives him the filthiest glare. I take hold of her arm. 'I need to go to the hospital. Pash is there. I need to be with her.'

When we get to A&E, we hang around for half an hour, only for the Staff Nurse to inform us Pash discharged herself an hour ago, they think. Think? Don't they know?

Cameron is all for seeking out his police chums and bagging another jaunt in their flying toy, but after I manage to convince him I'm likely to throw up before we've even left the ground, he relents and we manage to bribe a kindly taxi driver to drive us the two hundred miles home for the princely sum of four hundred quid.

Three and a half hours later, I totter up to the door of Bean My Guest, where Enid greets me with open arms . . . and an obscenely large brandy.

When we switch on the TV, the incident is the highlight of the local news channel, with Geraldine Strickland emerging as some kind of anti-

284

hero, which I don't bloody understand at all. Then I have to witness Mother, in all her finery, being beamed live from ruddy Sark, cooing to the interviewer how "abundantly proud" she is of her youngest daughter.

Enid tells me it's lovely.

I go to the loo and make myself puke.

43

I've never considered crutches to be a particularly sexy look, but hey, against the odds, she's managed to pull it off yet again. There really is no need to remind me, I'm a sucker for a vulnerable woman.

'Blasted knee's busted,' Pash says. 'They want me to have an op, but we'll see. I've just opened some wine. Come through.'

I trail her into the living room, which is a complete and utter mess. Papers everywhere.

'I went to the hospital. So why did you discharge yourself?'

'I'm allergic. Hospitals bring me out in a fever,' she says, lowering herself onto her recliner and handing me her crutches to park.

'But you're a doctor.'

'So, I'm more educated than most. This is where I get to order you about. Could you fetch the wine from the kitchen?'

'Yes ma'am. I can see you're going to make the most of this.'

On the cork clipboard fixed to the kitchen wall, there's a prescription for some painkillers and a hastily scribbled note that says: 'Visiting: 14.00-16.30.' Pash's handwriting. I pour two glasses of Chablis and take them through, with the bottle wedged under my arm.

'Hell of a day,' she says, running her hands through her hair.

'Isn't that the bloody understatement of the year. When did you know it was Strychnine doing this?'

'I had a hunch a little while ago. Wouldn't let myself acknowledge it. She's been odd with me lately, when we've spoken on the phone.'

'So, when I called you today . . .'

'I was in the middle of a paper chase. She was sending me cryptic messages, like she used to when we went on dates. I told you, didn't I? I was kind of hoping I could calm her down before she did anything rash. If I thought for a second she was going to take your kid . . .'

'She must have used police resources to trace her.'

'I guess.'

I perch on the footstool beside her feet. 'Can I come to Karachi with you?'

'Serious?'

'Yep.'

'What about Lola?'

'She doesn't need me fucking up her life. Hardly a suitable role model, am I?'

'I beg to differ. You did well . . . on the bridge.'

'Don't. Just thinking about it makes me shudder. I never want to see that place again as long as I live. Unless it's to see the puffins.'

'I still think there's a place in Lola's life for you.'

'So do the Masseys evidently. They said I can take her out by myself. How's that for a result?'

'Well then.'

'Whether Lola needs me or not,' I take a deep breath, 'I need you.'

She leans back in her chair. 'It's not that I don't want you along, Jes, don't think that. But I can't see your probation officer sanctioning it.'

'Sod him.'

'Unfortunately we need him on side.'

'That note on the board outside – visiting times – is that for her?' I say accusingly. 'The fragrant Gerry?'

'Yes.'

'She abducted my daughter, Pash. She could have killed Lola – and you for that matter.'

'But she didn't. She saved my life, Jes. She pulled me out of the river when I was going under – got me to the raft. Without her I wouldn't be here enjoying a glass of exceptionally classy Chablis – with you.' She sticks her tongue out at me.

'It's gone.'

'Yeah. They removed it when they were trying to get me to breathe properly. Somehow I don't think I'll miss it.'

I get up. 'You were fucking mental going in after Geraldine like that. She could have drowned you both. Personally, I'd rather have you as a living, breathing coward, than a dead hero. You *do* realize you could've ended up paralysed. Or a vegetable.'

'We know from studies involving this type of suicide,' Pash says in that bloody irritating lilt, 'of the people who survive, eighty per cent of

287

jumpers regret doing it the moment they leave the bridge. I took a calculated risk. Gerry knows I'm not a strong swimmer, whereas she is. She used to swim for the Kent county. She could probably have swum the channel if she'd put her mind to it. I figured if I got into trouble . . .'

My fist thumps the wall. 'You and your fucking warped theories. What kind of a fucking idiot relies on a suicide jumper to save them from drowning? You need your head, examining, Doc.'

'You wouldn't be the first person to say that. Like I say, I've always erred on the side of radical. Anyway, if she'd really wanted to kill herself, she'd have chosen Britannia. Or Clifton. It was one of our haunts back in the early days. People don't come back from that one.'

'Honestly, you think she was that rational?'

'Rational and organized. Geraldine always planned everything with military precision.' She laughs, 'including our dates.'

I rub my head. 'The second you'd gone over the edge I knew I should have stopped you.'

'Your first priority is your daughter. I understand.'

'I was scared, Pash. I froze up there. You've got more balls than me. Both of you. Really I hate to admit that about *her*.'

'Geraldine's not a bad person. She should have got help after that hostage episode in the bank. That was the catalyst. She bottles things up until they get too big for her, then she's too proud to admit she can't cope.'

'She killed someone, Pash. She murdered Melissa.'

'And you killed someone. The only difference was, as far as I am aware, you were well at the time.'

'And you're still bloody sticking up for her. I was telling God what an exceptional person you are, but I never thought you'd be like this. I can't fucking handle it.'

'It turns out, she and Melissa were having secret trysts. Mel wasn't interested in Gerry like that, only for what she could get out of it. She was something of a tease. Gerry wanted to break off their arrangement – she reckoned she could still get back with me. Mel realized she had her exactly where she wanted her and tried to extort money from her. Gerry knows how much store I place on fidelity. She knew if Mel told me they'd slept together, there would have been no chance. The sad truth is, there would have been no chance, either way. What a terrible waste of a young life.'

'But how did Geraldine know about the car?'

'Now this I find really quite perverse. After we got burgled a year ago, Gerry arranged for security cameras to be fitted in every room in the house. She thought it would give me peace of mind whenever she was away. She went away a lot – police training.

'What I hadn't realized until the investigators told me, was that, far from focusing on intruders, the cameras were monitoring my every move – what's more she could view the content of the recordings remotely. At any time, wherever she happened to be, she could tune in to her laptop and find out what was happening in our living room, bathroom and . . . I'm afraid . . . the bedroom.

'She wanted to know if anything was going on behind her back. If I was bringing anyone home.'

'You mean, she saw us? That night?'

'It makes my toes curl thinking about it.'

'So when you were . . . doing that to me . . . oh shit.'

'And worse still, she could hear everything.'

'Double shit. No wonder she was boiling mad.'

'And the night Melissa came to my room and sat on my bed, intent on seducing me.' She raises her hand. 'Stop right there – she didn't get anywhere with me. The only thing she got was the keys to my car. Geraldine would have heard me agreeing to lend it to her the next day. Seen her taking the keys from my jacket pocket. And something in her snapped.

'Right then and there she decided to put a stop to it. Gerry convinced herself it was the solution to her problems . . . dispose of Melissa . . . and get you out off the scene at the same time. And it almost worked.'

'Here's me thinking all along it was Eva Rowe getting to me and it was bloody Strychnine all along. She had my cell ransacked. She took my things. She had poor Tess sent down the block. If it wasn't for her, Tess would still be alive. I'd have made damn certain of it.'

'I'm sorry,' Pash says. 'For your loss.'

'So what happens now?'

'I suggest more wine.' She waves the empty glass at me.

'I meant, about us.'

'Are you free tomorrow?'

'Darlin', I'm free forever – for you.'

'Excellent. Because there's something I want us to do.'

44

'What happened to the fashion accessories?'

'I sent them back. Grey is *so* not my colour.'

'Want me to drive?'

'It's an automatic. I can manage. I've hired it for a couple of days.'

'Still don't trust my driving, huh? Don't believe everything that twisted sister of mine spouts. She's prone to exaggeration.'

'It's not that,' she says. 'It's just, I would prefer us both to arrive in a tranquil frame of mind.'

'Sounds interesting. Tell me more.'

'We're going to see a house that's up for sale.' She takes an envelope from her bag and rattles it. 'I have the keys.'

'But . . . you already have a house. And besides, you're going away.'

'True. Sit back and relax, we'll be there in no time.'

'You're not serious, Pash. I'm not bloody going in there. It might be haunted.'

'Don't be silly. Come on.' She clutches my arm. 'Nothing's worked so far. You want to know, don't you?'

'If I agree . . . which, frankly, I'm not at all convinced about . . . what's going to happen?'

'We'll go through to the back garden, I'll hypnotize you, then we'll go inside.'

'What if I freak out?'

'You won't. If you do, we'll deal with it.' She opens the door. 'There's a picnic rug in the boot. Can you fetch it please.' She drops the car keys into my hand. 'And lock up after you.'

She hobbles to the back gate and undoes the latch. When I get there the walled garden is overgrown. Unkempt. Not like when prissy Lizzy had it, though the wilderness gives it a certain charm.

'Pick your spot,' Pash says. 'The rug is doubling as my couch for the afternoon.'

'I'm really not sure.'

She takes hold of my hand. 'We're here now. We're going to lay this down wherever you choose and I'm going to do some subliminal relaxation on you. Then we'll go to the front of the house and we're going to walk through it together exactly the way you did on that day. We're going to find out exactly what happened.'

'What if nothing comes?'

'We still have a few days. No pressure. If necessary I'll put a deposit on the place.'

'You'd do that for me? Really?' I think she was kidding. 'Here then.'

She rolls the rug out. I kick off my shoes. She tries to sit cross-legged on the grass, but her damaged leg refuses to comply, so she stretches it out in front of her.

'Get comfy.'

I lay on the rug, beneath the gaze of a pleasantly warm sun. She gives me one of those eye masks – the sort they give you on long-haul flights.

'What do you want me to do?'

'Nothing. Just relax.'

I pull the mask over my eyes and she begins talking me through the 'beach' scenario. All there is in this beautiful remote world, is my breathing . . . and her voice . . . soft and mellow. Time has stood still.

My body feels still . . . my limbs light . . . tingly sensations dancing around my tummy . . . like I am floating on the tender breeze . . . drifting away into nothingness.

After a while, I can't say how long, she eases the mask off me and I stand up. She takes hold of my arm. We walk towards the house.

'Tell me what you see. What you hear.'

'I'm being drawn to the conservatory. Raised voices.'

'Take me there.'

'The pair of them arguing – Ewan and Lizzy. They don't know I'm watching them.'

'Can you hear what they're saying?'

'No. But it's heated. And my name is mentioned. At first I hide. I duck down beneath the ledge and try to listen in. I can see him holding her wrists and her struggling. I bang on the window. He releases her. She brushes herself down, runs her hand through her hair and lets me in through the back door. When I get inside, Ewan's in the kitchen prepping the vegetables, like nothing's happened and Lizzy has this air of breeziness like she isn't affected, only her eyes betray her.'

'What do you mean by that?'

'They're shifty. Uneasy. She takes my coat off me and goes to hang it up. It's so pretty outside, as the droplets of snow settle on the evergreens. If it keeps snowing like this, we may not get to leave at all. When Lizzy leaves the room, Ewan whispers in my ear, "She's on to us. Keep cool." He pulls a knife out of the block and flips it several times, catching it by the handle. So I take one out. The biggest one . . .'

'Go on.'

'I make a fist around it – I'm about to tell him off for shouting at Lizzy, but then he makes a joke about something I don't get and the doorbell goes and I can hear Lizzy in the hallway. Then . . . I don't know. Shit. I can't see.'

'I'm Ewan Stafford. When you look at me, you see him. His features . . . his mannerisms . . . his voice . . .' She puts her mouth to my ear. 'She's on to us. Keep cool.'

'You're laughing . . . stop laughing at me.'

'What? What am I doing?'

'I turn away from you. You come after me. Put your arms around my waist. Kiss the back of my neck.'

'Again.'

'Your hands go under my top. Feeling my breasts.'

'Like this.'

'Yes, but . . . rougher. Better. You tell me Lizzy will be taking her afternoon nap soon and we can have some time together and I say, she won't because mother's coming over, but are insistent. You make a joke about me going upstairs and taking my knickers off. The moment you run your hands over my protruding tummy, you know. You rub the bump, round and round . . . over and over.'

'Like this?'

'Yes.'

'Am I happy?'

'Ecstatic. You tell me it's what you always wanted. Your hands stay pressed against my tummy like you're trying to feel the little person inside. And for a moment I don't notice. When I look up, she's standing there watching us . . . silently . . . tears streaming down her cheeks. She doesn't speak. The heat is flooding my face like I'm on fire.

'I'm aware of your skin leaving mine as you release me. I hear the clatter of the knife as it leaves my hand and in those few brief seconds of consciousness, I remember asking myself why I was still holding it. I feel my knees buckle as my vision goes fuzzy and then black. And when I wake up, I'm lying on the sofa. Mother's gloved hand is on my brow . . . and I know there's no point in fighting.'

'No point in fighting what? Your mother?'

'Destiny.'

'What else do you remember?'

'A very kind policewoman who told me her name was Rena. I didn't mind being handcuffed to her. She said it was necessary. She was reassuring . . . '

'Who else drinks Manhattan?'

'Just me and Lizzy.'

'At the police station, were you drugs tested? Did you give a blood sample?'

'I wasn't asked.'

*

'Thank you both for coming here today,' Pash says, pouring coffee. 'We do appreciate it.'

'My pleasure,' Mother says, crisply. 'You have a very nice house, Doctor Khan. Minimalist, in the extreme.'

'Decided to de-clutter,' Pash says. 'I'm going away for a while.'

Lizzy shoots me a concerned glance.

I say, 'I've asked Pash to act as a witness.'

'Witness?' Mother says. 'Whatever for?'

'Because Octavia, I have a favour to ask of you. And I thought it only right and proper that Lizzy be here as support for you.'

294

'Do, please get to the point,' Mother says. 'I have a luncheon arranged with my agent in an hour.'

'I want you to patch things up with Dad. Tell him you were having a delayed mid-life crisis and you were mad to want to divorce him. Tell him you love him more than ever. Beg him to take you back – lie your silk stockings off if that's what it takes.'

Mother looks like she's about to choke on her coffee. 'Have you taken leave of your senses, girl?'

'We don't know how much time Dad has left, but what's clear to me is that he needs his family around him. That's me, you and Lizzy, and we're all going to pitch in and make more of an effort from now on.'

Mother sighs. 'You're quite deluded, Jes, if you think I have any intention of cancelling my impending divorce. Even to please you. I love Leo with all my heart and I intend to marry him as soon as it is legally possible. I've already begun making arrangements.'

'Well un-make them.'

'No thank you.'

'Fine. Go ahead. Many people marry in jail, Octavia. I'm sure he'll wait for you. Understanding bloke, is Leo.'

'I beg your pardon, Jesamine. Doctor Khan, can you please talk some sense into my daughter.'

Lizzy's eyes twitch from side to side nervously.

'The thing is,' Pash says, 'Jes and I have been doing some sessions under hypnosis.'

'Yes and she can't remember anything,' Lizzy says firmly.

'Oh but I can. I remember plenty. We went to the house, Lizzy. Your old house. And it all came flooding back.'

Lizzy's mouth gapes open.

'You saw us. You stood there watching us.'

'Don't say anything, Lizzy dear,' Mother says.

'Ewan's hands on my belly.'

'Shut up,' Lizzy says.

'You heard us talking. And you swapped the drink Ewan had prepared for you, with mine, because you knew he had drugged it with your tranquilizers. How am I doing so far?'

Lizzy starts to sob. Pash pulls a bundle of tissues from a box and presses them into her hand.

'Don't upset yourself, my dear,' Mother says. 'There is such a thing as False Memory Syndrome. It's well documented.'

'Want to phone a pal, Octavia? I doubt whether even the silky skills of Damien Locke will save you from the gallows this time.'

Mother turns to Pash. 'I suggest it is you who has planted these outrageous notions in my daughter's head.'

'That will be for the CPS to decide,' Pash says, in her usual understated manner. 'But we're confident we have enough substance for a retrial. Certainly we shall be asking for a transcript of the original case, because in the expert opinion of Harriet Bryher, QC, elements of the trial were almost certainly unfairly conducted.'

Mother looks totally crushed – like she just done ten rounds with Lennox Lewis.

I bite my lip to stop myself laughing. 'I don't suppose Trevor Nunn has anything for an over-the-hill, old lag.'

'Please, Mummy,' Lizzy says, panicking, 'do something.' She sounds like a frightened child.

'I refuse to be blackmailed,' Mother says, taking out a monogrammed handkerchief and sniffing into it, theatrically.'

'I can just see the headlines. "Grande Old Dame frames daughter for son-in-law's murder."'

Mother says, 'I will stand by my opinion, that the memories you believe you have recovered are entirely false, Jesamine.'

'In that case, you have nothing to worry about,' Pash says. 'Thanks for your time.'

'Mummy,' Lizzy pleads.

'So do we have a deal?' I say. 'In which case, I'll keep my mouth shut. Swallow the fact that I've had eight and a half years of my liberty snatched away without so much as an apology from either of you.'

Mother says, 'I'll agree to your demands, Jesamine, on one condition. That, when we are together like this, none of us ever mentions this matter again.'

Lizzy nods.

I look at Pash, then back at Mother. 'I'm in. Though I have to say it's more than you deserve.'

296

Mother says crossly, 'And another thing. I do intend marrying Leo Hendry once this damned awful business is over, so don't think you can renegotiate the rules to suit yourself later on.'

'Octavia, you just don't get it, do you? I really don't give a fuck what you do with your life once Dad's passed on. All I'm asking is that for once you do what's right for our family.'

Lizzy rakes at my arm. 'I'm sorry, Jes. I wouldn't have survived in prison. I'm not strong like you.'

'Don't say any more,' Mother says, gripping Lizzy's arm.

'Go on, Lizzy,' I say. 'Let your sister take the rap for this. It's what she deserves. Anyway, they'll never convict a pregnant woman.' Isn't that what you told her, Mother?' I realize I've said it at last . . . the dreaded 'M'-word.

'I don't have to sit and listen to anymore of this nonsense,' Mother snaps. 'I have far more pressing things to do with my time. Come on, Lizzy.'

'Oh just more thing. We'll keep that girl on Dad's fond of. The one with legs that go all the way up to her arse. Still *"abundantly proud"* of me, Octavia?'

Mother shakes her head at me. 'I hope you're satisfied.'

When they go, Pash offers to take me to lunch. I'm amazed to hear myself decline.

'Being alone with you – it's starting to hurt.'

'I know,' she says. 'Me too. Bad suggestion. In any case I have lots to do. At least, lots I should be doing. You know I'd love to be with you for your long weekend with Lola. I'd give anything . . .'

'Not quite.' I feel like punching something.

'Want me to pop by in the morning?'

'No. I'm going to call and see Lizzy before she heads to the States on Saturday. I still need to know stuff.'

'Yeah, well don't press it. You've made such incredible progress. All of you.'

'You think so? Just do me one last favour, Pash.'

'Name it.'

'Don't ever say you and me . . . we wouldn't have made a go of it.'

'Wouldn't dream of it.' She winks at me. 'I'll see you.'

'Not if I see you first.'

45

'You shouldn't be sitting in with me Enid. I'm a big girl. I can look after myself. I don't need a babysitter.' That last bit came out rather unkindly.

'It's only an evening class,' Enid says, fiddling with her hands. 'I can catch up with the gang next week. Besides, this week it's house plants – can't say I'm awfully enamoured at the prospect. I was going to take along a cactus.'

'Do you ever get to draw nudes?'

'No. Bowls of fruit sometimes . . . copper kettles . . . the occasional ewer . . . never nudes.'

'That's what I'd want to look at if I signed up for a class. A beautiful, naked woman, stretched out on a chaise longue. Don't know if I'd be able to keep the brush steady . . .'

'You're tormenting yourself unnecessarily, Jes.'

'Why do I want what I can't have, Enid? I swore to God I wouldn't ask for anything else as long as Pash's life got spared. I'm always so bloody ungrateful.'

'It's only natural,' Enid says. 'You're too hard on yourself.'

'How did you get over Mr Rhubarb and that Richard bloke.'

'Richard was easy to get out of my mind. I was livid when I found out he'd been cheating on me – and as for Mr Rhubarb . . . I left him stewing in his own juice.'

I don't feel the need to apologize for not laughing.

'Get off to your *Still Life* class, Enid. I'm going out for a bit. Need some air.'

'Are you certain, my dear? Don't you go doing anything rash now. Not when you're seeing Lola tomorrow.'

'I just need to work off some steam, that's all. I'll be fine, really.'

'If you're sure,' she says, scuttling to get her coat . . . and her cactus.

Thank God she's gone. It was doing my head in the pair of us sitting there, staring at the four walls, not knowing what to say, when we both know we'd rather be elsewhere.

What I need right now is meaningless sex. Casual. No strings. Anything to keep my mind off Pash Khan. *"Drop by anytime"* – that's what she said. I despise myself for being so weak. And for using the kid like this. But there are times when doing it by yourself isn't enough.

So I make my way over to Mack's on the bus and find myself plastered to the hairy forearm of a bloke not dissimilar to Mr Moron. That event seems like a lifetime ago now.

What does Mr Moron's life consist of, I wonder, when he's not assaulting women on trains. Is he married? Divorced? Gay and fighting it. Does he have a brood to provide for? Is he your *Relatively Normal* average bloke? Has that incident on the train impacted on him in any way? Does he have nightmares about me? Green slime trickling off his shiny head . . . seeping into his eyes . . . blinding him . . .

I peel myself off my bus companion's arm and ring the bell for the next stop. It's not actually a bell these days, it's a buzzer . . . like they have on TV quiz shows. Maybe I'll have to answer three questions correctly before the driver will open the doors.

Obviously not.

I step up the pace. Whatever happens, I don't intend staying the night. Why not? I'm a free agent after all. Because I care what Enid thinks of me, that's why. I don't want her to think I'm still a slapper.

An hour at Mack's, tops – do the business – grab a quick coffee, or a beer . . . or a glass of wine . . . whatever's on offer, then back to Enid's for a shower and plenty of rest, before the most important day of my life.

Mack answers the door wearing the broadest smile I've seen on her. At least someone's pleased to see me.

'Jes, hi. What a surprise. You look nice.'

'Thanks.' Not that I intend having these clothes on for very long. 'You know you said – '

'Me first,' she says, leaning across the doorway so I can't get in. 'Fantastic news – Immo's ditched Davy – for good this time. We're having another crack at the relationship.'

'Hi,' Imogen says, peering over Mack's shoulder, in a state of slovenly undress. 'Would you like to come in for a drink? Celebrate with us? We've got some bubbly. It's Jasmine, isn't it?'

'Jesamine. Kind offer, but . . . I can see you're busy. Another time.'

Mack says, 'So . . . what did you want?'

'Erm, nothing. I was passing and I just thought I'd call by and see if you were OK – and you so obviously are . . .' I step forward and hug her, impulsively. 'Thrilled for you . . . both.'

A girl can lie, can't she? To save face.

Imogen hooks an arm protectively around Mack's neck, as if staking her claim.

'Must fly,' I gush. 'People to see and all that.'

'See ya then,' Mack says, like she can't wait to close the door on me and be alone with her lover.

Not allowing myself to give in to the temptation of Enid's dwindling brandy supply, it's gone two in the morning when I finally drift off to sleep.

*

When I get to the cottage, Lizzy is cleaning blinds. She beams at me. I check my reflection in her pristine windows, to make sure I haven't got some silly splodge on my face, or something.

'Coffee?'

'No, I won't stop. Just popped by to wish you a good trip. And to say, if you want anyone to look after the bistro . . .'

'Piss off,' she says playfully. 'Leave you in charge and I won't have a restaurant to come back to.' She looks at me seriously. 'Yesterday . . . the business with Leo . . .'

'I don't intend apologizing.'

'I was about to say, I think you're right in a way.'

'Bloody hell, Sis, you're on my side.'

'I've always been on your side,' Lizzy says, 'it's just – I wasn't always allowed to show it. And I'll do my bit for Dad. Promise. Even if it means I have to leave Cam cavorting with the pretty young sirens of Santa Monica.'

'Cameron loves you.'

'I know,' she says, blinking tears from her eyes. 'God knows why.'

'Because he's a decent bloke. So stop testing him. And you're a good woman.'

'Thank you, Jes.'

'What kind of mother destroys the bond between her daughter and her daughter's husband? She played on your insecurities, Lizzy. And do you know why? Because she couldn't bear for you to leave her. She wanted you at home with her for ever.'

'That's not true.'

'You have to face up to the truth sometime.'

'What kind of sister sleeps with her sister's husband?'

'I know what it must seem like to you, Lizzy, but Ewan and I had a pact.'

'Pact? What pact? I don't understand.'

'I said I'd let him act out his fantasies on me if he'd leave you alone.'

'Leave me alone. Why would he leave me alone? What are you talking about?'

'You know full well. The bumps. The bruises. All the things you always had an excuse for. Like the time you dislocated your wrist. He was rough with you, wasn't he?'

'You thought Ewan was knocking me about?'

'Well you sure as hell didn't do them yourself. Did you?'

She drops the soapy cloth in the bucket.

'I was the one who got angry – threw things. Slapped his face occasionally when he stepped out of line. Or when he embarrassed me by flirting with our friends' wives. When I dislocated my wrist, it was because he was trying to restrain me. For my own good.'

'He didn't hurt you?'

'No.'

'What never?'

'He shouted sometimes – we both did – but Ewan would never have laid a finger on me. If he had . . . just once . . . I'd have walked out.'

'Then he was playing us both for idiots, Lizzy.'

'This is madness,' she says, scratching her head. 'Unbelievable madness.'

'And poor old Ewan paid with his life.'

'I always thought you were selfish, Jes. I thought you wanted everything I had – the love of a good man – because Ewan did love me in his own way, no matter what I put him through. And Mother's love . . . isn't that what you wanted?'

'God, Lizzy, how wrong can you be? I never wanted any of that. The last thing a raving dyke like me needs is "*the love of a good man*." The only reason I got into Ewan Stafford's bed was to protect you. How warped is that? And as for bloody Mother . . .'

We start to laugh . . . and laugh . . . and laugh . . .

As I go to leave, Lizzy presses a small red box into my hand. With trembling hands I lift the lid. It's a half of a silver heart. It has a jagged edge and is inscribed with the initials 'LO.' Fighting back tears she says, 'I think you'll find Lola has the other half somewhere.'

We stand on the doorstep for what seems like an eternity, just holding one another and not speaking, because for the moment, there's nothing left to say.

46

When I get back to the B&B, Enid has left a note on the fridge saying she's running late, but will be back at around five to prepare a special tea for Lola and me. She's arranged for a taxi to pick me up at three. And, yes, I know I ought to feel on top of the world – it seems bloody ungrateful not to, considering everything that's happened – and I know like I said I'd never ask for anything again – but right now – right this minute, I've never felt so miserably alone. It's like all the people I care about have abandoned me. All I need now is for Octavia to put in an appearance and make my misery compounded.

I switch on the radio for company and the announcer is saying that Eva Rowe has been spotted at Ascot on Ladies Day, parading around in a bright saffron dress and four inch heels, with a pink creation resembling a wedding cake on her head.

Circling the paddock astride Shergar, no doubt . . .

I've got exactly an hour to kill before the taxi is due, so I have a bath that lasts forty minutes. I keep topping it up with hot water, until it dawns on me there will be none left for Enid's guests this evening.

I change my clothes three times because I haven't the first clue what to wear to impress Little Miss Perfect. In the end I settle on the smartest jeans I can find and a *Save the Planet* T-shirt. Organic cotton, naturally. Then I fetch myself an obscenely large brandy, take one sip and pour the rest back in the bottle. Instead I console myself with a cup of ginger tea – the stuff Enid swears by – surprisingly soothing.

Ploughing through the classifieds in the local paper, I spot an ad for a PA to a professor. It's twenty-five grand a year and five weeks paid holiday. I wonder if it's for a male or female boffin. It certainly wouldn't hurt to enquire. I find a pen and circle the ad.

The taxi driver honks his horn just as I'm checking my armpits for the third time for sweat marks. Bloody lazy bastard, can't even be bothered to walk up the path and ring the bell.

As I wriggle onto the back seat, clutching Lola's half-heart in my hand for luck, she turns and lifts her sunglasses. 'Where to, Missy?'

'Pash! What the hell . . .? I told you not to come,' I say, leaping out and jumping into the front alongside her.

'I know what you said . . . this is all Enid's doing. Proper little matchmaker is that landlady of yours.' She holds my face in her hands and whispers, 'It's OK, I'm not going anywhere.'

'You're going to bloody Karachi in three hours.'

'I've put the job on hold for six months. See how things go. They were very understanding. Considering.'

'Because of me?'

'Several reasons. There's you . . . obviously. Then there's the practice . . . what with poor Melissa, I can't leave Jeff in the lurch. Also I need to make sure Geraldine gets the care she needs to recover fully. Use my influence . . . call in some favours . . . whatever it takes to get the right people on the case.'

'So this is really all about the Geraldine Strickland show. Still. Bloody marvellous.'

She clutches my hands – binds her fingers tight to mine. 'Listen to me, Jes. If you want to play a big part in my life – which personally, I'm hoping for too – you're going to have to accept certain things about me.'

'You're unbelievable. Next you'll be telling me the pair of you are getting back together.'

'No, of course not. Do you still want me?'

'You know I do. More than anything.'

'Then you'll need to respect the qualities I value. Fidelity: while we're in a relationship, I'll be faithful to you and I'll expect the same back.'

'Fair enough.' I think about my non-starter with Mack last night and feel the teeniest bit tarnished. 'I don't want anybody else,' I say, my voice catching.

'And, loyalty: I don't write someone out of my life because they have a problem, be it drink, drugs, a breakdown, whatever. Particularly with people I have known intimately over a number of years. I'll stand by Gerry – be a friend to her for as long as she needs me. Can you accept that?'

'I don't know. Oh Pash . . . what you're asking . . .'

She takes hold of my shoulders, firmly, like she's about to shake me. 'We're together, aren't we? Why can't that be enough for you? Or do you always need something to fight against? Don't you believe you deserve to be happy, Jes? Because that's what I believe in for you.'

'That, law of attraction crap pisses me right off.'

'Give it a go. Try it for a month. Indulge me . . . *please*,' she says, in that seductive tone that reduces my legs to mush.

'Pash?'

'Mmmm.'

'On the bridge, when you said you loved me . . . before, you told me you never say that to anyone until at least the fourth date.'

She smiles. 'I said it then, in case we didn't make the fourth date.'

'But you meant it?'

'I never say anything I don't mean.'

At last the tears come. Only this time, they're not tears of pity, or self-loathing, despair, or loss, like I've experienced throughout the last eight years of my life. These, my friend, are tears of pure joy.

I begin to blub uncontrollably. 'Nobody I've loved has every loved me the same back.'

'Well there you go,' she says, hugging me. 'That, "law of attraction crap," is working already. I've got some tissues somewhere.' She rakes around the glove compartment hopelessly. 'Oh sod the tissues, we can stop at the garage shop,' she says, firing up the engine. 'Let's go fetch your daughter.'

Printed in the United Kingdom
by Lightning Source UK Ltd.
136221UK00001B/212/P